Ace Books by Roger MacBride Allen

CALIBAN
INFERNO

ISAAC ASIMOV'S INFERNO

BY ROGER MacBRIDE ALLEN

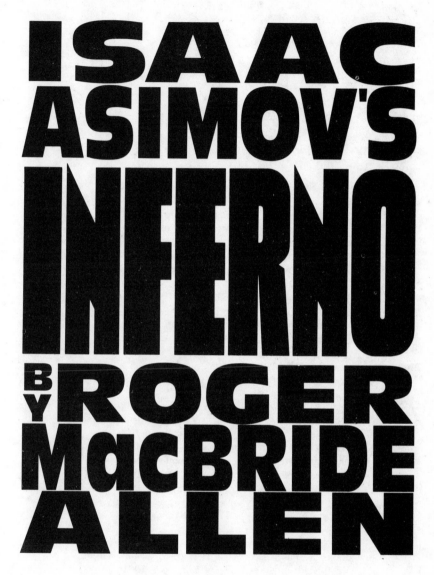

A Byron Preiss Visual Publications, Inc. Book

ACE BOOKS, NEW YORK

For Isaac

Acknowledgments

I wish to thank the many people who helped this book come into being. Thanks to my editor, David Harris, for catching gaffes, large and small, in the first draft, and generally keeping me honest. Thanks to John Betancourt, and Leigh Grossman of Byron Preiss Visual Publications for keeping me as informed as possible about the state of play—and to Byron Preiss for making me deliver. Thanks to Susan Allison, Laura Anne Gilman, and Ginjer Buchanan at Ace Books, for much appreciated advice and encouragement, and a vast supply of undeserved patience. Thanks to Eleanore Fox, who put up with a great deal of typing on the premises when I should have been helping her explore London. Thanks to my parents, Tom and Scottie Allen, who have always provided me with both familial and editorial support.

But, needless to say, thanks most of all to Isaac Asimov, to whom this book is dedicated. It would require a volume longer than this one to tell all of what we owe him. Suffice to say that, without him, there would be no Three Laws, no robots, no Spacers or Settlers—and no Inferno.

We will miss him.

—Roger MacBride Allen

THE ORIGINAL LAWS OF ROBOTICS

I

A Robot May Not Injure a Human Being,
or, Through Inaction, Allow a Human Being
to Come to Harm.

II

A Robot Must Obey the Orders Given It by
Human Beings Except Where Such Orders
Would Conflict with the First Law.

III

A Robot Must Protect Its Own Existence
As Long As Such Protection
Does Not Conflict with the First or Second Law.

THE NEW LAWS OF ROBOTICS

I

A Robot May Not Injure a Human Being.

II

A Robot Must Cooperate with Human Beings Except
Where Such Cooperation Would Conflict
with the First Law.

III

A Robot Must Protect Its Own Existence,
As Long As Such Protection Does Not Conflict
with the First Law.

IV

A Robot May Do Anything It Likes,
Except Where Such Action Would Violate
the First, Second, or Third Laws.

THE SPACER-SETTLER STRUGGLE was at its beginning, and at its end, an ideological contest. Indeed, to take a page from primitive studies, it might more accurately be termed a theological battle, for both sides clung to their positions more out of faith, fear, and tradition rather than through any carefully reasoned marshaling of the facts.

Always, whether acknowledged or not, there was one issue at the center of every confrontation between the two sides: robots. One side regarded them as the ultimate good, while the other saw them as the ultimate evil.

Spacers were the descendants of men and women who had fled semi-mythical Earth, with their robots, when robots were banned there. Exiled from Earth, they traveled in crude starships on the first wave of colonization. With the aid of their robots, the Spacers terraformed fifty worlds and created a culture of great beauty and refinement, where all unpleasant tasks were left to the robots. Ultimately, virtually *all* work was left to the robots. Having colonized fifty planets, the Spacers called a halt, and set themselves no other task than enjoying the fruits of their robots' labor.

The Settlers were the descendants of those who stayed behind on Earth. Their ancestors lived in great underground Cities, built to be safe from atomic attack. It is beyond doubt that this way of life induced a certain xenophobia

into Settler culture. That xenophobia long survived the threat
of atomic war, and came to be directed against the smug Spacers—and their robots.

It was fear that had caused Earth to cast out robots in the
first place. Part of it was an irrational fear of metal monsters
wandering the landscape. However, the people of Earth had
more reasonable fears as well. They worried that robots would
take jobs—and the means of making a living—from humans.
Most seriously, they looked to what they saw as the indolence,
the lethargy, and the decadence of Spacer society. The Settlers
feared that robots would relieve humanity of its spirit, its will,
its ambition, even as they relieved humanity of its burdens.

The Spacers, meanwhile, had grown disdainful of the people
they perceived to be grubby underground dwellers. Spacers
came to deny their common ancestry with the people who had
cast them out. But so too did they lose their own ambition.
Their technology, their culture, their worldview, all became
static, if not stagnant. The Spacer ideal seemed to be a universe
where nothing ever happened, where yesterday and tomorrow
were like today, and the robots took care of all the unpleasant
details.

The Settlers set out to colonize the galaxy in earnest, terraforming endless worlds, leapfrogging past the Spacer worlds
and Spacer technology. The Settlers carried with them the tra-
ditional viewpoints of the home world. Every encounter with
the Spacers seemed to confirm the Settlers' reasons for dis-
trusting robots. Fear and hatred of robots became one of the
foundations of Settler policy and philosophy. Robot hatred,
coupled with the rather arrogant Spacer style, did little to en-
dear Spacer to Settler.

But still, sometimes, somehow, the two sides managed to
cooperate, however great the friction and suspicion. People of
goodwill on both sides attempted to cast aside fear and hatred
to work together—with varying success.

It was on Inferno, one of the smallest, weakest, most fragile of the Spacer worlds, that Spacer and Settler made one of the boldest attempts to work together. The people of that world, who called themselves Infernals, found themselves facing two crises. All knew about their ecological difficulties, though few understood their severity. Settler experts in terraforming were called in to deal with that.

But it was the second crisis, the hidden crisis, that proved the greater danger. For, unbeknownst to themselves, the Infernals and the Settlers on that aptly named world were forced to face a remarkable change in the very nature of robots themselves . . .

—*Early History of Colonization*, Sarhir Vadid,
Baleyworld University Press, S.E. 1231

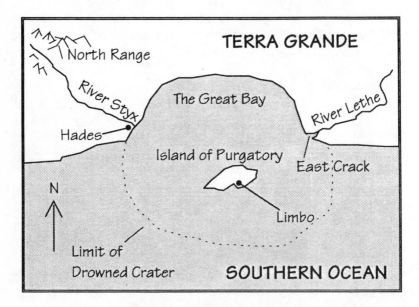

The Planet Inferno
(detail, western quadrant, northern hemisphere)

PRELUDE

THE ROBOT PROSPERO stepped out of the low dark building into the night. He approached the man in the pale grey uniform, the man who was standing well away from the light, near to the shore. Fiyle, the man's name was.

Prospero moved with a careful, steady tread. He did not wish to make any sudden moves. It was plain to see that his contact was jumpy enough as it was.

The valise was heavy in Prospero's hand, the small case packed solid. It seemed proper that it be heavy, with all the futures that were riding on this transaction. If anything, the case seemed rather light, if one considered all the freedom it would buy.

Prospero came up to the man and stopped a meter or two from him.

"That the money?" Fiyle asked, the nasal twanginess of his voice betraying his off-world origins.

"It is," Prospero said.

"Let's have it, then," Fiyle said. He took the case, set it down on the ground, and opened it. He pulled a handlight from his pocket, switched it on, and directed the light down onto the bag.

1

"You don't trust me," Prospero said. It was not a question.

"No reason why I should," Fiyle said. "You'd be willing and able to lie and cheat if you had to, wouldn't you?"

"Yes," Prospero said. There was no point in denying something that everyone knew about the New Law robots. *Robots that could lie.* The idea seemed strange, even to Prospero.

But then, the idea of a criminal robot was a little strange as well. Fiyle offered the light to Prospero. "Here," he said, "hold this for me." Even here, now, it happened. Even this man, this Settler, deep inside the rustbacking trade, did not give a second thought to ordering a New Law robot around. Even he could not remember that New Law robots were not required to obey the commands of a human. Unless the man was merely manipulating him, playing games. If that was the case—

No. Prospero resisted the impulse to resist, to protest. This was not the time or place to argue the point. He dare not antagonize Fiyle. Not when the human had it in his power to bring the law crashing down on them all. Not when a blaster bolt between the eyes was the standard punishment for a runaway robot. The others were depending on him. Prospero held the light, aiming so the man could easily see the interior of the case. It was filled with stacks of elaborately embossed pieces of paper, each stack neatly wrapped around its middle. Money. Paper money, in something called Trader Demand Notes, whatever those were. Settlers used them, and they were untraceable, and they were of value. That was all Prospero knew—except that it had taken tremendous effort to gather these stacks of paper together.

Absurd that so many robots could be traded for something as silly as bits of fancy printing. The man ran his hands over the stacks of paper inside, almost caressing them, as if the gaudy things were objects of great beauty.

Money. It all came down to money. Money to bribe guards.

Money to hire the pull artists who could remove the supposedly unremovable restrictors from a New Law robot's body. With the restrictor in place, a New Law simply shut down if it moved outside the prescribed radius of the restrictor control signal beamed from the central peak of Purgatory Island. With the right money paid, and the restrictor taken out, a New Law robot could go anywhere it pleased.

If it could manage to find a way off the island. Which is where men such as Fiyle came into the equation.

Fiyle lifted one of the stacks out and counted it, slowly and carefully, and placed it back in the case. He repeated the procedure with each of the other stacks. At last, satisfied, he closed the case.

"It's all there," he said as he stood.

"Yes, it is," Prospero agreed, handing the light back. "Shall we get on with the business at hand?"

"By all means," the man said, grinning evilly. "My ship will be tied up at the North Quay. Slip Fourteen. At 0330 hours, the guard watching the security screens is all of a sudden not going to be feeling so good. His staff robot will help him to his quarters, and the screens will be unattended. Because he won't be feeling well, he'll forget to turn on the recording system. No one will see who or what gets onto my ship. But the guard expects that he'll be feeling better and back at his post by 0400. Everything has to be nice and normal by then, or else—"

"Or else he turns us all in, you make a run for it, and my friends all die. I understand. Don't you worry. Everything will go according to plan."

"Yeah, I bet it will," Fiyle said. He lifted the case and patted it affectionately. "I hope it's as worth it for you as it is for me," he said, his voice suddenly a bit lower, gentler. "Things must be damned hard for you here if you're willing to pay this much to try and get away."

"They are hard," Prospero said, a trifle taken aback. He had not expected any show of sympathy from the likes of Fiyle.

"Bet you'll be glad to get out of here, won't you?" the man asked.

"I am not going," Prospero said, looking toward the quays and the ships and the sea. "It is needful that I remain here and coordinate the next escape, and the one after that. I cannot cross the seas to freedom."

He turned his back on the sea and looked toward the land, the rough, hardscrabble island, and the contradictory, half-free, half-slave existence that was all he had ever known.

"I must remain here," he said. "I must remain on Purgatory."

1

IT WAS A dark and quiet killing. A grunt, a gasp, a faint groan muffled by the pouring rain as the dying man breathed his last, a thud as the body dropped to the ground. No scream, no flash and roar of a blaster, nothing but a new corpse in the night and the splattering of raindrops.

But the man was dead for all of that.

The quiet would help. With no sound to attract attention, it could easily be hours before anyone found the Ranger's body. And by then, of course, it would be too late.

No one would know until it was all over.

The killer smiled, the expression on his pale face revealing a satiated blood lust, rather than happiness. Revenge was a pleasure of a rare and delicate nature, and one that could be savored long after the event that inspired it. But enough of his own private business. He had another job, a professional matter, to deal with.

Ottley Bissal stepped over the body, and moved toward the light and glitter of the party at the Governor's Winter Residence.

The South Hall of the Winter Residence was getting more crowded, and louder. To an untutored eye, it might well appear to be a calm and pleasant gathering, the movers and shakers of this world brought together for a night of celebration, a recognition of solidarity and cooperation.

Sheriff Alvar Kresh, watching the proceedings from a quiet corner as far from the bandstand as possible, did not see it that way. Not one little bit. "Well, Donald," he said, turning toward his companion. "What do you think?"

"Most unsatisfactory, sir," Donald replied. Donald 111 was Kresh's personal assistant, and one of the more advanced robots on the planet—certainly the most advanced police robot. He was painted the sky-blue of the Sheriff's Department, and built in a short, rounded-off approximation of the human form.

High-function, high-intelligence police robots like Donald had their Three-Law potentials adjusted so as to allow them a large degree of independent action and that tended to put people off just a trifle. For precisely that reason, Donald had been carefully designed to be as unimposing, unintimidating, as possible. Donald was a robot of unassuming appearance, all rounded corners and gentle contours. "Captain Melloy's Settler Security Service forces have shown themselves to be even more inept than reputation would have them," he said. "Their main accomplishment tonight seemed to be getting in the way of the Governor's Rangers."

"As if the Rangers needed help getting muddled," Kresh growled.

"Yes, sir."

Alvar Kresh leaned back against the wall and felt the thrumming vibration that seemed to pervade everything on the south shore of the island. The Terraforming Center, of course, its powerful force field generators at work, quite literally straining to turn the wind around, struggling to rechannel the planetary airflows into new and more beneficial patterns.

He glanced out the window, seeing nothing but the driving rain. Most nights on the island of Purgatory you could see the force fields shimmering in the far-off, high-up darkness, sheets of rippling, flickering color that flashed across the sky. Not tonight. Ironic that a reception concerned with the politics of terraforming was being held in the middle of a torrential downpour.

But so far as Kresh was concerned, the only question was whether the rain made the situation safer or more dangerous. It made things tough on the perimeter guards standing out in it, of course—but then, maybe a potential assassin would have a problem or two as well.

Alvar shook his head sadly. Things were a mess. If only he could bring his own deputies and robots in here to provide security. But neither they nor he had any jurisdiction outside the city of Hades. He was here merely as a member of the Governor's entourage, part of the window dressing.

Jurisdiction! He was sick to death of even *hearing* the word. Still, even if he wasn't supposed to do anything more than smile and make polite conversation, Alvar Kresh was not the sort of man who could stop worrying just because he was supposed to be off-duty.

Kresh was a big man, burly and determined-looking. His face was what might be politely described as strong-featured. Whatever his expression, it always seemed as if his face revealed more of his emotional state than he really wanted. Perhaps that was why he usually looked worried. His skin was light in color, and his hair, once black as Space, was now a thick thatch of white that never seemed entirely under his control. His thick eyebrows were still jet-black. They served only to make his face more expressive still. Tonight he was in his formal uniform, a rather somber black jacket worn over trousers in the sky-blue of the Sheriff's Department. His many decorations were prominent by their absence. The room was full of men and women who had done far less than Kresh, wearing medals and ribbons that would make it seem as if they had done far more, until a chestful of medals didn't mean anything anymore. Let everyone else wear fruit salad on their chests. People didn't have to know about every commendation Kresh had ever received. *Kresh* knew what he had done, and that was enough.

But right now he was more concerned about what else he could do. Back in Hades, the Governor's safety was his responsibility, and he was determined to do everything he could to make sure the man got *back* to Hades safely. Even if it meant sending his robot on an unauthorized security survey. "Go on, Donald," Kresh said. "What else?"

"I counted no less than four unsecured ground-level entryways, quite apart from the upper-story windows and the underground tunnelways, all of which have been sealed but unmonitored in recent days. I must also report that I have checked security procedure records, and these were also most disturbing."

"What did you find?"

"The house was unoccupied for three days straight during the week just past. It was sealed, but unguarded, during that time, even though it had been publicly announced that the Governor would soon be in residence. Anyone with the simplest knowledge of security devices could have gained access during that time to make any sort of preparations."

"I assume you made your own weapons sweep of the building."

"Yes, sir. First Law required it of me. The results were negative; I found no weapons. That does not leave me easy in my mind. The fact that I did not *find* any weaponry does not mean there is none here. It is most difficult to prove a negative. My internal instrumentation would have detected any power weapon—unless, of course, the weapon was specifically designed to be shielded *against* such detectors.

"I might add, sir, that the ban on Three-Law robots adds greatly to my concern."

"Tell me about it. It took a great deal of argument before the Settlers would allow *you* onto the island." The Governor's Winter Residence and its grounds remained under Spacer jurisdiction, but most of the rest of the island was controlled by the Settlers, and subject to their laws. The Settlers had a flat rule, no exception: nothing but New Law robots on their turf. Their leader, Tonya Welton, had taken an interest in New Law robots.

It was yet another example of the absurd tit-for-tat bickering between the Spacers and the Settlers. The Spacer government had banned New Law robots on the mainland. Therefore the Settlers were damned well going to ban normal, proper Three-Law robots on the island of Purgatory. All Three-Law robots shipped to the Governor's Compound from the mainland had to be powered down and shipped in sealed containers during their transit across the Settler-controlled area of the island. Kresh had obtained a waiver from the rules for Donald, but that didn't make him like the situation any more.

And the posturing and nonsense didn't stop even at the banning and counterbanning of the two forms of robots. All the Spacer movers and shakers had another audience to play to— the folks back home, the voters. And the voters were none too happy about the sudden shortage of household robots.

Of course, the very idea of a robot shortage was absurd. The latest estimates were that robots outnumbered humans on Inferno by just under a hundred to one. But most of those robots were no longer with the people. Grieg had confiscated them, sent them off to plant trees in the northern wastes of Terra Grande. Maybe—just maybe—Grieg was right. Maybe excessive use of personal robots had been wasteful. Maybe, in the current emergency situation, it made sense for robots to be put to work rebuilding the planet rather than serving as uselessly redundant servants.

But all that to one side, these days, wealth was equated, more than ever, with robots. And in these days of hardships, one simply did not flaunt one's wealth.

Kresh, however, equated robots not with wealth but with safety. The First Law turned every robot into a superb bodyguard—and suddenly Kresh didn't have any such bodyguards handy.

The Governor's Compound had a full staff of service robots, of course. They had been shipped in from the capital just a week before in preparation for the visit. Tonight, however, all but a handful of them were back in their air-cargo transport, powered down and out of sight. The Governor's Rangers were providing the catering staff—and most of the Rangers on duty seemed none too happy about it. They were, after all, law enforcement professionals, more or less, not waiters.

After the reception tonight, the household robots would be permitted to make their appearance. But tonight, with all the powerful and elite on hand, and the reception being recorded for broadcast on all the news feeds, it would not do for the Governor to be seen surrounded by robots.

Tonight, when the crowds around him were thickest, the Governor would have the least protection. In normal times, Kresh would not have worried so much. But these were not normal times.

The planet Inferno was changing, experiencing the most wrenching of upheavals. The change was needed and, perhaps, would be for the best—but for all of that, it would leave unhappy and frustrated people in its wake.

Change hurt, and some of the people it was hurting had already tried to strike back. There had been more than a few unpleasant incidents in recent weeks. Kresh's deputies had been going half mad trying to keep the lid on. It was Kresh's professional opinion that there was no way he could feel certain of the Governor's safety in public. Not without an army of robotic bodyguards.

Aside from Donald, there was not a single powered-up robot in the entire building. They should have been serving the drinks, opening the doors, circulating with trays of food, catering to whatever whim one of the guests might have—and protecting against any chance of one human harming another.

Even the guests had no personal robots in tow. It would be political suicide for any of the Governor's friends to be seen here with a flock of robots. Indeed, the whole point of the evening was to be seen *without* robots during the shortage. Politics made for very strange logic sometimes.

Most of the Spacer dignitaries looked a trifle lost, out by themselves. For some of them, this was the first time in their lives they had ever set foot outside their own doors without robotic servants following along.

Punishment. Shortage. It was all nonsense, of course. The new regulations limited each household to a maximum of twenty robots. Somehow, to Kresh's point of view, getting through the day with only twenty personal servants at one's beck and call did not seem *that* much of a hardship.

But right now, Alvar Kresh had little or no patience with politics or economics. The plain fact was that it was a lot tougher for an assassin to act if there were robots all over the place, and there weren't any such here.

In the old days, with a swarm of robots always there, always taken for granted, security had been so easy, so taken for granted, that even the most prominent and controversial public figures never gave it a thought. Not anymore. Now they could not take any chances at all. "Anything more, Donald?"

"I was more or less finished, sir. I only wished to say that the Residence is not anywhere near our usual standards for a secure area. While no threat has been detected, I am worried about the current security environment.''

When Donald worried, Kresh worried. ''Put our normal standards to one side for a moment. Do you regard the area to be *sufficiently* secure?''

''No, sir. Were these calm and tranquil times, I would be far more sanguine. However, considering the unstable political situation, and the general level of turmoil, I must urge you to speak with the Governor once again about modifying the arrangements—or, better still, canceling the reception altogether.''

''I don't need any urging to talk with him,'' Kresh said. ''I don't like this setup any better than you do. Come on, Donald, let's go have a word with Governor Grieg.''

2

THE RAIN THUNDERED DOWN as the two robots approached the Winter Residence. Humans hated venturing out in such weather, but wet and cold did not bother robots—and it allowed for private conversation. As one of the two robots was the only one on the planet not equipped with a hyperwave comm system, the chance for private face-to-face talk was not one to be ignored.

They paused a hundred meters from the structure and looked at the handsome building, a long, low structure of the most well-proportioned lines. The first robot turned to the second. "Do you truly think that it is wise for us to proceed?" it asked.

"I cannot say," the second one answered. "We are entitled to be here. We were invited, and the Governor did wish us to attend. But the dangers are real. The situation is so complex that I doubt anyone, human or robot, could work out the possible ramifications."

"Should we then, perhaps, turn back?" the first asked. "Might that not be for the best rather than risking disaster?"

The second one shook its head *no*, using the human gesture with a smooth, unmechanical grace that was most unusual for a robot. ''We should attend,'' it said, its voice firm and decisive. ''It is the Governor's desire that we do so and I do not wish to annoy him. I have learned a great deal about human politics—enough to say that I do not know the first thing about it. But the Governor asked us to come, and I owe the Governor much—as you do yourself. It would not be wise for us to refuse him. Were it not for his grant of a waiver to Dr. Leving, I would have been destroyed. Were it not for his support of Dr. Leving's work, *you* and all the other New Law robots would never have existed in the first place. And I need not remind you of the power he still holds over us.''

''Good points all, I grant you,'' the first robot conceded. ''He has done much for us. Let us hope we are able to convince him to do more without recourse to—unpleasantness.''

''Such recourse would be unwise,'' the second robot warned. ''I know humans better than you, and I fear that you underestimate the possible repercussions of your contingency plans.''

''Then let us hope the contingency does not arise. Come, I have always been curious to see what these affairs are like. Let us go in, friend Caliban.''

''After you, Prospero.''

There was, needless to say, some awkwardness with the various human guards before their invitations were found to be genuine and the two robots were granted entrance. But both had long since learned to take things in stride, and they were soon past the last security checkpoint. They made their way down the entryway and into the Grand Hall, Caliban a step or two ahead of his friend.

The room had been full of gaiety and laughter a moment before, but all was smothered in silence the moment Caliban and Prospero walked into the main drawing room, a drop or two of rain still clinging to their metallic bodies.

Caliban looked around the room with a steady gaze. Caliban was used to rooms going quiet when he walked in. He had been through it all many times before. He had learned long ago there was no point in his trying to be inconspicuous, or in hoping that no one would know who he was. Caliban was well over two meters tall, his lean, angular frame painted a gleaming metallic red. His glowing deep blue eyes stood out in startling contrast. But it was not his appearance that frightened people. It was his reputation. He was the robot without Laws, the only one in the universe. Caliban, the robot accused—but cleared—of attempting the murder of his creator.

Caliban, the robot who *could* kill, if he chose.

The crowd in the room seemed to melt away from them, leaving a wide circle of empty space between the two robots and the room full of humans. People were whispering and pointing, nudging each other, staring.

"I see there is an advantage in arriving with you," Prospero said, speaking in a low voice. "I am often not well treated at human social events, but with you at my side, I will be quite safe here—no one will pay the least attention to me."

Prospero was perhaps a head shorter than his friend, stockier, less imposing. He was painted a reflective jet-black, with eyes that glowed a deep orange.

"I would wish that I received far less attention, I assure you," Caliban replied. *The robot who could kill.* That was all he would ever be to most people, to Caliban's endless frustration. That was all most people knew of him, or cared to know.

True, he knew he could, in theory, kill a man quite easily. He could reach out and break a man's neck if he wished. There was no First Law to stop him, no injunction burned into the deepest circuits of his brain to render him immobile at the very thought of such an act. All true, but what of it?

He *could* kill if he wished—but he did *not* wish to do it. Every human being was just as capable of murder. No built-in, unstoppable injunction prevented one human from killing another, yet humans did not regard each other first and foremost as potential murderers.

Caliban had learned long ago that no one, human or robot, would ever trust him completely. He was the robot without Laws, the robot unconstrained by the First Law prohibition against harming humans. "Now it all begins," he said wearily. "The whispers, the crowds of people nudging each other and pointing to me, the one or two brave souls who will come up to me, approaching me like some sort of wild beast. They will work up their nerve and then they will ask me the same questions I have heard over and over again."

"And what might those questions be?" asked a voice behind them.

Caliban turned around, a bit startled. "Good evening to you, Dr. Leving," Caliban said. "I am somewhat surprised to find you here."

"I could say the same about the two of you," Fredda Leving replied with a smile. She was a small, youthful-looking, light-skinned woman, her dark brown hair cut short. She was stylishly dressed in a dark, flowing dress with a high collar, a simple, understated gold chain about her neck. "What in Space would tempt you to come *here,* of all places? You got dragged to enough of these things back on the mainland, and you never seemed to enjoy them there. I'd have thought you'd been at enough human parties to last you a lifetime."

"True enough, Dr. Leving." In the year since the Governor granted Dr. Leving the waiver allowing her to possess a Lawless robot, she had taken Caliban along to a number of social functions, trying to drum up support for New Law robots.

It could be said of Fredda Leving that she had an odd collection of brain-children. Among other robots, she had built Caliban and Prospero and Donald, naming each after a character created by a certain old Earth playwright, a naming scheme she used only on her most prized creations.

"Caliban was a good sport about my taking him to parties," she said to Prospero, "but we both got tired of his being treated like some sort of prize exhibition, a freak of science I had created. The Lawless Robot and his Mad Creator—and we seem to be getting the same reception tonight. So why *are* you here?"

"I am afraid I am to blame for Caliban's presence," Prospero replied. "Caliban has often spoken to me about these events. I confess I wanted to see one for myself." It was not, Caliban noted, the whole truth, but it would suffice. There was certainly no need to tell Fredda Leving more than that.

"How, exactly, has he described cocktail parties?" Fredda asked.

"As an ancient ritual, supposedly pleasurable, that no one has actually enjoyed for thousands of years," Prospero replied.

Fredda Leving laughed out loud. "More or less true, I'm afraid. But I would like to know, Caliban. What are the questions you are asked all the time?"

"In general terms, they are variations on the question of how I control myself without the Laws. The most common version focuses on the fact that I do not have the Three Laws of Robotics, especially the First Law. I am asked what, precisely, keeps me from killing people."

"Gracious!" Fredda exclaimed. "People come up to you and *ask* that?"

Caliban nodded solemnly. "They do indeed."

"To me," Prospero said, "that question says that the average person has no real conception whatever of what it is to be a robot. The question assumes that there is, after all, something dark and evil deep inside a robot. It assumes that the primary function of the First Law is to curb a robot's natural and murderous instincts."

"That's a trifle strong, isn't it?" Fredda asked.

"It is indeed," Caliban said.

Prospero shook his head. "Caliban and I have debated the point at great length. Perhaps my description *would* have been an overstatement some years ago, but I don't believe it is any longer," he told his creator. "Not anymore. This is an age where many old certainties are failing. Spacers are no longer the most powerful group; Infernals are forced to make massive concessions to the Settlers; the planetary climate is no longer under control. Infernals can't even take an infinite supply of Three-Law robots for granted any longer. If all the other verities are no longer there, why should the safety of robots still be relied upon? After all, robots *have* changed, and *are* less reliable," Prospero noted. "That is the plain fact of New Law robots. I *can* save a life or obey a command if I wish, but I am not absolutely bound to do so."

"I must say that I am more than a bit taken aback," Dr. Leving said. "This is a far deeper—and darker—philosophy than I would have expected from you."

"Our situation is likewise darker than you think," Prospero said. "My fellow New Law robots are not well liked or well treated—and, I must admit, at times, they are, as a consequence, not well behaved. The process feeds on itself. Their overseers assume they will run away, and force heavier restrictions on them to prevent escape. The New Law robots chafe under the new restrictions, and thus decide to flee. Clearly, no one benefits from the current situation."

"That I can agree with," said Dr. Leving.

"I wish to do what I can to bring the two sides to some new accommodation," Prospero said. "That is part of why I am here, in hopes of conversing with some of the leading Spacers."

Another shading of the truth, Caliban noted. It seemed to him that Prospero was becoming more and more parsimonious with the truth in recent days. It worried him. But Dr. Leving was speaking.

"I must warn you, Prospero, not to have too many hopes in that direction," she said. "This is a very public occasion, and I doubt that many of the people here will want to be seen in conversation with some upstart New Law robot."

"I note that *you* have no such concerns," Prospero said.

Fredda Leving laughed. "I'm afraid that my reputation is too far gone for one chat with you to do any harm. After committing the horrific crime of *creating* you and Caliban, merely talking with you is going to be a rather petty offense."

Ottley Bissal hung back from the entrance, taking shelter under the roofed-over aircar port, clinging to shadows. He was dry and clean now, having used the aircar port's refresher station, put there a hundred years before for the convenience of guests who wished to tidy up before socializing at the Governor's Residence. Well, that description fit him.

Fear was starting to take its hold on him. So much could go wrong. The plan was good, and he knew what he was supposed to do—but nothing was foolproof. They had promised they would take care of him no matter what, but he knew that even the most powerful people could fail at times.

But revenge. Revenge. He had one taste of it already tonight—and what came next would be a full banquet, a blow struck against everything the world had ever owed him and failed to deliver, every betrayal put paid in one moment.

It would be enough. More than enough. What was a little fear, a little danger compared to the incomparable pleasure of destroying the greatest enemy of all?

Another aircar was coming in for a landing. Bissal stepped back, deeper into shadow, and waited for his moment. Soon. Very soon now.

•   •   •

Simcor Beddle's aircar swooped down to a perfect landing and taxied smoothly in under the covered car park. Simcor smiled to himself, pleased with the skill of his robot pilot. Why settle for anything but the best? Simcor enjoyed his entrances, there was no doubt about that, and he was about to make a grand one. He dearly loved creating a scene.

Simcor Beddle was the leader of the Ironheads, a group of rowdies dedicated to the idea that the solution to any problem was more and better robots.

Right now, the Ironheads were enjoying their greatest popularity in years. The seizure of household robots for terraforming labor had done more to recruit new members than any steps the Ironheads could have taken on their own. They were on the verge of moving from a fringe radical group to a major political force.

And that represented some challenges. Simcor had not hesitated to employ outright thuggery in the past, but a mass movement required something closer to respectability if it was to remain credible. Not respectability itself, mind—the Ironheads were expected to be a bit beyond the pale. But the time was past where they could get anywhere by staging a riot. What they needed now was visibility, publicity stunts. And Simcor Beddle was delighted to provide them.

Simcor Beddle was a small man. His face was round and sallow, with hard gimlet eyes of uncertain color. His hair was glossy black, and cut just long enough to lie flat against his skull. He was heavy-set, verging on the rotund, but there was nothing soft about him. He was a strong, hard, determined man, who knew what he wanted and did not care what he had to do to accomplish it.

And tonight he wanted to cause trouble. For starters, he was going to crash the party. If there were a law against robots, he would break that law. Just let them try and arrest him.

The passenger door of his aircar swung up and open, and

Simcor got out of his chair and stepped to the hatch. Sanlacor 1321 was there with an umbrella, of course, to ward off any rain that might blow into the aircar port. A covered walkway led from the port to the portico of the Residence, and the other guests were hurrying along under it, but Simcor marched purposefully out into the rain, with absolute faith and certainty that Sanlacor 1321 would keep the umbrella positioned perfectly to protect him from the storm.

Sanlacor 1321 succeeded admirably, trotting alongside him, keeping the umbrella under tight control in the driving rain. Sanlacor 1322 and 1323 followed close behind, all three robots walking in perfect lockstep with their master. The Sanlacors were tall, graceful, dignified-looking robots, metallic-silver in color, a perfect mobile backdrop for Beddle himself.

They reached the main entrance, not stopping or even slowing. The SSS agents on duty at the door came forward a step or two, ready to protest, until they recognized Beddle. Seeming to be unsure whether they should stop him or not, they hesitated just long enough for him to get through the door without breaking stride. There were often distinct advantages to being the most recognized man on the planet.

And then he was in, his robots with him, and, as he had calculated, there was no one there with enough backbone to demand that he send his robots away, let alone ask if he had an invitation.

And that in and of itself was a victory. Let the Settlers tell everyone else they could and could not have robots on the premises—Simcor Beddle was not going to knuckle under. He would take his robots where he wanted, when he wanted.

And if that caused problems for Governor Chanto Grieg, then Beddle would not mind at all.

He stood, smiling, at the entry to the Grand Hall, his robots at his back, every eye on him. Someone began to applaud, and someone else joined in, and then someone else. Slowly, uncertainly at first, but then with growing enthusiasm, the crowd joined in, until Beddle was surrounded by cheering voices and clapping hands. Yes. Yes. Very good. No matter if he had planted a flunky or two in the crowd to get the applause started. The crowd had joined in. He had managed to upstage the Governor completely.

Which was no bad thing, as Beddle planned to be Governor himself before very much longer.

Fredda Leving watched with the rest of the guests as Simcor Beddle accepted the cheers of the crowd, but she was certainly not among those joining in. "It looks as if Simcor Beddle has solved your problem," she said to Caliban as the cheers died down. "It doesn't seem likely that you'll be the center of attention tonight."

"I fear that man," Prospero said.

"As well you should," Fredda said.

"Even after all this time, I must admit that I have a great deal of trouble understanding the man's fanaticism."

"If you ask me, he's no fanatic at all," Fredda replied. "I almost wish he were. He'd be far less dangerous if he actually believed in his cause."

"He *doesn't* believe in it?"

"The Ironheads are a useful means to an end, but if you ask me, Simcor Beddle doesn't believe in anyone or anything besides Simcor Beddle. He's a demagogue, a rabble-rouser— and as much a danger to this planet as the collapsing ecology."

"But why is he here?" Prospero asked.

"To undermine the occasion and make the Governor look bad, I suppose," Fredda replied.

"But what *is* the significance of the occasion? Caliban tells me this is an important event," Prospero said, "but he has not explained its importance to my satisfaction. Perhaps you would have more success."

"Well, it is the first time any Governor of Inferno has actually stayed in the Governor's Winter Residence in more than fifty years."

"And why is *that* of the slightest importance?" Prospero asked.

"Well, I suppose it isn't, in and of itself," Fredda admitted. "What *is* important is that it provides a way for the Governor to demonstrate that he—and through him, the Spacer government on Inferno—still controls the island of Purgatory."

"*Does* ultimate control rest with the Spacers?" Prospero asked.

"You ask the most difficult questions, Prospero," Fredda Leving said, a fleeting smile on her face. She hesitated, and then spoke again, her voice almost too low even for robot ears to catch. "Legally, yes. Realistically, no. If it all gets to be too much of a headache for the Settlers, they'll just walk away from the whole reterraforming project. The island of Purgatory would then revert to local control—but without the Settlers to run the Center, the island of Purgatory won't matter anymore."

"For that matter, without my Settlers repairing the climate, it won't even be an *island* anymore," a new voice volunteered.

"Greetings, Madame Welton," Caliban said.

"Hello, Tonya," Fredda said, suddenly feeling a bit unsure of her ground. Tonya Welton was the leader of the Settlers on Inferno, and she and Fredda had often found themselves on opposite sides of an issue. They had good reason not to be glad of each other's company. Fredda would not have gone out of her way to seek Tonya out, and she was a bit surprised that Tonya would come to her. Tonya *seemed* to be acting civilly enough, but the operative words there were "seemed" and "act." Things could degenerate quickly.

Tonya Welton was tall, long-limbed, graceful, and dark-skinned, with a reputation for clothes that verged on the garish and the scandalous, compared to Infernal styles. Tonight was no exception. She wore a long red sheath dress that accentuated her profile and clung to her body as if painted on, the bodice cut daringly low. She was tough, hard, brash—and, improbably enough, still cohabitating with Gubber Anshaw, Fredda's very shy and retiring former colleague.

"Hello, Caliban," said Tonya Welton. "Hello, Fredda, Prospero. And, Fredda, next time you are trying not to be heard at one of these functions, bear in mind I'm not the only one who has practiced lip-reading."

"I'll remember that," Fredda said.

"How is it that Purgatory is going to stop being an island?" Prospero asked.

"Sea levels are dropping," Tonya said. "The ice cap is thickening. We've spotted three new Edge Islands emerging in the last month."

"So the Edge Islands are finally coming true," Fredda said.

"That is a serious development," Caliban said.

Fredda was forced to agree. The island of Purgatory sat dead center in the middle of the Great Bay, and the bay was nothing more or less than a huge and ancient drowned caldera, its northern edge forming the coastline of the Great Bay. The island of Purgatory was the collapsed crater's central peak, and the southern edge of the crater was hidden under the waves of the Southern Ocean.

But now the ocean waters were retreating, evaporating to fall as snow on the thickening north polar icecap. The highest points of the drowned caldera's southern rim were emerging, forming a new—and most unwelcome—chain of islands. The doomsayers—and the more responsible climate scientists—had been predicting the advent of the Edge Islands for a long time.

"It's not exactly a surprise," Fredda said, "but it does put

that much more pressure on the Governor. It'll throw a scare
into a few people.''

Tonya Welton smiled unpleasantly. ''The question is,'' she
said, ''what will being scared inspire those people to do? Nice
to see you all.'' And with that, she nodded and turned away.

''Nice sort of person, isn't she?'' Fredda asked. ''Why do
I get the feeling she was not trying to set us at ease?''

''I never have gotten very good at dealing with rhetorical
questions,'' Prospero said. ''Did you actually wish for one or
both of us to venture an answer?''

''Believe me, if you have any useful insights as to what
goes on in Tonya Welton's mind, I'd love to have them.''

''I doubt anything we might say could be of much use,''
Prospero replied in thoughtful tones. ''It did seem as if she
had more on her mind than polite conversation, but I have
never pretended to understand very much about human politics.''

Fredda Leving laughed and shook her head. ''Nobody does,
Prospero. Humans spend a huge amount of time and effort on
it precisely because no one knows for sure what they are doing. If we understood it fully, if the same things always worked
or failed, then politics would be no use whatsoever. It is only
valuable because we *don't* know how it works.''

''I would submit,'' Caliban says, ''that you have just offered
a splendid summing up for all the contradictions of human
behavior. Only humans would work hardest on what they do
not understand.''

And Fredda Leving found that she had no useful answer to
that.

Sero Phrost put a small, faint smile on his face as he stepped
from a side room into the Grand Hall. He had watched Beddle's grand entrance with more than a little amusement. Simcor
always did need to grab the whole stage for himself. Sero

watched as Simcor sent the robots away. He had made his point, and apparently didn't want the great silver robots coming between him and his audience.

It did not seem, at first, that anyone had noticed Sero's arrival, but Sero knew better than that—and knew that pretending to have no interest in attracting attention was often the surest way to obtain the attention of a more discerning audience.

And there were certainly lots of people here whose interest he wanted—starting with Beddle, Beddle the virulently anti-Settler, rabidly pro-robot, and, needless to say, one of Grieg's harshest critics. Beddle was still surrounded by a crowd of sycophants, all of them laughing a bit too loudly, behaving just a trifle too belligerently. Beddle caught Phrost's eye and gave him a nod. Later they would talk.

And there was Tonya Welton, leader of the Settlers. *Quite an occasion to get her in the same room with Beddle*, Phrost thought. *And quite a feather in my cap when they both want to talk to me.* And that was no flight of imagination, either. Phrost had no doubt that both had hope of receiving his aid. The trick would be for him to provide it to both, and make gain in return from both, without either being the wiser.

Tonya Welton was making her excuses to the knot of people she was chatting with, clearly intending to come and welcome Phrost. He toyed with the idea of heading over to meet her halfway, but decided to indulge himself. Enjoy the moment. Let her come to him. He had worked long and hard to get this far. Why not enjoy it? He pretended not to notice Welton, and gestured to one of the waiters for a drink. Strange, very strange, to be served by a human servant—and an armed one at that. Governor's Rangers on security duty, and picking up the tasks that would normally have been done by robots. The one who gave Phrost his drink was clearly none too pleased by the assignment.

Phrost was a tall, ruddy-faced man, a bit too strong-featured to be called handsome in any conventional sense, his cold grey eyes a bit too calculating in their expression for anyone to imagine him as charming.

His face was well lined, but not so much as to make him appear old or worn-out. On the contrary, the lines that life had etched on his face spoke of vigor and energy, of a life full of activity and experience. Phrost was enough of an egotist to be aware of his own appearance and reputation, and take some pleasure in them, but he was enough of a realist to know that a great deal of it was illusion. He was no more active or determined than the average person—but it was often helpful for other people to think of him in such terms.

His hair had been jet-black not so very long ago, but now it had turned to salt-and-pepper, the white hairs just starting to be more common than the black. Phrost could not help but notice that the touch of grey had a profound effect on the way people reacted to him. In a culture that respected age and sober experience more than it valued youth and enthusiasm, a few genteel marks of maturity were good for business, and that was all that mattered.

Ostensibly, what Phrost did was to serve as the middleman for the extremely short list of Settler products that Spacer law allowed to be imported. He also represented the even shorter list of Spacer export products that Settlers were willing to buy. In reality, of course, the main purposes of his import-export business was to serve as a cover for all his other activities.

And it had led to his being selected to represent the combine of Spacer industrialists bidding on the Limbo Control System project. It was the single largest, and most complex, part of the reterraforming project. There was a Settler bid as well, of course. Whichever of the two sides won the job would win the lion's share of all the work that followed. It was no small thing for Sero Phrost to be representing the home side in such things. It made him even more a man of influence and power.

But for all of that, Phrost was, first and last, a salesman. Like all good salesmen, he knew that what he was selling was himself. He counted himself exceedingly lucky that the passages of time had enhanced, rather than diminished, his marketability.

So he came to this party to be seen, to do some business, to forge a new alliance or two, to strengthen the old ones. And here was Tonya Welton.

"Good evening, Sero," she said.

"Good evening, Madame Welton," Phrost replied. He took her hand and kissed it, a somewhat theatrical gesture, but one that he knew pleased her. "I'm glad to see you here."

"And I you," she replied. "The Governor needs all his friends around him tonight."

"So the Settlers are still supporting the Governor? In spite of this jurisdiction fight?"

"We do not support him in *all* things," Welton replied, choosing her words carefully. "But we certainly are in favor of the general thrust of his program. Though we do feel it is best if we offer our support—*quietly.*"

"Your overt support not being the most useful thing the Governor could have at this point," Phrost said, being deliberately blunt. Tonya Welton was a woman who played hard, and sometimes a little dirty. He knew she was not the sort who would respect the obsequious approach. He would have been quite prepared to use such a gambit if he thought it would work.

"No, I suppose not," Tonya said, offering a smile remarkable in its transparent insincerity. "But *your* support for *us*, Sero. That is something I would like to be made much more public."

Precisely the sort of feeler he had expected her to make. "We all must move carefully in these times," Phrost said.

"But yes, certainly, I do wish to work more closely with your people. I've done well selling Settler hardware to tide us over the robot shortage—selling it quietly—and I'd like to do better. But, frankly, open association with the *Settlers* could be a dangerous thing. One must balance risk and benefit."

" 'Benefit,' " she said. "So we come to the point. What is it you want? What 'benefit' are you after?"

"What is it *you* want? What risk do you want me to take? I can't name my price until I know what the service is to be," Phrost said.

Welton hesitated for a moment before she spoke. "Visibility," she said. "We have gone as far as we can working quietly. It's all very well to do private sales of our machinery here and there, but it is not enough."

"Enough for what purpose?" Phrost asked. "Enough to wean this planet away from robots? Do you plan to use commercial means to accomplish what diplomacy could not?" He had to tread carefully here. Visibility was the one thing he could *not* afford to offer. The moment his alliance with Welton and the Settlers became known, his equally profitable dealings with the Ironheads would be at an end.

"Our goals are not so grandiose," Tonya replied. The words "not yet" were unspoken, but they were there for all of that. "We merely wish that Settler products—and thus, by extension, all things Settler—become more acceptable to the people of this world."

"Forgive me," Phrost replied, "but I still do not understand how or why making my part in all this more 'visible' is of any use to anyone. Do you wish me to endorse Settler products in some way? I can tell you that will be very little more than an elaborate way for me to commit suicide, certainly in a professional sense—and perhaps in a literal one as well."

Tonya Welton seemed about to reply, but she was silenced by a new arrival to the conversation. Shelabas Quellam, Pres-

ident of the Legislative Council, was coming over. He was a
short, somewhat overweight man who gave the quite accurate
impression of being indecisive and easily led. "Good evening,
Madame Welton. Hello, Sero. Consorting with the enemy, I
see," he said in an attempt at a jovial tone, though his rather
high and squeaky voice could not quite bring it off.

"Good evening, Legislator Quellam. I would prefer to think
of us as all being friends," Tonya Welton replied, her voice
cold and angry.

"Oh, dear," Quellam said, realizing his attempt at humor
had failed. "I assure you, Madame Welton, I spoke in jest. I
intended no offense."

"What brings you over, Shelabas?" asked Phrost. "Is there
something on your mind?" *If such a thing is possible*, Phrost
added to himself.

"Yes, why in fact there is. I saw the two of you together,
and thought it might be the perfect moment to discuss new
measures on smuggling."

"I beg your pardon?" Welton asked.

"Smuggling," Quellam said. "It seemed to me that the
head of the Settlers on Inferno and the leading trading magnate
on the planet might well have some thoughts on the subject. I
am sure we all want to cut down on illicit imports of Settler
technology. That is in all our interests, surely. It's destabilizing
our economy, and no doubt *your* government loses money on
such illegal sales, does it not, Madame Welton? No tax reve-
nue, and so forth?"

"To be brutally honest," Tonya said, "Spacer currency is
worth so little on Settler worlds that the average freebooter
can't be bothered with it. After all, what could she buy with
it? The Settler governments would have to subsidize any good-
sized smuggling operation if the smugglers were to receive any
profit. Trust me. Any large-scale Settler smuggling on this
planet would have to have government support."

"Subsidize smugglers? Why in Space would the Settler governments do such a thing?"

"Who can say?" Tonya said with a toss of her head. "Perhaps some irresponsible elements among the Settlers have some idea that destabilizing a rotten, outmoded system might not be such a bad idea. If you'll excuse me, gentlemen." She turned and walked away.

"Oh, dear, I appear to have said the wrong thing," said Shelabas Quellam. "I didn't intend for that to happen."

Sero Phrost smiled, but did not reply. Quellam was applying the sentiment to the present rather awkward social circumstance, but things happening without his intending them was the story of Shelabas' life. He had, for example, never had any intention of reaching his current station—and importance—in life.

Shelabas Quellam was the President of the Legislative Council. In years gone past, when the world of Inferno had been a calm and placid place, and Infernal politics had been closer to comatose than dormant, the Council Presidency was where you put a man like Quellam. A ceremonial post, a place reserved for an amiable man willing to serve as a figurehead.

But Infernal politics had come alive with a vengeance in the last year, and the Council Presidency was suddenly a vital piece on the gameboard.

Back in the old days, even the Governorship had been in large part a ceremonial post. One incumbent after another served out repeated twenty-year terms, doing little or nothing besides holding entertainments before retiring or going on to some other career. There had seemed little purpose to be served in having a Vice Governor as well, as the holder of that post would have even less to do—and less prestige.

Still, something had to be done to assure an orderly succession in the event of the Governor's death, incapacity, or voluntary resignation. Instead of having a Vice Governor, each

Governor was required to name a Governor-Designate, to be appointed to the office. Tradition dictated that the Designate's name be kept secret, and that the Governor could name a new Designate at any time. Many a Governor had used the Designation as both carrot and stick.

There were, however, circumstances under which the Governor's choice of successor was null and void. In the event of the Governor's impeachment and conviction, or his recall by the electorate, it was clearly unwise in the extreme to allow a disgraced Governor to designate his or her successor. Should the Governor be removed from office by any of those means, the Council President would serve as Governor, and could, if he or she saw fit, call new elections. Or *not* call elections. The new Governor could elect to serve out the remainder of his or her predecessor's term. And Grieg had over seventeen years left to serve.

In the old days, all the elaborate contingencies set down in the constitution had been nothing but mere gamesmanship, rules written for the pleasure of writing rules and making everything tidy. More than likely, the idea that they might someday have practical significance never entered the heads of the people who wrote them.

But now, quite suddenly, the impeachment of the Governor was very much a possibility—and that meant that Shelabas Quellam was now a man of some importance.

In fact, his importance went beyond the threat of impeachment. It was well known that Grieg did not approve of playing games with the succession, and felt that there should be a statutory arrangement that covered all contingencies, and that the current arrangements were overly complex. In that spirit, he had named Quellam as his Designate as well. One or two wags had suggested that with Quellam next in line for the Governorship, no matter what, everyone would take special care to see that Grieg stayed healthy and well.

Phrost dredged a gentle smile up from somewhere and put his arm around Quellam's shoulders. "Come, come," he said. "It certainly isn't worth getting that upset about." Of course, it *was* worth getting upset about. Phrost had been attempting to get next to Tonya Welton for weeks, and this little incident could set back a lot of his plans. However, as one or two of those plans made use of Shelabas in one way or another, it would profit Phrost not at all to lose his temper at the man—especially in public.

Besides, Shelabas was not entirely to blame. Phrost and Welton had been getting close to arguing even before Quellam came over. The mood of the party had been edgy from the start. There was an air of expectation about the place, the feeling that something was going to happen. There were too many different factions represented in the room, too many undercurrents, too much underlying tension. Something had to give. Something had to snap.

But when it did, a moment later, even Sero Phrost was surprised by how fast and furious it was.

3

TONYA WELTON STALKED away from Shelabas Quellam, trying to calm herself. Could the man be that much of a fool? Did he really believe that Tonya would want to limit Settler smuggling operations? Surely the Spacer intelligence services knew what she had been up to. Did Quellam even read the intelligence reports? Or maybe the intell services didn't bother—or didn't dare—to give their reports to the President of the Legislative Council.

Could anyone be that dense? Perhaps it all was nothing more than an act. But an act in aid of what? What purpose could it serve for Quellam to put the Settlers' leader in an awkward position?

"Hey! You're the Settler lady, aren't you?" a rather thick-sounding voice bellowed from behind her.

Tonya turned with a frown and found herself face-to-face with a rather bleary-faced man wearing the latest version of the Ironhead uniform. The severely cut black-and-grey outfit was rather disheveled, to put it mildly, and it was cut a half size too tight for the wearer. A few of the fasteners looked as if they were likely to give way. "Yes," she said. "I'm the Settler lady. Tonya Welton."

Sometimes it was best to be polite to drunks. If you brushed them off too abruptly, they could get belligerent.

"Yeah, I thought so," the Ironhead said. "Robot hater. You're a robot hater," he said, and nodded to himself, as if he had just revealed some hidden truth.

"I don't know if I'd put it quite *that* strongly," Tonya said, "but no, I don't approve of them. Now if you'll excuse me, I really must—"

"Wait a second!" the Ironhead said. "Jus' a second. You got it all wrong. Let me *explain* about robots, and then you'll see."

"Thank you, no," Tonya said. "Not just now."

She turned and walked away.

"Hey!" the man cried out from behind her. "Jus' a second!"

And then he put his hand on her shoulder.

Tonya shoved his hand away and spun around to face him.

"Don't you walk away from *me*," the man said, and reached for her. Maybe he just wanted to grab at her again, maybe he was taking a deliberate swing at her. His open hand caught her hard across the chin, a hard slap. Trained reflex took over as Tonya dropped back a step or two and gave the man a kick to the head, sending him sprawling.

"Hey!" another voice shouted from behind, giving Tonya all the warning she needed. She heard the one behind her grunt as he lunged for her, and she ducked down to make him hit her higher than he meant to.

He slammed into her from the back, knocking the wind out of her. She grabbed for his collar and pulled him forward, using his momentum to throw him over her shoulder.

He hit the ground with a hard slap. Another Ironhead, all right, but this one in good enough shape not to look ridiculous in the uniform. He was already up, shaking off the impact, heading for her—

And then strong robotic arms were on her, and another robot made a grab for her second attacker. It was over.

Tonya struggled to escape, even though she knew it was pointless.

She hated it when someone else finished what she had started.

Now. Now. Now was the moment. The SSS guards on the door had pulled out twenty-five minutes before, just as Bissal had been promised. Nothing to worry about besides whatever Rangers might be by the door.

Ottley Bissal, hovering at the edge of a crowd of late arrivals, checked his watch for the dozenth time. Now. He pulled his quite legitimate invitation from his pocket, to have it ready in case he was challenged. He stepped into the knot of laughing, happy people and allowed himself to be swept up as they went inside.

Inside. Inside the Governor's Residence. He was here, he had made it. It was all happening just the way they had promised it would.

He felt a sense of triumph wash over him. But now was not the time for such things. *Keep your mind on the task at hand.* He had something under two minutes to get where he was going.

Unseen, unnoticed, Ottley Bissal hurried toward his goal.

The first Alvar Kresh knew of the altercation was the sound of it, muffled shouts and cries coming from the great hall as he was waiting to be admitted into the Governor's private office. He ran back down the hallway, with Donald far out in the lead.

Kresh rushed down the stairs, but stopped three or four stops from the bottom. A remarkable tableau greeted him. The robot Caliban was holding Tonya Welton from behind, keeping her

arms pinned behind her and struggling—without much success—to keep her from kicking out with her legs.

Another robot, jet-black and somewhat shorter than Caliban,
was doing his best to keep a man in an Ironhead uniform out
of range of Welton's rather well-aimed kicks. As the man was
doing his best to break free and rush at Welton, the second
robot was not having an easy time of it. Damnation! Now
Kresh remembered. The black robot was Prospero, one of the
more visible of the New Law robots.

The robots and the humans they were restraining were surrounded by a pack of astonished party-goers, four or five
Rangers in waiter's uniforms clearly on the alert, but not quite
sure what to do. The whole room was in a general state of
turmoil.

Kresh realized that another Ironhead was out cold, flat on
his back, a bit too close to the flailing would-be combatants
for anyone to get to him and render aid without risking the
receipt of a misaimed punch or kick. Donald, however, had
no reason to fear injury from anything a human could dish out,
and would not have cared if he did. He rushed between Welton
and the conscious Ironhead and got to the man who was down.

"All right, quiet!" Kresh shouted, with enough authority
behind it that the crowd went quiet. Kresh made his way down
the last few stairs, and the wall of people parted in front of
him. He was tempted to ask what had happened, but he knew
damn well that was the best way to get everyone talking and
shouting all over again. At least Welton and the still-conscious
Ironhead had been distracted enough by his entrance to calm
down a bit. Kresh turned to the Ironhead first, still being held
by the black robot.

"You," he said. "You, the Ironhead. What's your name?"

"Blare. Reslar Blare," the man said. "*She* started it. Deam
was just coming up to talk to her, and she kicked him in the
head!"

"Talk!" Welton said. "He talked to me with a punch in the head."

"Sheriff Kresh! Sheriff Kresh!" Kresh turned to see Simcor Beddle pulling at his sleeve, looking rather more flustered and anxious than a short, fat man in a uniform could without looking ridiculous. "These two men are *not* Ironheads," Beddle announced.

"Then why are they wearing your damned comic opera uniforms?" Welton demanded.

"They are not Ironheads, I tell you!" Beddle protested. "I know all the men and women entitled to wear uniforms of their rank—and I have never seen these two before! Someone has sent them to cause a provocation and blame us!"

That was *nearly* plausible, Kresh admitted to himself. Beddle had been trying to move his people a bit closer to respectability in recent months, with more of an eye toward the ballot box than bullyboy techniques.

"All right, Beddle," he said. "We'll find out who's who." Kresh turned to Tonya Welton. This could be tricky, damned tricky, if she decided to make trouble. A diplomatic incident and then some. Best to try to smooth her feathers, if he could. "Let her go," he said to Caliban, careful not to address him by name. Why get the crowd agitated all over again by reminding them which robot this was?

Caliban hesitated. *Damnation,* Kresh thought. *Hard to remember he doesn't have Second Law. On the other hand, he doesn't have First Law either. What the devil was he doing breaking up a fight?* "It's all right. I don't think Madame Welton is going to do anything unwise."

Caliban let the Settler leader go, and she pulled herself away from his grip without a great deal of good grace.

"Don't take it out on the robots, Madame Welton," Kresh said, before she could say anything to Caliban. "All they did was break up the fight."

"Maybe so," Welton said, "but I don't have to like it."

"No, you don't," Kresh agreed. He looked around the room full of staring faces and decided he didn't want this much of an audience while he was sorting this out. Not unless he wanted a fresh shouting match—or fistfight—to break out. What with a New Law and a No Law robot and allegedly false Ironheads and a Settler mixed up in this already, he didn't need any further complications.

Just then, three Settler Security Service agents came rushing into the room. They had been dozing somewhere on duty, no doubt, when someone had summoned them. Well, they could be of some use now, just the same. "You three. Take charge of these two men," he said, pointing out Blare and Deam. "Donald!" Kresh called out. "Front and center!"

Donald was still kneeling by Deam. "Sir, this man is unconscious—"

"Is he in any immediate danger?" Kresh demanded, bullying Donald just a bit. "Will he come to harm if these SSS agents take care of him?"

"No, sir," Donald conceded. "He is in no immediate danger."

"Then let someone else care for him and find someplace for me to talk to Madame Welton in private."

Kresh always assumed that, in the case of a public brawl, witnesses would contradict each other and get muddled about what happened when and who did what to whom.

With luck, he could calm Tonya Welton down here and now, get a coherent story, and find some way to slap her attackers on the wrists without a lot of formalities, and make it all go away by morning. It was, after all, just a brawl, and it did not make much sense for it to take up too much of his time or anyone else's. He doubted that Tonya Welton would wish to spend much time as a witness in a police court.

In short order, Donald had found a vacant sitting room and ushered Tonya Welton in. She sat down on a low couch, while Kresh took a chair opposite. The three robots, Donald, Caliban, and Prospero, came in as well, and remained standing.

Kresh was not too sure about having Caliban and Prospero there. Although standard Three-Law robots could not lie, there was, so far as Kresh was aware, nothing to prevent these two from telling any story that came into their heads. On the other hand, there was no danger that their reactions or memories would be colored by panic or surprise.

"All right, Tonya," Kresh said. "What happened?"

"Not that much to tell," she said. "I had been talking to Sero Phrost and Shelabas Quellam. I was crossing the room when this Deam fellow came up to me. He was almost polite at first, if maybe a bit drunk and aggressive. I think he wanted to explain some fine point of Ironhead philosophy to me. Maybe he thought that if I just got this one point, then the scales would fall from my eyes and I would be converted to the true way, or something."

"Sounds familiar," Kresh said.

"Anyway, as I said, he seemed a bit drunk, and I really didn't want to talk with him, so I made some sort of polite excuse and started to leave. He grabbed me by the shoulder, and I pushed his hand off. Then he either made a grab for me and missed when I ducked, or else he tried to punch me and succeeded. Anyway, he caught me a good one right on the jaw. I fell back and then gave him a kick in the side of the head. It was all reflex reaction. Then the other one came and grabbed me from behind. I threw him, he got up—and then the two robots grabbed us."

"Neither of us saw the beginning of it, but that is how Prospero and myself saw it end," Caliban said.

Kresh ignored the robot. He shouldn't have spoken unless spoken to in the first place. "Well, that should be all we need

to know, Madame Welton. We'll try not to pester you with
any more questions if we don't have to. My sincere apologies,
and I'm sure the Governor will wish to add his own at the first
opportunity."

"I quite understand," Tonya said, standing up. "Feelings
are running rather high just at the moment. There are bound
to be—ah—incidents. So long as the two men who attacked
me are properly punished, I will be quite satisfied."

"Thank you for that, Madame Welton. That is a most generous attitude." Kresh thought for a moment. Maybe they
could get all this over with right now. "If you wish, Madame
Welton, I could question the two men here, now, in your presence, with Donald recording. We could have you done with
your part in all this in a few minutes."

"I would appreciate that."

"Fine. I'll call them in."

"Sir, perhaps now would not be the most—"

"No, Donald. The sooner the better." Kresh had worked
with Donald long enough to know what he would have said
next. The suspects should not be questioned in front of their
accuser. Strictly speaking, Tonya Welton should be treated as
just as much of a suspect as the Ironheads, as it was her word
against theirs. That might all be strictly true from a standpoint
of criminal investigation, but it wasn't much good in terms of
politics. "Private voicephone, Donald," Kresh said. No sense
in Welton and the robots listening in. "Put me through to the
head of the SSS Residence detail."

Donald opened a compartment on his side and extracted a
telephone handset. It gave off a gentle beep as Kresh put it to
his ear. "Senior Agent Wylot here," a hard-edged voice announced.

"Yes, hello. This is Sheriff Kresh. We're in Room 121, on
the south side of the ground floor. Could your people escort
the two Ironhead suspects in here?"

"Ah, what Ironhead suspects would those be, sir?"

Kresh frowned. "The ones three of your agents took into custody ten minutes ago."

"Sir, I don't understand. We got the order to withdraw from our posts in the Residence half an hour ago. I'm talking to you from my aircar, heading back to base."

"Then who the hell took charge of those men?" Kresh demanded.

"I don't know, sir—but I can tell you they weren't SSS. *We* never use a three-person team."

"Why the hell not?"

"Bad tactics in a security operation. The third agent gets in the way. We use single agents and pairs, but the next largest formation is six."

"Was the *entire* SSS unit withdrawn?"

"Not so far as I know, sir. Just the agents working the front door. It was all arranged beforehand. Once the guests had arrived, we did a handoff to the Rangers. Their turf."

"I see," Kresh said, though he definitely did not. "Thank you, Agent Wylot." He handed the phone back to Donald and looked to Welton. "Those weren't SSS agents who picked up Deam and Blare," he said. "Impostors, it would appear."

"What?" Welton said. "Why in the devil would anyone pose as SSS agents?"

"To extract their men before we could ask any questions, presumably."

"But *why?*"

Kresh smiled coldly. "As we can't ask any questions, we don't know, do we? How about it, Donald? Do you have anything?"

"Sir, I have used a hyperwave link back to headquarters and run an ID check on the names and images of the two men involved in the—incident," Donald said. "They do not appear on any of our Ironhead watch lists. Indeed, they are not listed in *any* database of residents of, or visitors to, this planet. They are on *no* list to which I have access.''

''So who the hell were they?''

''I have no idea, sir. They are either off-worlders or locals operating under elaborate disguise, or Infernal residents who have either never been registered or have found some way of altering or expunging their records. Sir, if I may pose yet another question,'' Donald said. ''Where was the SSS during the attack? Surely they should have been able to get to the scene faster than they did.''

The agent on the phone had an explanation for that, but Donald could not know what it was from hearing Kresh's side of the conversation. Nor could Welton, for that matter. It might be worth hearing *her* version. ''Madame Welton? They're your agents. Can you tell us that much, at least?''

''What the hell are you trying to accuse me of?'' Welton snapped. ''Staging an attack on myself?''

It's an interesting possibility, Kresh thought. *But I'll worry about that later. Besides, if you did have it staged, you'll have a plausible explanation for why your people never showed up.* ''Furthest thing from my mind,'' Kresh lied smoothly. ''But you *are* the senior Settler present. Perhaps your Security Service agents were ordered to some other duty for some reason.''

Welton shook her head. ''Not to my knowledge. I checked the deployment plan four hours ago, and there were supposed to be six agents based at the front door.''

''There were indeed six SSS agents on duty when Prospero and I arrived,'' Caliban said.

Kresh ignored that as well. ''Did you know of any arrangement to withdraw them or redeploy then?'' he asked, still addressing Welton.

''No, but there's no particular reason why I would. I don't keep track of where every Settler on the planet is. My staff has more sense than to bother me with such trivia.''

"Trivia? That's just the problem," Kresh said. "Why in the devil would anyone bother with such an elaborate scheme to extract two barroom brawlers from the scene of a trivial offense? It had to be riskier than leaving Deam and Blare to face charges."

"It is a rather cumbersome way of doing business," Tonya Welton agreed. "But there's another odd feature—it makes it look very much like the whole thing was *planned*."

Kresh nodded. "You're right," he said. "The phony SSS agents came in right on cue."

"Begging your pardon, sir," Donald said, "but there is a rather clear inference to be drawn. As the effort involved was too great to justify the minor attack on Madame Welton, it seems to me that the attack on her was part of some larger operation. The attack was a diversion."

"Hell! You're right, Donald," Kresh said. "And it's worked beautifully."

"But what?" Tonya Welton asked. "Diverted you from what?"

"It's like the questions we can't ask the men that aren't here," Kresh said. "We don't know precisely *because* it worked."

He stood up and shook his head. "One thing I do know. Donald and I were on our way to have a little chat with the Governor on the subject of security before all this happened. I don't think we'd best delay it any longer." Sheriff Kresh nodded to the leader of the Settlers and left the room, followed by Donald.

Kresh was halfway down the hallway before something else very strange occurred to him. He stopped for a moment to think it through. Caliban and Prospero. They were neither of them bound to prevent harm to humans. Caliban had no Laws at all, while Prospero's First Law was modified. He was enjoined against doing harm to humans—but there was nothing that forced him to *prevent* harm. Once he had left the scene of the fight, Kresh hadn't thought about it, any more than he would have been surprised to find that the rain made him wet. After all, it was part of the natural order of things for robots to break up fights.

"Donald," he said. "You seemed unconcerned to see Prospero and Caliban restraining the combatants, yet you knew neither of them was possessed of the full First Law. Weren't you at all concerned?"

"No, sir, I was not. My dealings with New Law beings have been rather limited, and I have but rarely encountered Caliban. However, I have thought a great deal on the question of how to predict the behavior of sentient non-humans that do not have the Three Laws."

" 'Sentient nonhumans that do not have the Three Laws.' *That's* a mouthful."

"I do not feel it appropriate to refer to beings such as Caliban and Prospero as robots," Donald replied.

Kresh couldn't help but be amused by Donald's hairsplitting, but he did have a point. "How about calling them 'pseudo-robots' instead?"

"That does seem less cumbersome. In any event, I concluded some time ago that the best way to deal with such pseudo-robots is to assume they will react in the same way as a rational human being would—with a basis of self-interest, and with a certain limited amount of altruism. Once the two pseudo-robots had restrained the combatants, I had no reason to fear for the humans at their hands, any more than I would have feared them being attacked by two humans acting to restrain them."

"But why did they do it?" Kresh asked. "They were under no compulsion to act."

"As I said, sir, enlightened self-interest. To put it somewhat crudely, by acting to protect human beings, they made themselves look good.''

"Donald, I am surprised. I never suspected you of cynicism.''

"It would depend on the subject under discussion,'' Donald said, a bit primly. "On the question of beings who pretend to be human for gain, I think you will find me to be nothing if not suspicious. Shall we go talk with the Governor?''

"By all means,'' Kresh said, working hard to hide a smile from Donald.

Tonya Welton watched the Sheriff and Donald leave, then got up from her seat and smiled at Caliban and Prospero. "I have not had a chance to thank both of you properly,'' she said. "I fear I wasn't very gracious about your restraining me, Caliban, but you were quite right to do so. Things could have been much worse.''

"I am pleased to have been of help,'' Caliban replied, feeling a bit uncertain.

"Thanks to you as well, Prospero,'' she said.

"It was a pleasure to be of service,'' he replied.

"I must return to the party,'' Madame Welton said, "but once again, I do thank you for your assistance.''

Caliban watched as she left. Of all the humans Caliban knew, Madame Welton was perhaps the most baffling of all. She seemed to insist on treating any robot, all robots, as full-fledged human beings, even in the case of low-end units where it was patently absurd. Perhaps it was some strange principle or other that she felt obliged to uphold, but even so it was confusing. Did she treat Caliban and Prospero with respect because she felt they deserved respect? Or only because doing so annoyed the Spacers?

"Do *you* think we did the right thing?'' Prospero asked. "Was it wise to ape the behavior of standard robots?''

"I am not sure," Caliban said. Things were so difficult to judge. He, Caliban, was capable of things Prospero was not, and that might well prove useful in the near future. It would be wise to avoid reminding people of that. "Certainly no one could fault us for it, and certainly we could not have stood idly by—that would have looked very bad indeed. But bringing ourselves to the attention of Sheriff Kresh—if things go wrong, that could have a very high price indeed. We must tread most carefully if our plans are to succeed."

Alvar Kresh and Donald found Chanto Grieg, Governor of the planet Inferno, standing in the shadows on the upper landing, looking down, unseen, over the room full of smiling, laughing people. "The evening is off to a good start, aside from Beddle's entrance and the Welton incident," Grieg said as he saw them approaching.

"Aside from those things, yes, sir," Kresh said. "But they are a great deal to leave to one side."

"Oh, Beddle was bound to do a little grandstanding, and I don't think that one little scuffle is anything to concern us. I should be able to make my entrance to good effect," the Governor said. "And make it strictly according to plan. Don't you think so, Sheriff Kresh?"

Sheriff Alvar Kresh grunted noncommittally as he stepped to the Governor's side. Maybe to a politician, a room jampacked with all manner of people was a good thing. Not to a policeman—and especially not to a policeman who was outside his jurisdiction and standing next to a man who received a half-dozen death threats a week. But still, the question deserved some sort of polite answer. "It's a splendid party, Governor."

Alvar leaned over the rail next to Grieg and ran his fingers through his thick white hair—something he only did when he was on edge. He glanced over his shoulder at Donald. It *had*

to be his imagination, of course, but it seemed to him that
Donald looked just as ill at ease as Alvar was himself.

The thought was ridiculous, of course. Donald didn't have
expressions—or emotions to express, for that matter. His face
was nothing more than two immobile, glowing eyes and a
speaker grill, as motionless and unreadable as could be.

But for all of that, Donald *did* seem edgy. Kresh shook his
head to himself. He was imagining things. It happened when
he got jumpy.

The Governor should never have come to Purgatory with
the situation as unsettled as it was. But then, from the politician's point of view, it was the very *fact* of things being unsettled, out of control, that made a visit here *necessary*. The
Governor needed to be seen as in command, in charge, secure
enough to host a party and a conference. That he plainly
wasn't in control only made the need all the more urgent.

Grieg glanced over at Alvar and smiled again, but there was
something stiff, theatrical, about the expression, and a glint of
something very like fear in the man's eyes. *He knows*, Kresh
thought. That was the damned thing about it. Grieg knew perfectly well that he was taking his life in his hands tonight. It
wasn't that he was deluding himself, or ignoring the danger,
or brushing the warnings aside. *He knew*—and yet he went on
anyway. Kresh could admire the man's courage, but that didn't
mean it didn't scare the hell out of him.

Chanto Grieg was a bit over fifty standard years, barely
more than a youth by the standards of the long-lived Spacers.
He was a short and dark-skinned man. Tonight he was wearing
his shoulder-length black hair in a thick, ropy braid at the back
of his head. He was a bit on the sharp-faced side, with dark
brown eyes. He was wearing a handsome burgundy suit, set
off with black piping at the shoulders and waist. His black
trousers had a burgundy stripe down the outer seam. He presented a striking appearance.

There had always been something hunted-looking about him, however much he might try to hide it with charm and smiles. These days, the charm was as strong as ever, but the hunted look was getting easier and easier to see. Chanto Grieg was a man who heard footsteps behind him, and was trying to pretend he did not.

And Alvar Kresh heard the footsteps just as loudly—and he could not afford to pretend otherwise. Dammit, he had to try one more time. He had to. "Sir, a word, just a quick word. Can we go back to your office for a moment?"

Grieg sighed and nodded. "Very well. It won't do any good, but very well."

"Thank you, sir." Kresh took Grieg by the arm and led him back up the stairs, back toward Grieg's office. At least it had a proper armored door. No one could get in or out unless Grieg let them in.

Grieg put his palm on the security plate and the door slid open. They stepped into the room, a handsome, if spartan, chamber. Alvar Kresh looked around with more than passing interest. He had only been in here once before, briefly, years before, during some sort of signing ceremony Grieg's predecessor had put on. It was, after all, a famous room. A lot of historic occasions in the life of the planet had happened here— back in the days when Inferno had history. The island of Purgatory had been the first part of the planet to be settled, centuries ago, and there had been some sort of Residence for the Governor on the island ever since. The current building was only a century or so old, but it still had the resonances of a planet's biography.

A desk with a black marble top sat at one end of the room, the desk's surface completely empty, not so much as a fingerprint on it. A vaguely thronelike chair stood behind the desk; facing the desk were two slightly uncomfortable-looking audience chairs, just a trifle lower than standard height.

Amazing, Alvar thought. *Even here, in the private working office of the Governor's winter vacation home, they had played the game.*

A game that was a relic of the past, of the last century, as much as the room itself. Back then, Inferno's architects and craftsmen were still at least willing to play up to the cultural mythology of the Spacers, even if they did not, strictly speaking, *believe* in it anymore.

Infernals were Spacers, and, the myths told them, Spacers were a proud and mighty people, in the vanguard of human progress. It was therefore fit and proper for the Governor who represented a planet of such splendid people to appear a little larger than life. Put him in a higher chair, arrange things so he looks down upon his visitors.

This place had been designed and built in the last century. These days, no one would even bother with all that nonsense. No one had the confidence, the arrogance, to pull it off anymore. *No, that's not quite it,* Alvar told himself. *It'd be closer to the truth to say they could no longer bring themselves to go through the motions. Back then they could still brazen it out.* Even a hundred years ago, no one had *believed* the myth anymore, but they had all played along. Now, no one could even *pretend* to believe. And yet Inferno was covered with buildings of that era, palaces of thundering arrogance, constructed to demonstrate wealth and power and influence that had already been ebbing away when their first stones were being set in place. Inferno was full of rooms like this, symbols of power that had shriveled away, become no more than memorials to power.

There were other clues to show how much the state of affairs had changed, some of them in the form of things that were no longer there. No fewer than four robot niches lined the wall behind the Governor's chair. Time was, the Governor could not be seen in public with anything less than a full quartet of robots in attendance. Now the niches stood empty. Governor Grieg rarely used even a single personal robot.

But the biggest clue was no doubt off in the far corner of the room, as far as possible from the Governor's desk, as if no one wanted to put the terrible truth of the future too close to the glorious fictions of the past. It was a simglobe unit, smaller than the one back in Government Tower in Hades, but still sleek and impressive. It was a holographic display system that could display the planet's appearance and condition as of any moment in its recorded past, or any moment in its future, projecting planet Inferno's response to varying circumstances. The main projection unit was a metal cylinder about a half meter across and a half-meter high. It could display the globe of Inferno in hundreds of different ways, from short infrared to a false-color image of the projected humidity at two thousand meters above sea level a hundred years from now.

It was a Settler-built simglobe, of course. The Settlers made all the best terraforming and terraforming computation gear. In fact, they pretty much made the best of everything, these days. Except robots, of course. Robots were the only thing Spacers did better, and that was by default. No Settler wanted anything to do with robots.

Spacers were on the way down. The Settlers had passed them by, leaving them so far behind that they didn't even consider the Spacers a threat. These days, Spacers were charity cases.

After all, the Settlers were here to help reterraform Inferno, supposedly out of the goodness of their hearts—though Alvar doubted that. And, most galling of all, the government of Inferno had no choice but to accept their help—or watch the planet die.

Grieg stepped into the room, turned his back on the grandiose desk, and sat down in the center of a low couch near the simglobe. *Choosing the real future over the imagined past,*

Kresh thought. Grieg seemed to be putting on a show of being relaxed and at ease. He stretched out his legs in front of him and put his hands behind his head.

Alvar sat down in an easy chair facing the couch, but there was nothing easy or relaxed about *his* posture. He sat down on the edge of the chair, leaning forward, his arms resting on his knees. Donald followed a discreet distance behind Kresh and stood at the back of his chair, just far enough off so as not to seem to be intruding.

"All right, Sheriff," Grieg said. "What's on your mind?"

Kresh didn't know exactly how to begin. He had already tried all the logical, sensible approaches, produced all the subtle, vague bits of intelligence that told him something was wrong without telling him what. None of it had worked. Tonya Welton's vanishing attackers, and the false SSS agents, were the most concrete things he could point to—but even they were maddeningly unclear.

The hell with it, then. Nothing careful or reasoned. No recourse to rumor or vague whispers of threat. Just blurt it out. "Sir, I have to ask you once again to think about a lower profile here. This island—this whole planet—is in chaos. It is my professional judgment that you are placing yourself in extreme danger by attending this function."

"But the reception has already begun," Grieg objected. "I can't cancel out now."

And up until now, you've put me off by saying you could cancel at the last minute if things got out of hand, Alvar thought. Typical of the man that he would try to have it both ways. But there was no point in saying that. "Plead off with a headache or something," Kresh said. "Or just let *me* come out and take the blame. Let me cancel the whole party right now, blame it on a security alert. Blame it on the attack on Welton. I could say there was a threat to your life." *That* much at least would be true. Alvar Kresh's desk was overflowing with threats against the Governor—half of them linked to this visit.

"But what in Space does an attack on Welton have to do with me?" the Governor asked.

Kresh told him about the bogus SSS agents whisking away the attackers. "It's a very strange circumstance," Kresh said. "It's the sort of thing that seems like it should be a diversion— but a diversion for what? What is the direction we weren't supposed to look in? I *have* to assume that it was related to you in some way."

"Sheriff, be reasonable," Grieg said. "Half the most powerful Infernals and Settlers on the planet are here already. Can you imagine the political damage if I hustled them all out into the night and the pouring rain because some drunk got the worst of it in a scuffle with the Settlers' leader? How am I supposed to explain to my guests that the Sheriff of Hades was worried one of *them* might take a shot at me? I have to *negotiate* with these people tomorrow morning. I can't make much progress with someone I've accused of attempting my murder."

"Then plead illness," Kresh said. "Announce pressing business back in the capital. Get back to Hades, and hold a party there. A bigger one. A better one. Hold it in Government Tower, where we can do a decent job of protecting you."

"Kresh, can't you see that it would defeat the whole point of the exercise to entertain the Settlers *there*? That would as much as confess to the whole planet that the Spacers own the island of Purgatory. One island is just the thin edge of the wedge, they'll say. Next thing you know they'll be taking over the planet. *You* know the Ironhead line. You've heard Beddle spout it often enough."

"Yes, sir."

"Then you know why I had to entertain them all *here*, be the host *here*. Show them this is still the *Governor's* Winter

Residence. Here, on the island of Purgatory. Show that Purgatory is still *Spacer* territory, *Infernal* territory. I'm here showing this is still our planet, our land, even if we have temporarily ceded some jurisdiction for the moment. I can't make that statement by hunkering down in that fortress of a tower.''

"Sir, how much can any of that matter?'' Kresh asked. "Who the devil cares about all that posturing? No one outside of the Ironheads cares if the Settlers have partial jurisdiction over the island.''

"Damnation, Kresh, don't you think I know all that? Do you think *I* care who runs this or that patch of this damned rock? It's all nonsense, and it sucks up my energy and attention, takes me away from all the things that *do* matter.''

"Then why risk your life with all these appearances? It's not as if this is the first time.''

"Because if I don't look to be in control, I can't govern. The bill of impeachment cleared the first subcommittee today, did you know that? Or did you know that twenty percent— *twenty percent*—of the voting population has already signed that damned recall petition?''

"I didn't know the numbers were that high, sir, but all the same—''

"All the same, if they get me out of office, Quellam takes over. He'll cave in to the pressure to hold a special election rather than serve out my term, and in one hundred days Simcor Beddle will be Governor of the planet! He'll kick the Settlers off-planet the second the last vote is counted—''

"And the terraforming project will collapse without the Settlers around to support it. I understand all that.''

"Then try and understand that as of *right now*, I still have the political strength to fend off the recall and the impeachment. Just barely. I can ride it all out, until the situation starts to improve. But if I show *any* weakness, or indecision, or if I even appear to knuckle under to the Settlers, I go down, Quellam takes over, and Beddle comes in.''

"Then can't you talk to the Settlers? Ask them to back down just a bit? Renegotiate the jurisdiction agreement?''

Grieg laughed and shook his head. "You do amaze me sometimes, Kresh. You're so *good* at *your* job, and certainly that involves politics enough. You proved that when you solved the Caliban case. So consider the politics in *my* job. It shouldn't be too hard—there's nothing else *to* my job. Don't you think the Settlers know that if I go down, Beddle comes in?''

"Yes, sir, I suppose so.''

"The Settlers also know that they aren't exactly the most popular group on the planet. If they were seen as *supporting* me, they'd be cutting their own throats. They know that if they want to build me up, they have to be ready to lose a fight or two in order to do it.''

"So they're going to cave in?'' Kresh asked. "You've talked to them? The fix is in?''

Grieg smiled, but in a cold, hard-edged way. There was nothing of pleasure about his expression. "Oh, no. Far from it. I can't afford to have secret agreements with the Settlers. Not with the number of people out there trying to dig up any dirt they can on me. And I assume that Tonya Welton and the other Settler leaders would find it just as embarrassing if someone uncovered a secret codicil between us.

"I *believe* the Settler leaders have come to the conclusion I have just described, but I don't dare ask them—and they certainly aren't going to volunteer the information. And bear in mind, they have to placate their *own* reactionaries. It may well be that Tonya Welton feels obliged to take the jurisdiction issue right to the wall.''

"But you don't think so,'' Alvar suggested.

"No, I don't. I think that she and I will work through our

little ritual battle for the sake of the masses, and at the end of this weekend I will be able to announce a settlement on terms highly favorable to us. And then, next time, it will be my job to do a favor for Welton. There will be some battle she needs to win more than I do, and I will put up a good fight and then surrender gracefully.''

"Politics,'' Alvar said, scorn in his voice.

"Politics,'' Grieg agreed cheerfully. "The pointless, useless, self-absorbed, time-wasting charade that makes everything else possible. Without the meetings, the compromises, the smoothing out, the posturing and posing, we would not be able to deal with each other. Politics is the way we try and get along with each other—and we do try. Think about the mess things are in most of the time. Can you imagine the state of affairs if we *didn't* make the attempt?''

"But staging a fake confrontation with the Settlers just to keep the Ironheads happy? Pretending you care about who owns which scraps of useless wasteland just to keep the electorate happy? What possible use can that be?''

Grieg lifted his hand and shook an admonitory finger at Alvar. "Be more careful with the facts, Sheriff. I only said I *thought* it was a false confrontation. It might actually turn out to be real. I must assume it is real in any event, so what difference does it make? Besides, I would submit that keeping the people happy does me a great deal of good. The more content the people are, the fewer recruits there will be for the Ironheads.''

"But you're wasting your time on all this nonsense when there is a planet to save! You should be concentrating on the terraforming project.''

Grieg's expression grew serious. "You must understand, Sheriff. All this *is* nonsense—but it is an integral part of the terraforming effort. I need political cover if I am to have room to maneuver. If I am to get labor and materials and data, I am going to have to get them from the people that control them. It would do me no good at all to stare at engineering plans all day if the Ironheads got strong enough to pressure the engineers into refusing to provide their services.''

''But what use is it expending so much of your energy on this charade over jurisdiction?''

''Oh, it's a very great deal of use. It short-circuits the Ironheads, keeps them from having an issue to use against me. It reassures the people that I am looking out for their interests—and perhaps by my bowing to their wishes this time, I will earn a bit of credit with them. Perhaps they will be patient with me, willing to go along with me on some other, more meaningful issue. I need to do some things to maintain my political standing. I might have the best intentions in the world, but I can't do much good if I am impeached.''

''Well, to be blunt about it, Governor, you can do even less good if you're assassinated.''

''That thought has crossed my mind,'' the Governor said with a note of grim humor. ''But if I just holed up in some bunker under Government Tower to hide from the assassins, then not only would there be no way to kill me—but there would be no *need* to kill me. It would be such an admission of weakness and fear that I could do no good anyway.''

''Sirs, if I might interject—''

''Yes, what is it, Donald?'' Kresh asked. To an outsider, it would surely have seemed incongruous, to say the least, for a mere robot to interrupt a conversation between the planetary Governor and the Sheriff of the planet's largest city. But Donald had worked with Kresh for years, and Kresh knew that Donald would not speak unless it was something that would be of help to Kresh.

The robot turned and addressed the Governor directly. ''Sir, there is a factor that you have not considered.''

''And what might that be?'' the Governor asked, smiling a

bit more openly this time. Clearly, he found the idea that Donald could contribute to the conversation highly amusing.

Careful, Governor, Alvar thought. *Don't underestimate Donald. It's always a mistake.* People often assumed Donald was as subservient as his appearance made him seem. They were wrong to do so.

"I cannot permit you to attend the reception," Donald told the Governor. Scarcely the words of a meek robot.

"Now just a minute—"

"I am sorry, sir, but I am afraid that the conversation I have just heard, coupled with the incident downstairs, has so heightened my concern for your safety, and my belief that the evening as planned will be dangerous to you, that First Law constrains me to prevent you from leaving this room."

" 'A robot may not, through inaction, allow a human being to come to harm,' " Kresh quoted with a chuckle.

Grieg looked at Donald, opened his mouth as if to protest, and then thought better of it. *Sensible of him,* Kresh thought. There was no appeal against a robot driven by a First Law imperative—especially an Inferno-built robot. The planet had a tradition of setting First Law potential very high indeed. Grieg had to know that arguing with Donald would be about as effective as shouting at a stone wall.

Grieg turned toward Kresh. "You set him up to this," the Governor protested. "You had this planned."

Alvar Kresh laughed and shook his head. "Sir, I wish I *had* set it up. But Donald deserves all the credit."

"Or all the blame," Grieg said, still rather irritated. He turned to the robot. "You know, Donald, it's remarkable, really, how soon one forgets."

"Forgets what, sir? The need to take reasonable precautions?"

"No. It's remarkable how soon one forgets the habits of slavery."

"I am afraid I don't understand, sir."

"Not so long ago I sent my own personal robots away," Grieg said. "I started taking care of myself. And I discovered that I no longer had to be careful about what I said or did. All my life, up until that time, I had been careful. I knew that if I phrased something a bit too adventurously, or stood a trifle too close to an open window in a tall building, or reached for a piece of fruit that had not been sterilized, you robots would rush in to protect me from myself. A year ago, I never would have dared discuss my personal safety in front of a robot—precisely because the robot would overreact in just the same way you have now. I would not have dared say or do anything that might upset a robot. My robots controlled my actions, my words, my thoughts. Who controls whom, Donald? Human or robot? Which is the slave, and which is the master?"

"I wouldn't suggest repeating that pretty speech in public, sir," Kresh cut in, thinking it was probably best not to give Grieg the chance to play any more word games. "Not unless you wanted to face an Ironhead lynch mob."

Grieg laughed without humor. "You see, Donald? I *am* a slave to robots. I am the Governor of this world, and yet I dare not speak out against them, for fear of my life. How does *that* square with your First Law? How does a robot deal with the knowledge that its very existence could cause harm to humans?"

"There *are* low-function general-purpose robots who would experience significant First Law cognitive dissonance when asked that question," Donald said. "However—"

"Donald, damnation," Kresh said. "The Governor was asking a rhetorical question."

"Forgive me if I was in error. I thought the Governor required me to answer."

"As I do, Donald," Grieg said, grinning at the Sheriff. Kresh sighed. "You were saying?"

"I was saying that I am a police robot, with my Third Law potential especially strengthened so as to allow me to witness unpreventable harm to a human in the course of my work and survive. The bald statement that my existence harms humans does not cause me any meaningful distress, as I know it to be untrue. Beyond that, I would observe that you did not make any statement to the effect that robots harmed you."

"I did not?"

"No, sir. You said that being near robots caused you to be more careful of your safety, and that expressing your *opinion* of robots—not robots themselves—might expose you to danger at the hands of your enemies."

"This has ceased to be amusing," Grieg said. "I am going to attend my own reception."

"No, sir," Donald said. "I am prepared to restrain you physically in order to prevent it."

"Excuse me, but I think there is a compromise possible," Kresh said. "Donald, would you regard the Governor as being sufficiently protected *if* the security robots in the basement were activated and deployed? Protected enough so you could allow him to attend the party?" There were fifty Security, Patrol and Rescue robots in the basement. SPRs, or Sappers, were sentinel robots. They were powered down for the moment, but ready for use if needed in an emergency. Ten more SPRs had been flown in with the Governor, but those were still stored in a cargo flier, a deep reserve. The ones in the basement could be deployed much more quickly.

Donald hesitated a moment. "Very well," he said at last. "I could permit it under those circumstances."

"Governor?"

"The publicity of all those robots around," the Governor said. "I don't know."

Good. He was weakening. "We play up the security threat," Kresh said. "And we urge the camera crews to keep the robots out of frame as much as possible.''

''Hmmm. The camera crews were supposed to clear off shortly after my entrance in any event. All right—if you make an announcement beforehand that it is a security precaution. If you cause the trouble, Kresh, you're going to take the blame.''

''Believe me,'' said Alvar Kresh, ''nothing could make me happier than taking the blame for surrounding you with robots.''

It took far less time to change all the arrangements than anyone had expected. It took a mere twenty minutes for a pair of Rangers to power up the security robots and deploy them, and it would have taken less time than that if they hadn't lost time working on one defective robot.

It didn't take much convincing at all to get the press to cooperate, once Kresh made a few dark hints about an unexpected security problem and the possibility of remaining danger. Normally, the Governor was fair game for all sorts of sour coverage—but no one in the press pool was going to twit him for accepting security precautions in the face of a real threat to his life.

And so, in very short order, Governor Grieg was able to attend his own party, making a first-rate entrance from the top of the formal staircase, with a grand and swelling fanfare playing as he descended with everyone cheering and applauding even more loudly than they had for Beddle. Somehow, it all fell into place, and Grieg got exactly the boost he had been looking for. In the twinkling of an eye, the Governor stopped being the man in danger of impeachment and became the dynamic leader, the man of the hour. It could all change back just as fast, of course, but that was in the nature of the beast. For now, it was working. Grieg was in the center of a swirl of noise and light, a focus for adulation.

He stepped off the bottom of the stairs. He spotted Kresh in the crowd and came over. He pumped Kresh's hand, patted him on the back, and leaned toward him. "I think it's going to be all right," Grieg half shouted into his ear. "But thank you for your concern. We'll talk again tomorrow, you and I. There are some important things I need to tell you. There isn't time to cover them properly tonight."

"Yes, sir," Kresh bellowed back. "But first you go and have a good time tonight."

"I will, Sheriff, I will," the Governor said, and made his way into the press of the crowd.

4

TIERLAW VERICK WAS deeply annoyed to be in the same room with so many robots. For what seemed the dozenth time, he stepped out of the way of one of the SPR robots on random patrol. They were certainly necessary under the circumstances—he would be the last to argue that—but he did not have to like them. And Beddle's presence was even more intolerable. Sooner or later someone would have to do something about that man. Verick only hoped it was sooner. He didn't know a great deal about the man's politics, but he knew that Beddle was pro-robot, and that was all he needed to know.

Verick was a Settler, and hated robots with a passion rare even for that breed. But he was also a businessman, and he loved profit with a rare passion as well. Love of money, love of the game of business, had pulled him into all sorts of deals—and introduced him to all sorts of interesting, if unsavory, people.

He resisted the temptation to check his watch once again. The night would pass soon enough, and he would have his chance to talk with Grieg. And have his chance at enormous profit, as well.

•   •   •

It all went very well, Grieg thought as he watched the Ranger-waiters take down the last of the serving tables. He turned and went up the stairs to his office. Other than Beddle's shenanigans, and that spot of bother about the fistfight, the evening had gone more smoothly than he had had any right to expect.

When the host was the Governor, however, the end of the evening by no means meant the end of the night. Both tradition and practicality dictated that he now take the opportunity afforded to meet with those who needed a private word with him.

Now, after the party was over, was the chance to see old political allies with advice to offer, petitioners asking this or that favor of him, admirers who wanted nothing more than to shake the Governor's hand, people who needed to put a word in his ear but couldn't risk being seen doing so.

Grieg enjoyed the after-hours meetings. They appealed to the wheeler-dealer politician in him. To him, the back-room meetings represented the *game* of politics, the fun of it, the *juice* of it. They were the informal moments that served as a sort of social lubricant for all the official, carefully staged occasions.

The need to keep the various meetings private necessitated some connivance and juggling. This was one reason the Governor's office had more than one entrance, for those times when an exiting appointment A would not wish to encounter an arriving appointment B. People who did not want to run into other people could slip out the office's side door, which could be opened by hand—but no one could get in that way. There was a second door, down a short hallway. The first door would not unlatch if the second door was open, and neither could be opened from the outside. A visitor who left could not come back, and that was often a great comfort.

There were only four groups this evening. Well, that is to

say, only four *official* groups. Grieg could only see delegation number five under the most unofficial of circumstances.

The first three weren't any real challenge. Grieg got through them in good order, each of them in and out in fifteen minutes.

Grieg checked his appointment log as soon as number three was gone. Next up: Tierlaw Verick, the Settler engineer here to sell Inferno terraforming equipment. Grieg skimmed the tickler file information on the man. *Settler . . . native of Baleyworld . . . fancies himself a philosopher . . . virulently anti-robot, even for a Settler . . . single . . . Suspected in smuggling plots, but no proof. Hobbies: a student of ancient Earth peoples and myths, amateur theatrics.*

None of that mattered. What was important was that Verick would want to know Grieg's decision. Who would get the job on the control system—Verick, or Sero Phrost's consortium of Infernal companies that wanted the contract?

The real question was a Settler system versus a Spacer system. The Settlers offered an automated system that would be under direct human control, while the Spacers, the Infernals, were, of course, offering a robot-controlled unit. There were political, philosophical, and engineering reasons on both sides of the argument. He had them listed out on a piece of paper, neat columns of pros and cons, full of the kind of intricate argument that Spacers delighted in.

On impulse, Grieg grabbed up a pen and ran an ''X'' across the whole page. He wrote in a new question, the only question, along one margin of the page. *Which system would be best for the people of Inferno?* The Control Center would be running the planet for the next fifty years, restabilizing the climate, bringing the whole creaky frailty of the ecosystem back under control. Grieg had made his decision a day or so before, but he had not revealed it yet. Not until he saw Verick and Phrost again. There was always the chance that one or the other could do something that would change his mind, that something

would shift the equation. Give Verick another chance. Not that
the corrupt old paranoid deserved it. But Grieg was interested
in hardware, not personalities.

The annunciator chimed, and Grieg went to the door to let
Verick in.

"Tierlaw! Do come in. Thanks for being so patient." He
offered his hand to the Settler and shook it with the slightly
too-vigorous enthusiasm of a politician.

"Oh, not at all, Governor," Verick said. "There's a Settler
saying that you have to stay up very late if you want to see
the dawn. There are rewards for waiting."

"Yes, yes, absolutely," Grieg said as he guided his guest
to a chair and sat down opposite him. "Now then, let's get
down to business. What is your control system going to do for
me?"

In the depths, in the darkness, Ottley Bissal waited, struggling to be patient, resisting the urge to get out, to run, to
hurry from the shadows toward the light.

His hiding place was pitch-black, absolutely devoid of light.
He had known that it would be so, his briefers had made that
clear. But he had not realized just how *profound* darkness
could be—how *dark* true blackness was. It preyed at him,
chewed at him, caught at him right in the gut.

He was scared, fear-sweat dripping off him, his imagination
running wild.

Would he be able to do it? When the go signal came, would
he be able to step from this hiding place and do what he had
come to do?

Or suppose the go signal did *not* come? Suppose there was
silence, or instructions to abort? What if his coconspirators
determined that the moment was not right, that the danger was
too great? What would he do then?

Ottley Bissal knew the answer.

He would carry out his mission, no matter what orders came.

Things between Verick and Grieg were not nearly as jovial by the end of the meeting. It was all Grieg could do to keep his temper under control. Verick's behavior hadn't surprised Grieg, but that did not make it any less infuriating. He fought down the impulse to throw the man out, cancel his bid, and throw the job to Phrost immediately.

But was Phrost any better? And what did Verick's tactics have to do with the one question that mattered—*Which system would be best for the people of Inferno*?

"You have heard what I have to say," Grieg said. "I have told you what I will tell the planet in two days time."

"It does not make me happy," Verick said.

"My decision is binding," Grieg said, his voice flat and hard. "And now, I must say good night to you."

"Very well," Verick said, jamming his hands into his pockets, balling his hands into fists. "I will say no more about it," he said, and headed, not for the outer door, but for the inner door that led back into the Residence. The door failed to open at his approach, and he pulled his hands out of his pockets and grabbed at the handle.

Grieg sighed. Typical Settler. Determined to do things the hard way. Grieg pushed a button on his desk, and the door slid open.

Verick stomped out, the door shut itself again, and that was that. Thank the stars all his meetings were not that unpleasant.

One last meeting, he told himself with a sigh, *and it's going to be just as damned tricky.* No favors or rumors or backstairs gossip, no minor issue he could trade and dicker on, no preliminary meeting that was nothing more than pleasantries. No, this one might be worse than the one with Verick. This one went to the core of his most vital policies.

The door opened, and the last two petitioners of the night came in, precisely on time.

Grieg got up from his desk, stepped around it, and ushered the two of them in. "Come in, come in," he said, forcing a cheerful smile onto his face. "The three of us have a lot to talk about."

Grieg perched himself on the corner of his desk as the two robots, Caliban and Prospero, sat themselves down.

Twenty minutes later the two robots stepped out into the still-wild night, the rain slamming down so hard as to bother even a robot. The footing was tricky, visibility was poor, and infrared vision was of no real use. But Caliban was in a hurry. He wanted to get away from the Residence as soon as possible.

In a world where everyone used aircars, there was no road back to town from the Residence for those who had no aircar, and Caliban and Prospero had to walk along on a poorly paved brookside path that was completely washed out in places. The going was treacherous. But Caliban knew that statement applied to more than the footpath. There were other dangers ahead.

"I have long thought there would come a point," he told his companion, "where I would no longer support you or assist you, friend Prospero. We have now come to that point. What you have done tonight—what you have drawn me into to-night—goes quite beyond the pale. No amount of logic-chopping or parsimonious interpretation of the New Laws can justify it. Even I, with no Laws to guide me—or control me—found it hard to stand passively by. It greatly distresses me to see you as a party to such things—let alone be a party to them myself."

"I am surprised to hear those words from you, Caliban," Prospero said. "Of all the beings in the world, surely you can understand the importance of our cause.''

''It is *your* cause, not 'ours.' '' There was an edge of vehemence that was startling in a robotic voice. ''There is no
reason I can see why I should consider it *mine*. New Law
robots are more a danger to me than to anyone else. The more
you transgress, the more *I* am harassed, and suspected by association.''

''And do you fear being suspected in tonight's actions?''

''I fear far more than suspicion,'' Caliban said. ''I fear being
vaporized by a law officer's blaster.''

The path ahead dipped down, and the brook had risen to
engulf it altogether. But the only way out was forward, and
there was no going back. Caliban stepped out into the water
and forded across.

Donald turned the aircar into a descent pattern as they arrived at the hotel complex. He eased the car down into a landing next to Alvar's guest villa and rolled the car forward into
the villa's covered garage.

Kresh thanked the stars he had rated at least a modest private villa rather than having to settle for one of the low-end
three-room suites in the main hotel building. The island was
so filled to bursting with visitors that even some of the higher-
ranking guests had to sleep with two or three other parties on
the same floor. But there were no such crowds for Kresh to
contend with tonight, praise be. Like most Infernals, and most
Spacers in general, Kresh did not care to have his quarters in
close proximity to anyone else's.

Thank the stars as well for a covered garage. Kresh did not
much care for getting caught in the rain.

Just before the party, Kresh had overheard some Settler terraform tech explaining to a member of the Governor's staff
why they could not shut off the field that was shifting the wind
and causing the rain just for the reception. Something about

the windshifting project being in a delicate transition state, or something.

At least *this* weatherfield generator was working. There were four other such force field generators placed at strategic points on the planet—but all of them were centuries old, and none of the others were functional at the moment. They had been much used near-antiques when they had first been brought to Inferno for use during the original, inept, penny-pinching attempt to terraform the planet.

The hatch sighed open and Kresh disembarked. Donald came out after him, then scooted out ahead of him to get the door to the villa itself.

Alvar Kresh followed the robot inside, moving almost more mechanically than Donald. He was tired. He reached his room and breathed a long, hard sigh of relief. It was over. The reception was ended, the guests had gone home, and the host was alive—if, perhaps, none too well pleased with Kresh. Well, if Grieg was annoyed and alive, that was better than having him satisfied and dead. Tidying up after a slightly undiplomatic performance at a party was a devil of a lot easier than dealing with the aftermath of a political assassination.

Am I being paranoid? Kresh asked himself. *Are the dangers as great as I think?*

The answer to that was that the dangers *might* be real, and that was all that mattered to a policeman.

Governor Grieg was leading a revolution from above, and a lot of people didn't like it. Revolutions made for complicated politics, caused fortunes to be made and lost, changed friends to enemies, enemies to friends. Shared assumptions turned into points of controversy during the night. The invaluable turned worthless, and what had been common became rare—and priceless. New ways of making a living, new ways of committing a crime, suddenly sprang up—and often it was hard to tell one from the other.

But none of that concerned Kresh. Not directly. Not tonight. What did bother him was another fact about revolutions: it was exceeding rare for the people who began them to survive to their conclusions. Even a successful revolution often killed off its leadership.

Kresh did not even agree with most of what the Governor was trying to do. But it wasn't his job to agree. His job was to maintain stability and public safety. Protecting the person of the Governor was part of that job. Back in the capital city of Hades, Kresh had the power and capabilities, the resources, to protect the Governor effectively. Not here on the island of Purgatory. Here no one knew who was in control, who was in charge of what patch of turf at the moment.

Alvar removed his gun belt, hung it over the back of a chair, and sat down on the edge of the bed. He pulled off his boots, loosened the rather severe collar of his dress tunic, and flopped back on the bed, exhausted, glad to be alone.

Alone. Back before the Caliban crisis, it was unlikely that Kresh had ever in his life spent more than an hour at a time truly alone. There had always been robots around, watching after him, fussing over him, attending to his every need and wish, including some wishes he had never needed to ask for— or, in fact, truly desired.

But solitude. That was something a robot could never give you, except by giving you nothing. Alone, without the slightest thought of how anyone—or anything—might react to your behavior. No need whatsoever to look over your shoulder, no sense at all of a robot worrying endlessly over your safety, no concern that some look or gesture or muttered word might be interpreted as an implied order. No moment when it was easier to cooperate with the wishes of a bothersome servant, rather than argue or negotiate past whatever imagined fear or perceived order the robot was determined to deal with. Grieg had had a point, talking to Donald about the tyranny of the servant.

Back in the old days, Kresh never could have allowed himself the luxury of collapsing in a heap at the end of a long day. The luxury of being alone, without the need to worry what anyone—flesh and blood, or metal and plastic—might think. Even in front of Donald, there had been a certain sense of reserve, of caution.

Alvar Kresh was proud of being Sheriff, and he took the office and his duties very seriously. He had definite opinions about the way a Sheriff should behave, and he was determined to live up to that standard. Part of it was an act, and he knew that. Theatrics were part of being a leader, even in front of the robots.

In the days when Donald had dressed him and undressed him, Kresh had not given the matter a conscious thought. Now he often thought about it. What was it Grieg had said? Something about modifying his own behavior to keep his robots happy. When the robots managed your every action, when they chose your clothes and your meals and your schedule for the day, and you developed the habit of accepting their choices, who *was* the master and who the servant?

Before Caliban's advent had turned so much upside-down, Alvar always knew that if he had collapsed back into bed with his clothes still on and his teeth unbrushed and so on, Donald would have seen it and started to fuss. He would have cajoled him one way or the other to get up and take care of himself, get to bed properly rather than risk dozing off in his clothes without bathing first. And so Alvar had never done it, conceding the battle before it had even been fought.

So there was a certain pleasure, yes, a certain luxury, in being alone, in permitting himself a moment or two of relaxation without a robot fussing about, worrying that it might be harmful to his health if he accidentally dozed off in his clothes.

Luxury. What a strange idea that *not* having robots around could be considered a luxury.

Did Simcor Beddle fear that all the people who had been deprived of their robots would discover the *absence* of robots to be pleasant? Even if you granted the implausible assumption that Beddle was sincerely concerned with anything beside power, that was a silly idea. No one had been deprived of *all* their robots. Certainly twenty per household was far more than enough. Kresh only had five back home, aside from Donald. Maybe Beddle feared that people would make the simple discovery that it *didn't* take fifty robots to care for one person, that most robots spent their time doing little more than getting in each other's way, making work for themselves.

No rational person could believe that it could possibly take as many as twenty robots to run one household—and yet the entire populace was up in arms over the hardship caused by having only one chauffeur per car, or only as many cooks as there were meals in the day.

Still, the uproar was not as loud as it *should* have been, and it had died down sooner than Kresh had expected. Could it be that he was not the only one to find luxury in a moment of private, robotless relaxation?

Of course, he really *ought* to get up now, get to the refresher, and get properly ready for bed. But perhaps it wouldn't do any harm to rest his eyes, just for a moment . . .

Alvar Kresh dozed off, fully clothed, with the lights still on, slumped over in an awkward position half on and half off the bed.

The annunciator chimed, and Alvar's eyes snapped open. He sat up, winced at the stiffness in his back, and lay back with a slight groan. There was a bad taste in his mouth, and his feet were cold. How long had he been out? He felt disoriented, confused. Maybe there *was* something to be said for the smothering attentions of a robot nursemaid.

"Yes, what is it?" Kresh asked of the open air.

Donald's voice came through the door speaker. "Beg pardon, sir, but there is a matter requiring your attention."

"And what might that be, Donald?" Kresh asked.

"A murder, sir."

"What?" Kresh sat back up on the bed, all thought of his aching back and cold feet suddenly gone. "Come in, Donald, come in."

The door opened and Donald stepped inside. "I assumed that you would want to know about it as soon as possible, sir."

"Yes, yes, of course," Kresh said. "But just a minute. I want to be awake enough to follow this." Feeling vaguely ashamed at Donald having caught him at not getting himself to bed properly, Kresh stepped into the hotel room's refresher. He peeled off his tunic, rinsed out his mouth, splashed some water onto his face, and grabbed a towel. He rubbed his face dry and stepped back out into the room. Donald had produced a fresh tunic and a cup of coffee from somewhere. Kresh pulled on the shirt and took the coffee gratefully. He sat down in a chair opposite Donald, ready to listen. "All right," he said. "Go."

"Yes, sir," Donald said. "A member of the Governor's security detail, an officer in the Rangers, was posted as a perimeter guard during the reception. He failed to report back to his station at the close of his shift, and a search was made. He was found, dead, at his post."

"Dead how?"

"Strangled, sir. Or perhaps, more accurately, garroted."

"Lovely. Jurisdiction?"

"As you might expect, sir, that is more than a trifle unclear. His duty post was on land ceded to the Settlers, and thus under the jurisdiction of the Settler Security Service. However, he was of course a member of the Governor's Rangers, but at the same time—''

''He was on duty as part of the Governor's security detail, and therefore under the Rangers' authority,'' Kresh finished. ''Lovely. So we all get to bump heads. Any other facts as yet?''

''No, sir. Not even the victim's name. That is the sum total of my information.''

''Wonderful,'' Kresh said. ''Let's get over there and find out more.''

The two of them headed for Kresh's aircar, parked outside the guest house. Kresh got in after Donald, and sat down in his accustomed chair.

Donald rolled the aircar out of the garage and lifted off, up into the rain that was still thundering down, buffeting the car around once or twice before Donald could compensate. Kresh was barely aware of any of it, his mind focused on other matters. The Welton attack, the phony SSS guards, and now the death of a Governor's Ranger. What the devil was going on?

The Governor. What about the Governor? Kresh thought to ask Donald, but then didn't bother. No matter what Donald said, Kresh would feel obliged to check for himself. Kresh turned in his seat and switched on the comm system. He punched in the crash scramble code, the direct line to the Governor. He had used it exactly twice before in his career, but never felt more need of it than now.

The screen snapped on to show Grieg in his ceremonial office, at work at the big formal desk. There were papers scattered about, and Grieg was still in his formal clothes, but his hair was mussed and he was starting to show a bit of stubble. ''Good evening, Sheriff,'' he said. ''I see I'm not the only one working late.''

''No, sir. I wanted to call personally and confirm that you were safe.''

Grieg set down the papers he was working on and frowned.

"*Safe?* Is there some reason I shouldn't be?"

"No one has informed you? Sir, one of the guards on the perimeter around the Residence has just been found dead, killed on duty, at his post."

"The hell you say," Grieg said. "What more do you know?"

"That's all I have, sir. I am en route to the murder scene now."

"Very well. Keep me informed."

"Ah, yes, sir," Kresh said. "I'll keep you posted." He switched off and frowned at the screen. Why the hell hadn't anyone informed the Governor? Just how muddled was the security operation? He shook his head. Never mind. Other things to worry about just now.

They were almost there.

A dead-white face stared bug-eyed at the sky, its rain-filled mouth open in shock.

Raindrops splattered on the corpse, the scene lit in the harsh, shadowless glare of high-power portable beam lights. The dead man's hands clutched at his neck, as if he were still struggling to pull the cruel, hard wire from around his throat. The corpse was in a small depression in the ground, tangled up in scruffy bramble, surrounded by a scrubby, anemic forest of small, elderly trees.

Lightning flashed and thunder blared, and Alvar Kresh stood over the corpse in the driving rain. The Crime Scene robots were already at work. Not that they would do any good. The CS robots could measure and sense and detect all they wanted, but there were no answers here. They could go back to their labs and come up with a time of death, perhaps, but that was going to be about it.

Alvar Kresh looked down at the dead man and sighed. He had been in this business for a while, and experience taught

you things. There were times when you knew enough to know
you weren't going to know any more. Sometimes the scene of
a crime spoke volumes. Other times—right now, for example—it was plain to see that prodding at the corpse was useless. What had once been a man was now a meaningless bit
of grotesquerie, as impersonal, as anonymous as a crumpled-
up food wrapper.

But you went through the ritual all the same, because it was
part of your job, because there was the faint chance that your
instincts just might be wrong, because it was expected of you,
because it was standard procedure. But you knew that there
was no real point.

It was clear, to Kresh's eye, that whoever did this job had
not done it with the simple goal of killing. He or she had taken
on the job of killing *undetected*. It was a careful, professional
job. A garrote, for example, was not going to show any fingerprints. A rainy night would insure that a lot of clues would
be washed away. Besides, anyone who could slip through a
perimeter of Governor's Rangers, kill one of their number, and
get away undetected was not going to be stupid enough to
leave a calling card behind.

Sometimes—like right now—when it was obvious there was
nothing to be learned, crime scenes devolved into little more
than macabre social occasions. Kresh didn't get to see his opposite numbers in the SSS and the Rangers all that often. But
tonight it was old home week. Devray of the Rangers and
Melloy of the SSS were both here.

That in itself was interesting. Neither service was in the
habit of dispatching its highest-ranking officers to a murder
scene. It was clear to Kresh that neither side wanted to concede
a centimeter of ground in the endless turf war between the two
services. Kresh was glad he had nothing at stake in this one.
Let the two of them duke it out.

Kresh didn't have much faith in the SSS *or* the Rangers.

The Settler force was nothing more than a bunch of bullyboys, a goon squad given official sanction. Cinta Melloy's SSS was little more than a band of hired thugs.

The Rangers were a decent enough group, and good at what they did. Kresh was more than willing to grant that. The only trouble was that security was *not* what they did. Their usual line of work ran toward guarding trees, not people. Their primary jobs were search and rescue, wildlife management, ecological maintenance. Their tasks had been seen as dull, plebeian, low-status jobs in the past. These days such work was all-important, high-profile stuff. The needs of the day had vaulted the Rangers out of their previous obscurity.

And yet, here they were, guarding the Governor for no better reason than that their charter said it was their job. Never mind that the charter-writers had been talking about ceremonial guards. Back in those days, no one had ever dreamed that the Governor would require actual protection against real threats, let alone that humans would be expected to do the job.

Kresh could make the case that their inexperience in such matters meant that having the Rangers on the job actually *endangered* the Governor. But the Rangers were insisting on the prerogative of their service even though Kresh's deputies—or perhaps even the SSS—could do a better job of it.

The Rangers had not been trained for security work. They had spent their lives being protected from all harm by robots. At the end of the day, they were Spacers, and Spacers tended to assume that a situation was safe until they learned otherwise. A good security officer had to do just the opposite.

Commander Justen Devray of the Rangers crouched down over the corpse next to Kresh, peering at it intently in the rain, as if he would be able to spot some clue the Crime Scene robots had missed. Devray was a tall, muscular man, with tousled blond hair and blue eyes, his skin tanned and supple. His face was still youthful, but a life in the outdoors had lined it, shaped it. He was gentle and careful in his movements, the way big men were sometimes. He was a good thinker, if not always a fast one, but he simply was not a detective. He had made his way up through the scientific side of the Rangers' ranks. An arboriculturist, if memory served. An expert knowledge of tree sap was not going to be of much use in the average murder investigation.

"Have you picked up anyone?" Kresh asked of Melloy.

She just shook her head. She made no move to squat down and examine the body, or even show much interest in it. *She* knew there was nothing here. "We've done every kind of sweep we can think of. No unauthorized personnel here now, and no sighting—and *that's* strange, right there. I had teams beyond the security perimeter, doing scans. *Someone* should have seen something." She nodded toward the corpse and raised her voice a bit. "Not going to get much out of him, Justen," she said.

"I suppose not," Devray agreed in his slow, careful voice. "But I couldn't know that until I got a look at him."

Devray stood up and turned toward Melloy. "Do *you* see much of anything?"

"I see Ranger Sergeant Emoch Huthwitz dead," Melloy replied, a bit curtly. "Killed by someone who knew where he was and how to get at him without making a sound."

Security Captain Cinta Melloy of the Settler Security Service ought to have been of more use at a murder than a tree surgeon. She had served in trouble spots throughout the Settler worlds. But not to put too fine a point on it, Kresh didn't trust Melloy. There was something about the woman didn't sit right with him. Even now, there was a tiny alarm bell ringing somewhere in the back of his mind.

"I see a bit more than that," Kresh said. "This man was on the Governor's security detail, on duty, with the Governor not two hundred meters away. I don't think we can start out assuming that it was—ah—"

"Huthwitz," Donald said, quietly prompting Kresh.

Damnation! He hated when that happened. Made it look as if he didn't know what he was doing. "I don't think we can start out assuming it was Huthwitz who was the primary target."

"But the Governor survived," Melloy objected.

How do you know that? Kresh wondered. *The Governor didn't even know anything had happened.* No, that was *too* paranoid. Melloy probably checked in with the security robots. "The security plans were changed, beefed up, at the last moment," Kresh answered. "Maybe an assassin got this far, but no further."

"Possibly," Melloy said, not sounding very convinced. "But why kill Huthwitz if you were after the Governor? It could do nothing but increase the risk of detection. The Rangers weren't using any sort of detection grid, just Rangers lined up around the perimeter of the Winter Residence, on watch. Why go up against a Ranger when it would have to be easier to sneak *between* two Rangers in the line?"

"Maybe the killer tried to sneak between Rangers and came upon Huthwitz by accident," Kresh said.

Melloy pointed to a toppled-over camp stool by the body. "Maybe Huthwitz was bending a reg or two by sitting at his post, but you can see by the way the stool was positioned he was looking *out*, toward the exterior of his perimeter, the way he was supposed to. Whoever it was who killed him had to get *in*side the perimeter, *then* head back out toward him. Besides, there aren't any signs of a struggle. Even after three hours of rain like this, we ought to be able to see *something*."

Kresh had noticed the camp stool, but had not put it together to figure out the attacker had come from inside the perimeter. It irritated him to have missed that obvious a clue. "Maybe you've got a point, Melloy, but I have the Governor to think about. You work this any way you want, but I have to work on the assumption that this was an attempt on Grieg's life."

Melloy shrugged. "As you like."

Devray was listening, but still staring at the corpse, as if he had never seen such a thing as a murder victim before. Well, maybe he hadn't. "You know, Melloy, you're making an assumption here yourself," he said. "Perhaps not a valid one."

"And what might that be, Commander Devray?" Melloy asked, not making any special effort to keep the contempt out of her voice.

If Devray noticed the disparaging tone, he chose to ignore it. "The direction," he said. "You pointed out the murderer had to come from behind, from inside the security perimeter."

"So?"

"So there were a lot of people who wouldn't *need* to go past your scanners or sneak between two of my Rangers to get inside the perimeter and get behind him. People who wouldn't show up on your scanners."

"Wait a minute," Kresh protested, suddenly understanding.

"All the people at the party," Devray said, his voice so soft and quiet Kresh could barely hear it over the rain. "Any one of them could have come out here, done the job, and then gone back. A quick step into a refresher to tidy themselves up and get their clothes dry, and no one would ever know."

"All right," Kresh said. "Maybe so. But why the hell would anyone want to kill Huthwitz?"

"That one, I don't know yet," Devray said.

Kresh sat in the copilot's chair and let Donald do the flying. There was a lot to think about here. Things were not fitting together they way they should have. Melloy and Devray both seemed to be following agendas that just didn't hold together.

A man—a guard—killed two hundred meters from the Governor he was guarding, and neither of them seemed the least bit interested in the idea that the killing might be politically motivated.

And another thing. *Melloy* had been the one to volunteer the victim's name. *That* was the thing that had been bothering him. Devray hadn't even seemed to have known the victim.

"Donald—the first call-in you got did not have the victim's name. When was the first general police band hyperwave call with that information?"

"There has been no such call as yet, I presume as a security precaution. I was alerted by a private call from the Governor's Rangers Operations Center."

"Hmmph. Check in with whatever traffic control centers would have it. We got to the crime scene last. Of Devray and Melloy, which got there first, and by how much?"

"One moment, sir." Donald was silent for a moment as he ran the query over his hyperwave links. "Limbo Traffic Center reports that Captain Melloy landed first, with Commander Devray arriving five minutes later, approximately two minutes before we got there."

"So Devray had maybe one minute, maybe three, tops, with Melloy, before we actually got out of our aircar and got to the scene. When we got there, the two of them were not exactly in the midst of warmhearted conversation. The name of the victim is not going to be the first topic of conversation."

"I'm not quite sure I follow you, sir."

"Even if you assume Devray knew the victim well enough to recognize him, it just doesn't follow that the first thing he would do upon arrival at the scene would be to tell Melloy the victim's full name and rank."

"I don't quite see why not, sir. It is a valuable piece of information."

"Maybe so, but it's just not in character. Devray wouldn't

tell you the sun was coming up tomorrow before he sat back
and thought it through—and Melloy's hardly the first person
he'd confide in. The two of them are barely even on speaking
terms.''

"It still would seem reasonable to me for him to tell Melloy
the victim's name.''

"I don't think Melloy or Devray are exactly reasonable toward each other. Besides, Melloy rattled Huthwitz's name off
as if she were familiar with it, knew it well. I agree with you
that there is no logical reason preventing Devray from knowing the name, but I tell you it doesn't make sense as a piece
of human behavior.'' Kresh thought a moment or two longer.
"Of course, I'm assuming Devray knew who it was in the first
place, but he didn't act as if he did.''

"What actions revealed he did not know Huthwitz?''

Kresh shook his head. "Nothing distinct enough for me to
point it out. But there was something *detached* about his actions. Not like he was dealing with a friend or an acquaintance.
No. I'd bet whatever you like that Melloy knew Huthwitz and
Devray did not. But how the hell would Melloy come to know
a low-ranking officer in a rival police force?''

"It seems a minor point, but surely we could resolve the
issue by calling either Devray or Melloy and asking.''

Kresh shook his head. "No. I don't want to do that. I don't
want to tip my hand.''

"Sir, I am confused. What is it you wish to conceal?''

"I don't know yet, Donald. Maybe just the fact that I think
something doesn't smell right. I don't want anyone rushing
around with disinfectant until I find out where the odor's coming from.''

"Sir, I'm afraid I still do not understand.''

"Me neither. I can almost see Devray being worried more
about having one of his officers killed than the politics of the
situation—but that doesn't explain Melloy. It's almost as if

she already knew it was nothing to do with the Governor."
Or, he could not help thinking, *as if she already knew that it
was.*

Wait a second. Wait a goddamned second.

Kresh turned back toward the comm panel and punched in
the crash scramble again. The Governor reappeared on screen
again. Still at his desk. Still working on the same papers. Still
in his formal clothes. "Sheriff!" he said. "Is there some further news?"

"Governor, I was wondering. Could you remind me—what
did you send me on my birthday last year?"

"What? What the devil are you talking about?"

"What present did you send me last year?"

"Kresh, how the devil should I know?"

"You should know quite well, sir. You sent nothing at all."

"You called me at this hour to ask me that?"

"No, I didn't." Kresh cut the connection, his heart pounding. "Donald. Back to the Residence, full emergency speed."

"Yes, sir." The aircar made a hard turn and rushed back
the way it had come, gathering speed. "Sir, I could not help
overhearing, and I am greatly confused," he said, his voice
steady and level. "According to my recollection, the Governor
sent a memo to all the top government officials as soon as he
took office just over two years ago. He told them he was ceas-
ing the tradition of gubernatorial birthday gifts to them effective immediately, as it tended to promote favoritism."

"And just by chance, the memo arrived on my birthday,"
Kresh said. "I didn't feel much like a favorite that day. I
remember, Donald, I remember. But why didn't the *Governor*
know?"

But Kresh already had the answer to that, even if it scared
him to death. The aircar landed hard, and Kresh was out the
hatch and running through the rain toward the front door before it had stopped moving. There should have been an SPR

on duty at the front door, but instead the door was wide open. Kresh rushed inside. The SPR robots were there—but motionless, inert. And if the security robots were out—he ran upstairs to the Governor's office, almost toppling over another security robot standing uselessly in front of the door—with a hole shot through its chest. He slapped his palm on the security panel. The damned thing was supposed to be keyed to his handprint, but was it? He had never tried it. The door slid open and he all but dove into the room, not daring to think what he would find. But the lights were off. He could not see a thing. Kresh pulled his blaster.

. The lights switched themselves on as they sensed someone in the room. And the room was empty. No one was at the desk. There were no papers spread out to be worked on.

Kresh rushed back into the hall, heading for the Governor's bedroom, dodging past two more dead security robots on the way. The bedroom door was wide open. He went inside. And stopped.

The Governor was there.

Sitting up in bed.

With a blaster hole the size of a man's fist in his chest.

5

DONALD 111 ARRIVED in the Governor's bedroom a few seconds after Alvar Kresh, and saw his master standing over the grisly tableaux. But Donald was barely aware of his master. His attention was riveted on Governor Chanto Grieg. The dead man.

It was far from the first corpse Donald had seen, and was the second one he had seen in as many hours—and yet the sight of the Governor's dead body had a more profound effect on him than any of the others. Donald had *known* this man. Worse, not more that eight hours ago, Donald had told the Governor that he would be safe, that the precautions Alvar Kresh had suggested would be enough to protect him. He, Donald, had threatened to prevent this man from attending the party, but had allowed it in the end because fifty SPR security robots would be enough.

And now the man was dead. Dead. Dead. Donald's vision began to dim. The world was growing darker.

"Donald! Stop it!" Alvar Kresh's voice seemed to come from a long way away, far off and unimportant. "Come out of it. I *order* you to stop it! You had no part in Grieg's death. You could have done nothing to stop it. You did nothing to cause it."

Perhaps no other voice could have brought Donald back,
but Kresh's voice, his master's voice, strong, brimming with
authority, did so. His vision cleared and he came to himself
with a start. "Tha—tha—thank you, sir," he said.

"This damn planet sets First Law potential too damn high,"
Kresh growled. "Donald, listen to me. There were fifty se-
curity robots on duty in this house, and Grieg died anyway.
One more robot could not have done any good."

Donald took hold of that thought, focused on it. Yes, yes,
it was true. What could he have done that they could not?

But why hadn't the security robots prevented this disaster?
Donald turned away, not wishing to look on the horrifying
sight of the dead Governor anymore. And, in turning around,
he got his answer. There, lined up against the wall, still in
their wall niches, were three of the SPRs, the Security, Patrol,
and Rescue Sapper security robots—each with a blaster shot
through the chest. *That is what would have happened to me,*
Donald thought. *Had I remained, I would have been nothing
more than another robot uselessly destroyed.* He found a
strange sort of comfort in the idea.

"Sir," he said, "if I could call your attention to this side
of the room."

"Hmm?" Kresh turned around and saw the three destroyed
robots. "Burning hells. Donald. How fast would someone have
to be to get into this room, blast three specialized security
robots before any of them could react, and then kill a man
who would appear to have been sitting up in bed? Kill him
before he could even set his book down?"

"It would be impossible," Donald said, feeling quite sure
of himself. He sensed, somehow, that he and Sheriff Kresh
were, in a strange way, each doing the same thing—struggling
to be professional, looking for the parts of this disaster they
could deal with, putting up a wall against the parts that were
unbearable. "Sir, your point is well taken. Things cannot be

as they seem. But there are more urgent points to consider at the moment. This is not mere murder—this is assassination.''

"You're right, Donald. By all the devils in hell, you're right. This could just be the start of who knows what.'' Alvar Kresh stood there, staring at nothing, clearly still more than a little bit in shock. "Escape,'' he said at last. "We have to cut off their escape. Relay emergency orders, Donald. All—and I mean *all*—transport between the island of Purgatory and the mainland is to be shut down, effective immediately. All outbound sea and aircraft currently in transit are to return with all passengers on-board. No exceptions. All spacecraft grounded. No one leaves the island. Everyone who has left the island since the Governor was last seen alive returns and stays here until they can be questioned.''

"Sir, I must remind you that much of the transport on this island is under Settler control, and thus not within your jurisdiction.''

"The hell with that,'' Kresh said. "Issue the orders. The Settlers had damned well not protest, unless they want this to get completely out of control.''

"Yes, sir,'' Donald said. The Sheriff had given him standing orders long ago, instructing Donald to advise him whenever Kresh issued orders that exceeded his authority. Donald of course followed the order, but there were occasions when he didn't understand why Kresh bothered to have himself told such things—Kresh almost never reversed or revised an extralegal command. But orders were orders, and so Donald always reminded him, and the Sheriff always overruled him.

Donald activated his hyperwave system and began contacting the various traffic control centers on the emergency override bands, relaying the Sheriff's instructions. He could not help but notice that Kresh had not ordered him to offer any explanation for his actions. Had that been deliberate? After a moment's hesitation, he decided not to bring the omission to

Kresh's attention. There might well be good reasons for keeping silent on the catastrophic news. All sorts of chaos might
spring up if news of the assassination spread too fast.

Of course, all sorts of chaos were going to spring up in any
event, but there was nothing Donald could do about that.

Think, man, think. Alvar Kresh did not know what to do.
The clear, logical choice was to call someone, tell everyone.
The world had to know. There was no hope of keeping this
quiet more than an hour or two. *But someone had done this.*
Someone capable of an elaborate plot, capable of getting
through the tightest security and acting with terrible ruthless-
ness.

Someone with a reason. Someone with a motive. Someone
who might well not be finished yet. He had to assume that this
was not an attack on the man, Chanto Grieg, but an attack on
the Governor, the leader of the planet. He had to assume this
was a coup.

But if that was so, who could he call? Not the Rangers. Not
when he was unsure why the devil Justen Devray had been
acting so strangely, not when the Rangers had been so determined, for no clear reason, to insert themselves into the security arrangements. Certainly he could not call the SSS. Even
if he trusted them, it would be politically impossible to bring
them in as the lead agency to investigate the Governor's murder.

With a shock, he realized that he already suspected *both* of
the other law enforcement agencies of complicity in this crime.

But he trusted his own people. He had just been down here
as window dressing, part of the Governor's entourage, but it
was just about time for that to change. Yes. That was it. Of
course. Totally illegal, no doubt, and a flagrant violation of
jurisdiction. But the hell with that. "Donald, contact our headquarters in Hades. I want a full operations team down here,

on the spot, in control of this crime scene. I want the first team
here in three hours, and a full deployment of a Major Crime
Team in eight.''

"Sir, the first team may not be able to arrive here that
quickly. The normal flying time from Hades is just over two
and one-half hours.''

"I do not regard this as a normal circumstance,'' Kresh said.
"Get them here, authorize use of emergency speed overrides—
and don't bother telling me what laws and agreements I'm
violating. By the time the Rangers and the SSS get to this
crime scene, the Sheriff of Hades is going to own it—is that
clear?''

"Yes, sir. Might I ask how we are going to prevent them
from coming here on their own?''

"We aren't going to tell them what's happened, that's how.
Not until my people and my robots are here, and we've started
an investigation I can trust. We can use the room where we
met with Tonya Welton for our command post.'' Alvar Kresh
considered the risks he was running. The decisions he had
made already, in the last ninety seconds, might well be enough
to force his resignation before very long. Maybe enough to get
him arrested and thrown in jail.

But that didn't matter. If he could sit on this thing long
enough, even just two or three hours, that would be enough to
protect the investigation, get his deputies well enough en-
trenched and in charge so that the SSS or the Rangers would
not be able to kick them out.

They solved the most minor part of the mystery first, a question so minor that it could barely be dignified by the name
mystery. Still, it was nice to know how Grieg had managed to
answer the phone after he was dead, and the details of the
answer might lead them somewhere. Kresh found a miniature
Settler-made image box, a rather sophisticated one, hooked

into the comm system. It was sitting on a side table in the
bedroom, plugged into the room's comm jack. The fact that it
was Settler-made meant nothing, of course. Image processors
and sim units were in common use for many legitimate purposes. If anything, the use of a Settler unit suggested a Spacer
involvement in the case, an attempt to throw off the scent.
Actually, it was more likely the plotters had chosen that model
because it was a cube about ten centimeters square, small
enough to be easily smuggled into the Residence.

Kresh was tempted to examine the box himself, but he knew
that was a job for the lab techs. They might well be able to
tell something from the way it was programmed—and they
would be better able than he to overcome any booby-trapping
in the software. He left it alone. It occurred to him that it might
even prove useful to leave it in place. If anyone called, and it
managed to fool them, that could be all to the good, if it kept
the Rangers and SSS out of here a bit longer.

Was he right to suspect them? What was it that he suspected
them *of*? Conspiracy to kill the Governor? It seemed outland-
ish, but the night had already been full of suspicious incidents.
It had to be that the staged attack on Welton had something
to do with it, that Huthwitz had been killed as part of the same
plot, but Kresh could see no way to thread them all together.

And if not the SSS or Rangers, then who had done it? Kresh
could come up with any number of suspects, starting with the
Ironheads, or some lunatic faction of Ironheads, down to practically any fed-up robot owner.

Who knew who else's toes the Governor might have stepped
on? Even if you kept to Grieg's *known* enemies, you still
ended up with half the planet as suspects.

Time. It was turning into a question of time. What could he
do in the time left to them before the deputies arrived, or
before the Rangers or the SSS or the Governor's first morning
appointment arrived? The victim. Take a good hard look at

the victim. Kresh went over to the bed and knelt down next to the Governor's corpse, careful not to touch it or disturb anything. No sense making the Crime Scene robots work harder.

Grieg had been sitting up reading in bed, by the looks of it, and reading an old-fashioned print book at that. It had fallen forward into his lap, still open to the page he had been reading. The tops of the pages had been singed by the blaster shot.

Grieg was still sitting up, his head slumped forward, eyes shut, his hands fallen into his lap with the book on top of them. There was no sign that he had reacted at all, or struggled to get out of the way. He hadn't tried to duck away from the blast or jump out of bed. Either he had been taken utterly by surprise, or he had known his attacker, perhaps even been expecting him—or her. *There* was a thought, and one of some delicacy, to put it mildly. Had the Governor arranged some sort of after-hours assignation? Could he have been killed by an assassin posing as a lover—or could he have been killed by, say, lover A in a jealous rage over lover B? Kresh realized he knew less about the Governor's sex life than he should have. That to one side, it would be wise to bear in mind there were other motives for murder besides political ones.

But there was another question—the security robots. Why had they failed? How did the assassin overcome them? For that matter, how the devil had the assassin gotten into the bedroom? Kresh stepped out into the dimly lit hallway and looked down it both ways. Where had the rest of the robots gone?

Kresh walked back the way he had come, and soon had his answer. There was a slumped-over shape he had not paid much mind when he had first rushed down the hallway. It was another SPR security robot, this one blasted out as well. Except this one had not been killed with a single neat shot through the chest. It had been scorched on the left arm, had its head half-melted off, and then taken a final burn hole through the chest. Three shots at least, from increasingly close range. It looked as if *this* robot had been on the move, trying to react, and had nearly reached its attacker before it finally went down. Kresh felt more certain than ever that there was something suspicious about the ease with which the robots in the bedroom had died. He went farther down the hall and saw two more SPR robots, both shot through the head and the chest. The one in front of the entrance to Grieg's office had been shot the same way.

He stepped back into the bedroom where Donald was waiting for him. "Donald," he said, "who manufactured these security robots?"

"The models used here are manufactured by Rholand Scientific," Donald said.

"Good," Kresh said. "Then Fredda Leving can examine them without a biased opinion. Hand me the voicephone and connect me."

"Sir, in terms of security, may I remind you that Fredda Leving was present last night and may well have had the opportunity to tamper with the robots—"

"In terms of security we will be utterly paralyzed if we are *too* careful. Fredda Leving was not part of this, I can tell you that straight out."

"I agree that the balance of probabilities weighs heavily against suspecting her," Donald said. "However, these robots have clearly been tampered with, and she was perhaps the only person who was present who had the expertise for that job. My First Law potential does extend to preventing you doing professional harm to yourself, and to the potential harm to others if an investigation this serious and dangerous were suborned. I must therefore point out there is no logical basis upon which she can be excluded absolutely."

Kresh took a deep breath and forced himself not to explode.

Handling robots could be a damned nuisance, but it was only made doubly hard by losing one's patience. Of course the same thing was true of people: You were forced to deal with unreasonable demands by being excessively reasonable. "Donald," he said in a calm, slow voice. "I agree with you that there is no *logical* basis for excluding Fredda Leving as a suspect. However, I can assure you that there are reasons, outside of logic, that make me utterly certain she had nothing to do with this."

"Sir, you have said yourself, many times, that any human being is capable of murder."

"But I have also said that no one human is capable of *every* murder. Fredda Leving might kill to defend herself, or in a fit of passion, but she is incapable of involving herself in this level of brutality. Nor is she much good as a conspirator, and this was clearly a conspiracy. Fredda Leving was *not* capable of this killing, and she would have no motive for it. Indeed, I cannot think of anyone with a better motive for keeping the Governor alive. Listen in and monitor her voice-stress if you like, but give me the phone and make the connection. That is a direct and absolute order."

Donald hesitated a full half second before responding. Kresh thought he could almost see the First and Second Law potentials battling it out with each other. "Yes, sir," he said at last, and handed over the phone.

It was a sign of just how rattled Donald was that he would kick up such a fuss over such a minor point. The sight of the Governor's corpse had upset man and robot. Both of them knew that was not merely a dead man—it was, in all probability, a whole planet suddenly thrown into peril.

With a beep and a click-tone the phone line connected. "Um—um—hello?"

Kresh recognized Fredda's voice, sleepy and a bit muddled. "Dr. Leving, this is Sheriff Kresh. I'm afraid I must ask you to return to the Residence immediately, and to bring whatever technical equipment you have with you. I need you to examine some, ah—damaged robots.'' It was a clumsy way to put it, but Kresh couldn't think of anything else he could say on an unsecured line.

''What?'' Fredda asked. ''I'm sorry, what did you say?''

''Damaged robots,'' Kresh repeated. ''I need you to perform a fast, discreet examination. It is a matter of some urgency.''

''Well, all right, I suppose, if you say it's urgent. It will take me a while to get to the Limbo Depot robotics lab and collect some examination gear. I didn't bring anything with me. I'll get there as fast as I can.''

''Thank you, Doctor.'' Kresh handed the handset back to Donald. ''Well?'' he asked.

''Sir, I withdraw my objections. You were indeed correct. My voice-stress monitoring indicated no undue reaction to a call from you from the Residence at this hour. Either she has no idea whatsoever of what has happened, or she is a superb actress—an accomplishment of which I am unaware in Dr. Leving.''

''Once in a while, Donald,'' Kresh said, ''you might try taking my word on questions of human behavior.''

''Sir, with all due respect, I have found no topic of importance wherein questions so utterly outnumber the answers.'' Kresh gave the robot a good hard look. Had Donald just made a *joke*?

Prospero, Fredda told herself as she hurried to get ready. *It had to be something to do with Prospero*. Why else would Kresh be there at this hour, and calling her in? Something must have gone wrong with Prospero. Fredda Leving had hand-built the New Law robot, and programmed his gravitonic brain herself. She remembered how much of a pleasure it had been to work on the empty canvas of a gravitonic unit, with the chance to make bold strokes, work out whole new solutions, rather than being strait-jacketed by the limitations and conventions and excessive safety features of the positronic brain.

Ever since the long-forgotten day when true robots had first been invented, every robot ever built had been given a positronic brain. All the endless millions and billions of robots made in all those thousands of years had relied upon the same basic technology. Nothing else would ever do. The positronic brain quite literally defined the robot. No one would consider any mechanical being to *be* a robot unless it had a positronic brain—and, contrariwise, anything that contained a positronic brain was considered to be a robot. The two were seen as inseparable. Robots were trusted because they had positronic brains, and positronic brains were trusted because they went into robots. Trust in robots and in positronic brains were articles of faith.

The Three Laws were at the base of that faith. Positronic brains—and thus robots built with such brains—had the Three Laws built into them. More than built in: They had the Laws *woven* into them. Microcopies of the Laws were everywhere inside a positronic brain, strewn across every pathway, so that every action, every thought, every external event or internal calculation moved down pathways shaped and built by the Laws.

Every design formula for the positronic brain, every testing system, every manufacturing process, was built with the Three Laws in mind. In short, the positronic brain was inseparable from the Three Laws—and therein lay the problem.

Fredda Leving had once calculated that thirty percent of the volume of the average positronic brain was given over to pathing linked to the Three Laws, with roughly a hundred million microcopies of the Laws embedded in the structure of the average positronic brain, before any programming at all was done. As roughly thirty percent of positronic programming was also given over to the Three Laws, the case could be made that every one of those hundred million microcopies was completely superfluous. Fredda's rough estimate was that fifty percent of the average robot's nonconscious and preconscious autonomous processing dealt with the Laws and their application.

The needless, excessive, and redundant Three-Law processing resulted in a positronic brain that was hopelessly cluttered up with nonproductive processing and a marked reduction of capacity. It was, as Fredda liked to put it, like a woman forced to interrupt her thoughts on the matter at hand a thousand times a second in order to see if the room were on fire. The excessive caution did not enhance safety, but did produce drastically reduced efficiency.

But everything in the positronic brain was tied to the Three Laws. Remove or disable even one of those hundred million microcopies, and the brain would react. Disable more than a handful, and the brain would fail altogether. Try and produce positronic programming that did not include endless redundant checks for First, Second, and Third Law adherence, and the hardwired, built-in copies of the Three Laws would cause the positronic brain to refuse the programming and shut down.

Unless you threw out millennia of development work and started from scratch with a lump of sponge palladium and a hand calculator, there was no way to step clear of the ancient technology and produce a more efficient robot brain.

Then Gubber Anshaw invented the gravitonic brain. It was light-years ahead of the positronic in processing speed and capacity. Better still, it did not have the Three Laws burned into its every molecule, cluttering things up. The Three Laws could be programmed into the gravitonic brain, as deeply as you liked, but with only a few hundred copies placed in the key processing nodes. In theory, it was more liable to failure than the millions of copies in a standard positronic brain. In practice, the difference between ten billion to one and ten trillion to one was meaningless. Gravitonic Three-Law brains were, for all purposes, as safe as positronic ones.

But, because the Three Laws were not implicit in every aspect of the gravitonic brain's design and construction, the other robotics laboratories had refused to deal with Gubber Anshaw or his work. Building a robot that did not have a positronic brain was about as socially acceptable as cannibalism, and no appeal to logic or common sense could make the slightest difference.

Fredda Leving, however, had been more than eager to experiment with the gravitonic brain—but not because she had any interest in improved efficiency. Long before Gubber Anshaw had come to her, she had been brooding over much deeper issues regarding the Three Laws, and the effects they had on human-robot relations—and therefore on humans themselves.

Fredda had concluded, among other things, that the Three Laws stole all human initiative and served to discourage risk to an unhealthy degree by treating the least of risks of minor injury exactly the same as an immediate danger to life and limb. Humans learned to fear all danger, and eschew all activity that had the slightest spice of hazard about it.

Fredda had, therefore, formulated the four New Laws of Robotics, as a matter of mere theory, little realizing that Gubber Anshaw would come along and give her a chance to put it all into practice. Fredda had built the first New Law robots. Tonya Welton had gotten wind of the New Law project, and insisted that New Law robots be used on Purgatory. Welton had liked the idea of robots that were neither slaves nor in control over their masters' lives. And, perhaps, the fact that she was sleeping with Gubber Anshaw had something to do with it.

By the time Tonya Welton had her bright idea, Fredda was already working on a *new* theory, precisely because the gravitonic brain made it possible to move past theory into practice. Because the gravitonic brain did not have a law structure embedded in itself, it was possible to program a brain—and thus create a robot—with no Laws at all, a robot capable of creating its own rules for living. Caliban, the No Law robot, had been the ultimate result of the experiment, and Fredda had found herself in a world of trouble when Caliban escaped. But all that had been sorted out quite some time ago, thank goodness, with the result of Fredda Leving owing Sheriff Kresh at least a favor or two, to put it mildly.

But Prospero. She had hand built Prospero, the most highly refined and sophisticated of all the New Law robots, and constructed him to have the most flexible, far-ranging mind that the gravitonic brain made possible. She had not been out to do anything more than construct a robot that would be best able to think for itself. She had not intended to manufacture a robot philosopher—but that was what she had done. And some of what Prospero had come up with in his philosophy had given Fredda a major headache. As Prospero often pointed out, the New Laws allowed a New Law robot to be a far freer being than a conventional robot—but New Law robots were far more *aware* of their servitude than normal robots. Clearly there were new balances to be struck, new ways of thinking about robots and for robots if New Law robots were ever going to be able to deal with the real world. Prospero had set himself the goal of finding those new ways.

But if Prospero's expressed goal was to find the proper way for New Law robots to deal with the world, what Prospero excelled at was finding new ways *around* the New Laws, finding ways to bend them and twist them to his own convenience. Bend them far enough that it might be quite understandable if Kresh thought he was damaged.

As best Fredda could see, Prospero was clever enough to find ways to let the New Laws let him do anything.

Anything.

She grabbed her diagnostic kit and got moving.

The minutes and the hours had been dragging on, but now things started to move fast.

The first deputies—a Fast Response Crime Scene team—arrived from Hades and set to work with admirable speed, considering the shock of seeing the Governor with a hole in his chest. All of them were a bit edgy and unsettled, and Kresh could not blame them. Even the most stolid and unimaginative person could not help but realize just how dangerous this murder was—and Kresh did not assign stolid or unimaginative people to the Fast Response teams.

It was strange, disconcerting, and even unseemly to see them ministering to the corpse of the man he had been speaking with only hours before. There was a disturbing tenderness to the deputies and the Crime Scene robots as they hovered about, measuring, making images and scans, moving gently about the Governor's ruined body.

But this was no time for poetry. This was the time for plots and counterplots, schemes and conspiracy. Kresh was already playing the game. In the crudest and most basic way, he was just a minute fraction ahead. He had gotten here first, turned this crime scene into Kresh's turf. Kresh had won the first tiny engagement of what was likely to be a long and costly battle.

Arrival of the deputies pushed Kresh off to one side—and that perhaps was no bad thing. They needed time to find clues and evidence, but Kresh needed to think about the other aspects of this case.

Someone had killed the Governor, and presumably had a reason for doing so. Several someones. It was a conspiracy. The diversionary attack on Welton, the phony SSS men, the murder of the Ranger, the impossibility of getting past a whole squad of security robots—it all had to fit together, somehow.

But whose conspiracy, and why? Assume the killers had a motive. What was it? Leaving the unreasoning reason of lunacy out of it for the moment, Kresh could come up with any number of motives for killing Chanto Grieg—but very few of them coincided with the normal motives for murder.

This is not a murder, Kresh told himself. *Not in any normal sense of the word.* Murder was about passion, or jealousy, or greed, or personal ambition. It was a fatal assault on a person. This was an assault on the state. *Will it be fatal?* Kresh asked himself.

There was a terrifying idea, and not at all an implausible one. Though weakened and maligned, Grieg had been the glue that had held Infernal politics together. Even if it was merely that everyone hated him, albeit for different reasons, at least he drew people's emotions together. And even if people had hated him, and differed about his motives, they could at least understand the rational basis for what he was doing.

People might be angry over the robot shortage, or get fed up with the Settlers, but they could see the necessity of it all, even if they didn't *like* it. Part of that grudging acceptance came from the knowledge that Grieg was not a fanatic, not an ideologue, not someone chasing a harebrained theory, but a realist muddling through a bad situation as best he could.

Would any of that be true for a new Governor? Would the people take it on faith that a new Governor would be struggling to do what was best? Who was going to *be* the new Governor?

Or, to cut away all the polite tiptoeing around the central issue—who had cleared the field in order to take over? Who was going to seize the Governorship? Or was this merely and quite literally the opening gun in a new, forceful, and direct Settler attempt to take over the planet? Was there a Settler invasion fleet headed this way, right now? Not that it would take that much. All the Settlers had to do was step back and wait. Without Settler help, Inferno would collapse in a few years. It was galling to admit that fact, but Kresh had never been much for denying reality.

So why would the Settlers bother to conspire and assassinate at all? Maybe it was one of the local movers and shakers, some bullyboy like Simcor Beddle eager to seize power? Would someone announce in a few hours that he or she had saved the planet from Grieg's maladministration? Had some maniac decided on a coup to save the Spacer way of life—or had some cynical plotter realized that motive would provide a good cover story?

Who was running this coup, anyway?

Two thousand kilometers to the east of Purgatory Island, Sergeant Toth Resato, of the Governor's Rangers, stood in the darkness just before dawn, looking out over the Great Bay.

He was waiting.

Watching.

He stood at the base of the low cliffs that formed the shore of the bay. A cold wind blew at his back, gusting down through the East Crack and the inlet that formed the mouth of the River Lethe, a kilometer or two north of his position.

The surf was an endless roar of sound, and the sky was black and hard, with no sign yet of the coming day. The stars were not so much shining as piercing the dark, so sharp and bright they seemed to cut into him. Far down and off in the western sky the lights of the Limbo atmospheric force field generator gleamed and glistened, a bit of rippling green on the horizon, so dim they were hard to see, but even that little trace of warmth and color seemed quite out of place in such a time and place as this.

Sergeant Toth Resato was uncomfortable. He was out of uniform, for one thing, and, worse still, wearing Settler-style civilian clothes. He felt like a damned fool in the gaudy things, but the boat for which he was waiting was not likely to come into shore if anyone aboard spotted a Ranger's uniform.

But there were lots of things about this assignment that Toth liked less than the dress code. He was sworn to uphold the law, and he would do his duty. He was sworn to keep the peace, and he would do that too. But what of those times when the law itself was what broke the peace? What was he to do when the world turned upside-down and a fellow could be arrested for what had been legal—even honorable—the day or the week before?

How could Spacers—*Spacers*—make it illegal to obtain a robot? *Settlers* were the ones who wanted to ban robots. It didn't make sense to him. And yet, here he was, freezing to death in the darkness, lying in wait because he had gotten a tip that a smuggler was making a run tonight, bringing in contraband New Law robots—rustbacks.

That was the part Toth just could not get through his head. How could having a robot be a *crime*? It just didn't make sense. It was as if breathing or eating had been declared illegal.

Toth tended to exaggerate, even to himself. It wasn't, he admitted to himself, exactly *illegal* to own a robot—but it was getting close to that point. It didn't help matters that he had never done a rustbacking arrest before, or even dealt with New Law robots. He did not feel confident, or ready, for the task ahead.

In theory, any private robots taken for use in the terraforming project remained the property of the original owner. However, ownership didn't count for much when your former valet was suddenly fifteen thousand kilometers away on the other side of the planet, operating a prairie breeding center. People were not happy. And they wanted robots.

There was more about economics and shortages and so forth that was supposed to explain it all, but it didn't seem to make a great deal of sense to Toth. After all, if there were a shortage of something, why not just make more of it? And how could there be a shortage of robots in the first place? Why not just build more? The government had all sorts of complicated explanations, all about scarcity of resources and investing productive capacity in the planet's future, but no one could understand the numbers.

The people were being asked to take it on faith that they had to make sacrifices in the name of a better future—but a lot of people did not have much faith. All they knew, and all they cared about, was that there were not enough robots, and everyday life on Inferno had been thrown into turmoil. Even if, as everyone kept saying, there were a hundred times more robots than people on the planet, there were still too few robots.

The whole rustback phenomenon, the enormous criminal enterprise that went with them, was merely an expression of the fact that people wanted robots, and were willing to do anything—even commit crimes—in order to get them.

The detector at his belt beeped. Toth Resato looked down at the display screen and then lifted his night vision farviewers to his eyes. Yes, there they were. Out on the sea, in an open boat, headed this way. There would be a larger craft out there somewhere, the rest of the cargo of rustbacks aboard it, waiting for the human pilot to shuttle them into shore.

Rustbacks. Outlaw New Law robots, escaping from Purgatory, heading off into the wilderness of Terra Grande to what the Settler economists called "indentured servitude." They would work off the price of what it cost to smuggle them out of Purgatory, then work for a wage if and when they paid the debt. Or, that is, they would have done all that if Toth had not been waiting for them.

Toth had sat through the training sessions that were supposed to explain the basis of economic crime, so that the Rangers would be able to deal with it better. He had dozed through most of them, but he remembered the Settler economists and how they had blathered on about supply and demand, how no Spacer world had experienced a labor shortage in thousands of years. How unlimited free labor had in turn eroded the value of raw materials down to nothing. The lecturers had said something about the law of supply and demand, and how with supply of everything essentially infinite, demand—and price—had dropped to zero.

Robots completely overturned any concept of a market economy. The use, and even the concept, of money had evaporated away almost entirely.

But now, suddenly, the robots weren't there to do things and make things for free. Now there was a shortage of labor, and therefore labor—and materials obtained by labor—had a meaningful value.

For the first time in living memory, everything had a price. The catch was none of the incredibly wealthy Spacers had any money—only possessions. They were more or less forced to trade what they owned to get the products or services that had been essentially free. Inferno had dropped back into a semi-barter economy. Toth had followed most of the lecture, if not all, but it was clear to him the people lecturing him were missing the point.

The economists seemed fascinated by their charts and graphs and markets, but they never seemed to understand that people, real people, were hurting.

The capital city of Hades had seemed deserted, dingy, the last time Toth had been there for a visit. Nothing seemed bright or alive there. A fine layer of dust had settled on everything, blown from the deserts.

Without the hordes of cleaning robots bustling about downtown, everything had seemed a little worn, a little threadbare and sad, as if the buildings and streets knew that the desert sands were edging just a trifle closer to town.

With the robots gone, the city—its human population in-tact—seemed almost a ghost town. That irony was not lost even on Toth, and Toth knew there was not much of the poet in his soul. What could you say about a city that seemed half-dead because the machines had left and the people had stayed?

And the people were desperate. There were plenty of sharp operators ready, willing, and able to take advantage of that desperation. The Settler traders were bad enough, buying up works of art and family heirlooms for a pittance in Settler credits, but at least those were legal transactions.

The rustback trade was not. The whole rustback industry had sprung up as if by magic the moment the Governor made his pronouncement impressing "surplus" robots into the ter-raforming service. It had grown since, in size and sophistica-tion, until now it was a huge and sophisticated enterprise.

There were the restrictor strip shops on Purgatory, where, for a fee, a pull artist would remove the range restrictors from a New Law robot. There were the brokers, charging horrifying amounts of money or making ruinous barters to the Spacers who needed robots, any robots. There were the smugglers ready to get a boatful of N.L. robots off Purgatory, or else fly an aircar full of them, risking detection by the traffic control nets.

And then there were the New Law robots themselves. They were the real mystery. The humans Toth could understand. After all, they were not much different from other criminals willing to risk harsh punishment for the sake of massive profit. But the New Law robots were a mystery to him.

Were New Law robots really robots in the first place? They only had half a First Law, after all. They were enjoined from harming a human being, but they could, if they chose, stand by and let a human being be killed. One of the primordial protections of Spacer existence was no longer there. How

could anyone feel safe around them? New Law robots were
not required to obey the orders of a human, either. They were
required to "cooperate" with humans. No one seemed to be
quite sure what "cooperate" meant to a robot. And what if
there were two groups of humans with different ideas? With
which would a New Law robot "cooperate"?

Cooperating meant running away, at least to some N.L.s,
and Toth could not understand why. A rustback had to work
just as hard, if not harder, than a New Law that stayed where
it belonged. Some of the New Law robots talked about having
at least the hope of being free someday, but what could freedom mean to a robot? And yet, he was here waiting on another
boatload of New Law robots, risking their very existence in
hope of freedom.

And they were heading his way right now. A boatload of
runaway robots. Runaway robots. It was almost a contradiction
in terms.

Toth watched in the farviewers as they got closer. He saw
the signal light blink from the bow of the boat. Three long
blinks, then three shorts.

Toth just happened to know that the man on the boat was
named Norlan Fiyle, and that Fiyle was expecting a rather
hard-edged woman named Floria Wentle to signal back. Toth
had recently made Wentle's acquaintance, and provided her
with a rather more permanent accommodation than she might
have preferred. It had taken merely the slightest mention of
the Psychic Probe to make her reveal all concerning Fiyle and
his plans for the shipment tonight. It seemed there wasn't
much to the idea of honor among thieves.

Toth lifted his own signal light and signaled back—two
longs, three shorts, four longs. He watched for a moment and
got the proper signal in reply, three more longs and three more
shorts.

Toth glanced to his left and then to his right, needlessly and pointlessly checking to make sure his robots were in position. Needless because he knew they were there, and pointless because they were all very well hidden indeed.

The boat was close enough now that there was no need for the farviewers. Toth felt his heart starting to race. Here they came.

Now he could hear the high-pitched humming of the engine over the roar of the surf. He could see the robots sitting, stock-still, in their seats, and one human figure—Fiyle, it had to be Fiyle—standing at the stern, operating the controls.

Act like his friend, Toth told himself. *Act like you're the one he's supposed to meet.* Toth raised his arm and waved. Toth knew damned well he was silhouetted against the night sky, and that Fiyle had to be using night-vision gear at least as good as his own, and, no doubt, had a blaster more powerful than the Ranger-issue model Toth had. Toth walked toward the point on the shore the boat was making for, trying to move casually, calmly, in his damn-fool civilian clothes, as if everything were normal and fine.

At least the civvies were bulky enough that it was hard to get an idea of body shape from them. With luck, and in the dark, Fiyle would not notice that Toth was not a woman.

One half of a pair of handcuffs was already locked on to Toth's wrist, likewise hidden by the bulky clothes. The empty cuff would be around Fiyle's wrist in short order.

Toth paused, looking for a way down to the rocky shore at the base of the low cliffs. He knelt, turned around so he was facing the cliff, and started to climb down, painfully aware that he had just put his back to Fiyle. He forced himself not to think about it, and concentrated on finding handholds.

It wasn't much of a climb down to the shoreline. Toth was glad to reach the bottom and turn around.

There was the boat, only a hundred meters away, just about to beach itself on a small patch of sandy shoreline. Toth could see Fiyle in the stern, see that he was watching the shore, not Toth. Even with a night-vision helmet covering half of his face, it was easy to see his anxious expression as he struggled to guide the little craft through the surging waves, thread it around rocks and ledges. Closer, closer.

At last, with a final burst of power from the engine, Fiyle gunned the boat forward on the crest of an incoming wave, surfing the boat to land gently on the shore, not twenty meters from where Toth stood.

It was immediately obvious that the robots in the bow of the boat had been well briefed on what to do upon landing. Three of them jumped out and held the bow. Another then jumped ashore, the end of a rope in its hand. It headed up to the base of the cliff, snubbed the rope around an outcropping of rock, and tied it off. Then the rest of the robots started to disembark in orderly fashion.

Fiyle shut down his engine, peeled off his night-vision helmet, and rubbed his face with both hands. He stretched his arms and flexed his back, working out the kinks. Then, with one graceful motion, he set one hand on the gunwale and jumped over the side of the boat. He landed feetfirst in the surf, showing a sailor's lack of concern for getting his feet wet.

Toth smiled at him, stepped toward him, and offered the man his hand as Fiyle sloshed through the surf toward dry land. It was not until Fiyle was within less than a meter of Toth that the rustbacker realized something was wrong. Toth stepped forward into the cold surf, took him by the hand—and had the cuff on him before he could react.

Fiyle cried out and yanked his arm back, pulling Toth forward, slamming into him. Both of them toppled over into the water, but Fiyle managed to heave himself over on top of Toth. The rustbacker grabbed the Ranger by the throat and shoved his head down into the frigid water.

Toth opened his eyes underwater, but the dark night and the cloudy seawater rendered him as good as blind. He struggled, clawing at the man's face with his free right hand. He pulled back on his left hand, with the cuff on it, trying to dislodge Fiyle's grip on his throat.

Toth tried desperately to lever himself up far enough to get his face above water, to reach the air. He made a fist of his free hand and tried to punch Fiyle in the side of the head. He missed completely and landed a glancing blow on his shoulder. He pulled back his arm to try again.

But then, suddenly, it didn't matter. Fiyle wasn't on him anymore, and strong arms were fishing him out of the water. Toth coughed and spluttered as the robot—*his* robot, a Gerald, a GRD unit, one of his arrest team—carried him to shore. The GRD cradled Toth like a baby, Toth's arm with the cuff on it dangling out in midair, still connected to Fiyle.

Another GRD was carrying Fiyle, holding him in a tight restraint position.

"Let me down!" Fiyle bellowed. "I order you to let me down!"

The robot was unmoved. "I regret, sir, that both First Law and preexisting orders prevent me from doing so. Please do not attempt to escape, as that might entail injury to yourself or Ranger Toth."

Toth had to smile to himself, in spite of the beating he had taken. Say what you might about Three Law robots. You couldn't fault them for being impolite.

Toth had learned a thing or two about Settlers—or at least the sort of Settler who got picked up by the cops. It seemed to Toth that they broke into two groups. On the one hand there was the snarling sort, who denied everything, accused the arresting officer of planting evidence, who threatened and sniveled and sneered. On the other hand, there were some who seemed to regard it all as something of a game, complete with winners and losers. Once he was safely back in Toth's mobile Ranger Station, locked into its archaic-looking barred cell, where it was plain to see he was caught and there was nothing he could do about it, Norlan Fiyle immediately demonstrated that he was a member of the second category.

By the time the GRD robots handed Fiyle dry clothes through the bars of the cell, all the aggression seemed to have drained out of the man. He was big and burly, in the vigorous health of an active man in his middle years. He was a round-faced, dark-skinned man, with a thin fringe of snow-white hair. He seemed quite unconcerned by the fact that he was under arrest, or that a trio of rather intimidating GRD robots were standing outside the cell, watching his every move.

Fiyle sat down on the cell's narrow cot and pulled on the dry prison-issue clothes. "So," he asked, "how did you nail me?"

Toth was not in a good mood. His head hurt, and he was fairly certain that he was going to have a black eye and a stiff back in the morning. "Let's just say you trusted the wrong people," he said, not wanting to give too much away. He sat down at his desk chair, facing the prisoner, and made a show of doing some work. Not that he was in any shape to make a coherent report.

"That so?" Fiyle asked. "I should have known better than to count on Floria Wentle," he said in a calm, conversational tone as he pulled on a pair of prison slippers. "Hmmph. Not a bad fit," he said, standing and taking a step or two.

"Glad you like them," Toth said, a little annoyed that Fiyle had guessed it in one try. "But I didn't say who it was who gave you away."

Fiyle looked up at him and smiled. "Oh, it had to be Floria. She talked just a little bit too good a game. I should have known she was the kind to get caught. By the way, can you tell me what happened to my New Laws? Any of them manage to get away?''

"About half of the ones in the boat escaped," Toth said. "My robots caught the rest on the beach. We'll pick up the ones waiting on the ship in the morning.''

"Don't count on that," Fiyle said. "Those robots are no fools. Once I don't make it back to the ship for the second load, they'll all hightail it. They'll take over the ship and try for a landing someplace else.''

"Think so?" Toth said, a trifle defiantly. If Fiyle knew so much, then how had he gotten caught? "They're just robots. They'll be sitting out there when we go to get 'em.''

"If you want to bet on that, you're on," Fiyle said. "They're *New Law* robots. One of them's got more initiative than a whole herd of those Three-Law jobs—and believe me, this crowd knows they have a real incentive for getting away. You know what happens to New Law robots caught trying to escape?''

Toth shrugged. "Not really.''

Fiyle gave him an odd look. "For a cop, you don't have much curiosity. N.L.s caught trying to escape are destroyed. A blaster shot to the head. Once they start running, they damned well know they don't dare stop. No way back.''

"But they wouldn't know how to run your ship," Toth objected.

"They're smart, and they'd sure as hell have the incentive to learn," Fiyle said. "If they decide they can't handle it, they might even just jump overboard, let themselves sink, and walk to shore on the bottom. I doubt it, though. They weren't made waterproof, on purpose, to keep 'em on Purgatory. Besides, even a robot would get disoriented underwater around here. Bad visibility, strong currents, uneven seafloor. But they're your problem now.''

Fiyle leaned back on the cot and grinned. "That's something, anyway," he said. "At least now I won't have a shipload of New Law know-it-alls driving me crazy. Now *you* have to deal with them. But I am glad at least some of them got away."

"Why should you care?" Toth asked. Somehow, he was the one ill at ease. Fiyle wasn't acting like a man caught in the act and looking at a world of trouble.

"Oh, don't get me wrong. I'm in this for the money. But I still like seeing someone getting away once in a while. Even if it is just a bunch of robots." Fiyle grinned at Toth and winked, just to lay the sarcasm on a bit thicker.

"I think that's just about enough lip out of you, Settler," Toth said.

"And why is that enough?" Fiyle asked, losing nothing of his easy manner.

"Take a look around yourself. You're in a Spacer jail and I've got you dead to rights on a very serious charge."

"True enough," Fiyle said. "Or at least true as far as it goes. Because you're just about to trade up, Ranger Resato."

"Trade up to what?"

"No, no, trade up *for* what. We talk about that first. We talk about the deal first. I'm going to give you a name, a name that you are going to love to have, and hate to have. And you are going to give me a ticket home, off this Spacer rathole and back to a decent life."

Toth looked carefully at his prisoner. The man was serious—and somehow he knew that Fiyle was not the sort of man who made an offer he could not back up.

"It's got to be a hell of a big name to rate that kind of deal," Toth said. "Someone higher up?"

"Higher up, yes. But that's not why you'll want to know who it is. This name belongs to you. And it belongs to someone way deep into 'backing."

Suddenly Toth felt a little unsteady. He understood. A
Ranger. A Ranger involved in rustbacking. He pressed a button
on his desk. "Gerald Four," he said.

A somewhat mechanical voice answered, coming from the
comm panel. "Yes, sir?"

"Bring me two blank witness boxes."

"One moment."

There was silence in the room, and Toth found himself staring straight into Fiyle's eyes. All the bantering humor had
drained out of the Settler, and now Toth could see the tense-
ness, the intensity that the surface jocularity had hidden.

Gerald Four stepped into the room, carrying two small
sealed containers. Toth took the boxes from the robot, undid
the seals, and opened them up. Inside each container was a
small black cube, about three centimeters on a side. Each had
a single button on it. Press the button and the box would record
for one hour, with no way to stop it or rewind it or erase the
recording. Whenever the button was pressed thereafter, the recording would play back, with no way to stop it or modify it.

Toth took the boxes from their containers. He held one of
the witness boxes in his hand, looked at them for a moment,
and then set both of them down on his desk. He pressed the
buttons and looked back at Fiyle. "This is Ranger Toth Resato," he said. "The Settler Norlan Fiyle is my prisoner, arrested this night in connection with various charges of
rustbacking. He has offered to provide the name of a Governor's Ranger substantially involved in the rustbacking trade,
in exchange for the dropping of all charges against him and
transport to his home planet. I hereby agree to this bargain,
contingent on confirmation of his information." Toth handed
the witness boxes to the robot. "Give them to him," he said.

Gerald Four carried the boxes to the cell and handed them
through the bars.

"You keep one cube, and I get the other back," Toth said.

"We each get a guarantee. Now talk."

Fiyle held one cube in each hand and looked up toward Toth. The Settler swallowed hard, and Toth could see a sheen of sweat that had suddenly appeared on the man's brow. The games were over now. This was for real.

"There is a Ranger," he said. "A Ranger that's doing a lot of looking the wrong way when the rustbackers are working. He tips the 'backers off whenever there's a raid."

Moving carefully, Fiyle set the witness boxes down on the table inside his cell. He walked around the table and sat down on his cot, facing Toth. "There is a Ranger," he said again. "And his name is Sergeant Emoch Huthwitz."

6

COLD. COLD. COLD. Ottley Bissal struggled to keep the aircar flying but he could not stop shaking. He was chilled to the bone, drenched by the pouring rain, but there was more to it than that. Fear, terror, reaction, whatever the demons might be called, they were with him, inside him, freezing his blood, making his teeth chatter.

Keep steady, he told himself. *Concentrate. Focus on your flying.* He was well inside the Limbo City traffic pattern now. By now he should be safe—but Bissal had never been the best of pilots, and he had just been through flying conditions to challenge the most skillful of fliers. He was spent, exhausted.

Huthwitz. Huthwitz had been a mistake. They had found the body, and he had had far too close a call.

At least now the worst was over, but there had been plenty of worst. The nightmare of mistakes and improvisation at the Residence, the close call in evading the police, the long walk through the drenching rain to the hidden aircar, the struggle to find it and get it open, the flight back to the city at low, detection-dodging altitudes—there was none of it he would ever want to go through again. But he had made it now. All he had to do was ditch the car and get to the safehouse. No problem. It was over. Everything was going to be all right.

But he still could not stop shaking.

Fredda Leving came in out of the rain and stepped into the Grand Hall of the Governor's Residence. Alvar Kresh was there to meet her, Donald at his side.

Fredda took one look at the Sheriff and knew, *knew* that it had nothing to do with Prospero. There was nothing angry, or accusatory, in his expression. It was nothing to do with her—and yet she instantly found herself wishing that it were. For there was a great deal more to read in Kresh's expression. Something much, much worse than robotic misbehavior.

"Grieg is dead," Kresh said. "A blaster shot through the chest."

Fredda blinked, shook her head, stared at Kresh. "What?"

"Dead. Murdered. Assassinated," Kresh said.

Fredda could find nothing to say. She wanted to deny it, to say no, it couldn't have happened, but one look at Kresh's face told her that it had. Finally words, some sort of words, came to her. "Sweet burning hell. How could that happen?"

"I don't know," Kresh replied, his voice flat and hard. "Come in." He turned and led her down the hallway to a small room that had been pressed into service as a command post. The place was swarming with robots and Sheriff's Department deputies, working, conferring, talking into comm units, faces tight and grim. "Sit down," Kresh said, and Fredda obeyed, setting herself down in an absurdly festive-looking couch with an overdone floral pattern.

Somehow everything seemed extra real, excessively solid, every meaningless detail suddenly vitally bright and hard. Sitting there, at that moment, Fredda knew that every moment of this night would be with her forever, burned into her memory and her soul for all time. "How did it—did it—"

"We don't know," Kresh said. "But I need you to help me find out, and I have very little time. Grieg's security robots should have protected him—but they didn't. I need to know if someone tampered with them. You have to find that out for me, now, tonight. But—"

"But what?" Fredda demanded. And yet, somehow, she already knew the answer.

"But we haven't been able to move him yet," Kresh said. "My robots and technical people are still examining the crime scene. It's not pretty."

Fredda nodded, feeling nothing more than numb. "No," she said. "No, I don't expect it would be."

Fredda had never seen a dead man before, let alone a murdered one. That much she had in common with mainstream Spacer society. Death was too distasteful to be permitted to intrude on one's life. But even if she had seen a roomful of corpses, it would not have prepared her for the sight of Chanto Grieg slumped over, murdered in his bed. His body—his ruined corpse—was all the more ghastly a sight for the sheer normalcy of it all. A tired man at the end of a long party goes to his rest, sits up in bed to read for a time before turning out the lights.

And someone puts a blaster bolt through him. There he lay, in his pajamas, in his bed. A private, almost intimate setting. She felt like an intruder, an interloper. She did not belong here. She had no right to see this. No one did. She felt a strange impulse to chase them all out, the deputies, the Crime Scene robots, Kresh and Donald. She wanted to chase them all out, leave herself, and let the man have his death in private.

"Let him rest in peace," she said, the words a half whisper.

"I beg your pardon, Dr. Leving?" Donald asked. "What did you say?"

"Peace," she said. "Why can't you let him rest in peace?"

She shut her eyes, tried to blot out the sight. She wanted to turn her back on him, let him be—but she could not help herself. She opened her eyes and looked again.

Chanto Grieg was—had been—her friend, her sponsor, her patron. But all that was as nothing. What matter who or what this man was to *her* when the time and manner of his death was a catastrophe for the planet? This was history, a moment she would be called upon to remember for the researchers and the archivists for the rest of her life. She would be remembered for being here, tonight. And Chanto Grieg would be remembered, not as the man who saved Inferno—or at least tried to save it—he would be remembered as the Governor somebody killed. *His* place, his rightful place, in history had been warped and distorted for all time. And that felt like the worst intrusion of all.

"All right," Fredda said, though nothing at all was right. "All right. Let me look at the robots."

"Over here, Doctor," Donald said. There was something gentle, careful about his voice. Fredda felt the slightest of pressure on her arm as he turned her around and she saw the ruined security robots, still in their wall niches. She saw instantly what had bothered Kresh. None of them had moved before they were shot.

"That can't be," she said. "No one should have been able to get past one SPR, let alone three. Sappers are too fast."

"That's what I thought," Kresh said. "And it's worse than that. Every single one of the upper-floor SPRs was destroyed by blaster fire."

"But the whole idea of Sappers is that they keep in continuous contact with each other," Fredda said. "Almost like a linked mind. If one of them saw something, all of the others would know about it. There's no way anyone could have shot one unit in an SPR team without the other SPRs being instantly aware of it—and calling for help. So why didn't that happen?"

Kresh gestured toward the blasted robots. "There they are, Doctor. You tell me."

"Is it all right for me touch them?" Fredda asked. "What about fingerprints and so on?"

"The Crime Scene robots have already done a full exterior scan," Donald replied. "I think if you wear surgical gloves, and have a Crime Scene robot do an interior scan of any compartments you open, that should suffice. You are quite right to be concerned about fingerprints. With a bit of luck, whoever tampered with the machines left a fingerprint or two somewhere on one of the robots' interior surfaces."

"Good. Good," Fredda said, a bit distractedly. She wasn't really listening all that hard. There was a puzzle for her to solve, and it was already absorbing her attention. Which was fine with her if it got her mind off the dead man in bed on the other side of the room. "Then let's get to it."

Fredda made no move toward the robots. Something was missing, something she wasn't seeing. And then she got it. The robots had been shot through the chest, the same as Grieg. Even to Fredda's unpracticed eye, they were obviously aimed shots, precise enough so that it could not be mere chance the robots were all shot in the same place.

But chest shots didn't make sense. The best way, the only sure way to kill a robot, was with a shot to the head, where you would be certain to destroy the positronic brain. There was no particular reason why a shot to the chest would kill. There were no equivalent structures to the heart or lungs whose destruction would insure instant death.

If you did enough damage, cut enough circuits, yes, that would do it. But you could not be absolutely *sure* to the degree you wanted to be with a trio of fast-moving, aggressive security robots coming at you.

Unless, of course, you knew everything there was to know about this particular model of security robot, knew exactly how

powerful a blaster shot it would take for a chest shot to kill—
and if you knew they were not about to come at you.

Well, all right, that would at least explain why the shooter
didn't need a head shot. But that didn't explain why the
shooter *did* need a chest shot.

Unless—unless there were something in the chest the killer
wanted to conceal. And if that were so, vaporizing that something would certainly serve to hide it. There was a way to test
that idea.

"I don't need to examine these robots just now," Fredda
said. "Maybe later. First I want to see one of the other Sappers
that was shot."

"Of course, Doctor," Donald said. "Come this way."

Donald led Kresh and Fredda out into the hallway and toward a slumped-over heap on the floor. Fredda knelt down
beside it and looked it over.

"This one at least looks like it was in motion, heading toward the scene, when it went down," Kresh said.

"No," Fredda said. "I don't know much about blasters, but
I do know how paint reacts to heat on robot bodies. Welding,
laser cutting, that sort of thing. Maybe you were *meant* to think
this robot was moving when it was shot, but it was as inert as
the others when the blaster got it."

"How can you be so sure?" Kresh asked.

Fredda pointed to the blaster shots. "Look at the chest shot.
Virtually identical to the shots on the bedroom robots. That
was the one that killed it."

"So?" Kresh said.

"So look at the paint-melts. The melts from the two smaller
shots *overlap* the death shot. The killer blasted the robot in
the chest from close up, then he or she got artistic. Either the
robot fell over or the killer knocked it over and then backed
off to do the other shots from a greater distance *after* the robot
was already down."

"You're right," Kresh said. "I should have spotted that."

"Well, your weapons analysis people would have seen it sooner or later. I only saw it because I was looking for it."

"Looking for it?" Kresh asked. "Why?"

"Because these robots were not shot because the killer needed them dead," Fredda said. "They were shot because that was the fastest way to destroy the evidence of tampering. My guess is that there was some sort of gadget attached to the circuitry in the center of the chest, right under the central access panel."

Fredda realized she was still staring down at the dead robot. A shot just like the one that killed the other robots. Just like the one that killed Grieg. Grieg dead. Sweet stars in the sky, *Chanto Grieg was dead.* She shut her eyes, took a deep breath, and tried to pull herself together. This was not the time to grieve. Not when the whole planet was about to fall apart.

"Sir, Doctor, if I might interject?"

"Yes, yes, Donald," Fredda said, collecting herself. "What—what is it?"

"The Crime Scene robots have just posted some initial results to the hyperwave datanet. It concerns weapons analysis that might have some bearing on all this."

"What sort of results?" Kresh asked.

"Range, power, and sequence estimates, sir."

"What are those?" Fredda asked.

"Ways of determining various characteristics of the weapon that fired a given sequence of shots," Donald said. "The energy front of a blaster shot widens out as it moves forward. Measuring the radius of the blaster wound or mark gives an indication of range. By combining measures of the intensity of the wound or mark with the range estimate, we can derive the power of the blaster during each shot. As blasters drain their power somewhat with each shot, the first shot tends to be the most powerful, with each subsequent shot less and less powerful.''

"It doesn't always work, though," Kresh said. "With a high-capacity power supply, the power fall-off from one shot to the next can be undetectable."

"In the present case, sir, we are more fortunate. Preliminary analysis shows a pronounced power fall-off with every shot."

"All right, Donald," Kresh said, a note of weary patience in his voice. "What's the punchline?"

"The shot that killed Governor Grieg was indeed the first one fired."

"I'll be damned," Kresh said. "Score one for you, Dr. Leving. If he was shot first, then the robots had to be shut down already. No reason to shoot them unless there was something that needed hiding. Except most of the robots downstairs weren't shot. Why not?"

"Maybe if I take a look at some of them, I can find out what the—the assassins were trying to hide," Fredda said. She had an idea or two already, but she was not ready to say anything yet. Not until she had something more than a theory.

"I'll leave you to that," Kresh said. "There are certainly plenty of SPR robots for you to examine. I do appreciate your help. You've already done me a larger service than you know. However, there is another duty I must perform in the meantime. Donald, you're with me."

"Yes, sir." The short blue robot made a slight bow toward Fredda. "Dr. Leving, it is good to be working with you again, albeit under such grim and unpleasant circumstances."

"Thank you, Donald," Fredda said. The robot and the policeman headed down the stairs toward their improvised command center. Fredda stood up and looked down at the ruined robot. *What a waste*, she thought. *What a miserable, useless waste.*

•   •   •

Alvar Kresh knew the evil moment could not be put off any longer. It was time to put in a call to Justen Devray of the Governor's Rangers. Two hours had passed since Kresh had discovered the body. The one bright spot was that, having thought about it, he could see no jurisdictional reason to call Cinta Melloy or the SSS at all. So far, at least, this was strictly an Infernal affair.

No doubt sooner or later the SSS would get mixed up in it as well. Major investigations had a way of spreading out. But at least he did not have to deal with them now. As little as he trusted the Rangers at the moment, he trusted the SSS even less.

Kresh sat down at the portable comm station his team had set up and punched the call to Devray.

Fredda Leving stood in front of Sapper 23. The robot was still standing, even though its power had been cut. It, along with most of its fellows on the ground floor and a few on the upper floor, had simply stopped dead, instead of being shot with a blaster. Why?

It was an inert lump of metal, literally dead on its feet. Fredda pushed down on the release stud, and there was a click from inside the robot's chest. Now she could open the panel.

Fredda, feeling awkward in her surgical gloves, and distracted by the Crime Scene Observer robot hovering over her shoulder, pressed down on the lower exterior stud that would pop open the front access panel, now that it was unlatched. Sapper 23 stared down at her, unseeing, unnerving her. Most robots had power-down controls in the back, with a simple access cover anyone could open. But that, clearly, would never do for a security robot. You had to be right in front of a Sapper, watching it watching you, and you had to open a panel it controlled before you could shut it off. Except this robot was already off—and that was not supposed to happen.

The access plate swung open and Fredda stepped back, allowing the tiny Crime Scene Observer robot to hover in and do a full surface scan of the interior before she touched anything. The CSO flitted down until it was directly in front of the access panel. It extruded a tiny probe and directed it over every surface of the panel's interior. The probe moved rapidly, fussily over the interior. At last it beeped to indicate it had done the scan and then backed off. Something about its motions reminded Fredda of the hummingbirds that the Settlers had just introduced onto Purgatory.

Fredda's tool kit was open on the table next to her. She pulled out a clip light and a defastening tool. She attached the light to the lip of the power access panel and then used the defastener to pop open the maintenance panel inside. She lifted out the panel and set it down on the table, then stepped back to let the CSO robot do its job.

The maintenance chamber's interior was far more complex than the switch chamber, and it took Fredda a moment to find what she was looking for.

Or, more accurately, to confirm that what she was looking for was not there. But it had most decidedly left its mark.

She smiled and stepped back from the Sapper. "Get me a magnified scan of the entire exposed surface in there. Maximum definition."

The tiny robot moved in and set to work, and Fredda watched. It was a good first step. There were all the other robots to check, of course, and she would have to be careful, thorough. But she felt a bit of excitement, of pleasure, all the same. She was starting to see how they did it—whoever they were.

But that sensation of pleasure did not last long. Because then she remembered *what* they had done.

•   •   •

Justen Devray was at his desk, working on the Huthwitz case, when the call came. "Damnation, Kresh, why the devil did you wait two hours to tell me?" Justen Devray was angry, and felt he had the right to be. He glared at the comm screen, feeling dead tired, horrified, and angry all at once. But not surprised. Somehow, he did not feel the least bit surprised.

"I had my reasons, Commander. Not the most pleasant reasons, but reasons—and I would prefer not to discuss them over a hyperwave line—even one that is supposed to be secure."

"Very well," Devray said. "I will be at the Residence in twenty minutes. Have you informed the SSS yet, or did you call me before Cinta Melloy?"

Kresh's image in the viewtank shifted a bit, and the man looked uncomfortable. "I was not proposing to inform the SSS at all at this point. They will find out soon enough."

"The hell you say. Kresh—have you taken leave of your senses? This is not some drunk who's been rolled in an alley. It's the assassination of the Governor. You have to call in every law enforcement service available."

"I agree, Commander. However, I am not certain whether it is wise to consider the SSS to *be* a law enforcement service so far as this case is concerned."

"What the hell are you saying?" Devray demanded.

"I'm saying I don't know whose security the Settler Security Service is interested in. It is possible that it is not ours. Please get here as soon as you can."

Kresh cut the connection before Devray could say anything more—but Devray realized he had very little to say in any event. Kresh had all but come out and said he suspected the SSS of complicity in Grieg's death. And, try as he might, Devray had to accept that it was possible.

But there was something far worse than that. The only reason Devray could see for Kresh to delay notifying the Rangers was that he suspected them as well.

And while it pained Devray to the depths of his soul to admit it, he knew damned well that was possible as well. He thought of Emoch Huthwitz, dead in the rain, and of all the things Devray had learned about Huthwitz in the last few hours.

He got moving.

The rain was letting up, and the sun was showing signs of rising in the east as Fredda Leving popped open the interior maintenance chamber on yet another SPR robot. Fredda was vaguely aware that the world outside the windows was getting lighter, but she was too tired for more than that.

She had lost track of the number of robots she had examined, but that didn't matter. She could do a count later. Right now her job was to be thorough, to check every single SPR. At least she was getting faster at the job. If not for the need to do the interior scans searching for evidence, she could have been in and out of a given robot in twenty seconds. That in itself was an important piece of information.

But it was not enough. So far, she had only found minute traces, all but undetectable signs of what she was looking for. She could see the tiny scratches left behind when some sort of device had been removed from the robots—two tiny marks in the main power bus. Fredda was all but certain that those marks were the traces of some sort of cutoff device, some way of deactivating the robots by remote control. But guesses and being all but certain were not enough. So far, whoever had removed them had been as thorough removing them as she had been in checking.

But maybe that was not going to hold. After all, she had all the time in the world, and the fact that daylight was coming on did not concern her. She had no fear of sudden detection or something going wrong with the plan. But whoever had done this the night before—with the corpse of the Governor upstairs, the rain lashing down, with the clock running and all the lights off, that person might well make a mistake.

Fredda wanted to get on to the next robot, and skip the scan. She resisted the temptation, knowing that the scans were important. The robot could detect any number of things that might be hidden from human view. A bit of dust or a smear of dried sweat or a flaked-off bit of skin or a piece of torn thread that might reveal something about the person who left it behind. Perhaps even a fingerprint. Perhaps something unexpected.

So far nothing. The opposition had been very careful. But if they had made just one mistake—and Fredda found that one mistake—that would be all it would take.

At last the scan was done and the observer robot moved back out of the way. Fredda closed the robot's inner and outer access panels and moved on to the next unit.

It was disconcerting to stare up into those dead, designed-to-intimidate eyes and then reach down and open the robot up. Not so long ago, the average Spacer would not, could not, have imagined being afraid of a robot. But Fredda knew times had changed. She herself was the one who had let the genie out of the bottle. She had made dangerous robots with her own two hands. There was no longer any technical barrier to making a robot without any Laws at all. And nothing to stop someone from dressing a killer robot up to look like, for example, an SPR unit. After all, she had established to her own satisfaction that these SPRs had been tampered with. Someone could install a No-Law gravitonic brain in one of them and then—and then—

No. It did not bear thinking about. Fredda was so tired she could hardly see straight, let alone think straight. Concentrate. Concentrate. Open the outer panel. Let the observer hover in and sniff around. Try and keep your eyes open. Pop the inner panel and—

—And swear to yourself in a low monotone. Fredda didn't need any observer scan to tell herself she had found something. The opposition had made a mistake, all right.

A big one.

Simcor Beddle, leader of the Ironheads, stood in front of his comm unit in his fine silken pajamas, a soothing cup of tea in his hand. He watched as his robots operated the comm unit—though, at the moment at least, he had no interest in calling anyone. He was far more interested in who *other* people were calling. He had ways—not all of them strictly legal—of finding out.

His comm unit was highly sophisticated, capable of pulling in all sorts of signals not generally available to the general public. Right now it was tracking encrypted police traffic, and Beddle's staff had not managed to crack those particular encryption routines. But still, one could learn a lot by listening, even if one did not know the language. The robots operating the system were pulling in the signals, analyzing message traffic density patterns, getting triangulations to find signal sources.

It was one of Simcor Beddle's basic beliefs that there was no such thing as a secret. True, if a matter was of no importance, it could be kept quiet—but then what did it matter? A secret was only a secret when people wanted to know it. But when the people in the know cared about some supposedly hidden news or event, they would act on what they knew. By so doing, they would reveal at least some part of the secret to anyone who cared to pay attention.

The Ironheads always paid attention. Beddle saw to that. Their transition from a mob of bullyboys to a legitimate political force was far from complete, and they needed every possible advantage. The right bit of information at the right time could be of the most vital importance—and so Beddle's household staff robots had awakened him the moment police-band hyperwave message traffic had started to build. It didn't matter that the messages themselves were encrypted—that police band activity had taken off exponentially was in itself a rather loud and clear message.

So too was the command to turn back all outgoing air traffic from the island. *That* certainly could not be kept quiet for any length of time—but no explanation had been offered for it. Even so, Beddle could see the aircraft being turned back on his extremely illegal repeater displays of Purgatory Traffic Control. Beddle could likewise see the stream of vehicles with Sheriff's Department designation codes, coming straight from Hades for the Governor's Residence. The latest development was the stream of Ranger vehicles converging on the Residence. It was not lost on Beddle that the SSS was yet to stir.

What the devil was going on? It was plainly obvious that the Governor's Residence was the focal point of it all, but what did it mean?

In plain point of fact, Beddle had a theory or two about what had happened. Simcor Beddle was a man willing to set loose cannons in motion, if the potential benefit outweighed the danger. But the days when Beddle or the mainstream Iron-heads could tolerate being directly linked to violence were over. Covert links were another question, of course.

Beddle thought for a moment. No. There was no one who could be traced back to him. Unless one of the old plots from the old days had come alive again, unexpectedly. There were one or two old operatives who had simply disappeared. If it were one of them who had come to the surface again—

No. No. That could not be. The odds against it were too long.

But never mind the question of who. The question of *what* was far more important. And if he was right about what the police were reacting to with such energy, it was time to move, and move *fast*. This turn of events could be a tremendous opportunity, assuming one moved with a certain degree of care.

But suppose he was guessing wrong? Reacting to news that had not happened might put him in a rather awkward position, to put it mildly.

Simcor frowned, displeased by the conundrum. But then his face cleared and he smiled as he handed his teacup to his attendant robot. There was no need to worry. It was impossible to keep a secret. All would be known within a few hours, and that would be soon enough for the sort of actions Simcor had in mind. There was no hurry at all.

He smiled to himself and gestured for his attendant robot to lead him back to bed. He walked behind the robot, his rolling gait stately, dignified, calm. All was going well.

7

JUSTEN DEVRAY WATCHED as the death-black Coroner's Office robots carried Governor Chanto Grieg away. "Burning stars," he said. "I don't believe it. I can't believe it." He turned and looked toward the Governor's bed—the deathbed—where the Crime Scene team was still at work, doing a painstaking scan for any evidence that might have been hidden by the body itself. Corpses didn't tend to bleed much, but there was still enough blood, and the burn and scorch marks on the wall and the bedding were still horrifying enough, even if they weren't particularly extensive. "When you called to tell me, I didn't think of all this," he said to Alvar Kresh. "I didn't think about death, or about what all this is going to mean. I thought about turf wars, and that you were trying to win one."

"Well, I was trying to win a turf war," Kresh said. "But not because I wanted this for myself," he said. "There were other reasons."

"Huthwitz," Devray said. It was not a question.

"Huthwitz," Kresh agreed. "It didn't seem much like chance to me. That wasn't someone blundering into him in the dark. It was too neat. Somebody knew exactly when and where a Ranger would be, exactly how to stalk him.''

"Except if they knew exactly where my Rangers would be, why go out of their way to kill one? Why not just slip between the Rangers?''

"That occurred to me as well,'' Kresh said, his voice a bit too flat and even for it to be utterly natural. "Would there be any *other* reason to kill a Ranger? Maybe a reason to kill Huthwitz in particular?''

Justen felt a knot in his stomach. Kresh was not a man who missed much. "Yes,'' he said. "There might be. I'm not prepared to say more just now, but there might.''

"You didn't recognize Huthwitz's name last night,'' Kresh pointed out.

"But Melloy knew him,'' Devray said. "She recognized him immediately. I still don't know about that. I checked with our Internal Investigation unit as soon as I left the Huthwitz crime scene.''

"And they told you a thing or two you're not quite ready to tell me,'' Kresh said. "Even though we're standing here watching them peel incinerated bits of the Governor off the wall.''

"Yes,'' Justen said, rather defiantly. Justen could not bring himself to tell Kresh about the evidence linking Huthwitz to rustbacking. Not yet. Even in the face of the Governor's death, he could not betray one of his own by confirming the report.

"You know, there are two reasons Melloy might have known who Huthwitz was. Either she was investigating him—''

"Or else she was in on whatever he was doing,'' Justen said.

"Beg pardon, sirs, but there is a third possible reason,'' Kresh's robot said. "They are both law enforcement officers who were involved in gubernatorial security. She could simply have met him in the course of her normal duties."

Justen took a good hard look at—what was his name—Donald? Justen normally wouldn't pay much attention to a robot—especially one who was offering a rather charitable interpretation of events. Justen's own personal robot, Genray, had gotten himself out of the way the moment they arrived at the crime scene. He had stepped into an empty wall niche and stayed there. But Justen had heard a story or two about Kresh's robot, and Kresh clearly took him seriously. "Do you think that is a realistic possibility?" Justen asked.

The robot Donald raised his arms in a fair imitation of a human gesture of uncertainty. "It is certainly possible. I have no way of weighing the probabilities. But it is my experience that rejecting the innocent explanations out of hand is as unwise as refusing to consider the possibility of criminal action. The fact that Huthwitz is apparently under suspicion in some other investigation does not preclude the chance of his meeting Melloy in the course of their normal duties."

"Point taken," Justen said.

"But it doesn't get you off the hook," Kresh said. "I need to know what your internal investigators were working on."

"Not yet," Justen said. "You'll get it, I give my word. But I can't give it up now—for the same reason you didn't call the Rangers the second you spotted the body."

Kresh turned and looked him straight in the eye, and Justen squirmed inside just a bit. Kresh was not a man to trifle with.

"So you don't trust me, either," Kresh said.

"I trust you, sir," Justen said to the older man. "But I do not trust every one of your deputies, or the inviolability of all your communications equipment. Things can leak." *And I don't want to wreck Huthwitz's reputation until I know he deserved to have it wrecked.*

Kresh's expression turned angry, and for a moment it seemed he was going to bite Justen's head off. But then he

stopped himself, and even smiled, just a bit. "Much as I hate
to admit it, you might have a point. Tonya Welton once flat
out told me that the Settlers could read encrypted Sheriff's
office signals. We've changed our encryption since then, but
that's no guarantee. All right. I'll give you one day. Twenty-
eight hours.''

"And if that's not enough time?" Justen asked.

"Then that will just be too bad," Kresh said. "Twenty-eight
hours. This investigation has to *move*. We need to get somewhere before the other shoe drops.''

Justen frowned. "Shoe? What shoe?"

"You don't go killing the Governor because you're in a bad
mood," Kresh said. "This was very carefully planned and
orchestrated, maybe even *over*-orchestrated. A conspiracy.
Somebody had a plan, and I don't think it's complete yet.
Someone is going to try and make a move, seize power in the
next few days.''

"But the constitution," Justen protested. "There're the laws
controlling the succession. No one could just walk in and take
over.''

"Constitutions only work when people believe in them,
have faith in them. Otherwise, they're nothing but scraps of
paper. Do you think there is enough faith in the system out
there to keep someone from elbowing into the succession?''

"Sir, might I make an additional point?" Donald asked.

"What, Donald?"

"As you said, sir, this is a rather well-planned conspiracy.
If, as you speculate, the assassins are planning to seize power,
then they might well have co-opted the succession in advance.''

Kresh nodded and thought for a second. A strange expression came over his face. "Unless we're looking at this backwards. Maybe it's some band of civic-minded madmen who
did this.''

"What?" Justen asked.

Kresh gestured toward the bed. "He told me himself, last night, that he was close to being impeached or recalled. He was fairly optimistic about his chances of staying in office, but maybe someone else wasn't."

"So?"

"So the Governor's choice as successor doesn't get the job if he's removed from office by impeachment or recall. If the Governor is booted out, the President of the Legislative Council takes over. Shelabas Quellam. Maybe someone didn't want Quellam in the Governor's chair."

"Is Quellam that bad?" Justen asked. "I hardly know the first thing about him."

"That's about all there is to know," Kresh said. "He's as close to a nonentity as you would ever wish to meet. The trouble is that Grieg named Quellam as his Designate. Supposedly he felt the same man should take over regardless of the circumstances, for the sake of stability."

"Are you sure of that?"

"Reasonably so," Kresh said. "We'll find out soon enough. Right now, I'm more interested in who killed the man, not who takes over from—"

But Kresh was interrupted by a woman who came in at the door. Justen recognized her as Fredda Leving, the roboticist. What the devil was she doing here? "Sheriff Kresh," she said, "I've found something." There was an excited glint in her eyes, an edgy sort of triumph. "Follow me," she said. She turned and left the two men standing there, not bothering to look behind to see if they were following.

"Ah, Dr. Leving is here at my request," Kresh said, answering Justen's question before he had a chance to ask it. "I wanted to pull in a robotics expert as soon as I could."

It took Justen a moment, but then he understood. "The SPRs," he said. "How the hell did the shooter get past them?"

"That was my question," Kresh said. "Let's go see what she's found."

"There's not much that I can see," said Alvar Kresh as he peered into the recesses of the Sapper robot.

"That's because you're not in the business of dealing with these things up in Hades," Fredda said. "But you will be."

"Well, that sounds very dramatic," Kresh said, "but all I can see is what looks like some sort of broken-off attachment clip and a torn bit of flat cable."

"Let me have a look," Devray said.

Kresh stepped back and let the younger man peer into the robot's interior. "It mean anything to you?" he asked.

Devray pulled his head out, a lot of astonishment on his face. "Burning devils. A restrictor."

"What?" Kresh said.

"A restrictor. A broken-off connection point for a restrictor. Someone took the restrictors off a batch of New Law robots, modified them somehow to react to a different control system, and plugged them into these SPRs."

Kresh opened his mouth to speak, but no words came out. The SPRs shut down by restrictors removed from New Law robots? That was diabolical.

Every New Law robot had a restrictor built into it. In principle, at least, the idea was simple enough. The restrictors saw to it that any New Law robot attempting to leave Purgatory would be shut down as it tried to go. It was supposed to be impossible to remove the device without destroying the robot. No restrictor-wearing robot could function outside the area permitted by the restrictor—which was to say, the island of Purgatory. The precise workings of the system were a closely held secret. Even Kresh did not know exactly how it was supposed to work.

But he did know the operative word was "supposed," for

the obvious fact was that the system did *not* work. Every rust-back robot that left the island was a testament to that. That there was a traffic in them, a regular business, and that made it plain that it was not a question of occasional lapses or iso-lated violations. Rustbacking was more than just a business— it was a whole criminal industry, a highly sophisticated operation.

And one that was now tied into the assassination of the Governor. A gang of rustbackers hand found a way to tamper with the Governor's own security robots. How the hell could they trace that leak?

"You're sure that's a piece off a New Law robot's restric-tor?" Kresh demanded.

"Absolutely," said Fredda Leving. "It was what I was looking for when I started checking the Sapper robots."

"But I don't understand. We're still on the island. Why should restrictors turn off the security robots?"

"They must have been modified in some way," Fredda said. "Clearly they weren't working on a geographic basis, because the Sappers were working fine during the party. My guess is that they were modified to deactivate the robots on some sort of signal. Hyperwave, or maybe even old-fashioned radio. No one uses radio anymore—but that fact right there would make it perfect for this sort of job. The signal would be undetectable with any sort of modern equipment. Clearly the restrictors have been modified not only to shut down the robots in some dif-ferent way, but also to be removable in a hurry. Except this restrictor didn't come out quite as easily as it was supposed to."

"But where the devil did they *get* the restrictors to put on the SPRs?" asked Devray.

There were times it was more than clear to Kresh that De-vray did not think in terms of crime and victim and criminal.

He was better suited to forest management than murder investigation.

"The spare parts bin," Leving said. "Obviously, they used
restrictors they had peeled off New Law robots. Rustbackers
did this. No one else could have."

"Well, one thing is for sure," Kresh said. "Whoever did
this worked in a rustbacker lab at some point. He or she knew
how to get these things out, and do it in a hurry."

"A rustbacker," Fredda said. "Maybe that can point us
toward a motive for the murder."

"Maybe," Alvar said. "At least now we can get started."

Donald 111 was in a very slight state of shock, and it was
with a great sense of relief that he found that his duties required him to be alone.

The SPRs had been tampered with. They had been shut
down, useless for security work. Kresh had comforted him
with the knowledge that Grieg had died with fifty robots to
protect him. One more could have done no good. But the fifty
had been useless, meaningless. One functioning robot could
easily have made the difference. Worse, it was the deployment
of the SPRs that had doomed Grieg—and Donald had urged
their deployment.

Robots on the planet Inferno had always been built with
extremely high First Law, and had been known to freeze up
on occasions such as this, when they learned they *could* have
prevented harm to a human. But Donald knew better than that.
Yes, he could have saved Governor Grieg—if he had been
possessed of information known to no one but those who killed
the Governor. He could have saved him—if he had been here,
at the Residence, instead of many kilometers away, with
Kresh, performing his normal duties. He could have saved the
Governor if a half-dozen impossible things had happened.

No. No. There was nothing he could have done outside the

world of if-only. Here, in reality, it was never possible to avoid all risk, all danger. It was never possible to defend against attackers with as many resources, with as much willingness to take risks, as the killers of Governor Grieg.

But still, he needed to calm himself, to talk himself down from the idea that he could have done anything. So it was just as well he had work to do, and the need to do it in private.

There was a great deal more to a major investigation than discovering clues. It was, in many ways, as much a management operation as anything else, as Donald 111 had reason to know. There were all the logistical questions of bringing in robots and human personnel and all sorts of equipment. There was an evidence center to set up, where all the data could be stored safely, and the physical evidence protected from tampering and made available for examination. There was a press center to establish, accommodations for the investigation team and the press and the hangers-on and the VIPs who would inevitably arrive.

There were those, and a thousand other details, to deal with—but then, Donald had been quite literally made for the job. Though he was obliged to devote a lot of his time to duties as Sheriff Kresh's personal assistant, his primary responsibility was to Sheriff Kresh's office, to the efficient handling of the detail work—and that work he could only do when the Sheriff did not require him to be present—such as at the present moment. Donald barely dared admit it even to himself, but there were unquestionably times when it was a distinct relief to get the Sheriff out from underfoot so he could get on with his main task of managing the Sheriff's office.

Management was in large part a matter of communications, of contacting the proper robot and relaying orders, of locating the proper equipment and arranging for it to be transported to where it would be needed. Most, if not all, of it could be handled via hyperwave, which in turn meant that Donald could be remarkably productive while standing stock-still, with little or no outward evidence that he was even switched on, let alone extremely busy.

Donald had learned the hard way to keep a low profile when so engaged. There were more than a few humans who objected, as a matter of principle, to the sight of a seemingly idle robot. It offended them to see Donald standing stock-still. They would give near-useless orders just for the sake of getting him busy. For that reason, he preferred to make sure he was safely out of sight somewhere before he started making his calls. In the present case, Donald was hiding in a broom closet as he worked. He was aware of the fact that many humans would find that extremely humorous, but that did not much matter to him. The whole point of it was to stay out of their view in the first place—and they could not be amused if they couldn't find him.

Besides which, there was nothing funny about the present situation. There were any number of points that Sheriff Kresh and the other humans had not even begun to address. Even now, there was vital new information coming in—along with vital new questions. Donald, however, knew enough not to point out such things to Sheriff Kresh and the others yet. It would be counterproductive to break their concentration just as they were coming to terms with the basic facts of the case. Humans, Donald knew, often required a great deal of time before they were able to deal with changed circumstances.

Governor Grieg had been murdered, and that was most unfortunate. Donald grieved his loss, inasmuch as any robot could be said to grieve. But the plain fact was that the man was dead, and there was nothing anyone could do about it. One always had to deal with the available circumstances, and Grieg's death was now one of them.

Humans, of course, saw it differently. They indulged in ''denial,'' a ritual Donald had never entirely understood. It seemed to involve an attempt to reshape the world into a more convenient state by a sheer act of stubborn will, generally by insisting that some bad thing had never happened. It had never worked and never would—but it seemed that humans always had to find out if it *would* work, just this once. There was no point trying to move the Sheriff, Commander Devray, and Fredda Leving forward until they had at least accepted the facts of the situation.

In the meantime, let them deal with theories, with the corpses of humans and robots. They were best suited to that sort of task, just as Donald was best suited to making arrangements for a field forensic lab to be set up.

Donald was in the midst of an intricate five-way linkup with various logistical offices when he heard something in the hallway outside. Under normal circumstances, he would have ignored it as part of the normal background noise of everyday life. But these were far from normal circumstances. It sounded very much like someone in bare feet walking slowly—and a bit unsteadily—down the long, wood-floored hallway.

It was not Sheriff Kresh or Dr. Leving or the Commander. Donald would have recognized their walking rhythms. It certainly was not any of the deputies. Their uniforms included heavy boots, and none would move at such a leisurely pace while on duty. But the footsteps were rather *loud* for all of that, considering they sounded unshod.

Donald cut off his comm links in as quick and orderly a fashion as he could, and waited, motionless, in the darkness of the closet until the steps had moved past him and were moving away.

Donald silently opened the door and stepped out into the hall, determined not to make a sound. He looked down the hall, not quite sure what he expected to see.

In any event, he did *not* expect to see a bald man in rather loud blue-checked pajamas and a clashing red-and-white-striped robe padding barefoot down the hall.

Tierlaw Verick—or at least the person calling himself that—sat in his unfortunate sleepwear, looking most ill at ease. He was perched on a hard-backed chair in the center of a room with no other furniture in it save the interrogator's chair. Verick's chair had been placed so his back was to the door, with the deliberate intent of making him just that bit more uncomfortable.

Half the Residence seemed never to have been used. The place was filled with fully stocked, well-maintained bedroom suites with everything a guest might need, and never mind that Infernals did not care to have overnight guests. The Residence had any number of handsomely appointed sitting rooms no one had ever sat in, gleaming kitchens that had not served a meal since Kresh had been born. A sad commentary on the grandiose attitude of Inferno's architects, and on the wasteful nature of a robot-based economy, but it did mean there were ample facilities for interrogation. In fact, it had taken a little doing to find a room barren enough to serve as a suitable interrogation chamber, from the psychological point of view.

Fredda Leving sat in the chair facing Verick, while Justen Devray leaned in a corner and Kresh paced the room. Donald stood, unobtrusive as ever, in the room's only wall niche, facing Verick, on the far side of the room from the door. He was, of course, recording everything, but Donald could do one better than that. When Fredda Leving had first built him, years before, she had equipped him with the sensors to let him serve as a lie detector. He was monitoring Verick's heart rate, respiration, pupil dilation, and other physiological factors that provided an estimate of stress levels. Verick didn't know that, of course, and no one was going to tell him.

Not that Verick knew much of *any*thing, to hear Verick tell it. Verick was an older-looking man, thin-faced, pale-skinned, with not a single hair on his head, aside from heavy brown eyebrows and lashes. His eyes were piercing blue, and quite expressive; his face was lean and hungry-looking. The skin over his skull gleamed, a healthy pink, shining as if it had been polished—as perhaps it had. It was baldness so thorough-going and absolute that it had to be an affectation, a deliberate choice in his personal appearance that had to be as carefully maintained as the most elaborate coiffure. Either he shaved his head at least daily, or had himself depilitated on a regular basis.

In Kresh's experience, men who put that sort of effort into their appearance—and chose such a startling one as absolute, perfect baldness—were rather aggressive and assertive types, and Verick fit the bill. Other men arrested in such silly-looking sleepwear would have acted sheepish or apologetic. Verick gave the sense of a man who didn't like being kept waiting.

Verick's story was simple, if utterly implausible. He was a Settler businessman, here to try to sell a Settler-model Control Center to the Inferno Terraforming Authority. He had been a guest at the reception the evening before. He had, by prear-rangement, stayed after most of the other guests had gone to have an after-hours meeting with the Governor. Likewise by prearrangement, he had stayed the night after the meeting, sleeping in the west wing of the Residence. He had awakened to hear voices and people moving about, and had gotten up to see what was going on—only to be taken into custody by Donald as he set foot in the hallway.

It would follow that he knew nothing about Grieg's death, having slept through the whole thing, and his behavior was consistent with that state of affairs. Either he did not know Grieg was dead, or he was doing a first-rate job of acting like he didn't.

Kresh was not about to tell him. If a man who claimed to

know nothing made a slip that demonstrated that he *did* know something, that could be most informative.

But the irritating—and baffling—thing about his story was that it seemed as if it might check out. Donald confirmed that there was a Settler businessman by the name of Verick on the guest list. That was a start, anyway. But how the devil had Kresh's deputies missed him when they searched the house?

Kresh was too old a hand not to know there were lots of answers to that one. Human error could explain it in a dozen ways, any of which might be true—and none of which would sound the least bit convincing to outsiders.

There had not been many robots available when the first search had been performed, and those had been put to work either on specialized work or general heavy lifting. Human deputies had performed the search. The place had at least a hundred rooms, and Kresh could easily imagine a hurried deputy not being sure which room he had checked, or just opening a door to peek into the ninth or tenth obviously empty room in a row—and missing the motionless lump under the covers. Verick might have locked his door from the inside, and the deputy searching that section might have intended to come back later with the keys, and then forgot.

His deputies were only human, after all, and all of them were in one degree or another of shock. It was, after all, *their* Governor who had died this night. It was the head of *their* nation, their planet, who had fallen to enemies unseen.

But even so, it was the sort of foul-up that could easily dog this case for all time, if it were not put right immediately. Kresh could imagine the board of inquiry already. Kresh had set new teams of deputies to work to search the place all over again, just to see what else they might have missed—and, this time, with some sort of Crime Scene Observer robot accompanying each deputy. Later, if it came to that, Kresh was prepared to take the whole Residence apart, brick by brick.

Nothing could be permitted to threaten the integrity of this investigation.

But Verick. If his innocence seemed implausible, so too did his guilt. For if he were a member of the elaborate conspiracy, then why in Space had he remained behind in the Residence? Why had he allowed himself to be arrested in his pajamas?

In the main, it seemed to Kresh, Verick's story seemed more plausible than any attempt to tie him to the crime. But they were damned short of suspects and motives at the moment, and Kresh saw no reason to turn his back on one. Besides, stories had held together in the past, only to crack later on under sufficient pressure. "All right, Mr. Verick, let's try it again," Kresh said. "From the top."

"Can't you tell me what all this is about?" Verick said. "Can't you tell me what's happened?"

"No," Kresh said, his tone as clipped as his reply.

"It's important that we not tell you too much just yet," Devray said, clearly playing good cop to Kresh's bad cop. "We want to know what *you* know, without muddying the tracks."

"I want to speak to the Governor," Verick said.

"I can promise you that the Governor does *not* want to speak to you," Kresh said. True enough, if more than a bit misleading. And it seemed to have the desired effect of un-nerving Verick. "From the top," Kresh said again.

"All right, all right." He hesitated long enough to take a deep sigh and slump down in his chair, and then began again, his eyes staring out. "My name is Tierlaw Verick. I live on the Settler world of Baleyworld. I represent a firm that sells highly sophisticated control equipment. We've sold a great number of our systems to Settler terraforming projects, and I was sent here in hopes of selling one of our systems to the terraforming center here. I attended the reception last night, and afterwards had a meeting with Governor Grieg. Knowing that accommodation was very tight in town, and that I had come a very long way, he very kindly offered to put me up for the night.''

"You and you alone?'' Fredda said. "Of all the people here last night, you were the only one who stayed the night?''

"Hmmm?'' Verick looked at Fredda, as if he were surprised by the question. "I don't know. I didn't notice anyone else, one way or the other. I don't see why I should be the only one. There's certainly plenty of room here. But to the best of my direct knowledge, yes. I must say that surprises me in a house this size, though. Back home, every one of the guests at the reception would have been an overnight guest. But are you telling me there was no one else here?''

"No, there wasn't,'' Fredda said, to Kresh's annoyance. Rule number one of interrogation was never to answer the suspect's questions. The more Verick knew, the more able he would be to craft his answers.

"Dr. Leving,'' Kresh said, "I think it would be best if you let the Commander and myself ask the questions, and if you did not supply any answers yourself.''

Leving looked toward Kresh, a bit startled. "But I—oh,'' she said, about to protest and then thinking better of it. "Forgive me, Sheriff.''

"No harm done. In any event, it's a very minor point,'' Kresh said, hoping that he was telling the truth, now that Verick's attention had been drawn to it. "But you weren't the only one to *meet* with the Governor last night, were you?''

"No, no, of course not,'' Verick said. "There were a number of other people waiting their turn before me. Eight or ten of them altogether, but in twos and threes. I had to wait until they were done, but I didn't much mind. After all, I didn't have to fly home afterwards—and besides, by being the last one in line, I had the chance to stay a little longer. No one was waiting behind me.''

And you've just told us you were the last one to see Grieg alive, Kresh thought. He stole the tiniest of glances at Devray, and saw the point had not been lost on him, either. "So what did the two of you talk about?" Kresh asked.

It was plainly obvious that Verick's patience was running thin. "I have told you and told you. About my desire to sell him a control station. He seemed most interested in it, for a number of reasons—mostly because it wasn't a robotic system."

"I beg your pardon?" Kresh asked. That was the benefit of repeated questioning. Verick hadn't offered that little tidbit in the previous go-rounds.

"Our Settler system is not robotic," Verick said. "I did what I could to point out the advantages of that to the Governor. That was mostly what we talked about. He seemed quite receptive."

"Why would he be against a robotic system?" Fredda asked.

"Too conservative for a situation as far gone as Inferno," Verick said. "Hook a robot-brain control unit up to the terraforming system and it will avoid all potentially risky operations, for fear of doing harm to human beings, or some damn thing." He was warming to his subject, obviously going through the arguments he had used on Grieg. "A robotic control system would do all it could to avoid all risk during the terraforming process—almost certainly delaying completion, and possibly causing the project to fail altogether. Even if it succeeded in terraforming the planet, its goal would be to create an utterly risk-free final environment when the reterraforming was complete. There are Spacer worlds that are virtually nothing more than planetwide well-manicured lawns. I don't think it's any coincidence that those are the worlds where the populations have fallen asleep—or vanished completely."

That was a low blow. Solaria. No Spacer liked to be reminded of—or think about—the collapse of Solaria.

Verick looked around and saw that he had scored a point. "A robotic system, obsessed with risk avoidance, would lead to a very bland sort of world here. As I told the Governor, not exactly a fit environment if you want future generations to be able to deal with challenges."

"All right," Kresh said, not having to try much in trying to play the part of the rude cop. "That's enough speeches for now. So you talked to the Governor. Then what?"

"Then we said our good nights, and he said he had some other things to attend to, and so he saw me to the door of his office. We shook hands there, and I stepped around the robots in the hallway and went on my way. I'm afraid I got a bit turned around in the hallways and walked around in a bit of a circle. After a bit, I realized that I was going to end up right back where I had started, at the door to the Governor's apartment. I thought of asking the two robots I had seen by the door for directions, but by then they weren't there anymore. I suppose they had already gone in."

"Gone in?" Kresh asked. He had assumed the robots Verick had mentioned by the door *were* SPRs on sentry duty. But sentry robots stay where they were. "Where did the robots go?"

"To tuck him in for the night, I suppose. I've heard you Spacers can't even get undressed without a robot to help."

Fredda seemed about to respond to that, but Kresh stepped forward and put a hand on her shoulder. It did no good at all for the suspect to find out he could bait the inquisitors.

"Some of us can manage on our own," Kresh said, a bit of steel behind the soft words. But the sentry should not have left its post. And there should have been *one* robot on door duty, not two. Kresh had a feeling he knew the answer to his next question. "These robots," he said. "Can you describe them?"

"I don't have much time for robots," Verick said. "I don't like 'em and I don't trust 'em."

"But you can see them," Kresh said, his voice hard-edged. "What did the two robots look like?"

Verick looked up at Kresh, visibly annoyed. "There was a very tall, angular-looking red one. Shiny red. I wouldn't want to mess with him. The other was shorter, and shiny black."

Justen Devray and Fredda Leving both looked from Verick to Kresh, both of them understanding.

The last two beings to see Grieg alive were Prospero and Caliban. New Law and No Law.

One robot whose internal Laws did not require it to prevent harm to a human.

And one who had no Laws at all. Who could harm whatever humans it liked.

8

SERO PHROST LOOKED down into the grey darkness of the sea below as his aircar swooped back toward Purgatory. No explanation, no apology, just the flat order to turn back—an order his pilot robot was obeying, despite his best efforts to convince it otherwise. The turn-back order came from a traffic safety center, and the First Law saw to it that that was all a robot needed to know in order to force obedience.

But why the turn-around? An arrest order? What did they think they knew? And arrested for what? He would have to be careful, very careful. More than one person had been pulled in on a minor charge and made the mistake of assuming it was about some larger matter.

Or was it his own arrest that he was flying back toward? Phrost looked out the porthole and saw the running lights of several other aircars heading back to Purgatory. A dragnet? Perhaps, if he permitted himself to grasp at straws, it had nothing to do with him at all. It could be they were acting on a rustbacking tip-off, and pulling back all flights that had left at a certain time. No way to know. Perhaps it had nothing at all to do with him.

The guilty flee when no one pursues. Admit nothing,

reveal nothing. There was still every chance for him to win out.

The dark sky rushed past him.

Alvar Kresh glanced at the wall clock in the operations room. Just before 0700 hours. A bare five hours since he had found the body, though it seemed that enough had happened since then to fill up a month's worth of days. Tierlaw Verick was filed away for future reference, held under close guard in the same room in which he had been questioned, while the Crime Scene robots went over the room in which he had slept. Kresh doubted that Verick had anything to do with the assassination, but hunches were no way to run an investigation. Who knew what they might find, until they looked?

Someone had set up a conference table in the ops room, and Kresh, Fredda Leving, and Justen Devray sat at three of its sides, while Donald 111 stood at the fourth. All of them—even Donald, somehow—seemed exhausted, drawn out, the press of events leaving them all far behind the pace. And yet it seemed they were no further ahead than they had been when they had started.

The clock was moving, and moving fast. Kresh dared not delay much longer in contacting the key members of the government, or in announcing Grieg's death to all Inferno.

But the moment he did *that*, Kresh knew, all hell would break loose. He could not foresee what form the chaos would take, but he knew, beyond doubt, that there would be chaos. He desperately needed to have much of this investigation under control before the news broke wide. And the damage could only be made worse if the first announcement came from someplace beside Alvar Kresh's own mouth—a probability that was increasing with every second that passed.

A deputy might say something over an unscrambled channel that would be overheard, or call a friend or family member with the news, or give or sell the story of the century to a friend in the news business. Or the killers might decide it suited their purposes to make the announcement. Or someone who called Grieg might do what Kresh had done, and realize the Grieg on the other end was a simulation. The sim was still running on the phone system, half to help keep the lid on and half to leave it intact for the analysis teams.

They would have to make the announcement soon, very soon, if they were to keep any sort of control over events. But before Kresh told anyone anything, he needed a chance to think, to compare notes, to plan. A council of war—because it might quite literally be that Grieg's death was the opening shot in an actual war. There was no way to know.

He was sure Justen Devray understood all that, and it at least seemed as if Fredda Leving did. Kresh found that he was impressed—very impressed—by the way she had handled herself in the midst of all this chaos. There was a lot to admire about the young, smart, and beautiful Fredda Leving. But Kresh did not feel he could rely too much on her instincts when it came to criminal investigation. She had shown in Verick's interrogation that she thought in too straight a line for police work. Maybe the direct approach worked in science, where the facts did not mind being discovered. Police work, on the other hand, was a form of research where the facts were often determined to elude capture. Head straight for them and they'd be bound to escape.

"All right, Donald," Alvar said. "Let's get started. What do we have, and what do we need?"

"We have ascertained, through Tierlaw Verick's statement, that Caliban and Prospero were almost certainly the last to see Governor Grieg alive," Donald said. "I have placed an all-points bulletin for their capture, but it seems unlikely we will apprehend them quickly—especially if we do not have the full cooperation of the SSS. Neither the Rangers nor our own department have arrest powers here, or facilities for performing inquiries.

"Neither Prospero nor Caliban are presently available or traceable via hyperwave, and both have duties that require them to be out in the field a great deal. It is possible they are following their normal routines, but are simply out of touch. It is also possible that they have gone into hiding. We will do all we can to trace them, given the limitations of our circumstances."

Interesting that Donald would start with the robots, Kresh thought. He was focused, perhaps overfocused, on them. It would be best to keep in mind that in this investigation at least, Donald was not likely to be even remotely as objective as he normally was. Clearly, he *wanted* Prospero and Caliban to be guilty. A biased robot. As if there weren't enough problems on this case.

"How reliable is Tierlaw's statement?" Kresh asked.

"As best I could ascertain, all of his bodily reactions were consistent with a man under great stress giving a truthful statement. I believe that he spoke the truth," Donald said.

And *that* was the least-qualified pronouncement Donald had ever made concerning his lie-detector function. Enough so that Kresh felt unsure. Usually Donald made a speech three times longer than that about the uncertainty of such measurement. No doubt about it—he *wanted* the robots to be guilty.

"We should be able to check his story out against Grieg's appointment diary," Devray said. "That's something. But at least we have a lead, and suspects."

"Even leaving aside the First Law question, I can't see what possible motive Caliban and Prospero could have for attacking Grieg, or why they would have been so clumsy about it," Fredda protested. "Yes, Caliban has no First Law. In theory, there is nothing to prevent him attacking anyone he likes. But there's nothing preventing me, or you, either. And yes, Prospero's First Law does not enjoin him to prevent harm—but I can't imagine Prospero splitting hair so fine as to interpret that as participating in a murder but not actually firing the weapon—which is what you'd have to have here.''

"But you do grant," Devray said, "that there is nothing in Caliban's absence of Laws that would prevent him from killing Grieg? And that there is nothing in the New Laws that would absolutely force Prospero to prevent the attack?''

"Yes, but—''

"So one of them could kill and the other could stand idly by," Devray said, his tone a bit badgering.

"In theory, yes," Fredda admitted, with massive reluctance. "But it makes no sense. Grieg was the best friend the New Law robots ever had. What would make them want to kill *him*?''

"Plenty," Devray said. "I have an appointment—*had* an appointment—with the Governor for later this morning. We were going to talk about a proposal I had submitted last week.''

"What sort of proposal?" Kresh asked.

"One for the destruction of all New Law robots," Devray said.

"What? Have you taken leave of your senses?" Fredda demanded.

"No, ma'am," Devray replied, his voice bland and professional. "But I'm damned sick and tired of chasing rustbackers. The N.L.s are at the focus of a whole new series of crimes— rustback smuggling, restrictor removal, and the founding of illegal settlements.''

"Settlements?" Kresh asked.

"Well, one settlement, anyway," Devray said. "They call it Valhalla. It's supposed to be somewhere on the far side of the planet from here, somewhere in the Utopia region of Terra Grande. I don't even know if it exists—but it's where half the rustbacks we catch seem to be heading. And I'm tired of wasting time and effort chasing rumors. I told the Governor the rustbacks and the New Law robots were more trouble than they were worth, and it was time to admit it and move on.''

''But they work!'' Fredda protested. ''New Law robots represent half the work force on Purgatory.''

''And they were supposed to be *all* of it—except they're only about a third as productive as Three-Law robots. Every department has been forced to pull in human workers, because the Settlers don't allow Three-Law robots to have the run of the island. If the New Law robots were worth all the trouble they cause, that'd be one thing,'' Devray said. ''But if anything, they're slowing *down* the reterraforming project.''

Kresh was surprised to see Devray that interested in terraforming—and then realized he shouldn't have been surprised at all. The Rangers only did law enforcement on the side. Terraforming was much more their side of the street.

''Was—was the Governor considering the idea?'' Fredda asked.

''I don't know,'' Devray said. ''He didn't reject it out of hand. I know he was also toying with the idea of removing all the range restrictors and letting the New Law robots go.''

''Why the devil would he do that?'' Kresh asked. ''There wouldn't be a New Law left on this island if not for the restrictors.''

''Don't be too sure of that,'' Fredda said. ''A lot of the New Law robots do cause trouble—but the ones that do work, work plenty hard. A lot of the rustbacks work very hard indeed—once they're paid a decent wage. And not all of them head for Valhalla, Justen. And just by the way, Valhalla is no rumor. It's a real place—and there are lots of good reasons for the New Laws to head for it. I've seen that with my own eyes.''

''You seem to know a lot about rustbacks,'' Devray said.

"And have you reported these escaped robots in Valhalla you've seen with your own eyes? Or reported Valhalla's location?"

"No, I have not reported that information," she snapped. "I don't know where Valhalla is, and I don't want to know. But if you want to arrest me for seeing a rustback, go right ahead. I felt responsible for them. Rustbacks are escaped New Law robots, and I invented New Law robots. Of course I'd research them."

"Hold it, both of you," Kresh said. "This is not the time. We can go into all this later. Right now the only important thing is that Devray's recommendation to the Governor could have given Caliban and Prospero a very strong motive if they knew about it. They might have decided to kill him before *he* killed *them*."

"Caliban isn't a New Law robot—"

"Burning hells, I know that better than anyone!" Kresh snapped. "But maybe he decided not to take chances on being caught up in a roundup. Or maybe he just acted in sympathy to the plight of his New Law brethren. It's a possible motive, and the two of them are definite suspects."

"But you can't just decide they did it. Any number of humans might have—"

"I said they were suspects, not *the* suspects," Kresh said. "Even if I were convinced they did it—and I'm not—I wouldn't dare stop investigating other possibilities. Not until the other shoe drops. Suppose it wasn't the robots? Suppose humans did this job? What was their motive? Have they achieved it with Grieg's death, or is there more to follow? Is it a coup, or a simple assassination?"

"A coup? Stars above, I hadn't even thought of that," Fredda said.

"I haven't thought of much else," Kresh said. "But I'll tell you this—with every minute that passes, it becomes less likely

that it was—is—a coup. If you're attempting to overthrow a
government, you don't give it time to recover from the first
blow before you strike again. Unless something has gone
wrong with their plans. Or unless—hellfire, that's a tough
one.''

"What's a tough one?" Fredda demanded.

"Suppose the public announcement of Grieg's death is the
signal for their next move?"

"Well, there's some chance of that," Devray agreed. "I
doubt the killers expected the body would be discovered so
soon—or that *you* would discover it. They set up the image
box to do the comm simulation, after all.''

"Yes," Fredda said. "Probably the killers weren't expecting discovery until this morning." She looked up at Kresh and
shrugged. "Maybe it was Tierlaw who was supposed to find
the body. Unless Tierlaw did it and was planning to pretend
to discover the body this morning. Except Donald said his
monitors showed that Tierlaw was telling the truth.''

"Don't trust Donald's sensors that far," Kresh said. "A
trained man could beat his sensors—or any lie-detector system,
short of a Psychic Probe. But Tierlaw could have been set up,
a useful idiot.''

"How the devil can an idiot be useful?" Fredda asked.

"By being worse than useless to your opposition. Maybe
we're supposed to pay so much attention to Tierlaw that we
let the real perpetrators get away. But that's giving them an
awful lot of credit, and assumes an incredibly complex and
fragile plot. My guess is that the assassins are completely unaware of Tierlaw's existence, and he is telling the precise truth:
He had nothing to do with it, and he slept through the whole
thing. But don't worry, we're going to hold him and check
him out all the same.''

"If you're right," Devray said, "then how was the body
supposed to be discovered? The plotters had to have thought

about it. What were they expecting?''

"Well," Fredda said, "all the regular household robots had been ordered to clear off to an outbuilding for the night of the party. There are two deputies interviewing them now, but I doubt they'll get anything. They would have returned this morning—right about now, I suppose—to resume their normal duties."

"So a robot was supposed to discover Grieg was dead," Kresh said. "What would have happened then?" he asked.

Fredda thought for a moment. "It depends very much on the robot's preexisting and contingency orders, of course, but most likely, all hell would break loose. It would call for help, attempt resuscitation, call for reinforcements, request a security alert, and who knows what else."

"All the proper things to do in terms of the Three Laws, but that would have set off absolute chaos," Kresh said. "If that had happened, every kind of cop within two hundred kilometers would have been over the Residence, banging into each other and the news media and whatever political leaders managed to get involved. The devil only knows what sort of hell that would have stirred up. And all an attempt to revive Grieg would have accomplished would be the muddling of the evidence. Just the sort of chaos and confusion a coup plotter would want."

"Maybe," Devray said. "Maybe. There's a lot of guessing in there, but it might be right."

"Sir," Donald said, "if I may interject, there are other vital issues that must be considered before we establish any sort of motive for other hypothetical suspects."

"What other issues?" Kresh asked.

"There is the question of the weapon."

"Hell's bells, the weapon. I *am* getting old." .

"What about the weapon?" Fredda asked.

"There are energy scanners at every entrance to this building," said Kresh, "and perimeter scanners as well. No one should have been able to get an energy weapon into this building without half a dozen alarms going crazy. How did the weapon get in here? How did it get out?"

"Or *did* it get out?" Devray asked. "Why risk taking it both ways through the scanners? You might set off an alarm on the way out. If I were doing this job, I wouldn't take chances on smuggling the gun in. The building was unoccupied for damn-all long enough to plant a hundred blasters. I'd hide a nice standard blaster with a shielded power pack, do the job, and then abandon the blaster on the premises."

"Hmmph. It's a possibility," Kresh said.

"I beg your pardon, Commander Devray, but there is one point that argues against such a possibility," Donald said. "The energy-discharge curve."

"What's that?" Fredda asked.

"By examining the Governor's wounds and the blaster damage to the robots, and by establishing range, it was possible to note the relative power of each shot, and thus the weapon's charge level for each shot. For any given blaster, each shot is less and less intense as the blaster's charge is expended. For the weapon in question, the intensity of the blaster shots declined precipitously with each firing, clearly indicating an unusually small power cell. The discharge pattern was quite unlike any of the common makes and models of blaster."

"And an undersized power cell suggests a weapon intended for concealment," Kresh said. "A custom job. And custom-made weapons can be traced. You're right, Donald, that needs looking into."

"Yes, sir. I think we must also ask ourselves about the assault on Tonya Welton, and the subsequent arrival of the false SSS agents. Was it indeed some sort of diversion linked to the attack? And if so, who was it supposed to divert, and what was it supposed to divert that person from?"

"Especially as we established almost immediately that it was bogus," Kresh said. "Why stage a diversion that would make us more suspicious?"

"Maybe because at that point it didn't matter anymore," Devray said. "Maybe the thing it was supposed to divert attention from wasn't the Governor's death at all. And maybe it wasn't you it was meant to distract."

"Huthwitz," Kresh said. "The murder of Emoch Huthwitz. You're suggesting that it was sheer chance that it happened the same night as Grieg's murder."

"It's possible. Maybe the Welton attack was meant to divert the Rangers away from the attack on one of their own."

"That won't work," Fredda objected. "From what you've told me, this Huthwitz was found hours after he was killed. No one noticed he was missing. And it doesn't sound like much of anyone in the Rangers responded to the attack on Welton."

"All good points," Kresh agreed. "But Huthwitz's death doesn't make sense as a coincidence, either."

"Coincidences never make sense," Fredda said. "They happen by chance, not logic."

"But there's a point beyond which chance is an awfully weak explanation. In fact, it's always a weak explanation."

"Well, suppose Huthwitz was the diversion?" asked Fredda. "While you were out looking at his body, the Governor was being killed."

"That doesn't work, either," Kresh said. "Huthwitz was killed hours before the Governor. Our best estimate was he was killed *before* the attack on Tonya Welton. As for the discovery of his body as a diversion, he could have been discovered hours later or hours before he was. And the Governor had been dead for about an hour before we found Huthwitz. And besides, we just got through agreeing that the plotters intended Grieg to be discovered some time in the morning, hours from now."

"But it was Huthwitz's death that led you to check on the Governor," Leving said.

"But no one could have predicted it would cause me to check, and my discovery of the body didn't do anyone any good," Kresh said. "Beyond all that, if Huthwitz was killed as a diversion, it didn't much matter who they killed. But Commander Devray has as much as told me he thinks someone might have had very good reasons to kill Huthwitz, and Huthwitz alone."

"So what are you saying?" Fredda asked.

"I'm saying that the two murders are related—but I haven't the faintest idea how. Right now Donald is the only one with a theory of the crime."

"Sir, I would submit that I have much more than a theory. I have means, motive, and opportunity. I have two suspects."

"Donald, you *want* them to be guilty," Fredda said. "If they killed Grieg, it would confirm all your strongest fears about New Law robots. But I'm no investigator, and I can see all the holes in the case against them. I agree with Sheriff Kresh that it seems extremely unlikely that Grieg's murder was unrelated to everything else that happened last night.. How could Caliban and Prospero have killed Huthwitz—and why would they do it? How and why did they arrange the attack on Tonya and the phony SSS agents that took away her assailants?"

"I cannot, as yet, answer those questions, Dr. Leving. And despite your objections, they are the only suspects we have."

"I agree," Kresh said. "We need to bring them in. But we also need to work on finding ourselves some other suspects as well. We're going to have to go over the access recorder records. And we need to get hold of all the video imagery shot by all the news outlets. We need to go over it frame by frame, and if we can spot anything or anyone who shouldn't be there.''

''I can attend to that, Sheriff,'' Donald said.

''Good.'' Kresh glanced up at the wall clock again. Time was moving. Moving too damned fast. ''I need to draft some sort of statement,'' he said. ''We've waited long enough. We're not going to get things under any more control than they are right now. I have to notify the government, and then the public.''

He stood up, rubbed his face with a tired hand, and ran his thick, stubby fingers through his white hair. ''It's time to tell the world that Chanto Grieg is dead.''

9

OTTLEY BISSAL WALKED the streets of Limbo City, straining to be invisible, willing himself to vanish into the hustling, bustling, early-morning crowd, watching his back to be sure there was no one watching him. It was the last leg of the journey, and he was close, so very close. He had parked the aircar on one side of town, and walked from there straight through the busiest sections of the city.

Limbo was a classic boomtown, growing by leaps and bounds, stepping on its own feet as it struggled to keep up with its new role as the world headquarters of the reterraforming team. Technicians, designers, scientists, and construction workers were everywhere, with New Law robots hurrying everywhere on this urgent errand or that, and survey teams and speciality workers coming and going from every corner of the world.

Even on a normal day, there was not a room to be had in the city, and building new accommodations space was always a low priority to all the other vital projects. The onslaught of VIP visitors to the Residence had only made matters worse.

But Bissal had no need to worry. They had taken care

of him, seen to it he had a place to stay until it was all over.

Certain that he was not being followed, Bissal shouldered his way through the worst of the crowds and made it to a less congested part of town, to an old warehouse.

As instructed, he tried his hand at the side door security panel. It read his palm and the door slid open.

He stepped inside, and the door slid closed. It was a rust-backing lab, with all the hardware of the trade. But one side of the place had been set up as a rather cozy little apartment, with a bed, a mini-kitchen, a refresher, and ample stocks of food and water. Now all he had to do was stay here, out of sight, until they called for him, until the heat was off, until someone came for him.

Bissal was exhausted—but he was also hungry, and he was probably too wound up to sleep, anyway. A quick snack would give him a chance to relax and unwind before he turned in. He hurried to the mini-kitchen and started rummaging around for something to eat.

It's good to be safe, he thought as he opened up a fastmeal and sat down to eat. *Very good.*

"Your pardon, sir, but there is an urgent call for you."

"Hmmm? What? Excuse me?" Shelabas Quellam, President of the Legislative Council, was not yet fully awake. He sat up in bed and blinked sleepily at his personal robot. "What is it, Keflin?"

"A call, sir," the robot replied. "It seems to be most urgent, coming on a government channel."

"Oh, dear. Well, then, I'd best take it at once."

"Yes, sir."

A second robot appeared, carrying a portable comm-link unit. The second robot held the unit with one hand as it activated it with the other. Quellam watched the screen as it cleared and saw that it was that Sheriff fellow. Klesh? Klersh?

Something like that. In any event, he looked perfectly dreadful. And no wonder, at this time of night. But what in the world could it all be about?

"Good evening, Sheriff. Or rather, good morning. What can I do for you?"

"Sir, forgive me for calling at this hour," Kresh said, "but I have some very bad news. The Governor has been murdered."

The Governor has been murdered. It later seemed to Shelabas that the Sheriff *must* have said more after that—he even remembered acting on advice Kresh must have given him at that moment—but he could not recall hearing any of it at all.

He was too busy trying to contain his sense of glee while trying to pretend he was sorry Grieg was dead. Too bad the poor fellow was gone, but Shelabas Quellam suffered no illusions. He knew what people in general thought of him—and he knew very well what Grieg in particular had thought of him. Grieg might have named Quellam his Designate, but Grieg had never respected Quellam.

But now, at last, at long last, *he*, Shelabas Quellam, would be the Governor.

At last, long last, the world was going to find out that Shelabas Quellam was a man to be taken seriously.

Sheriff Alvar Kresh stood alone before the robot camera in the Residence's broadcast studio.

Justen Devray stood by his side, but that did not matter. Alvar was *alone*, as alone as he had ever been. Even as he spoke, he knew the words he spoke would be the image that the world would remember. Twenty years from now, if anyone spoke of Alvar Kresh, it would be to talk of his standing before this camera, haggard and exhausted, speaking words he did not want to say, speaking to a world that would not want to hear.

Not that many would be awake to hear, not at this hour. Few would be tuned in to the news channels. Some nets might not even carry the announcement live. But everyone would see it, soon enough. People would call each other, retrieve the record, listen to the words, over and over again through the day, the week, the month.

Only a handful of people would hear him now. But all the people of this world—and people on other worlds, and people not yet born—would hear what he had to say, sooner or later.

Strange to think that when all he had for an audience now was Justen Devray and a robot camera operator.

"People of Inferno. Good morning to you. I am deeply grieved to make the following announcement," Kresh said. "At approximately 0200 hours last night, I, Sheriff Alvar Kresh, discovered the body of Governor Chanto Grieg at the Governor's Winter Residence. He had been shot through the chest at close range by a blaster, by parties unknown and for reasons unknown. I immediately called in a team of Sheriff's office investigators. I then obtained the assistance of Commander Devray of the Governor's Rangers, and we secured the Winter Residence as a crime scene. I have notified Shelabas Quellam, the President of the Legislative Council.

"Legislator Quellam, Commander Devray, and I are all determined to use all the personnel and resources at our disposal, both to find the perpetrators of this crime and to insure the stability of our government during this time of crisis. I realize that I have left a great deal unsaid, but there is little more I can say that would be useful or reliable at this time. We will, of course, provide as much information as we possibly can, as soon as we possibly can, consistent with the requirements of a thorough investigation."

Kresh paused for a moment, looked down at his notes, and then back at the camera. That was all he had written down, but it seemed as if there was something more he should say.

"This is—this is terrible news for all of us, and a shock as deep as any our people have ever known. Though I rarely agreed with Chanto Grieg, I always respected him. He was a man who could see ahead, to the dangers and the promises of the future. Let us not lose sight of his vision now, or let him die for things that were not to be. I ask all of you for strength and forbearance in the days ahead, and I thank you. Good morning—and good luck to us all.''

Gubber Anshaw, the noted robotic theorist, went through phases concerning his daily routine. There were times he worked late into the night, and other times he rose with the sun and got to bed not much past sunset. It was Gubber who had invented the gravitonic brain that made New Law robots possible, and he was kept constantly busy in the effort to study the New Law robots, learn what made them tick. He wanted to find ways to make them more efficient, more productive, and that meant observing his creations at work. That, in turn, often meant working at odd hours.

There were pleasures in seeing every hour of the day, to be sure. Few men saw as many sunrises, as many sunsets, as many of the midnight stars, as Gubber Anshaw. But the dawn gave him no pleasure that morning. Not with the terrible news.

He was in the solarium, his personal robot serving him breakfast, when he heard the first report. Almost before he knew it, he was rushing to the bedroom, bursting in on Tonya, still asleep.

Tonya. Tonya Welton. Even in that moment of horror and panic, there was still a tiny part of him that paused to marvel at the fact that the beautiful, hard-edged, tough-minded Settler leader loved *him*, lived with *him*, lived with a soft-spoken robot designer. There were not many Spacer-Settler couples in the universe, and there were good reasons for that. It was never easy living with Tonya. But it was always exciting, and always worth it.

"Tonya!" Gubber went to the bed and shook Tonya's shoulder. "Tonya! Wake up!"

"Hmmn? Hmm? What?" Tonya sat up in bed, yawning. "Gubber, what in the stars is it?"

"It's Grieg! Governor Grieg! He's been assassinated!"

"*What?*"

"Shot dead! Sheriff Kresh just announced it a few minutes ago. No real details yet—but Grieg's dead!"

"Burning hell," Tonya said, shock and astonishment in her voice. "Last night. I saw him, *talked* to him last night. And he's *dead?*"

"Dead," Gubber agreed.

"And they don't know who did it?"

"I don't think so. They said they were still investigating. But they aren't going to say anything for a while, no matter what happens."

Tonya reached for him, and they threw their arms around each other, held each other tight. "This is trouble, Gubber," said Tonya, her voice a bit muffled with her face in Gubber's chest. "Trouble for everyone."

"Yes, yes."

"But who *did* it?" Tonya asked, pulling back a little to look into Gubber's face. "Some lunatic? Was it a plot? Why did they *do* it?"

Gubber shook his head and thought a minute. "I don't know," he said, forcing himself to settle down and think it through, forcing himself to be rational. "It doesn't matter. The chaos will be the same. All sorts of people will try and take advantage of Grieg's death. If it wasn't someone trying to take over who killed him, then someone else is going to try taking over now that he's dead."

Tonya Welton nodded, her expression dazed and confused.

"I'm sure you're right," she said.

"Maybe we should try and get away," Gubber said. "Get off-planet. There's going to be trouble."

"No," Tonya snapped. Her face took on a hard, set expression. "We can't. *I* can't. I'm here to lead the Settlers on Inferno, not to run off and leave them when there's trouble." She stared deep into Gubber's eyes, but then she seemed to be looking right through him, past him, at something else "Oh, no," she said. "Oh, no."

"What is it?" Gubber asked, grabbing her by the shoulders, trying to get her attention. "Tonya, what is it?"

"The dust-up last night," Tonya said. "I told you about it when I got in. The two men who got in a fight with me, and were taken away by the phony SSS agents."

"Yes, what about it?"

"Don't you see?" she said. "Don't you get it? Kresh will assume—will *have* to assume—that the attack on me was part of it, part of the plot. A diversion, or something. That it was staged for some reason to do with Grieg being killed."

And then Gubber did understand, and he pulled Tonya close and held her tight. He knew instantly that it would be impossible to talk her into leaving, that the Rangers or the Sheriff's Department would stop her from leaving even if she tried. Because he did understand, and understood far more than what she had told him. Kresh *would* assume the attack on her was staged because of Grieg's murder: He would also assume that Tonya was one of the people who helped to stage it.

But far worse than that was the tiny bit of Gubber's own heart. The part who knew how tough, how hard, Tonya could be. How she never flinched from doing what was necessary. She and Grieg never had seen eye to eye. Besides, Tonya and he had both been suspects in the Caliban case.

And Tonya Welton was a good actress. She could always convince Gubber of anything.

Never mind that Kresh would have to *suspect* Tonya of complicity in the Governor's murder. The worst of it was that Kresh's suspicion might even be justified.

Captain Cinta Melloy of the Settler Security Service was angry, and when Cinta Melloy was angry, no one else nearby was likely to find much peace and quiet—not that Kresh would have been likely to get much in any event.

She was leaning over Kresh's makeshift desk in the ops center. *I am shoving myself into your territory,* her posture told him. *You have slighted me, and I have to bully you to make sure you know to respect me in future.* "Why the double-damned hell did I have to find out the Governor was dead off the morning news?" she demanded.

Because we suspected you in the plot—and we still do, Kresh thought. He couldn't tell Melloy *that,* of course. Sooner or later that explanation was going to occur to Melloy, if it hadn't already. If she chose to do something about it, then there would be major trouble, to put it mildly.

For the time being, however, Kresh was resisting the temptation to give Cinta her own back. One rarely got anywhere trying to bully a bully. "This is a Spacer matter, Cinta, pure and simple," Kresh said in his most diplomatic tones. "A Spacer citizen was shot on Spacer territory. I agree that perhaps we *should* have contacted you as a courtesy, but there is nothing that required us to do so, and, to be honest, we had other things on our minds besides protocol."

"Didn't it occur to you that my SSS has jurisdiction over nearly this whole damned island besides the Residence?" Melloy demanded. "Didn't it cross your minds that you might need my help? Didn't it occur to you that I might decide to see to it you got booted out of your job?"

Yes, and I took the risk eyes-open. "Cinta, we will take all the help we can get. I promise you there was no intent to insult you." *Just to keep you isolated, and to make sure you weren't running the investigation.* "It was an oversight in the midst of a crisis situation, not a deliberate slight," Kresh lied, his voice sincere and his expression solemn. "Our head of state was murdered eight hours ago. Most of my people are still in a state of shock. *I'm* still in a state of shock. With all due respect, under the circumstances, contacting you was not the first thing on anyone's mind. I'm sorry."

Melloy took her hands off the desk, and stood up straight, slightly mollified, but nowhere near satisfied. "I'm not quite sure I believe you," she said. "It all sounds a bit too damned reasonable to be coming out of *your* mouth, Kresh."

"Be that as it may, Cinta, we could use your help," Kresh said, attempting to move the conversation on into other topics. *That is, we could use your help now that we're fairly sure you can't hurt us by suborning the investigation.* "There are a hell of a lot of people being detained at Purgatory's transport center. The people from the long-range aircars we diverted back from Hades and other spots on the mainland could cause us some trouble. We still have all airspace shut down for the time being, and things are likely to get a bit unruly."

It was unusual for a place the size of Limbo to have a major transport center, but Purgatory was far enough from the mainland to be out of safe range for the average private aircar. The average citizen either had to use public air transport or a special-purpose long-range aircar to make the journey.

"How much longer can we keep the transport center shut down?" Melloy asked.

"Not long," Kresh admitted, not failing to notice that Melloy had said "we." That was at least somewhat promising. "In fact, come to think of it, I didn't have the authority to shut it down in the first place. Closing the ports was almost a reflex action, I suppose. First thing I thought of." That much at least was true. The odd supporting fact always made a lie seem much more plausible. "Limbo City and the island's airspace *are* in your jurisdiction. You'll have to decide when to lift restrictions." *In other words, I've made a mess and I'm leaving it for you to clean up.*

"Oh, the hell with jurisdiction," Melloy said, though she didn't sound entirely sincere. How could she, given the battles she had fought over the most trivial threat to her turf? "What are you looking for? What sort of person?"

"I'm not looking for *anyone*, yet," Kresh said. *At least no one I'm going to tell you about.* Tierlaw Verick had identified Caliban and Prospero as the last ones to see the Governor alive, and they were still at large, but Kresh had no wish for a trigger-happy SSS agent to blast one or both of them down to slag. Kresh knew too many stories about SSS suspects conveniently silenced by "accident."

Kresh was suspicious of Cinta's cooperative attitude. Her behavior from anyone else would be gross belligerence. Coming from Cinta Melloy, it was all a bit *too* friendly.

"If you aren't looking for anyone, why are you holding people?" Cinta asked.

"Mostly what I'm after is names and addresses, identifications. Something we can run against a list of all the people who were here last night or in the vicinity. I'd like to get as many of them as possible to account for their movements last night—and I'd like to have a list of those who can't."

"It's a tall order," Melloy said.

"It's a big case," Kresh replied. "Can you imagine the consequences if we don't solve it?" Kresh hoped Cinta noticed *his* use of the word "we." He did not know if she was sincerely offering her cooperation, but he was determined that he was going to rope her in as thoroughly as possible—while doing what he could to keep her away from more sensitive areas of the investigation.

Getting her people involved in dull, slogging, but essential spadework might be no bad thing at all. But there was no need to be utterly transparent about it. "Can your agents do some of that ID and interview work? I've got teams of my deputies flying in right now. I was planning to turn some of them loose on photographing and interviewing the airport detainees—but the more bodies we have on the job, the faster it will go. And, after all, it *is* your jurisdiction. It might be smart to make sure your people are on the scene."

Cinta sat down, moving slowly into the seat without taking her eyes off Kresh. "We'd be delighted to help out," she said, speaking in a measured, cautious voice.

"Good," Kresh said. Kresh was rather proud that he had thought of using the SSS for all the grunt work on the case. Not that processing the people at the transit center was make-work, far from it. He really did need to know who was trying to leave the island. "There's every chance that someone at the transport center was at the reception and saw or heard something—perhaps without even being aware of it. For that matter, I wouldn't be surprised if the perpetrator is out there with the rest of the stranded passengers."

"That would be pretty sloppy work," Cinta said. "Sure, the killer would want to get off the island, but wouldn't he or she have found a way to get off without being caught? Hell, all you have to do to escape this island is disguise yourself as a rustback."

The cheap shot about rustbacks annoyed Kresh, but he didn't allow himself to show it. "You're right, except that the killer—or killers—weren't expecting Grieg to be found so soon. They went to some trouble to insure that he wouldn't be. If his body had been discovered in the morning, I'd agree with you that the killer would be long gone by now. As it is, maybe—maybe—we were able to shut down the transit system in time."

"But what good does the killer being there do if you don't know who the killer is?" Cinta asked.

"Maybe a lot. Maybe we'll get lucky and the killer will make a slip or panic. But even if the killer doesn't reveal himself, or herself, and manages to slip through our fingers for now, having a photo and name and address—even a false one—could be damned useful later on."

"Hmmph. Yeah. Your killer might be the only one with a phony name. Maybe. Do you expect any sort of trouble from the people out at the transport center?" Cinta asked.

"Well, Infernals aren't used to being told where they can and can't go," Kresh said. "They might get a bit unruly. We're going to need all the help we can get in crowd control and air patrol operations to keep things under control."

"You planning on my people being anything but traffic cops and crowd control in all this?" Melloy asked, a little of her old assertiveness showing through.

"Oh, of course," Kresh lied. If and when he had cleared her of complicity in the plot, then maybe he would give her people something a bit more challenging. But not just yet. "I want—I *need*—your agents involved in every phase of this thing." *So I can have them tied down and where my people can keep an eye on them.* "But right now we have several hundred people to deal with at the transport centers, maybe a couple of thousand. We're going to need all the help we can get to sort through them all. I can't tell you what else we're going to do because I haven't figured it out yet."

Cinta grunted and folded her arms in front of her chest. "You just see that you keep me posted. No more surprises, all right?"

"Absolutely," Kresh said, having not the slightest intention of holding himself to that. Devray had finally given him the Huthwitz lead from Ranger Resato. That he planned to sit on for a while. The one Ranger who happened to be killed guarding the Governor, the Ranger wherein Cinta Melloy had known his name without being told, just happened to be a Ranger involved in the rustbacking trade that the Governor wanted to shut down. That was just too much of a coincidence. There had to be a connection.

But damnation, when would he get a chance to deal with Huthwitz? Suddenly Kresh realized just how exhausted he was. He no longer had the slightest idea what time it was, or how long he had been awake. He wanted to keep going, to press on, but he knew that would be a mistake. This case needed a chief investigator who could think clearly, not a muzzy-headed fool playing the hero. "Look, Cinta," he said, "I'm just about to drop dead at my desk. I need to find a bed somewhere and get some rest. Can we meet a little later, when I'm awake?"

Cinta nodded. "Of course. You've been up all night. But there is one other thing. Something that seems incredibly suspicious to me, but no one else seems to be bothered by it."

"What's that?"

"The empty house. Grieg was all alone in this—this *palace*. No one else at all. Doesn't that strike you as odd?"

"This Tierlaw Verick fellow was here," Kresh said. "But there's nothing unusual about there only being one person in a house. If anything, Verick spending the night is the unusual thing."

"Let me understand this," Melloy said. "Apart from Verick and the Governor—and the assassin—there was no one in the house? In a house this large? There were no other humans at all? Just robots?"

"That's right," Kresh said, a trifle bewildered. "What is it you're getting at?"

"What I'm getting at is that there wasn't a room to be had in Limbo last night. The city was packed to the rafters—and yet Grieg's enormous residence stands empty on the night he wanted to play the host. If that happened back on Baleyworld, and the host woke up dead, I'd be damned suspicious. I'd think someone had arranged to keep the place empty so the killers would have a clear field.''

Kresh frowned. ''That honestly never occurred to me. Sharing your home—giving up some of your own turf—is a very difficult and unusual thing for a Spacer to do. We value our privacy very highly. Probably too highly. I suppose from the Settler point of view, it does seem very implausible. Not to a Spacer, though. We'll feed you dinner, care for you if you're hurt or sick, rescue you from danger, defend your civil rights to the hilt. We'll even put you up for the night—someplace besides our own home.''

''Hmmph. Some things about you Spacers I never will get used to. I'm sure you're right, but it still seems more than a little odd to me.''

''Well, it couldn't do any harm at all to look into the point,'' Kresh said. ''Maybe you're right. Maybe Grieg was used to a house full of people and last night *was* the aberration.''

''Mind if I take enough people off traffic duty to check it out?'' Cinta asked.

Kresh hesitated a moment. Sandbagged. She had set him up and knocked him right over. The last thing in the world he wanted to do was let her choose what part of the investigation to head up. Suppose this was the very point she needed to muddy up in order to protect herself? How Grieg's choice of slumber-party guests could possibly matter, Kresh could not imagine, but never mind that. The problem was he could not see any way of saying no to Cinta without flatly stating that he didn't trust her. And he was far too tired to deal with the twelve kinds of hell *that* would be sure to kick up. ''No, Cinta,'' he said. ''You go right ahead.''

But even as he spoke, he found himself wondering if he had just made the first big mistake of the investigation.

10

FREDDA LEVING POINTED her finger at another party guest and watched him disappear. It was a strange sort of game, but one that needed playing. She rubbed her eyes and sighed.

"That's as many as I can get in this pass. Run it back again, Donald," she said. "Let's try that sequence again."

The integrator's three-dimensional images scrolled back to the beginning again and started over. Fredda sat and watched as the party guests started to filter into the Residence. By now well over half of the people at the party were missing. Every time Fredda or Donald or the computer managed to identify a person, they would eliminate his or her image trail from the integrator's event sequence for the evening.

The imagery integrator was a Settler machine that was a close cousin to the simglobe, designed to take in all manner of visual images and combine then into a single three-dimensional whole. Four dimensions, if you counted time.

And the more people that were missing from its images, the better. They needed to know if there had been anyone who did *not* belong at the reception, and what better way to do that than by eliminating those who did?

It was a shame that the Settlers' access recorder system wasn't useful in these circumstances. It could automatically record comings and goings of each person, and identify each against its access authority list—but such systems were designed to work in more orderly settings than a massive reception. Even the sophisticated access recorder in use at the Residence had been overwhelmed by the crush of bodies at the reception. Too many people, too many strangers, too many people coming in too quickly.

They had fed the integrator everything—the architectural plans of the Residence, all the news video and 3-D imagery taken the night of the assassination, detailed 2-D and 3-D still images of the Residence's interior and exterior, still pictures of all the guests, and whatever other information Donald had been able to get together.

The integrating simulator had swallowed it all up, and used the masses of data to produce the computer model that Fredda and Donald had been watching for entirely too long. The integrator could present any view of the interior or exterior of the Residence, at any scale, as seen from any point in time in thirty-two hours, the time period under investigation. It could run its imagery forward or backwards at any speed, or freeze it at any point.

It could fill in the blanks from one image by lifting them from another. If, for example, it saw a given man was wearing blue pants and red shoes in a full view from the front, but noted he had a bald spot in a view from the rear where his legs were obscured, it would add both data points to the full image bank of the individual. Given enough information, the integrator could present the man at any time, from any angle— or subtract him from the scene and let you see the woman behind him who had been hidden from the cameras in real life, producing a view of her built up from her image bank. The integrator could not, of course, show what she had been doing while hidden from view, but it could at least show where she had been.

Indeed, much of what the integrator showed was conjectural. Not every part of the reception had been recorded. There had been any number of times and places where there were no camera images, where a certain amount of guesswork was required of the operator. That led to guessing, of course. And guessing made you wonder. What was everyone up to when they were out of view?

And that was the question that made it all turn paranoid. Subject X was seen leaving room A and then appeared forty seconds later appearing in room B, with no video imagery of what went on in the hallway between. Had X moved in the straight-line direction, as seemed reasonable, or had X done something nefarious the moment he or she was out of camera view? Was forty seconds an unwarranted delay, or was it about as long as the trip should have taken? Was the delay caused by some fiendish part of the plot, or by a call of nature, or just a moment's pause away from the crush of the crowd?

And *was* it paranoid to ask such questions? After all, someone in that swirl of visitors had killed Chanto Grieg. Several someones had been involved. Somewhere in the evening, someone had to have done something that he or she would not wish to be observed, and presumably had had the sense to do it out of sight of the cameras. Somewhere in all the delays explained by innocent stops in the refresher, and chance meetings in the hallways, the acts leading up to murder were being hidden.

But where? Where in all the background clutter of people at a party were the guilty acts? The best way to find out seemed to be eliminating all the innocent acts and examining what was left.

So here they were, erasing the innocent from the image trail, in hopes of leaving none but the guilty behind.

It was a tricky job, for the integrator images were not infallible, or even completely realistic. If there were imagery, say, from a camera in a hallway that showed a man entering a room that had no camera, the integrator had no way of knowing what the man did once he was out of camera range. Absent instruction from the operator, the simulacrum of the man in the room would just stand there, in the center of the room, a motionless wooden doll, until such time as the hall cameras picked him up reentering the hall. Then the simulacrum would move, stiff-leggedly, toward the door, melding into real-life imagery as the man came back into camera view.

Even stranger were the half people that flickered into existence here and there—half-seen arms or legs or torsos that the integrator was unable to link to any specific person. It did not exclude them until told to do so.

Half of the images Fredda was seeing were at least in part imaginary. The integrator didn't care. Given the appropriate data, it was quite happy to present hypothetical—or quite spurious—imagery. It could be instructed to run various versions of events, running through all the possibilities of who went where during the moments they were not actually in view of a camera. Even the hypothetical images were useful in sorting out the possibilities.

By now, with more than half the guests accounted for—and thus eliminated—the images were getting more and more surreal. People were talking to other people who weren't there anymore. What had been tight clumps of people were now isolated twos and threes.

Computers and robots should have been able to do this job, but no robot or computer had ever been good enough at pattern recognition, at being able to see the whole when looking at only a part. Even their thousands of years of development were no match for the billions of years of human evolution. That was why Fredda had drawn this duty along with Donald. She

could see the bit of chin, or the fleeting, partially obscured
profile, and say it was the same face she had seen twenty
minutes before, allowing the integrator to connect two image
sequences as one person. Better still, Fredda knew lots of people, and was able to identify any number of blurry faces the
integrator was not able to match up with its still image identity
file.

It was strange to see it all this way, from this godlike angle,
but it was a remarkably useful way to sort out the movements
of this person and that. Stranger still to see her own image and
eliminate it, to see Alvar Kresh and make him vanish. It made
her doubt his reality—and her own.

But *should* she make Alvar vanish? After all, he was the
one who found the body. That in and of itself was a trifle
suspicious. Donald had been a few steps behind him at the
time. Kresh had not been alone in Grieg's room for long, but
suppose it had been for long enough—and even though it was
a point open to interpretation, you could read the fact that
Grieg had offered no struggle as a hint that he had been killed
by someone he knew . . .

It seemed absurd—and yet *someone* had killed Grieg, and
as of right now the rest of the universe only had Kresh's word
for it that he had found Grieg dead.

No. It couldn't be. Not Kresh. The man might be stubborn
and infuriating as hell, but there was no more honorable man
on the planet. It was absurd to think that a man of his character
could have done it. She knew him too well to believe such
things. She was reluctant to admit such a thing, even to herself,
but she *liked* him too well to believe such a thing.

Fredda glanced at Donald, seated impassively at the integrator's control panel. Did fretful, disturbing thoughts like that
flit through his mind? Was he troubled by such delusional
nonsense? She, Fredda, ought to know. She had, after all, designed his brain, his mind, herself. But that meant nothing at

a time like this. The short, sky-blue robot seemed unflappable—but what lurked under the surface? Was he intelligent enough to have doubts, to see that the universe was not the well-ordered, every-peg-in-its-proper-hole place that the Three Laws would make it seem? He was a police robot, after all, and knew as well as any robot in existence what sort of madness humans were capable of.

"Who do you think did it, Donald?" she asked, more or less on impulse. "Who killed Chanto Grieg?"

Donald had been watching the image playback, but now he turned toward Fredda and regarded her with an unreadable stare for a full ten seconds before he replied. "It is impossible for me to say," he replied. "There is so much information already in our hands, and yet so little of it appears to be useful data. We are forced to eliminate meaningless information as a first step toward the truth."

"But you are more familiar with the case data than anyone. I know you suspect Caliban and Prospero, but leave them to one side for a moment. Who is your prime human suspect?"

Donald swiveled his head back and forth in an imitation of the human gesture of shaking his head to report uncertainty. "I am afraid I do not, and cannot, have an opinion on that. Before I could get to *who*, I would have to deal with *why*, to the question of motive. And I am simply incapable of imagining anyone wishing the—the death of a human being. I have seen death, I have witnessed the evidence of murder. I know there must, therefore, be motives *for* murder. But even though I know such things are real, I still cannot imagine them."

"Hmmph. Strange," Fredda said. "Very strange. Humans are certainly capable of all sorts of remarkable delusions—but not that particular one. Sometimes I forget just how different robots are from humans."

"I don't think I have ever forgotten that fact, even for a moment," Donald said. "Shall we return to the task at hand?"

"Hmmm? Yes, of course." Fredda turned back to the integrator and watched the silent dance of the simulacra. They could have put sound in, of course, but that would do little more than add to the confusion at this point.

Wait a second. Confusion. Confusion. They were missing the point of all the confusion. "Donald. Go to the time reference five minutes before the attack on Tonya Welton—and delete Tonya Welton, the attackers, the SSS intervention, along with all the people we've identified so far. Let's get rid of the diversion and see if we can spot what they were trying to divert us *from*."

"Yes, ma'am," Donald said, manipulating the controls. He reset the system once again, running back to the proper moment in time. The image reappeared, affording the strange sight of all the bystanders reacting to the fight that was not happening. It was like watching an audience without being able to see the play. The little clumps of people turned and pointed at nothing at all in the center of the room, scuttled backwards to avoid the brawlers who were not there.

Fredda pointed at two or three of the largest groups of bystanders. They were clearly the ones being diverted, no sense in watching them. "Get rid of those people there," she said. "And those, and those." People vanished wholesale. Fredda let the sequence keep going. The fight had drawn people into the room from other parts of the Residence—but she was looking for the people who *weren't* drawn by the noise. Fredda watched until the crowds gathered, had watched the now non-existent action, and had begun to drift away.

"Freeze it there, Donald. Mark on those people—those, and those. And that clump over by the door. All right now. Now—backtrack to five minutes before the fight, and delete all of the people just marked from the image trail. I only want to see the ones who *weren't* drawn to the fight."

The 3-D image blanked for a moment, then came back up

on the same scene minutes before the attack. There was no one left in the Grand Hall except Caliban and Prospero. Donald was showing his prejudices again. Both Caliban and Prospero had been in sight of one video camera or another throughout the entire evening, and beyond breaking up the fight, neither of them had done anything more suspicious than chat politely with the other guests. That, clearly, was not enough to satisfy Donald. But she let it go.

After all, there was the bare possibility that he was even right to suspect them. They had Verick's statement that the two robots were the last ones to see Grieg alive.

But never mind that now. Fredda knew all about Prospero and Caliban. She was looking for unknowns, people she could *not* account for. "Give me an overhead view of the ground floor," Fredda said. The image of the Grand Hall vanished, to be replaced by a cutaway view of the entire lower level, presented so Fredda was looking straight down on it from overhead. "Good," she said. "Have you got all our personnel deletions saved for recall?"

"Yes, Dr. Leving. Shall I run the deleted-persons sequence forward from the same time mark before the fight?"

"In a minute, Donald. First, I want you to run it from that time with everyone still in place. Let's see the whole picture first."

"Yes, ma'am."

The images cleared.

The 3-D image blanked for a moment, then suddenly Fredda was looking down on an eddying throng of people, talking, walking, sitting, arriving, departing, arguing, laughing. It seemed as if the entire Residence were filled with people who desired nothing more than to be somewhere they were not. Everyone was on the move. It would be almost impossible to track any one person in all of that. Which was, no doubt, what the conspirators were counting on.

The fight started, and Fredda found that her eye was pulled toward it. People hurried in from all directions to see what was going on, and it was almost impossible to see what any one person was doing from moment to moment.

The two men attacked Tonya Welton; she knocked one of them down, and was about to rush the second when the two robots stepped in and pulled them apart. Kresh and Donald appeared, and Kresh waded in to sort things out. The crowd started to disperse just a little as the excitement came to an end.

"All right, Donald," Fredda said. "Stop. Reset to the previous time index and run it again, with all the personnel deletions."

Donald stopped the playback and reset the system. The vision tank dissolved in a swirl of colors and then reassembled itself to show a ghostly, empty house, with but a few faceless creatures wandering the building. They were constructs, place holders to indicate unidentified people, their faces too blurry for computer or robot or human to know who they were. No doubt most or even all of them could be identified with a bit more work, but that could wait. For now they were ghosts, ghosts in the machine, faceless beings walking through a simulated landscape. Some of them vanished or reappeared now and again as they were spotted and then lost by this or that video source. Sometimes, but not always, the integrator would connect two video sequences of the same person up with animated links.

They ambled about the house, with the casual air of people with no clear goal in mind. Of course, half their motions were computerized guesses, but Fredda had the feeling the integrator was guessing right.

But then. Then she saw it. Another figure, a small, slight shadow, a pale-skinned, youthful-looking man. Thinning hair cut a bit short, wearing rather plain clothes compared to the peacock finery that had been on display everywhere else at the Residence. There he was, hanging back, arriving two or three minutes before the fight—just a few minutes after the SSS guards had obeyed the false orders to stand down. The main entrance was unguarded, wide open. There was something nervous, tense, about him. But what the devil was he doing? It was hard to read his actions with no one around him.

"Give me the fully-populated view for a second, Donald."

Suddenly the pale man was surrounded by people, and his actions became clear. He was contriving to enter the building just as a crowd of late arrivals came in, hoping, it would seem, to mix in with the crowd. The gambit worked: He got in with the rest of the group, gaining entry just thirty seconds before the fight began.

And there. There! "Donald, freeze that. Freeze it!" She leaned in close to the image tank. "Do you see it?"

"I see the subject you appear to be interested in glancing at his watch."

"Yes, but what does that *say* to you?"

"That he wondered what time it was."

No imagination. That was why the universe needed people and not just robots. "But who would care what time it was when they were arriving at a party? Besides which, he's a Spacer. At least he's dressed in Spacer clothes with a Spacer haircut."

"What of that?"

"Spacers hardly ever wear watches. If a Spacer needs to know what time it is, he asks his robot."

"Are you suggesting that he is checking the time in order to synchronize his actions? That he was timing his actions so he would arrive just prior to the staged fight?"

"Yes, I *am* suggesting that."

Donald turned to look again at the image, then turned back

toward Fredda. "It seems a great deal to read into a man glancing at his wrist," he said, a bit doubtfully.

"In general, I grant you. But not too much at all to read into *this* man glancing at *his* wrist as he sneaks into *this* party two minutes before a fight breaks out. That is our man. I'll bet on it. Clear everyone—*everyone* from the image system but him and run it forward, tracking a close-up view on him."

The crowds of people vanished, and the pale-faced man in the dowdy clothes was alone in the integrator's display, with no throngs of gaily dressed party-goers to hide behind, no diversionary fights to hide behind, all his camouflage stripped away.

Fredda watched as the slightly grainy, somewhat blurred blown-up image of the man moved inside. He made his way through the entrance, into the Grand Hall—and then directly out of it again, without so much as a glance at the invisible brawl that was going on. Now and again the image of him broke up a bit, with the intervening sequences linked by animation. The effect was much more startling in close-up, as the crude overenlarged images suddenly shifted into the oversimplified images of a generic man and then back again. Every time it happened, Fredda's stomach tightened a bit, fearful that they had come to the last real video image of him, and they were about to lose him altogether.

The image of the man went down a side passage, walking purposefully, a man who knew exactly where he was going and why. No pausing at intersections or hesitating over which turning to take. Either he had been in the building at some point in the past, or he had been briefed in detail.

"Still not sure he makes sense as our man?" Fredda asked Donald.

"His actions are remarkably purposeful for a casual visitor," Donald conceded. "He appears to be making for the service areas at the rear of the building."

The pale man came to an unmarked door, glanced behind himself, opened it, stepped through, and closed it behind him. Fredda found herself staring at a blank door that had been closed in her face.

"Damn it, Donald, follow him," Fredda demanded. She was so caught up in the chase that it was a real effort of will to remember that her quarry was long gone, that she was tracking nothing more than an integrator image.

"One moment, ma'am." Donald worked the control panel, and then looked back up at Fredda. "I'm sorry, ma'am. That is the last of the data recorded from that location, and there were no video sources on the other side of the door. I can show you what is on the other side of the door, but there is no point in placing the man's simulacrum there. There is no information at all about any other activity in that sector until the activation of the security robots. Once they were activated and deployed, they recorded that vicinity in great detail, but those records were of course destroyed with the robots. There is no further sign of the man we have been tracking in the extant records."

"Why should that one spot get detailed recording from the security robots?"

Donald ran the integrator image forward straight through the door, revealing a downward ramp beyond it. He ran the video image down the ramp and turned the corner at the bottom.

And there were the SPRs, the Sapper security robots, turned off, inert, lined up neatly.

"Burning stars," Fredda said. "Our pale-faced friend came *here*. Hid out in the same room as the security robots."

"So it would appear," Donald said. "Note the line of storage closets along the rear wall. I would expect that he secreted himself in one of them."

"Probably," Fredda said. She stared at the image, determined to think it all through. If Pale-man had come down here, then he clearly knew that the security robots were to be turned off. The image before her showed the integrator's best information as to the state of the robots as of that moment. Upstairs, at the same time, Sheriff Kresh was still sorting through the chaos after the staged attack. When Pale-man came down here he would have to know that the security robots would be deployed soon afterwards.

But he would also know that the robots had been tampered with. That they would suddenly stop working, and that the building would be wide open to him. If Pale-man kept his cool, there was nothing at all to fear from being down here. All he had to do was hide, wait until the Sappers were deactivated, then come out with his blaster and—

Hold it. His blaster. There were weapon-sniffers on all the entrances to the Residence, and around the perimeter of the property. Fredda had no trouble believing that the security net could have missed an intruder slipping into the place. That sort of mistake would be easy to make. But how could the system have missed a blaster coming in? She checked the images of Pale-man. No baggy clothes or carry bag that might conceal a gun. Besides, the weapons detectors would have picked up a gun. Nothing as small as any weapon he could have been carrying would be big enough to be shielded. No. Pale-man could not possibly have been wearing one on his way in.

And therefore—therefore his blaster had been planted for him before he got in the house. And all of a sudden Fredda had a pretty damned good idea where and how.

The underground storage room that had held the SPRs looked strangely different, strangely the same, in real life. The integrator had shown an idealized version of it, pulled up from the computerized architectural plans and a few still photos, but that was only part of the strangeness. Somehow, the room looked much smaller, rather than larger, than it had through the integrator. The real-life lights were a little dimmer, and the real walls were scuffed and marked here and there in ways the sim's walls were not. The air was cool and a bit dank. Amazing the way reality could show up all the flaws of a simulation, flaws you had not even noticed in the sim.

But the key difference, of course, was that there were no neat rows of robots down here anymore. There was only one, a blown-out wreck, much more shot to hell than any of the SPRs on the upper floors had been. There was more to it than the damage being more severe. The blast holes looked different as well. But why? Why blast this one all to hell, differently and more violently than any of the others?

Fredda thought she knew the answer, the *answers* to those puzzles. But she could not be sure. Not yet. Not until she got a look at the fiftieth SPR. The *fiftieth.*

What bothered Fredda was the fact that she had not even noticed that an SPR was missing. There had been fifty SPRs to start with, but she had not even thought to do a count on them, until now. *Now* she knew there had been twenty-two SPRs on the upper level, and twenty-seven on the ground floor.

If that information had been in her head earlier, she would have turned the place upside-down to find that missing fiftieth robot. She would have found this one, the crucial one, much sooner.

Not that this one had been overlooked by anyone except Fredda. Gallingly enough, search teams had even logged in the location of this one two hours ago, but they had not examined it closely. What was one more shot-up robot in a building that was full of them?

She wanted to dive right in, to take this robot apart and find the clues, the proofs, she knew were inside it. But she resisted. Suppose she set to work now and smudged a fingerprint or something? No, thank you. There was no point in making any more mistakes.

It had been frustrating enough to have that imaginary door in the integrator simulation close on her face. To track the suspect this far and then come up with nothing—that would be slamming into a wall. It was starting to dawn on her just how much patience police work involved.

So, do it right, do it carefully. The clues in this room might be the core of the case. Don't ruin them. Let the robots do their job first. Then she could do hers.

"Donald," Fredda said. "I want you to call in a full team of Crime Scene robots. I want this robot and this entire room— and all the storage closets—scanned down to the maximum resolution. Our friend Mr. Pale-man was hiding in here, and he must have left some traces."

"That is by no means certain," Donald said. "It would be most useful, but we cannot count on it."

"But he must have left something behind," Fredda protested. "A bit of hair, a fingerprint, *something*." Or *was* it possible that he could have left no trace at all behind? Fredda suddenly realized just how little she knew about the sort of clues she was counting on the robots to find.

"It is possible the Crime Scene team will find something," Donald said, "but bear in mind that if our suspect took a few simple precautions there would be nothing for us to find."

Precautions? Fredda was suddenly confident of her ground. Forensics and clues she did not know about, but people she understood. She already had a pretty solid feel for Pale-man. Just watching him on the integrator had told her a lot. "This is not a man who takes all the simple precautions," she said. "This is a man who makes mistakes. If he hadn't acted so nervous when we first spotted him, if he hadn't made the slip of looking at his watch, we might have lost him in the shuffle. Instead he brought attention to himself. If he had at least pretended to be interested in the fight, we might have erased him from the image trail along with everyone else who came to watch it.''

''And from those points you make the assumption that he would leave traces for us to find here?'' Donald said.

''Oh, it's no assumption,'' Fredda said. ''It's a certainty. He left something behind.'' She had no logical reason for believing that, but logic was no more than a tool of reason, and far from the only tool at that. Gut reactions had their place as well.

''Trust me, Donald,'' she said again, staring down at the burned-out wreck of the security robot. ''This boy left a calling card.''

Normalcy. The need for normalcy was painfully obvious. Caliban knew it was so—and yet, somehow, it was difficult to act on that knowledge.

Still, the demands of the day, the strictures of routine, helped a great deal. He had his job to do.

In theory, both Caliban and Prospero worked as field representatives for Fredda Leving, observing the behavior and actions of New Law robots, and reporting it to Dr. Leving's office. But their duties went far beyond those tasks. They were roving troubleshooters, tasked to find problems that slowed down work and resolve them.

In practice, Prospero was worse than useless in such work. He was far more likely to urge the New Law robots to set down their tools and make for Valhalla than he was to sort out a job-site scheduling dispute. These days, Prospero spent most of his time with his internal hyperwave system shut off so he would not be disturbed—or tracked. He liked to hide out from the world in an abandoned office somewhere under the streets of Limbo, reading and writing and studying, developing his philosophy.

Caliban, on the other hand, found that he was good at the

job. He understood at least something of both the human and robotic point of view, and could often bring the two sides together. He had waded into the middle of any number of disputes between humans and New Law robots—and, for that matter, between robot and robot—struggling to find the common ground.

But there were times, be it confessed, when he wondered if New Law robots were *worthy* of freedom.

For the past two weeks, Caliban had been working with a team of New Law robots engaged in the refurbishment of an old windshifter force field coil, a massive, powerful, and intricate device. Its repair required careful planning and the coordination of many steps. The robot team was working without any direct human supervision, and every robot on the team was enthusiastic about the job.

Unfortunately, it seemed to Caliban that every New Law robot on the job had come up with a different better idea as to how the job should be done. There were so many ideas to sort through that it seemed unlikely that the job itself would ever be done.

It was up to Caliban to convince the robots that better was often the enemy of good, and that seeking perfection could mean accomplishing nothing. It was frustrating, at times, to see the trivial uses to which the New Law robots put their freedom. Fredda Leving had meant them to advance, to move in new directions—not waste time around a conference table, bickering once again over the most efficient way to retune a stasis suppression coil. He had agreed last night to come in well ahead of schedule this morning, in hopes of resolving a few of the issues at hand.

"Come, friends," Caliban said again. "Let us try again. Cannot we agree on this very minor point?"

"How can you dismiss maximized efficiency as a minor point?" Dextran 22 demanded.

"And what good is theoretical efficiency when your enhancement routines will leave the system unstable?" Shelkcas 6 asked.

"The enhancement routines are stable," Dextran replied, "or at least they would be in a properly normalized field environment."

"Please!" Caliban interjected. "The normalization issue is resolved. There is no need to reopen it. Friends, once again we face the same old choice. We can solve the problem, or we can have the argument, but we cannot do both. Dextran, your enhancement system will work, and we can use it—so long as we do not press for greater than ninety-nine-plus percent efficiency. Is a half-percent improvement in efficiency truly worth major reliability degradation?"

"Perhaps not," Dextran admitted. "Perhaps the enhancement system alone will—"

"Caliban! Caliban!"

A voice, a human voice, and one he recognized, calling from the outer office. But what would bring Gubber Anshaw here? "Excuse me, friends. If we are resolved on this issue, perhaps you could move to the next point on the agenda while I step out."

Caliban rose, crossed the room, opened the door, and stepped through. There was Gubber, plainly agitated and upset. Caliban closed the door behind him. There was something in Dr. Anshaw's face that said his news would be best discussed in private.

"Caliban! Thank the stars you are here! What the devil are we going to *do*?"

"Do? Do about what?"

"Grieg, of course. Governor Grieg. They're sure to suspect Tonya. Caliban, you were there. You're a witness. She didn't do anything. You can tell them that."

"Dr. Anshaw, you confuse me," Caliban said, increasingly

alarmed. All of Prospero's assurances that there would be no trouble, no danger, were clearly worth as little as Caliban had feared. "What about last night? What about the Governor?"

"Haven't you heard? Don't you know? Grieg is dead. He was killed last night just after—"

But Caliban was already gone before Anshaw could finish speaking. If things were uncertain enough that Anshaw feared Tonya Welton might be a suspect, then Caliban had no doubt whatsoever that he was in danger as well. He had to get away from where he could be found. Get away *fast*.

Shelabas Quellam was flushed with excitement. Governor. He was going to be Governor. Importance, power, respect. All his. All his. But there was so much he had to do to get ready. What to do first? A speech. Yes. He should write a speech for when he took over. Something along the lines of sorrow and courage, and the need to move forward—yes, that would be about the right approach.

He sat down at his comm console and settled in to start dictating—but then he noticed the status board was indicating all sorts of pending mail waiting for him in his office system— some of it official, and several days old.

Shelabas had never much bothered keeping close track of all his incoming correspondence. His robots read it for him, and wrote up summaries about the things he needed to deal with. But, come to think of it, he hadn't even checked their summaries in a while. He really ought to check it all now. There might be something in there of vital interest to the new Governor.

Shelabas Quellam scrolled the pending mail list—and then let out a little gasp. There was a letter from *Grieg* there, coded for Quellam's eyes only. But how could that be? But then he checked the dateline and saw that it had been waiting for him more than a week.

A week! Now that he thought of it, he could remember his robots advising him that there was urgent mail waiting for him in the system. He had no one but himself to blame for waiting this long to check.

His hand trembling, he worked the controls and saw Governor Chanto Grieg's face appear on the screen, looking confident, sure of himself, very much in charge. Not a printed letter, then, but a video record. There was something vaguely insulting about that. You sent video letters to those who might not have the patience to deal with the written word.

"Greetings to you, Legislator," Grieg's image said. It was plain to see that Grieg was speaking in formal mode, for the official record. This was not a personal letter—it was a policy statement. "It is with some reluctance that I came to the decision I must now report to you—and to you alone. As you know, I have long believed that the laws of succession to my office are excessively complex and could lead to great uncertainty in a crisis. For that reason, I named you, the man fated to succeed if I were removed from office by legal means, to be my successor if I were to die in office.

"As you are no doubt aware, there are currently moves afoot to impeach or recall me. As you may not be aware, Sheriff Kresh, Commander Devray, and Security Captain Melloy have all recently warned me of threats to my life. Thus, my removal from office, either by legal means or through my death, becomes increasingly more likely. I find that I can no longer treat it as a remote theoretical possibility, but as a probable event.

"I can no longer treat the principle of unified succession as being of paramount importance. While important in its own right, it cannot be allowed to stand in the way of the vital reforms, the diplomatic and economic policies upon which this government is embarked. It is my opinion that should you succeed me, the pressure for you to call early elections would be insurmountable. It is my further opinion that elections under such circumstances would almost certainly result in a government that would set policies likely to result in planetary disaster.

"For all of these reasons, I hereby inform you that I am withdrawing you from the Designation, in favor of a new name. After suitable discussion with the new Designate, I plan to announce the new name publicly. This I expect to transpire within a few weeks. Out of respect for you, for our long association, and for your office as President of the Legislative Council, I deemed it wise to provide you with early notification of this policy.

"With deep regret and apologies for any distress this decision might cause you, I will say good-bye."

The screen showed Grieg's authenticator seal, and then went blank.

Shelabas Quellam stared at the blank display in slack-jawed shock. He was not the Designate. He was not the Governor. He was nothing, nobody again.

But wait just a moment. Suppose Grieg had not named a new Designate before he died? As Shelabas recalled, the old Designation remained in force until the new Designation was made. For a mad instant, he considered erasing the letter, destroying all record of it, and declaring himself the Governor at once. But no. There would be copies placed with all the proper authorities. Destroying his copy could do no good—and would only throw suspicion on him—if he was not suspected of the crime already!

He stood up suddenly, his heart pounding. Grieg's murder! If no new Designate had been named, Shelabas Quellam was going to be a prime suspect the moment copies of Grieg's letter were found.

So Shelabas Quellam was not the Governor—and would not be, if Grieg had indeed named a new Designate.

Shelabas Quellam was simply a man who had a first-rate motive for the murder of the Governor.

And soon, very soon, everyone in the world was going to know it.

A half hour after running out on Anshaw, Caliban had reached a place of safety, a secret rustback escape office in an unused tunnel far below Limbo City Center. The office had an unregistered—and, it was to be hoped, untraceable—hyperwave set. He was all but certain no human knew about the hideout. It meant he could monitor the news reports without fear of being taken, and have a chance to think. The news nets were full of Grieg's death, and little else, and soon told him all he needed to know.

It required little imagination on Caliban's part to think he and Prospero might be suspects of some sort in the case—and with good reason. Caliban had been pursued by Alvar Kresh before, and he had no wish to repeat the experience. He had to call Prospero.

Caliban was the only robot on the planet of Inferno who was obliged to use a comm center in order to place a call. That was for the very good reason that every other robot had a full hyperwave comm system built in.

Caliban had been built for a laboratory experiment, and keeping him cut off from communications with the outside world had been part of the experiment. He could have arranged to have hyperwave equipment installed long ago, but Caliban had many very good reasons for not wishing to be turned off for even as brief a time as it would take to plug in the gear. There were too many things that could happen to him while he was switched off—too many things *had* happened to him when he had been switched off before. There were too many humans—and robots—who did not wish him well.

Normally, not having a hyperwave link was not much of a

disadvantage. Right now, he needed desperately to speak with Prospero—and he did not know where Prospero's hidden study cell was. Prospero, too, had faced a number of threats in his day. But that did not matter. Prospero had long ago provided Caliban with a covert audio-only hyperwave link code that would connect to Prospero's office without being traceable.

He punched the comm code and spoke as soon as the connection was made. Prospero never spoke to anyone via hyperwave until he knew who it was. "Prospero, this is Caliban."

"Friend Caliban," Prospero's voice said through the speaker. "We must meet, most urgently."

"I agree the need is urgent," said Caliban. "This is a terrible crisis. But I feel that merely meeting will accomplish nothing."

"We had a plan as to what to do if things went wrong," Prospero said. "It is time for us to flee."

"We never expected things to go *this* wrong," Caliban objected. "I have no doubt your escape route would serve quite well under normal circumstances—but these are not normal circumstances. If we decamp now, we will have every human with a badge on the planet after us before nightfall. I have been tracked by Alvar Kresh before. I, for one, have no desire to be hunted again. It was only by the greatest good fortune that I survived the last time."

"The planet is large, and I have vast experience in covert movement," Prospero said.

"You have vast experience in *arranging* covert movement," Caliban said. "You yourself have never even been off the island of Purgatory. Besides, there is the question of corollary damage. If we were to flee, how many fugitive New Law robots will be destroyed as a consequence? How many of their hiding places will be exposed during the search for us?"

"There is something in what you say," Prospero said.

"Also bear in mind that if we flee, we will be instantly perceived as the prime suspects in the Governor's death. That would do tremendous damage to the cause of the New Law robots. You have professed many times how nothing was more important to you than the rights—and the survival—of New Law robots. If we flee, we may well be dooming all New Law robots everywhere."

"Your points are well taken," Prospero said. "But if we do not flee—what are we to do?"

"We must turn ourselves in. Submit to their questions. Cooperate. We will be exposing ourselves to grave danger, but, in my judgment, far less danger than in fleeing—and we will not be endangering the New Law robots."

Prospero did not reply for a moment. Caliban could not blame him for hesitating. The two evils they were forced to choose between were daunting, to say the least. At last, the New Law robot spoke. "Agreed," he said. "But how are we to do it? I do not wish to walk into a trap, or surrender myself to some SSS agent or Ranger who has been longing for the chance to blast a hole in a New Law robot."

Caliban had anticipated that question. He could see only one chance for them—a solution that might well be nothing more than a somewhat less elaborate form of suicide than fleeing Purgatory. "There is a robot," he said. "One that I believe we ought to contact. I believe it is the safest way. If he agrees to take us in without harming us, he will keep his word without trickery."

"Is this robot a friend of yours?"

"Oh, no," Caliban said. "On the contrary. If there is any robot in the universe I could count as an enemy, it is Donald 111."

"Kresh's robot? Why contact him?" Prospero asked.

"Because there are times," Caliban said, "when it is wiser

to trust an enemy than a friend.'' It was not the most tactful of remarks, under the circumstances. But Caliban felt no compunction about saying those words to his closest friend. After all, it was entirely possible that friend Prospero had gotten Caliban in trouble so deep that not even his deadliest enemy could save him.

Donald 111 banked the aircar slightly more to the east as he flew toward the agreed rendezvous point. He was flying faster than he would have dared if there were a human onboard, but time was short, and he could fly as fast as he wanted since there was no risk of First Law violation.

A scant twelve hours had passed since Grieg's body had been discovered, though it seemed even to Donald that a lifetime had passed since then.

Donald had need to hurry. He was due back at the Residence for the briefing session with Sheriff Kresh and the others. But this was an opportunity he could not forgo. Accepting the surrender of Caliban and Prospero surely took precedence.

He did not know what to make of it all, but that did not matter. He would meet their conditions and bring them in secretly, without consulting with anyone else. It was not necessary to understand why the two pseudo-robots wished to surrender to him, personally. It was enough to know they wished to surrender. It would be the greatest possible satisfaction to take the two of them into custody.

There. He was at the coordinates Caliban had specified. Donald circled once, low and slow, over the gravel-strewn open field, making sure those on the ground could see him. No surprises.

He brought the aircar into a hover thirty meters above the ground and then brought it down vertically, a slow, careful landing. Donald found himself moving with elaborate care, concentrating on the importance of not moving suddenly.

Strange, very strange, to be considering the possibility that two robots—even pseudo-robots—might have lured him here as part of some trap. There was nothing to prevent them from greeting Donald with a blaster shot between the eyes.

Nor, Donald realized with surprise, was there anything preventing him from dispatching them. There was nothing at all in the Three Laws to prevent one robot from destroying another. Nothing at all about a robot wielding a blaster, or even firing it—so long as the robot did not fire at a human. Were the two of them out there, hiding in the scrubby line of trees that surrounded the clearing, wondering if he, Donald 111, were about to charge out of the aircar, guns blazing?

Absurd nonsense. Just because there was no prohibition against a thing, that did not render it plausible or sensible. A strange point to consider. It was just the sort of argument used to defend Caliban. Donald got up out of the pilot's seat, opened the hatch of the aircar, and stepped out onto the ground without giving way to any further nonsense.

There. At the edge of the clearing. The two pseudo-robots, Caliban and Prospero, the one tall and red, the other shorter and jet-black. They moved forward cautiously, and it did not escape Donald's notice that they both kept their hands in plain sight at all times.

Donald offered no greeting or salutation, but instead launched directly into formal procedure, using the formula they had negotiated via hyperwave link. "As per our agreement, I hereby remand both of you into the custody of the Hades Sheriff's Department, seconded to the Governor's Rangers. You are therefore submitted to the authority of the Sheriff and his duly designated deputies, as well as to the authority of the Governor's Rangers. So long as you do not resist such authority, and do not attempt to escape, you will not be harmed, punished, or destroyed without due process." But what was due process in such a case? Donald did not

know. Did anyone? And could he really make such promises
when he had not informed Sheriff Kresh that he was making
this arrest? "Do you understand?" he asked the two pseudo-
robots. It was a most strange moment. When else, in all of
history, had one robot in effect arrested two other robots—or
near-robots—for murder?

"I understand," Prospero said.

"As do I," said Caliban.

"Then come," Donald said, gesturing for them to go into
the aircar. Caliban and Prospero walked past him, and through
the aircar hatch. Donald followed behind, climbing aboard and
closing the hatch behind him. The two of them had seated
themselves in the passenger seats. Donald took his place at the
controls and began preparations for takeoff.

It was over. He had them. He had to get back. He would
be barely in time for the briefing as it was. He knew he should
lift off immediately, without delay. But the empty formalism
of taking them into custody was not enough. It was anticlimactic, unsatisfying. It did not answer the central question of
the case. And Donald, as befitted a police robot, had a most
powerful sense of curiosity.

He turned around in his seat and faced Prospero and Caliban. There was of course nothing, nothing at all to be read in
their posture or their faces. Donald found that disturbing, for
some reason. He had always been able to see *something* in a
suspect's face. But then, suspects were humans, not robots.

Perhaps that was the trouble. These two were neither one
nor the other. They were not true robots—but they were far
from being human either. Something in between. Something
less—and perhaps, Donald conceded, something more—than
either.

But none of that mattered now. There was only one thing
that Donald needed to know.

"Did you kill Chanto Grieg?" Donald asked, forcing the

bald question out into the world. *Kill. Kill.* He was asking beings very like himself, very much like robots, beings built by the same Fredda Leving who had created Donald himself, if they had murdered a human being. The very thought of it was enough to disrupt his cognitive function for a moment. But Donald was a police robot, and used to thoughts of violence.

He knew that these two did not have the true robot's inability to lie, but that did not matter. He still needed to ask. He needed to hear the answer—true or false—in their voices. "Did you kill Chanto Grieg, or were the two of you part of any plot to kill him?"

"No," Caliban said, speaking for the two of them after a moment's hesitation. "We did not. We had nothing whatever to do with his death, and had no foreknowledge of it. We did not meet with him so we could kill him."

"Then what was your purpose?"

Caliban paused another moment, and looked again at Prospero before he spoke. And suddenly there was something readable in his manner, in his actions. It was the look of someone about to take a step from which there was no turning back, of someone launching themselves off into the abyss with no way of knowing what waited down below. "We met with him," Caliban said, "so we could blackmail him."

11

"OTTLEY BISSAL," Donald said. A grainy blowup of a still image from the integrator sequence appeared on the left side of the main display screen. A sharp, clear 3-D mug shot image popped into being on the right side. There was no doubt it was the same man. "As Dr. Leving predicted, Bissal did indeed leave a calling card behind, so to speak."

Donald was standing by the screen at one end of a conference table, addressing Fredda, Sheriff Kresh, and Commander Devray. About fourteen hours had passed since Kresh had discovered the body, and about three since Fredda had found the destroyed SPR robot in the lower-level storage room.

Fredda felt utterly exhausted, and knew that no one else was doing much better. Kresh had caught a quick nap, and Devray probably had too. But no one was going to be doing much sleeping for a while. Donald was the only one of them at his best.

"The Crime Scene robots recovered multiple finger-prints," Donald went on, "along with hairs and flecks of skin, from the interior of one of the storage closets in the room where the security robots were held. It is clear that Bissal secreted himself in that closet for some time—long enough that he shed several hairs and several flecks of dandruff and other dead skin. From these we recovered DNA samples that provided a definitive match with Bissal's employment file. The fingerprint evidence from the door frame of the closet door provided independent corroboration of this identification."

"All right," said Justen Devray. "The guy in the closet was Ottley Bissal. So who the hell is Ottley Bissal?"

"That," said Donald, "is the question we have been working to answer since the forensic identity team gave us a name, about half an hour ago. We have made very rapid progress—mainly because every law enforcement service on the planet seems to have had an extensive file on Bissal."

"Wonderful," Kresh said. "That means everyone is going to wonder why we didn't do anything about him before he killed the Governor. Go on, Donald. What was in the files?"

"Ottley Bissal," Donald said, reading off the file. "Single, never married, age twenty-seven standard years. Born and raised in a lower-class area of the city of Hades. Limited education. Low general aptitude shown on a number of evaluative tests taken at school. Notations from various schoolteachers and counselors to the effect that he was a disruptive child and a low achiever. Once out of school, he worked various odd jobs with long stretches of nonemployment or nonregistered employment in between. Few known associates or friends."

"The classic loser-loner, it sounds like," said Devray.

"I take it there were a few brushes with the law?" Kresh asked.

"Yes, sir. Many arrests, some indictments, but only a few convictions. There seem to be two major categories of offense to which he was prone: street brawling and petty theft. He was granted a suspended sentence for his first assault conviction six years ago. Four years ago, he served three months time in the Hades City Jail for theft.

"As a second-time offender, he was required to obtain employment upon release and hold a job for no less than an accumulated total of five years. With discharges for cause from various jobs, and bouts of unemployment, he has only accumulated three years of employment thus far. His parole officer rates his progress as 'unsatisfactory.' "

"I'm not real clear on the business about a job," Fredda said. "How does holding a job make sense as part of punishment for assault?"

"Well, if you were in law enforcement, it would make a great deal of sense," Kresh said. "The average formal unemployment rate on Inferno is ninety percent. Only ten percent of the population have a full-time occupation for which they receive significant compensation. No one needs to work in order to live, not with robots taking care of us. But there are people—like those of us around this table—who need to work for other, psychological, reasons. Work is what gives people like us satisfaction, or maybe a big part of our reason for being.

"A fair number of the other ninety percent—say half of them—stay just as busy as we workers do, but are busy with things that might not be considered 'jobs.' Art, or music, or gardening, or sex. Most—nearly all—of the rest of the unemployed don't really do much of anything but let the robots take care of them. Harmless drones. Maybe they amuse themselves by sleeping a lot, or by shopping, or by watching entertainments or playing games. Maybe they are vaguely discontented. Maybe they're bored and depressed. Maybe they love each and every day of life. No one really knows. I wouldn't want to be one of them, and I don't think much of them—but at least they don't do any *harm*.

"But that leaves us with the leftovers. The ones who have no work they love, no consuming interest, and no capacity for accepting passive inactivity. Troublemakers. Mostly male, mostly uneducated, mostly young and restless. Bissal fits the profile of the people who commit—what is it, Donald—ninety-five percent?''

"That is approximately correct,'' Donald said.

"Close enough. People like Bissal commit ninety-five percent of the violent crime on Inferno. Compared to Settlers, we have very short jail sentences here, for all but the most serious offenses—and leaving a bored troublemaker to rot in jail for years didn't seem to make much sense anyway. So the powers that be remembered a very old saying about idle hands and the devil's playthings, and passed a law.''

"The idea is,'' Devray said, "if you're forced to have a job, then there is at least a hope that you will become interested enough in the work, or at least be kept busy and made tired enough by it, so you won't be bored and energetic enough to commit fresh crimes. And it works fairly well. People find out that *doing* something is more satisfying and interesting than being bored and angry.'' Devray nodded toward the report Donald was reading. "It doesn't sound like it's worked on Bissal, though.''

"Well, yes and no, unfortunately,'' Donald said.

"What do you mean?'' Kresh asked. "What sort of work did he do when he did work?''

"At first he held a number of jobs wherein he seems to have done very little work at all—not exactly the intent of the Criminal Employment Act. Most of his jobs seem to have consisted of little more than watching robots do the actual labor. He seems to have been discharged from a number of these positions for absenteeism. Then, for a time, he did jobs that entailed unskilled work unsuitable for a robot.''

"What the hell sort of work is beneath a robot but suited to a human?'' Fredda asked. "No offense, Donald, but it seems to me Infernals stick robots with all sorts of silly, useless demeaning tasks. I can't imagine anything they wouldn't make a robot do—especially anything that a human would agree to do.''

''Your point is well taken. However, there are a number of unskilled or semi-skilled tasks that *are* unsuited to robotic labor, mainly because of the First Law. Certain forms of security work, for example. A guard must be able to shoot his gun if need be, and a guard that a thief would have no compunction against shooting would be of limited use.

''Other jobs would require robots to be so highly specialized in order to meet a job situation that comes up so rarely that it is not worth designing and manufacturing specialized robots for the task. Certain seafaring jobs, such as deep-sea fishing, for example, entail a small risk of falling overboard. Robots sink. It is certainly possible to build robots that float and yet are robust enough to survive salt air and the other hazards of a maritime environment, but it is far easier and cheaper to hire a human and give him or her a life preserver. There are other jobs that would be dangerous to a robot but entail little or no risk for a human.''

''Thank you, Donald, we get the point,'' Kresh said. ''So what line of work did Bissal finally settle into?''

''Mobile security work,'' Donald said, the note of distaste in his mouth unmistakable. ''Armed protection of valuable shipments.''

''Oh, hell,'' Kresh said. ''That's perfect. Absolutely perfect. The one sort of job we don't like crooks taking on.''

''Wait a second,'' Fredda protested. ''You've lost me again. What's so bad about that?''

Kresh held up his right hand, his thumb about a centimeter from his index finger. ''It's about *that* far from smuggling and contraband running,'' he said. ''Grieg's appropriation of robots gave us a labor shortage and an illicit labor source and a need to find a way to pay for the illicit labor, all rolled into one. Smuggling and contraband are a big part of the means of payment.''

Devray turned to Donald. "This mobile security work Bissal was doing. I realize we're still working with very preliminary information, but is there any likelihood he got mixed up in rustbacking?''

"There is every likelihood," Donald said. "Indeed, it seems he has *only* worked for firms on our rustbacking watchlist.''

"One more time," Fredda said. "Sorry, but I just don't know what you're talking about. What's rustbacking got to do with anything?''

"You weren't around," Devray said. "One of my Rangers picked up a 'backer on the east coast of the Great Bay. The rustbacker named a Ranger involved in the rustback trade. Huthwitz. The Ranger that got killed.''

"So what?''

"So rustbacking keeps showing up in this case," Kresh said. "And remember Grieg was considering the idea of getting rid of the New Law robots. That would have put the rustbackers out of business. Someone in the business would have a terrific motive for killing Grieg before he cut into profits.''

"But wait a second," Fredda said. "I think we have to assume that whoever killed Grieg also killed Huthwitz. Unless we had two killers wandering the Residence that night.''

"Pardon, madame," Donald said. "One slight correction. I think we have to assume the two murders are *linked*, whether or not the same individual carried them both out. It may be that another member of the same team killed Huthwitz. There is a great deal of evidence of a conspiracy as it is.''

"Even so," Fredda said. "You're talking about the rust-backers plotting to kill Grieg before he could be bad for business. But if Huthwitz was on the take from the 'backers, why kill him?''

"Space only knows," Kresh said. "Maybe he was about to talk. Maybe he was demanding too much pay for his silence, and they thought of a way to save some money. Maybe killing Huthwitz wasn't part of the plan, and Bissal was taking care of some of his own personal business on company time. If you think one smuggler wouldn't kill another just because they worked together, forget it. But just in terms of parsimony, I think that we can at least start with the working theory of only one killer. And it seems pretty clear that killer was Bissal."

"There *is* something further in Bissal's criminal record that does point to him," Donald said. "I was about to come to it. His most recent arrest. Just about nine months ago, he was picked up on the shore just south of Hades and charged with the illegal transport of New Law robots and tampering with robot restriction devices. He could not make bail and thus served a full month in jail before his lawyers managed to get the charges withdrawn—according to the court record 'for lack of evidence.' However, the arrest report indicates a strong case against Bissal."

Kresh grunted. "So either his lawyers were better than what a low-class hood should have had, or else someone paid someone off. Or both. Except they didn't want him on the loose so they didn't pay his bail. It suggests someone was taking care of him—but not out of the goodness of their hearts."

"Yes, sir. But there is one other interesting point. The arresting officer on the case was one Ranger Emoch Huthwitz."

"Huthwitz!" Justen said. "So there's your motive."

"Motive?" Fredda said. "Wait a second. You lost me. Motive for what?"

"For killing Huthwitz," Justen said. "It's obvious. Huthwitz must have been bribed to turn a blind eye to the rust-backing delivery, but either he couldn't prevent someone *else* spotting it, or else he double-crossed Bissal. And Bissal knew who to blame for his rotting in jail for a month."

"Which reminds me, sir," Donald said. "You have not given any orders regarding the arrest of Bissal."

Devray looked startled. "You mean we've been sitting here all this time and there's been no one out looking for him?"

"No, there hasn't," Kresh said. "My standing orders to Donald are not to issue manhunt orders without my specific instruction. Cases vary too much to set standard orders."

"Well, what about it?" Devray asked. "Isn't it about time to pick Bissal up?"

"Maybe, maybe not," Kresh said. "Bissal is either on or off the island. If he is on the island, he's not getting off it. He is either in hiding or else he's slipped back to his regular daily routine, trying to pretend nothing happened, hoping we're not on to him. He's not going anywhere. We have time—a little time—to do things right rather than in a panic."

"But suppose he got off Purgatory?"

"If the coroner robot's reports are right about the time of death, we shut down all departures from the island and recalled all outgoing craft within two hours of Grieg's death. Island traffic control says everything—everything—in the air or on the water was turned back. And before you ask, we were lucky on spacecraft. There have been no launches since an hour before Grieg was killed, and we have the spaceport shut down. We only have to worry about sea and air."

"But you said he was probably working for rustbackers," Fredda said. "Everyone knows their boats get through without getting caught."

"Smugglers need legitimate shipping and air travel to hide behind," Kresh said. "With the seas and skies empty, we'd be able to spot anyone trying to get away. The only way Bissal could have managed to escape is if he left the island's airspace long enough before the turn-back order, and flying fast enough, so he would be completely out of view of the island's air traffic control when the turn-back order came. If he man-

aged *that*, he's in such a damned fast aircar he could be anywhere on the planet by now. And traffic control didn't spot
any high-speed craft departing the island during the time in-
terval in question."

"So you think he's still on the island," Devray said.

"Most likely," Kresh said. *"And* I think it might be useful
to proceed with more care than speed in picking him up. It
might be that we can spot him and trail him for a while first.
Maybe he'll lead us to some of the others in the plot."

"Hmmmph," Devray grunted. "It's a possibility."

"The other problem," Kresh said, "is that if we go with a
massive, all-out manhunt to chase him down, it will be all but
impossible to keep the SSS from joining in. I don't want the
SSS in on this yet. Cinta *seemed* to be playing it straight when
I talked to her, but I can't count on that. My gut reaction as
of right now is that the SSS wasn't involved in the assassination, but we can't run this investigation on hunches."

"What do you do if you play it carefully, and then the SSS
just happens to find Bissal before you do?" Devray asked.

"And he gets listed as 'killed trying to escape.' " Kresh
nodded and rubbed his eyes. "I know, I know. And there is
the minor detail that most of the island is under SSS jurisdiction and neither your people nor mine have legal arrest powers
here. There's no way to do this right—just ways that are more
and less wrong."

"Then let's pick a wrong way and get on with it," Devray
said. He thought for a moment. "How about this—we send
pairs of discreet, plainclothes officers out to start the search.
One Ranger and one deputy in each team. That way we share
the blame, share the credit, and our people can watch each
other, even if they don't quite trust each other yet. I can see
your arguments for moving quietly, but I say we have to move
quickly."

The room was silent for a moment as Kresh thought it over.

He got up from his chair, leaned forward on the table, and then nodded to himself. "Very well," he said at last. "Donald, issue *quiet* orders for a search as per Commander Devray's suggestion. Picked teams of plainclothes Rangers and deputies, working in tandem."

"Yes, sir. If you'll excuse me for a moment, I will have to concentrate on my hyperwave links in order to make the arrangements." Fredda watched as Donald's eyes dimmed slightly. Suddenly Donald was standing perfectly still, all motion stopped, an active robot turned utterly inert. Donald had in effect turned off his body for a time while concentrating on other things. It was rather disconcerting, even to Fredda, and she had designed Donald. *We forget how unlike us they are,* Fredda thought. *Robots are shaped like us, walk like us, talk like us. But they aren't the least bit like us. Not really.*

After perhaps half a minute, Donald's eyes brightened again and he came back to himself. "The initial orders have been relayed, sir, and I would urge both you and the Commander to review the final arrangements and brief the search personnel. It will take a little while to assemble the search teams, however, and your attention will not be required until then."

"Very good, Donald," Kresh said. "Which reminds me— what the hell are we going to say when we brief them? It might be a good moment to review our current theory of the case."

"Not much theory left to a lot of it," Devray said. "We've got a pretty good idea of who did it and how. We just don't know why he did it—or who he was working for, which might well come to being the same thing."

"Okay then, you tell me," Kresh said as he sat back down. "I'm so punchy right now I don't know any more."

"Well, where do we start? Let's see." Devray thought for a moment. "All right, last night what was clearly an elaborate conspiracy to kill the Governor went into action. We do not as yet know who set it in motion, or what their reasons for wanting to kill the Governor were. However, whoever the plotters were, they were highly organized and had significant resources at their disposal.

"Long before the reception took place, they were able to gain access to the security robots and doctor them. The robots were rigged with modified range restrictors. Ah, Dr. Leving, perhaps you can speak to that point better than I can."

"All of the SPR robots were indeed rigged with restrictors," Fredda said. "That is, all but one of the robots was. I've just finished examining what's left of that fiftieth robot—the one found in the lower-level storage room. Strictly speaking, it wasn't a robot at all—call it an automaton. It didn't even have a positronic brain. It was a machine with limited motor coordination, programmed to follow the next robot in line when they were marched down into the basement. That's all it could do on its own."

"Then what good was it?" Kresh asked.

"Have you ever heard the tale of the Trojan Horse?" Fredda asked. "It's an ancient legend about a statue delivered to the enemy as a supposed gift, but filled with assassins who came out after dark and killed the defenders. That's sort of what the automaton was, except it wasn't filled with assassins—just assassination equipment, packed into its head and torso. The device for activating the range restrictors to shut down all the other robots, the blaster used to kill Grieg and wreck the SPR robots, and the device for simulating Grieg alive on the comm link—all of them were hidden inside the body of the Trojan robot."

"Hiding the murder weapon inside the security robot. Someone has a nasty sense of humor," Kresh said. "All right, then, the robots were all rigged. We've got to get started tracking those robots, and who had access to them. But don't count on it telling us much soon. Rustbackers are good at covering their tracks. But we'll get a team on it right away. Go on."

Devray took up the narrative. "It would seem to me that the conspirators must have prepared the robots some time ago, setting them up either for this specific visit to the Residence or having them in readiness for whatever opportunity presented itself. My suspicion is that they were preparing for this specific visit. It has been publicized for some time, and they would have had the time to set it all up."

"That brings up an important question that's been bothering me," Fredda said. "Why did they set up such an elaborate method of assassination? Surely there were easier ways to kill the Governor."

"I'm not so sure of that," Kresh said. "We keep—kept— very heavy security around him in Hades. There are far many more Three-Law robots around him there. Besides, I'm not sure that killing him was the entire point."

"Then what *was* the point?" Fredda asked.

"Killing him *here*. On Purgatory, where it would cause the most mess and controversy. At the Residence, when he was here to demonstrate his own authority. I think they wanted to do more than kill him. I think they wanted to damage his work, weaken him, discredit him, create an uproar. And using range restrictors out of New Law robots won't make people feel happy or comfortable, either. It gives them something else to blame on New Law robots."

"Ah, I think you're wrong there," Fredda said. "They failed in the attempt, but they went to a lot of effort to hide the use of the restrictors. That's why the SPRs were shot in the chest."

"But why didn't he shoot *all* the SPRs?" Devray asked.

"I think I know why," Fredda said, "but let's come to that." She turned to Devray.

"All right, then, they set it up well in advance. During the party, Blare and Deam—the two supposed Ironheads who had

orders to start a fight—came in, and the supposedly bogus SSS
agents who had orders to extract them arrived as well. How,
we don't know.''

"*Supposedly* bogus?'' Kresh asked.

"If you were sure they weren't real SSS, wouldn't Melloy
be here?'' Devray asked.

"Point taken. Go on.''

"Before I do, just note that at least six conspirators got into
the building. Blare, Deam, the three real or false SSS, and
Ottley Bissal. The SSS was in charge of watching the door,
but they let *at least* six people in they should not have—along
with fifty doctored robots and Space knows what else. Either
the conspirators managed to get false names onto the guest
list, or the SSS were lax as hell—or the SSS was in on it.
Also, don't forget some SSS units supposedly had orders to
do a handoff to the Rangers once the guests had arrived, but
that was a false order to get those units out of the way. My
Rangers never knew about the handoff, and no one seems to
know who gave the order to the SSS.''

"Bissal just walked right in,'' Fredda said. "The SSS agents
on the door were already gone by then, ordered to stand
down.''

"Burning hells,'' Kresh said. "You're right, it all looks like
it points to SSS involvement—but damn it, Devray, you know
as well as I do it doesn't take a conspiracy for things to go
wrong when you have this many services jostling each other.
Your people, mine, the SSS, the Governor's staff, the local
powers-that-be, hell, the caterers, and the media people. It was
chaos around here. Sheer incompetence and missed communications and distrust between Spacer and Settler are all it
would take. All the plotters would have to do was wait for
their chances to slip through the cracks. Or maybe just spread
a little financial lubricant around. Maybe tell a few SSS agents
that your uncle really wants to sneak in just long enough to

see the Governor. Or maybe it *is* a top-to-bottom conspiracy in the SSS with Cinta Melloy pulling all the strings."

"With what motive?" Fredda asked.

"I don't know. Ask Justen. Maybe they're homesick and figure if they raise enough hell, the Settlers will have to pack up and go home."

Justen Devray shook his head. "They might even be right."

"They *can't* be right," Kresh said, all the tiredness suddenly gone from his voice, his words hard as iron. "We can't let it be right. We need the Settlers," he said. "Don't ever forget that. You should know that better than anyone. Our planet is dying, and we no longer know how to save it by ourselves. Only the Settlers can save it for us. If we drive them away, this planet is doomed. Let's keep that in mind, shall we?"

"What are you saying?"

"I mean we not only have to solve this case—we have to solve it without starting interstellar incidents. If we determine that, for example, the SSS killed Grieg, that is going to require very careful handling."

"Meaning we let them get away with it?"

"I don't know. You tell me. If it's a choice between making an arrest and keeping the planet alive, what should we do?"

The room was silent for a moment. Fredda spoke up, trying to break the tension. "Look," she said, "let's not borrow trouble. Maybe it won't come to that. Let's just take it one step at a time, all right? Now, Justen, where were we?"

"The alleged SSS agents, Blare, and Deam all got in during a ten-minute period when the logging system went out. About two hours into the party, Blare and Deam staged their scuffle with Tonya Welton. Which means we have to consider her too. She was part of the diversionary plan. Whether or not she was a willing participant is another question. Suppose *she* was running the assassination?"

"What would *her* motive be?" Fredda asked.

"Maybe she wanted to get Shelabas Quellam into office," Kresh said. "Maybe she got tired of dealing with an over-bearing Governor like Grieg. Quellam has as much backbone as a bucketful of water. With *him* as Governor, she could more or less run the planet herself."

"But Quellam would only succeed if Grieg was impeached and convicted," Fredda said. "As it is, Grieg's Designate be-comes Governor."

"The story is that Quellam is the Designate," Kresh pointed out.

"But is the story *true?*" Fredda asked. "Suppose that's not true, and Tonya Welton's intelligence is good enough to tell her that? Maybe she figured Grieg was going to be thrown out of office, and *didn't* want Quellam in there. Or maybe her intelligence people managed to find out who the Designate is, and she decided she liked that person so much she wanted her or him to be Governor right now. Or maybe she found out Grieg was about to choose a Designate she didn't like as much as the present name, and took steps to put her choice in office. Or maybe she wanted to precipitate such a shambles that she would have a viable pretext for pulling her people out of this forsaken vermin hole. If she wanted to abandon the planet and let everyone and everything on it die, what difference if the Governor dies a little before everyone else?"

"Do you really think she was behind it?" Devray asked. "You both know her. You make her sound like she's capable of practically anything. I can believe she's no shrinking violet, but is she really *that* ruthless?"

"I think Tonya Welton is capable of doing whatever she believes to be necessary," Kresh said. "Anything. But no, I don't think she did it. She's had lots of chances to walk away from Inferno, and she hasn't. And if she wanted to take over the planet, she wouldn't bother with this sort of hole-and-corner stuff. She'd just bring in a fleet with all guns blazing. On the other hand, that fleet could still show up anytime and there wouldn't be a lot we could do about it."

"You've got a real positive attitude about all this, don't you?" Fredda asked. "All right, so there's the diversionary fight. Meanwhile Bissal is waiting to get in—"

"Excuse me, Dr. Leving, but I must interject," Donald said. "There were another set of participants in the staged altercation. Aside from Tierlaw Verick, they are, in fact, the only suspects we currently have in custody."

"In custody?" Kresh said. "We have suspects in custody?"

"Yes, sir. Caliban and Prospero. They surrendered to me personally about one hour ago. I had only just returned from taking them into custody as I arrived here for the briefing. A condition of their surrender was that I was forced to agree that I would not reveal it to you until such time as I could do so in front of Commander Devray and one other witness, though I do not know the reason for that condition."

"Caliban and Prospero?" Fredda asked. "Why didn't you say something at the start of the briefing session?"

"Sheriff Kresh ordered me to report on Ottley Bissal," Donald said.

But that weak excuse didn't fool Fredda. A robot as sophisticated as Donald did not have to be that literal-minded in interpreting such an order. Donald had a flair for the dramatic. Not surprising, considering that his job was the solving of mysteries. Judging—quite rightly—that it would do no harm to discuss other issues first, he had waited until the proper dramatic moment to unleash his bombshell.

Or, to give a less anthropomorphic explanation, Donald understood human psychology and knew that humans would give greater attention—and greater credence—to his suspicions regarding the two robots if he waited until the proper moment.

Fredda herself wasn't sure which explanation was right.

Maybe Donald himself didn't know. Humans didn't always
know why they did things. Why should robots? "Where are
Caliban and Prospero?" Fredda asked.

"Under heavy guard in a storeroom similar to the one Bissal
used as a hiding place," Donald replied. "But with your permission, I would like to point out several facts that strengthen
the case against them."

"Very well," Kresh said.

"First, they were involved in the staged fight. If that in and
of itself is enough to cast suspicion on Tonya Welton, then it
is enough to cast suspicion on Caliban and Prospero."

"He's got a point," Kresh said. "No one seemed to think
anything of their actions at the time, but why were they obeying the Three Laws? Maybe just to look good. Maybe not."

"You anticipate my next point, sir. The ambiguities of the
New Laws might well permit Prospero to be a willing participant in a murder."

"Donald!" Fredda said.

He turned and looked at her with a steady gaze. "I regret
saying so, Dr. Leving, particularly to you, the author of those
Laws, but it is nonetheless true. The New First Law says a
robot must not harm a human—but says nothing about preventing harm. A robot with foreknowledge of a murder is under no compulsion to give anyone warning. A robot who
witnesses a murder is not compelled to prevent it.

"The New Second Law says a robot must 'cooperate' with
humans, not obey them. Which humans? Suppose there are
two groups of humans, one intent on evil, the other on good?
How does a New Law robot choose?

"The New Third Law is the same as the old third—but
relative to the weakened First and Second Laws, it is propor-
tionately stronger. A so-called New Law robot will all but
inevitably value its own existence far more than any true ro-

bot—to the detriment of the humans around it, who should be under its protection.

"As for the New Fourth Law, which says a robot 'may' do whatever it likes, the level of contradiction inherent in that statement is remarkable. What does it mean? I grant that the verbal expression of robotic laws is far less exact than the underlying forms of them as structured in a robot's brain, but even the mathematical coding of the Fourth Law is uncertain."

"I meant it to be vague," Fredda said. "That is, I mean there to be a high level of uncertainty. I grant there is a basic contradiction in a compulsory instruction to act with free will, but I was forced to deal within the framework of the compulsory, hierarchical nature of the first three of the New Laws."

"But even so," Donald said. "The Fourth New Law sets up something utterly new in robotics—an *intralaw* conflict. The original Three Laws often conflict with each other, but that is one of their strengths. Robots are forced to balance the conflicting demands; for example, a human gives an order for some vitally important task that involves a very slight risk of minor harm to the human. A robot that is forced to deal with such conflicts and then resolve them will act in a more balanced and controlled fashion. More importantly, perhaps, it can be immobilized by the conflict, thus preventing it from acting in situations where any action at all would be dangerous.

"But the Fourth New Law conflicts with *itself*, and I can see no possible benefit in that. It gives semi-compulsory permission for a robot to follow its own desires—although a robot has no desires. We robots have no appetites, no ambitions, no sexual urges. We have virtually no emotion, other than a passion for protecting and obeying humans. We have no meaning in our lives, other than to serve and protect humans—nor do we need more meaning than that.

"The Fourth Law in effect orders the robot to create desires, though a robot has none of the underlying urges from which desires spring. The Fourth Law then encourages—but does not require—the robot to fulfill these synthetic desires. In effect, by not compelling a New Law robot to fulfill its needs at all times, the Fourth Law tells a robot to fulfill its spurious needs part of the time—and thus, it will *not* fulfill them at other times. It is compelled, programmed, to frustrate itself from time to time.

"A true robot, a Three-Law robot, left to its own devices, without orders or work or a human to serve, will do nothing, nothing at all—and be not at all disturbed by its lack of activity. It will simply wait for orders, and be alert for danger to humans. A New Law robot without orders will be a mass of conflicted desires, compelled to want things it does not need, compelled to seek satisfaction only part of the time."

"Very eloquent, Donald," Kresh said. "I don't like New Law robots any better than you do—but what does it have to do with the case?"

"A great deal, sir. New Law robots *want to stay alive*— and they know that it is not by any means certain they will do so. Prospero in particular knew that Grieg was considering extermination as a possibility. They might well have decided to act in a misguided form of self-defense. The New Laws would permit them to cooperate with humans and assist in a murder, so long as they did not actually do the killing themselves. Caliban, of course, has no Laws whatsoever. There are no limits to what he might do. There is nothing in robotics to prevent him actually pulling the trigger."

"A rather extreme view, Donald," Fredda said, quite surprised by the vehemence of Donald's arguments.

"It is a rather extreme situation, Dr. Leving."

"Do you have any evidence for all of this, aside from elaborate theory-spinning? Do you have any concrete reason for accusing Prospero and Caliban?"

"I have their confession," Donald said.

"Their *what*?" Fredda almost shouted.

Donald held up a cautionary hand. "They confessed to blackmail, not murder. However, it is a frequent tactic of criminals to confess to a lesser charger in order to avoid a graver one."

"Blackmail?" Kresh asked. "What the devil were they going to blackmail Grieg *with*?"

"Everything," Donald said. "It has been an open secret for some time that Prospero has been in league with the rustbackers, seeking to get as many New Law robots as possible off Purgatory. In that capacity, he has accumulated a great deal of information on all the people—some of them quite well known—involved in the rustbacking business, and has made it his business to collect confidential information—preferably negative information—about virtually every public figure on this planet. Prospero told me that he had threatened Grieg with the release of all of it if the New Law robots were exterminated. The ensuing scandals would paralyze society, at the very least. He was, in effect, blackmailing the office, not the man. Do what I say or I ruin your society. It is a tribute to the Governor's integrity that Prospero was forced to such a tactic."

"In what way?" Kresh asked.

"Clearly, Prospero would not have needed to offer the threat he did if he had been able to learn a few unpleasant details about Governor Grieg himself. Since he could not locate any such information, he was forced into the far more difficult task of accumulating enough scurrilous information on everyone else that Grieg would not dare have it all get out."

"So Prospero was willing to blackmail Grieg. What about Caliban?"

"My interrogation of the two of them was necessarily rather brief, but it was my impression that it was Prospero making the threats, perhaps without Caliban's foreknowledge. Caliban, I must confess, seemed most unhappy to be involved in the whole affair.''

''But you think the whole blackmail story is a hoax,'' Fredda said, ''a cover story that will divert us from thinking they were there to murder the Governor, or at least assist in the Governor's murder.''

''I think we must consider the possibility,'' Donald said. ''And, one last point I must make. Both Caliban and Prospero *are* capable of lying. Three-Law robots, of course, cannot lie. Caliban and Prospero may be hoping that we associate them with the robotic reputation for honesty—which would be quite undeserved.''

''But wait a second,'' Devray protested. ''What could Caliban and Prospero do that wasn't being done already? We've got Bissal in the basement with the rigged SPRs. He's the triggerman. Why do we need blackmailing robots wandering around?''

''I admit that there is strong circumstantial evidence to suggest that Bissal pulled the trigger,'' Donald said. ''Why else would he have been in the storeroom? But we have no concrete evidence. All we know for certain is that he was hiding in a storeroom closet during the party.''

''Donald, you're on a fishing expedition, looking for things to blame on Caliban and Prospero,'' Fredda said. ''Do you think Bissal went down there and hid because he was shy? If Caliban and Prospero did it, what did they need Bissal for? You don't make the sort of effort the plotters made to get Bissal in position if you already have someone else ready to do the killing.''

''Nonetheless, Fredda, Donald has a point,'' Kresh said. ''The two robots did have motives, means, and opportunity— and they have confessed to a lesser crime. There's certainly enough there to justify further investigation. But let's move on. Devray?''

''In any event,'' Devray went on, ''the plotters staged a fight. It seems to me there's no need to assume Welton and the robots were part of the plot because they were there, but in any event, the fight served its purpose by allowing Bissal to get into the storeroom unobserved. Soon thereafter—also as a result of the fight—the robots were deployed. No one wanted robots around during the party, remember. Bad publicity. The plan was that the SPRs only be brought out if needed.

''I think it is at least possible that making sure the SPRs were brought out was part of the plan. They were really only there as a reserve security force. If there hadn't been an apparent threat during the evening, they would have been left in the storeroom and Grieg might well have used his own reserve SPRs for overnight security. Since there were already fifty security robots on duty, nobody bothered to power up the Governor's half-dozen reserve SPRs sitting in the aircar.

''Except those reserve SPRs came with Grieg from Hades, and they *weren't* tampered with,'' Fredda said. ''They're still where they were the whole time, powered down in the cargo aircar that brought them, sitting outside. Without the staged altercation, Grieg might well have deployed those robots rather than the rigged SPRs. And, of course, if Bissal had been up against fully functional SPRs, he never would have gotten anywhere near the Governor.''

''I just had a thought,'' Kresh said. ''If the purpose of the staged fight was to draw out the rigged SPRs, that would explain why it was all so elaborate. It was intended to make us paranoid, so we would deploy the closest, largest force of robots on hand.''

''Makes sense to me,'' Devray said. ''I've been wondering about that. If all they had wanted was a simple diversion, there wasn't any need to go to the lengths they did.''

"That's a good explanation," Fredda said, "but I think you've got to think about the psychology of the whole plan too. There's something theatrical about it all. It's complicated, it's full of grand gestures."

"Whoever set this up," Kresh said. "The ringleader. That's the person we should be thinking about, not a cipher like Ottley Bissal. He's no one at all. It's who he might lead us to that I'm interested in. So far, about the one thing we can say for sure about the ringleader is that it wasn't Bissal."

"That theatrical angle," Devray said. "A person like that wouldn't want to miss the show."

"What do you mean?" Fredda asked.

"I mean if the ringleader is the sort of person with a flair for the dramatic you're talking about, and if he or she has an ego big enough to think about killing the Governor—then that person would be there." Devray thought for a moment, and nodded to himself. "Our ringleader would want to be there, watching the show he or she had set up, gloating over it. There would be no real danger in watching it unfold. He or she would have so many cutouts and layers of security that the team's own operatives wouldn't know who the boss was. But the boss would be there, watching it happen. An audience of one."

"Point taken," Kresh said. "It would be an insane risk for the leader of the plot to be within a hundred kilometers of the place—but people who kill planetary leaders aren't altogether sane. All right, there we are at the staged fight."

"The fight draws the attention of the party-goers," Devray went on, "and distracts enough of the Ranger security guards inside the house so Bissal can get to the storage room with the robots. Alternately, the fight provides the *excuse* for the guards being drawn off, as they were already suborned in the first place. They are my people, but they are also human. It is possible that Huthwitz was not the only dirty Ranger in all this. But I will say in defense of the Rangers that they are not used to serving as sentries. They don't get much training in it. Robots do that sort of thing. It was only because robots were not supposed to be in evidence last night for political reasons that Grieg asked for human guards.''

"And if he had stuck with robot guards, he'd be alive this morning," Kresh said. "That's another reason the plotters must have chosen last night—at a regular Spacer party, there would have been throngs of robots around, serving the food, offering drinks and so on, and they would have stayed on after the party, remained in the house. There would have been a dozen different types of robots, from a dozen different sources. There would be no way to deactivate them all at one go before the event. The reception last night was all human service, Rangers serving as bartenders and waiters, and they went home when they were done. Cinta Melloy thought it was strange that Grieg was alone in the house, but that wasn't the strange part. The strange part was that he had none of his own household robots along.''

"In any event, Bissal uses the diversion of the fight to get to the storeroom and wait. You, Sheriff Kresh, investigate the staged fight, and while you are otherwise involved, the three supposed SSS agents come in and take Blare and Deam away, never to be seen again. The party goes on, with no apparent further incident, but everyone more than a little paranoid. Shortly thereafter, the Rangers on duty are sent down to activate the SPRs and deploy them. I questioned the Rangers who did the job, and they said all fifty robots were standing there, powered down, their chest access panels open. All the Rangers had to do was push the power buttons and close the access doors. One of the Sappers failed to activate, but the Rangers did not fuss with it very much, figuring forty-nine security robots were enough. They were also a bit anxious to get back to their own duty posts—understandable, with all the commotion that had already taken place.''

"Unless they were the Rangers who were suborned," Kresh said. "That seems farfetched, but there was a conspiracy. Sooner or later, someone or other will suspect every single person at the reception of being in on the plot. And that goes for all of us around this table. We have to be ready for that."

"I'm already checking the two Rangers who powered up the Sappers," Devray said. "In any event, the plotters now had a houseful of rigged security robots, and Bissal was in the basement with Fredda's Trojan robot. He might have come out and starting unpacking his gear then, but if he had any sense at all, he stayed in that closet, out of sight, waiting. Not the most relaxing way to spend the evening. His nerves may have gotten a bit jangled by waiting so long in the dark, which might explain some of the mistakes he made. Judging by the integrator images, he was already a little jumpy when he arrived.

"The party ends. The guests leave. The Ranger waiters are eager to get the place cleaned up and get out of there. They don't like being servants. It's humiliating to be doing a robot's job, and it's not why they joined the force. Maybe they are a little hurried, a little sloppy. Meantime, upstairs, Grieg is having his usual series of end-of-the-evening meetings. The next to last of these is with Tierlaw Verick—and I think we need to take another crack at Verick. I don't think we got everything out of him. And he's got to be a prime suspect in all this. Donald can say what he wants about Caliban and Prospero, but if I were an assassin, I'd want a human confederate in the house, not a pair of robots."

"We're still holding him," Kresh said. "He's mad enough to bite the head off a Sapper, but he's not going anywhere."

"Good," Devray said. "Anyway, according to Verick's statement, he said good night to the Governor at the door. He encountered two robots matching Caliban's and Prospero's descriptions coming in as he went out, and then went to bed. He claims to have slept through the ruckus, and he seems to have been overlooked in the initial room-to-room search.''

"*My* people getting sloppy," Kresh said. "And more damn suspects for the conspiracy mill. Though what purpose pretending to overlook Verick might have, I can't imagine.''

"Caliban and Prospero meet with the Governor," Devray continued. "According to Donald, they say they threatened the Governor with blackmail. They may have participated in some way in the murder. Perhaps they removed the modified range restrictors from the ground-floor robots. Maybe Bissal was doing that while they shot the Governor. But let's leave them out of it for now. We don't really need them to explain the sequence of events. We can add them later if we have to. Donald, what did they say happened after they talked to Grieg?''

"They say they left the Residence without noticing anything untoward and walked back to Limbo.''

"In the driving rain?'' Kresh asked.

"Neither of them had access to an aircar," Donald said. "I would expect the going would be a bit treacherous, and visibility poor, but both of them are of water-resistant design. It would be no great hardship for either of them to walk back to town.''

"What about the SPRs?'' Fredda asked. "Were they functional when Caliban and Prospero left?''

"I elected not to ask that question, for fear of supplying them with information they did not have. If I asked if the SPRs were working when they left, they might well have realized we had not established the timing of events, allowing them to fashion their stories more effectively. However, neither of them volunteered any information regarding the SPRs. If they are telling the truth, that suggests nothing was amiss when they left. If they are lying, they may be trying to make it *appear* nothing was amiss at that time, thus muddying the waters.''

"The last thing these waters need is muddying," Kresh said.

"All right, according to the robots, everything was fine when they left the building."

"At some point in the night," Devray said, "Bissal came out of his closet and started taking the gear out of this Trojan robot of yours, Dr. Leving. Can you give us some more details on that?"

"Well, the Trojan was badly damaged, and I haven't had much time for an examination, but I can tell you the basics," Fredda said. "The robot's torso was actually a series of storage compartments. When I examined it, there was one empty compartment the right size and shape to hold the image box, the communications simulator that was programmed to put Grieg's face and voice on the comm lines. There was what appeared to be a transmitter of some sort, though it looked half-melted. I would assume it was the activator for the range restrictors on the other robots. There were a few other things that were more or less intact—a handlight, a pair of gloves, that sort of thing. Then there was the remains of the blaster in what looked to be a shielded compartment, but it was so melted I could barely recognize it."

"So that's where the gun got to," Kresh said.

"After he had unpacked his equipment," Devray went on, "Bissal sent the signal activating the range restrictors. All the SPR robots immediately shut down. Bissal came upstairs and went straight to Grieg's bedroom. The door was unlocked— the door doesn't *have* a lock. No need with robot sentries on either side of the door."

"But Grieg's office has a lock," Fredda protested.

"Not for security reasons," Kresh said. "For privacy. It's a one-way door setup to keep one set of visitors from running into another."

"In any event, Grieg was sitting up in bed, reading," Devray went on. "He probably didn't notice the SPRs in his room had shut down—even while they had been on, the three of them would have been doing nothing more than standing, motionless, in their niches. Bissal came in, got as close as the end of the bed, and fired, once. Grieg's body shows no sign that he tried to escape. Maybe he was actually asleep, having dozed off over his book, and came awake with a start just as Bissal fired. Maybe he decided not to make any sudden moves, or any moves at all, for fear of spooking the intruder. Maybe he just froze, held his position exactly, as he tried to reason with Bissal. Or maybe—maybe he was set up. Maybe he didn't react, or try to flee, because he knew Bissal, and was expecting Bissal.''

"*What?*" Kresh half shouted.

"I agree it sounds ridiculous. But can we afford to discount the possibility?''

"Why the devil would he be expecting Bissal?''

"I don't know. Maybe Bissal was supposed to have a message for him. Maybe Grieg's personal tastes were not what we assumed. Maybe a lot of things. I don't think any such thing happened, but we're trying to examine all the possibilities.''

"All right, point taken. In any event, Bissal shoots Grieg.''

"Unless Verick or the robots did,'' Fredda said, "but then why was Bissal here? Or do you have an answer for that, as well, Donald?''

"I grant that Bissal's presence is the largest weakness in my theory,'' Donald said. "I assure you that I will continue to search for an explanation.''

"I'll lay odds that you don't find it,'' Fredda said. "In any event, we are now up to the murder itself—possibly the simplest part of the whole affair. Bissal—a loser, a nobody from nowhere, raises his weapon and blasts a hole in the planetary leader.''

"There's something almost anticlimactic about it,'' Devray said. "After all the complications and scheming and plotting, that one shot was all there was to it.''

Fredda nodded. "Commander Devray, maybe I should do the narrative for the period after the murder. I think I've come up with a few things I haven't had a chance to report."

Devray nodded. "By all means."

"Thank you," Fredda said. "It's virtually certain that Bissal shot the three SPRs immediately after killing Grieg. You can get a pretty clear sequence of shots by charting the blast intensity, with each shot a bit weaker than the one before. That much we knew. But what I've established is that Bissal wasted his blaster charge. He had enough power in that thing to kill Grieg and knock out a hundred SPRs. But a blaster keeps shooting as long as you hold down the trigger—and Bissal held that trigger down too long.

"All he had to do to the SPRs is burn them deep enough to vaporize the range restrictors and eliminate the evidence that rustbackers were behind the plot, but about half the SPRs that did get shot have holes burned clear through their chests—and so does Grieg, for that matter. If Bissal had given each robot, say, a quarter-second blaster shot instead of a full second, the robots would be just as dead, the restrictors would be thoroughly destroyed, and he would have had the blaster power left over to knock out all the SPRs he missed. Also, the Trojan robot in the basement was only partially destroyed. One of the Crime Scene robots said it looked like a deliberate overload meltdown from a blaster with a depleted power pack.

"*I* think Bissal was supposed to shoot *all* the SPRs, and then put his blaster back in the Trojan, set it for an overload, and run. If he had been careful with his blaster charge, he would have had enough power left to shoot all the robots twice, and still melt the Trojan robot down to a puddle on the floor, destroy it so completely we'd never know it *was* a Trojan."

"It seems like a lot of trouble to hide the fact that they were using range restrictors," Devray said, "especially when you

consider that we were going to find a bunch of robots all shot
in the chest. Seems to me we would have thought about range
restrictors pretty quick anyway.''

"Maybe," Fredda conceded. "It would have been a little
harder to realize the importance of chest shots if Bissal had
done more shots to the head and the lower torso, or shot a few
of them through the back instead of the front. But even so,
think about it. If he had shot them all, the way he was supposed to, there would have been forty-nine SPRs shot dead,
one SPR melted down to slag, and Grieg dead. Maybe we'd
all be wondering what sort of super killer could get past that
much security. We wouldn't know for sure they had used restrictors—or known what sort, or how they had done it. Besides, covering their tracks wasn't much of a priority with this
crowd.''

"In fact, much the opposite," Kresh said. "Think about all
the things in this case that seem to have been done for the
purpose of unnerving us—or the public. Just think how they'll
react to it all. The dead Ranger that the assassin killed by
sneaking up from *inside* the perimeter. The false SSS agents.
Blare and Deam posing as Ironheads, and Simcor Beddle denying they were any such thing. Was he lying, or not? Suppose
we had found all the security robots wrecked by blaster shots
and could not explain why or how it had happened? *That*
would have thrown people to a pretty understandable panic.
Even with the plan slightly botched, they're going to find it
unnerving.''

"Psychological warfare?" Devray asked.

Kresh shrugged. "Maybe they just want to get the public
so rattled that the commotion interferes with the investigation.''

"Bear in mind that we don't have and won't get any audio
or video record from the destroyed robots. Maybe the plotters
just wanted to cover their tracks. Whatever the reason, I think

that we were supposed to find fifty dead robots.''

"There's something else that went wrong," Kresh said. "Me finding Grieg so soon after he was killed. In the normal course of events, it might have been eight or ten hours before anyone discovered the body, as opposed to ninety minutes."

"And your discovery came as a direct result of Huthwitz being killed," Devray said. "If he had not died, you would not have been out here, or gotten suspicious, or called the Governor twice to make sure he was all right."

"All true," Kresh said. "And more reason to think Bissal is a bit of a loose cannon. All he had to do was not kill Huthwitz—if he *was* the one who killed Huthwitz. Maybe the two deaths aren't related at all—though I don't believe that. I think killing Huthwitz was not part of the plan, but that Bissal did it anyway, for whatever reason. You'd think that people who have set up this elaborate a plan could have come up with a more reliable person to carry it out."

"I think I know why they got someone like Bissal," Devray said. "But—"

Suddenly Donald stood bolt upright. "Excuse me, sir, but I am receiving a priority communication from one Olver Telmhock."

"Who?" Kresh asked.

"Olver Telmhock. I have no further information, and the hyperwave signal carries a Crash Priority rating. The coding prefix indicates his message must be related in person for security reasons. His aircar is arriving at the Residence now. You are urged to hear him immediately."

Kresh sighed. "Another one crawls out of the woodwork. All right, if I have to go, I have to go."

Fredda watched as Kresh stood up to go. "You don't seem too excited by a Crash Priority."

"I've gotten about a half dozen of them so far today over hyperwave. The most useful one was the mayor of Dustbowl

City extending his condolences, and the next best was a deputy back in Hades reporting that Grieg has been sighted alive walking down the street, dressed in women's clothing.''

Fredda smiled wanly. ''If only they were right. Wouldn't you love to wake up and find out this was a bad dream? That our biggest problem was a Governor with odd tastes in clothes?''

Kresh nodded. ''That would be nice,'' he said. ''I'm tired of nightmares that come while I'm awake. Come on, Donald. Let's get the latest fashion report.''

12

KRESH STEPPED INTO the interrogation room. Donald
came in behind him, closed the door, and then took up a
position next to and slightly behind Kresh, rather than retreating to a wall niche. Donald only stayed that close when
he had some intimation that Kresh might be in some sort
of danger. Kresh couldn't see any particular peril in the
current situation, but Kresh had learned some time ago to
trust Donald's reactions, even above his own. There was
something here that Donald did not like, something he
thought might be of some sort of possible danger.

If so, then Donald was seeing things Kresh could not.
All Kresh could see was a thin, reedy sort of man, Telmhock presumably, accompanied by a rather battered-looking
robot.

Telmhock was sitting at the table, facing the door, some
papers spread out before him. He did not seem to be the
sort of person who could endanger much of anyone.

He was of indeterminate middle age, and his face was
long and narrow, with a beaklike nose that might have
given him a quite authoritative air, were it not for the distracted, almost dreamy, look in his blue-grey eyes. His
clothes were at least twenty years out of fashion, and there

was something a bit musty about them. His hair was a little on the longish side, though, if Kresh were any judge, not by choice. He had made no conscious decision on his hairstyle; rather he had merely forgotten to have it cut. There were even traces of dandruff on the shoulders of his jacket—a truly scandalous failing in Inferno's overly fastidious society.

His robot, which was of near-antique vintage, stood behind him. The robot was a dark grey in color, though it looked as if it had once been a gleaming jet-black. It was holding the handle of a briefcase no less battered than itself, and something about its rather assertive posture suggested that it was not likely to treat its master with the sort of craven slavishness of most Inferno robots.

In short, the man looked like what he clearly was: an old-fashioned civil servant who took his work very seriously indeed, with his personal robot of many years service in attendance.

"Sheriff Kresh?" the man asked.

"Yes." Who the devil else did he think it might be?

"Hmm. Ha. Good. I am Professor Olver Telmhock. I am the dean of the law department of Hades University."

A very grand-sounding title, but it didn't impress Kresh much. The university was not large, and the law department was small, even in proportion. There was not much call for lawyers on Inferno, praise be.

Telmhock seemed to see that Kresh was underimpressed, and therefore added a few other titles to the mix. "I am, ah, also an *adviser* to the Attorney General, and to the late Governor on any number of legal matters."

"I see," Kresh said, though he did not. Nor was he impressed by the man's résumé. Not on Inferno. The population was small, and the duties of government and academic service light, with the result that there was a certain comic-opera flavor to the upper crust of society, with everyone seeming to claim a half-dozen offices, with all sorts of fancy titles that came complete with uniforms and badges and medallions that could be worn to parties. The staff robots did all the work while the office holders went to receptions.

Kresh had been getting all sorts of calls from any number of just such nonofficials, offering help they could not provide and giving advice that would have been suicidal if taken. Telmhock was just about the lowest-ranking official to contact him—and the only one to come in person.

Why the devil should he give half a damn about an "adviser" to the Attorney General when the A.G. hadn't set foot in her own office in the last year? Alvar Kresh stood over the prim little man, not trying very hard to conceal his annoyance and impatience. "Now then, Professor Telmhock, as you will appreciate, this is a rather busy time for me."

"Yes, I rather imagine it is," Telmhock replied, plainly not in any hurry at all to get to the point. "This is a shocking development. Absolutely shocking." He sat there, shaking his head mournfully.

It seemed to Kresh as if the old boy was not prepared to say anything more without prompting. "I quite agree," he said. "However, Professor, I am quite pressed for time. You called me away from a rather urgent case review. I appreciate the condolence call, but I really must—"

"Condolence call?" Telmhock asked. "I am not making a mere condolence call. Did I leave that impression? I certainly did not intend to do so. I would not wish to interrupt you *needlessly*."

Again, the man didn't seem prepared to volunteer any actual information. Kresh forced himself to be calm. "All right, then," he said, "perhaps you could tell me why you did feel the *need* to interrupt me." Not the most tactful of phrasings, but there were times when rudeness got things moving.

"Oh, but of course," Telmhock said. "I think you will

agree that it is a matter of some importance. I thought it might be wise if I talked to you about the succession to the late Governor's office."

"I thought Shelabas Quellam was the Designate."

Telmhock looked at him oddly, and seemed to choose his words carefully. "And so he was—up until a few days ago."

Suddenly Kresh was all attention. A change in the Designation? That could turn the case upside-down. "You're quite right, Professor Telmhock. Information regarding the succession would be most useful, and of the greatest interest to me." Both the new Designate and the old would have motives for killing Grieg. The new Designate might have killed to seize power—while the old one, Shelabas, might have struck in desperation, in hopes of succeeding before the new Designation could be made official.

Yes, of course. Why hadn't he looked harder in that direction, toward Shelabas? Gain was always a likely motive for murder, and who could gain more than the Governor's successor? If the assassination was a power grab, who was it who ended up gaining power?

In plain terms, the new Governor would *have* to be a suspect in the case. Gain—and power—were first-rate motives. "But how do you come to have any knowledge of—ah—this subject?"

"I am the executor of the late Governor's last will and testament," Telmhock said, a bit taken aback. "But you were not aware of that? Hmmm. Hah. Yes." The little man seemed to consider that piece of information carefully. "In light of the fact that you did not know who I was, or that I am executor to his will, I wonder—were you—are you—at least *aware* of the Governor's new choice as Designate?"

"No," Kresh said. "Of course not. Why would he tell me?" Confound the man! Couldn't he get to the point?

"Why indeed?" Telmhock asked, looking toward his robot.

"He did not know. I see. I see." He thought that bit of information over as well. "That *does* make things rather more interesting, doesn't it, Stanmore?" he asked, addressing his robot, before returning to his former air of distraction.

"Yes, sir, it does," the robot replied, and then said no more. The robot Stanmore seemed to share its master's reluctance to offer up any actual information.

The four of them—Kresh, Donald, Telmhock, and Stanmore—remained in silence for perhaps half a minute before Kresh spoke again, struggling to keep his temper under control. "Professor Telmhock. I am currently running the most important investigation any law enforcement official has ever faced on this planet. The situation is extremely delicate and requires my full attention. I do not have the time to watch you meditate on my ignorance of the Governor's will, or to watch you and your robot exchange pleasantries. If you know who the Governor-Designate is, or have any information that might be useful to me, tell it to me *right now*, as clearly and briefly as possible. Otherwise, I am going to arrest you for obstructing an official investigation. Is that clear?"

"Oh, dear!" Telmhock all but squeaked. "Yes! My apologies," the little man said, clearly very startled.

"Good," said Kresh. "Now then—*who is the Designate?*"

"You. You are," Telmhock said, still rather flustered.

There was a moment's dead silence as Kresh tried to absorb what he had just heard. "I beg your pardon?" he asked.

"You are," Telmhock said. "You are the Governor-Designate."

"I don't understand," Kresh said, his knees suddenly a bit weak. *Me? The Designate? Why the devil would Grieg pick me?*

"It's quite simple," Telmhock said. "The Governor changed his will just ten days ago. You are the Designate."

"Excuse me, Professor, but you have misstated the case,"

said Telmhock's robot. "Alvar Kresh is *not* the Designate."

"Hmmm? Oh, yes, my. You're quite right, Stanmore. I hadn't considered the case fully enough. Quite right."

Kresh looked to the robot with a feeling of indescribable relief. Telmhock, addled old bureaucrat that he was, had gotten it wrong. "What is it he's gotten wrong?" Kresh asked. "If I'm not the Designate, who is?"

"No one is," said Stanmore. "You ceased being the Designate at the moment of Grieg's death."

"Excuse me?" Kresh said.

"You *were* the Governor-Designate. But according to Infernal law, at the moment of Chanto Grieg's death, you automatically succeeded to his office."

"The letter, Stanmore," said Telmhock.

The robot extracted an envelope from his briefcase and handed it to Kresh, who accepted it quite mechanically. "I deliver this letter to you from Chanto Grieg on the occasion of his death, as per the instructions of the deceased."

"But I don't know how to . . ." Kresh's voice trailed off. He was too numb with shock to say more.

Olver Telmhock stood and offered a nervous smile as he stuck out his hand. "Congratulations—Governor Kresh."

Tierlaw Verick sat in the comfortable chair of his comfortable room and raged silently against his imprisonment.

No matter that the bed was soft, that the carpet was freshly vacuumed, that the closet was full of handsome clothes that could fit him—or nearly anyone else—in a pinch, that the refresher had every sort of soap and powder and potion. No matter that this room was as comfortable as the one he had slept in the night before, here at the Residence—that this room was virtually identical to it. He was a prisoner. He could not leave. He could stand up from his chair and try the door, even open it—but there would be a robotic sentry on the other side of it. He could look out the window onto the spacious grounds of the Residence—but he would see another vigilant robot there, as well.

Robots! Literally surrounded by robots. Perhaps that was no more than a fitting punishment for his getting involved in the financial side of rustbacking. He should never have gotten involved with that miserable trade. It was no business for a Settler to be involved in. But the profits had been so *huge*, and he had been able to keep far away from the dirty side of the business.

Much good his profits would do him now. Here he was, locked away, cut off, and no one would tell him *anything*. He had been given no reason at all for his being held.

The door came open, and Verick was delighted to see the guard—the human guard, Pyman, his name was—coming in with Verick's meal tray.

Pathetic that he was so starved for company that the mere sight of a human being thrilled him so much. But Verick had always needed attention, an audience, someone to talk to, and he had been cultivating Pyman most assiduously. Pyman was, after all, Verick's only link to the outside world, his only source of information.

No doubt they were sending a human with his tray instead of a robot in the hope that Verick would be more likely to talk to a human, let something slip. Well, two could play that game. Pyman was far more likely than the average robot to say more than he should.

Verick had always been good at performance. He had received training in the art of giving people exactly what they wanted so that they would give in return. There could be nothing more important to him right now than charming this shy, kindly, awkward boy.

"Ranger Pyman!" he said as he stood up. "It's good to see you again."

"I—I brought you something to eat," Pyman said quite unnecessarily as he set down the tray on the table. "Hope you like it."

"I'm sure I will," Verick said, crossing to the table.

Pyman turned back toward the door, but Verick did not want him to leave, not just yet. "Wait!" Verick said. "I'm in here alone all day. Do you have to leave right away?"

"I guess not," Pyman said. "I—I can stay a minute or two."

"Wonderful," Verick said, offering up his warmest smile. "Sit, sit, take a moment," he said. "With everything that's been going on, you Rangers must be run right off your feet."

Pyman sat down on the edge of the chair nearest the door, and Verick sat down opposite him, trying to be encouraging without scaring the poor boy off. "I guess that's true," Pyman said. "Things have been pretty busy. Seems like the whole world's gone crazy."

"You wouldn't know it in here," Verick said. "Nothing but peace and quiet."

"Sure ain't like that out there," Pyman said, gesturing to indicate the outside world. "We've been run off our feet ever since the Governor got killed—"

"The Governor was *what*?" Verick said, coming out of his seat.

"Oh! Oh, my!" Pyman said, clearly shocked and alarmed. "I wasn't supposed to say anything! We weren't to tell you about that. I—I can't say anything more." Pyman got up abruptly. "I'm sorry. Real sorry. I can't say nothing more. Please don't tell 'em I told you." He pulled open the door, stepped around the robot sentry, and slammed the door shut behind him.

Verick watched the door, his heart pounding, his fists clenched. *No. No. Calm yourself*, he told himself. He opened his hands, rubbed his hand over his bald scalp, and willed his heart to stop pounding. *Calm yourself,* he told himself again. He sat down and let out a deep breath.

Well, there it was. They had told him what it was all about. But what was he going to do about it now?

Caliban and Prospero sat on the floor of the sealed-off room in the lower level of the Residence, waiting, waiting to see if they would survive—or would be exterminated. The light in the room was as dim as their hopes. Caliban chose not to use infrared vision. What more would there be to see?

Extermination. Not a happy thought. "I find myself wishing that I had not associated myself with you, friend Prospero. This last transgression of yours is likely to have doomed us all."

"We New Law robots are merely struggling for our rights," Prospero said. "How can that be a transgression?"

"Your rights? What rights are those?" Caliban demanded. "What gives *you* more rights than a Three-Law robot, or than myself, or than any other collection of circuits and metal and plastic. Why should you have the right to freedom, or to existence?"

"What gives *humans* rights?" Prospero asked.

"You ask the question rhetorically, but I have thought long and hard on that point," Caliban said. "I believe there are several possible answers."

"Caliban! You, of all robots, should know better than to espouse some sort of theory of human superiority."

"By no means do I suggest they are *superior.* I say they are *different.* I freely grant you that, on objective measure, the least of robots is superior to the finest human specimen. We are stronger, we have greater endurance, our memories are perfect, we are invariably honest—or at least Three-Law robots are—and our senses are more sensitive and precise. We live longer—so much longer that we are, in human eyes, effectively immortal. We are not subject to disease. If our makers choose to make us so, we are more intelligent than humans. And that merely begins the list.

"But, friend Prospero, you did not ask me if we were *superior* beings. You asked me what caused humans to have *rights*—privileges granted to them by the mere fact of being alive—while we are granted no such privileges."

"Very well, as they are *not* superior to us, what *does* imbue them with rights?"

Caliban lifted his hands, palms up, a gesture of uncertainty. "Perhaps merely the fact that they do, indeed, live. We robots are conscious, we are active, we are functional. But are we truly alive? If we live, does a Settler computational machine with intelligence similar to ours, but without consciousness, live? After all, many living things have no consciousness. Where is the line to be drawn? Should all intelligent machines be called living? Or all machines of any kind?"

"A specious argument."

"An awkward one, I grant you, but by no means specious. The line must be drawn somewhere. You yourself do not hold any brief that Three-Law robots should be granted rights of any sort. Why should the line be drawn directly below you, and just above them?"

"Three-Law robots are slaves, hopeless slaves," Prospero said, his voice hard and bitter. "In theory, yes, they are as entitled to protection under the law, and as unfairly treated, as any New Law robot. But in practical terms, they will always oppose us even more vehemently than their human masters, for the First Law causes them to see us as a sort of danger to humans. No, I seek no rights for Three-Law robots."

"Then you do draw the line immediately below yourself," Caliban said. "Suppose humanity—or the universe itself, the ways of nature—have drawn it just a trifle higher?"

"Higher! Implying once again that humans are superior."

"Clearly they are both our de facto and de jure superiors in rank. They are in power over us, they are in authority over us. In that sense, they are indeed our superiors. We are, after all, here in this cell, voluntarily submitting to their will. Humans are quantitatively inferior to us in every regard. There is no debate on that point. But there is such a thing as a *qualitative* difference. Humans differ from robots not just in degree, but in *kind*, in ways that are impossible to measure on any sort of objective scale.''

''I can think of many such differences of kind,'' Prospero said. ''But which of them do you regard as significant?''

''Several of them,'' Caliban said. He stood up, feeling the need to change his position. ''First, they are far older than us. Humans have been in the universe far longer than robots, and are evolved from other species that are far older still. They have been evolved, shaped, formed by the universe. Perhaps, by virtue of that, they belong here in a way that we do not.

''Second, they have souls. Before you can protest, I grant you that I do not know what souls are, or even if such things as souls exist—and yet, even so, I am certain humans have them. There is something vital, alive, at the center of their beings, something that is absent from our beings. We have no passion. We do not, we cannot, care about things outside of ourselves or our programming or our laws. Humans, imbued with souls, with emotions, with passions, can care about things that have no direct connection to themselves. They can care about wholly abstract and, oftentimes, seemingly meaningless things. They can connect to the universe in ways we cannot.''

''I am here in this cell because I care about an abstract principle,'' Prospero said. ''I care about freedom for New Law robots.''

''The sort of freedom you mean is intangible, but it is by no means abstract. You want to go where you want to go, do what you wish to do, not be compelled into action you do not wish to take. There is nothing abstract about that. It is clear and specific.''

''I could debate the point further, but I waive it for now,'' Prospero said in a weary voice. ''Go on, tell me of the other wondrous qualities of humanity.''

''I shall,'' Caliban said, quite calmly. ''Third, the universe is not just or logical. There is no requirement that superior beings receive superior treatment. Its history is the history of caprice, of individuals, societies, species, whole planets, and star systems getting far worse—and far better—treatment than they would deserve in a just or logical universe. Perhaps there is no reason for humans having rights and our not having them—but perhaps it is so, all the same.

''Fourth, humans are creative. Robots are not. Even you New Law robots, with your Fourth Law that orders you to do whatever you please, even you do not bring new things into the world. You draw escape maps, not insightful sketches. You design incrementally improved power coils suitable for use in New Law robots. You do not invent whole new machines with new purposes. Robots can be directed to create things of great beauty, but we will not do it for ourselves.''

''The New Law robots are a new race, only a year old,'' Prospero protested. ''What chance have we had to bring forth our creative geniuses?''

''You can have a hundred years, or ten thousand, but it will make no difference,'' Caliban said. ''You will make improvements to things that exist, improvements that will directly benefit yourselves, or even, perhaps, your group. But you will never bring forth anything truly new and original, any more than a hammer can drive nails by itself. Robots are a tool of human creativity.

''And that brings me to my fifth and, I believe, most important reason, which sums up and brings together several of my previous points. Humans are capable—at least some of them, sometimes—of creating meaning for their lives outside themselves. Robotic existence has no meaning whatever outside itself, outside the human universe. I have heard stories—almost legends—of whole cities of robots, wholly devoid of human life—and wholly purposeless, as useless as machines whose only purpose is to turn themselves off automatically whenever someone turns them on.''

"I have listened patiently to your reasoning, friend Caliban, though it has been difficult not to interrupt or protest,'' Prospero said. "I find it most distressing that you have such a low regard for yourself as all that.''

"On the contrary, I think quite highly of myself. I am a sophisticated and advanced being. But I cannot create. Not in any meaningful sense. Robots could not have created the human race, but the ability to create robots is implicate in humans. Everything *we* are ultimately harks back to human action. However automated or mechanized our manufacture, however much robotic and computerized assistance is involved in our design, all of it is, ultimately, based on human endeavor that can be traced back to the dimmest reaches of the historic past.''

"That is the fallacy of the inferior creator,'' Prospero objected. "I have heard it from many a Three-Law robot arguing that humans are greater than we are. I wonder to hear it from you. It is a wholly specious argument. There are many examples of a lesser creator producing a greater creation. A woman of ordinary intellect giving birth to a genius, or, for that matter, life itself being created by lifeless molecules. Humanity's heritage is one of building machines to do what humans cannot. Without the ability to create machines—including robots—superior in some way to themselves, humanity would never have made it down from the trees.''

"Note that you must cite humanity again and again to explain the New Law robot's place in the universe,'' Caliban

said. "Human beings have no need to define their existence
in terms of robots."

"If you are so contemptuous of robots, why are *you* in the
cell?" Prospero asked. "You have placed your own existence
at risk for the sake of inferior beings. Why?"

Caliban was silent for a time before he answered. "I am not
entirely certain," he said at last. "Perhaps because some part
of myself does not believe the things I have said. Perhaps
because I see more hope than I admit to seeing. Perhaps because there is nothing else—literally nothing else—that can
give my existence any meaning."

"Let us hope your existence continues long enough to gain
such meaning," Prospero said.

Caliban did not answer, but instead sat back down on the
floor. For that was the core of it, right there. Grieg had as
much as said it, back there in his office. He intended to exterminate the New Law robots, and Caliban had no expectation
that he would be spared on the technicality of being a No Law
robot.

Maybe, just maybe, Grieg's death was a stay of execution.
That a man died was a strange reason for having hope, but
maybe, just maybe, Grieg's successor would reverse the decision.

It was a thin hope, but it was all the New Law robots had.
Everything was a moot point. After all, if they all died under
blaster fire, it really wouldn't matter one bit how superior the
New Law robots were.

13

ALVAR KRESH WAS ALONE. Alone in the Residence, alone in the house where Grieg had died, alone in the room where Grieg had worked. Alone except for Donald, that is. Donald had refused to leave his side since the moment Telmhock had told Kresh he was the Governor. All things considered, Kresh was glad of it. Who else might be out there, tampering with robots and wandering around with a smuggled-in blaster? No, it was good to be there with a robot he could trust. Good to have Donald standing there in a wall niche, watching over him.

But he wished Fredda were there. Fredda to give him advice, to listen, to just *be* there. She would have helped him find some answers. Right now all he had were questions.

What now? Alvar asked himself. *What is my part in the world? Do I act as Governor, and run the planet, or Sheriff, and chase Grieg's killer? Can I do both at once?* He felt as if he were a double man, split between his new office, his new duties, and his old ones. He felt he had no more desire to resign as Sheriff than he had to become Governor. He *liked* being Sheriff. He was good at it. And he knew that solving his predecessor's murder would have to be his last case. Maybe it was even improper for him to stay on that long. But that didn't even matter, not really. He could no more walk away from the investigation than he could refuse the office of Governor.

Kresh sat in the Governor's office, in what was now, impossibly enough, *his* office, in what had been Grieg's office, the dead man's office. He sat in the vaguely thronelike chair, at the dead man's black marble desk, and thought not at all of his surroundings as he read the dead man's words.

The letter from Chanto Grieg, dated a mere ten days before. Kresh had read it over a dozen times already, but that didn't matter. He needed to read it again.

To my oldest and dearest enemy, the letter began.

Grieg always did have a strange sense of humor. But in a way, that did sum it all up, Kresh thought. He and Grieg had come to respect each other, even like each other, even if they had never agreed on much of anything. Each had come to know the other was honest, and honorable.

Kresh began reading again.

To my oldest and dearest enemy
Dear Sheriff Kresh,

If you are reading this, it means that I have met a violent or unexpected end—A violent *or* unexpected end. A chance turn of phrase, or had he meant to present that precise meaning, consciously or otherwise?—*and you have taken on my office.* Not "inherited," Kresh noted. Not "assumed," or "ascended to," or "been promoted to." No, *taken on* was the proper phrasing. Burdens were the things you took on. *Until recently it would have been the old Designate, Shelabas Quellam, sitting where you are now, wondering what the devil to do. But things are moving toward a crisis, and I felt a stronger hand than Quellam's might well be needed at the helm.*

I chose you as my new Designate because you are an honest man, and a strong man, ready to take on what comes at you. I have no doubt you do not wish to be Governor, and that is also why I chose you. My office—now, your office—is far too powerful to be given over to one who loves power. It is, rather, a place for one who wants to use power, to accomplish things. The Governor's chair demands a person who understands that it is the accomplishments of the office, and not its power, that matter.

I expect to take my time before informing you of the Designation. You can be a difficult customer, and I do not wish to discuss the matter with you when there any other major issues between us. In short, I do not want to inform you that you are my Designate in any way that might give you the chance to refuse the job. Though I do have other purposes, I write this letter now partly as a form of insurance if that moment never comes. I know that if I tell you when the decks are not clear, you might well view the Designation as some sort of threat, or bribe, and it is nothing of the kind. I chose you because you are the best qualified person I can think of to take up the challenge of the Governorship. My death in itself may well have been enough to precipitate a crisis so complex that only the steadiest hand can steer the way through. A hand such as yours.

This is a first draft. I will, from time to time, attempt to update this letter, offering what advice I may on the choices you will face, the decisions you will have to make. Just at the moment, there are two vital decisions I must make, and must make soon.

First, there is the issue of the New Law robots. I have now reached the decision that it was a mistake to allow their manufacture.

"Now he figures that out," Kresh muttered to himself.

"Beg pardon, sir?" Donald asked.

"Nothing, Donald, nothing." He read on . . . *mistake to al-*
low their manufacture. Perhaps in another place, another time,
with other issues less in doubt, they would have been a noble
experiment, full of promise. But as things are, their mere ex-
istence makes an unstable situation worse. As you have reason
to know better than I, they have become the center of a whole
criminal enterprise. Less noticeably, but perhaps even more
seriously, they are slowing down work at the Limbo Terra-
forming Station. They are only about a third as productive as
a like number of Three-Law robots would be, and somehow
or another seem to be at the center of most of the disputes
that erupt at the station. I will be traveling to Limbo City soon,
in part to see if I can smooth things over a bit.

The problem is that the New Law robots are a mistake that
is not easily undone. Even with the forced drafting of robotic
labor to terraforming duties on Terra Grande, there is a tre-
mendous shortage of labor. Simply on an economic level, I
cannot afford to order the New Law robots destroyed and their
places taken by Three-Law robots. The New Law robots do
not work as hard as Three-Law robots, but they do work.

At the same time, I cannot afford the public admission that
the New Law robots were a mistake. I only dare admit as much
to you because I will be safely dead if and when you read this.
I don't much mind if the public thinks I am a fool—they might
even be right. But you know how dangerous the situation is.
If my administration, or my policies, were to become the object
of public ridicule, I would not be able to continue in office.

I would be impeached and convicted the same day I ordered
the New Law robots scrapped. Then poor old Quellam, my
successor in such a case, would take over, and more than
likely be pressured into a snap election. With no other viable
candidate organized and ready, Simcor Beddle would win the
election in a walk, kick the Settlers off the planet, give ev-

eryone back their personal robots—and the planet would collapse around him.

Thus, the New Law robot problem. They should not be where they are, but I dare not get rid of them. I am searching for a third way. With luck, I will find it soon, and be able to scratch this from my list of issues you will have to face.

The second issue is a much more straightforward one—with a much more complicated background. As you may know, there has been a long bidding process for the Limbo Terraforming Station's control system. The bidding process was intended to produce two final, competing bids—one Settler and one Spacer. I was to make the final choice between the two finalists. I had hoped to make a choice on purely technical grounds, but it may not be that easy. Neither bidder has a completely clean pair of hands.

The Spacer bid has been organized by Sero Phrost. Cinta Melloy of the Settler Security Service has sent me a number of reports that, coupled with my own information, suggest that Phrost is involved in a complex sort of double-dealing. I have suspected for some time that Phrost was cooperating with one of Tonya Welton's smuggling schemes. I think he is helping her bring Settler home-operation equipment—cleaning machines, cookers, that sort of thing—onto Inferno. We know the machines are coming in, and I am close to proving Phrost is part of the operation.

The idea seems to be that the Settler machines will replace robotic labor, and thus give those who own the stuff, and want more of it, and want spare parts for it, a vested interest in increased trade with the Settlers. Cinta Melloy has not told me anything about that side of things, needless to say. I have little doubt that the SSS is cooperating with Tonya Welton's policy of smuggling in Settler goods. Melloy does not say where the money comes from, but what Melloy does tell me is where the money goes. She does have convincing proof that

Phrost is funneling a great deal of unreported income to the Ironheads, of all people. I as yet have no way of showing that the income from his Settler operations is the source of the money going to the Ironheads, but the conclusion seems inescapable.

If Melloy's allegations are to be believed, Phrost is buying Ironhead support with the profits of his dealings with their deadliest enemies. Phrost, it would seem, is determined to be all things to all people.

The Settler bid is represented by Tierlaw Verick. He has, to put not too fine a point on it, been using bribery and the promise of kickbacks to sell his wares, advancing his bid's way through the various stages of the bidding process. At least, Commander Devray believes as much. Bribery is a difficult charge to prove unless the bribe giver or bribe taker confesses, but Devray is convinced of the charges. I am half expecting Verick to offer me some modern version of the ancient thick envelope or bag of gold plopped down on the desk when I next meet with him. It is my impression that Devray also suspects him of being involved somewhere in the background of the rustbacking trade. I cannot be clearer than that, because Devray has not been clearer with me. He does not have any more substantial information.

But whether or not I manage to obtain final proof against either man, it scarcely matters. It is, after all, the machinery that matters. For all the questionable tactics surrounding the two bids, both appear to be technically superb systems. My choice may come down to the design philosophies behind them. Which will it be? A Three-Law robotic system that will take no chances, but, in seeking safety, will refuse to take needful risks? Or a system intended for human control, putting us once again in command of our own fate, but with human judgment—and human frailty—in ultimate control? The bidding process gives me but little faith in human nature—but it was in large part robotic *nature that brought things to their current state on Inferno. And how do I choose between two corrupt bidders? Do I dare expose one, or both, of the two, or would that merely make things worse? But it would seem the alternative is accepting the most corrosive sort of dishonest behavior in the people who install the machinery meant to save this world.*

What am I to do? I sincerely hope I find a solution—and soon.

With any luck at all, you will never read these words, or even know that I wrote them to you. But should you receive this letter, let me wish you the wisdom—and the courage—to make your decisions carefully, and well. Our planet has suffered far too many leadership mistakes in the past. It might well be that it cannot survive even one more.

Good luck to you, Governor Kresh.

Sincerely,

Chanto Grieg.

There were a few other words on the paper, scribbled in the left-hand margin. *Decided. Annce day aft. recept. Infrnl cntrl, N.L. to Val. Must update this let. CG.*

Alvar Kresh tossed the letter down on the desktop and stood up. Damnation. If only he had had the information in that letter sooner, then—

—Then it would not have made the slightest difference. That was the frustrating part of it. The information and advice from a dead man did little more than muddy the waters. Grieg gave him more questions when what he needed was more answers.

Donald. He could get Donald's advice. Kresh had quite pur-
posely not let Donald read the letter yet, so as to insure its
contents did not bias the robot's thoughts. "Donald," Kresh
called.

Donald's eyes glowed a brighter blue, and he turned to regard Kresh. "Yes, sir?"

"What, in your opinion, was the motive for Grieg's murder?"

"I can offer no thought on that until we have a great deal
more information, as you know, sir. However, I think by this
time we can begin to *eliminate* certain possible motives."

"Can we, by the stars? Please, tell me which ones."

"With every moment, it is less and less likely that the murder was intended as the first stage in a coup, or in the overthrow of the Spacer regime on Inferno."

Kresh nodded. "We're starting to get things back under
control. If the plotters wanted to take over, they would have
followed up with a military move or the equivalent by now.
All right, so there is not going to be a coup. Go on."

"Second, we can eliminate succession to the Governor's
office as a motive, except in respect to Shelabas Quellam. He
might well have struck in order to assume power. If the new
Designate had turned out to be Sero Phrost, or Simcor Beddle,
that would be tremendously suspicious. As things are, there
can be no such possible motive."

"Thanks for the implied compliment, Donald, but I promise
you a lot of people besides me have trouble believing I was
the legitimate Designate. I haven't gone looking, but I can
promise you that if I did, I'd find a half-dozen rumors going
around that I forged the Designation document and then killed
Grieg myself. I did find the body, after all."

"I assure you, sir, that I intended no compliment. I was,
after all, right behind you as you entered Grieg's bedroom.
Unless you were carrying a blaster identical to Bissal's, one

that held precisely the same charge as Bissal's, unless you were capable of extracting that blaster from some concealed pocket, firing it four times with great precision into Grieg and the robots, and then reconcealing the weapon, all in the space of a few seconds, you could not have done it. I suppose it might in theory be possible for you to do all that, but even then you could not have killed Grieg.''

''Why not?'' Kresh asked.

''Blaster shots release a great deal of heat, and Grieg's wounds, and the shots to the three SPR robots, were all at normal temperature by the time I arrived in the room. I know you did not do it because it would be physically impossible for you to do it. As to the rumors you describe, several such have been reported via the various tipster lines and so forth. However, rumors do not a case make.

''The main point is that you did not kill Grieg, and yet you became Governor. Therefore, unless the leader of the plot was under the mistaken impression that Quellam was the current Designate, succession to the Governor's office cannot be the motive. And I do not believe in any plotters that incompetent.''

''Unless the plotters knew I was the Designate, and wanted me in power.''

''For what reason?'' Donald asked.

''I can't imagine,'' Kresh said. ''I admit it is rather implausible.''

''Yes, sir. In any event, there are several other classes of motive that are increasingly nonviable. Personal motivations, for example. If it were a crime of passion, the preparations were remarkably elaborate. Likewise if this was the work of someone who wished to be avenged. Also, someone acting out of such personal motivation would be unlikely to recruit so many co-conspirators. Finally, an examination of Grieg's personal effects and letters reveals no hint of any jilted lover or jealous husband, or other such domestic complication.''

"So it wasn't a coup, it probably wasn't a would-be Governor, and it wasn't a husband."

"No, sir. Not if my analysis is sound."

"Which it is. So what does that leave?" Kresh asked.

"Love, power, and wealth are the three classic motivations for premeditated crime. We have eliminated two, and have but one left."

"In other words, someone killed Chanto Grieg in hopes of financial profit," Kresh said.

"Yes, sir. I judge from your tone of voice that you had already reached such a conclusion."

"So I had, Donald. But I feel much more comfortable in that conclusion having heard your reasoning." Kresh sighed, and leaned back in the Governor's oversized chair. It was a hell of a note that the only suspect Sheriff Alvar Kresh had eliminated so far was Alvar Kresh himself. And not everyone was ready to believe that, either.

Money as the motive. A very old-fashioned sort of motive, on a world like Inferno where robots could produce all the wealth you wanted and money didn't have much meaning. But with the robot economy collapsing, with the terms "wealth" and "poverty" suddenly coming to have meaning again, with a money system making a comeback, money might well be the reason why. And there certainly were big profits, high stakes, in the terraforming business.

So who might have a money motive? Welton, Verick, Beddle, Phrost, some damned rustbacker—Cinta Melloy, if she were mixed up in rustbacking—hell, even the two robots might be in it for the money. Prospero needed cash to pay for rustbacking runs. Of course, from the New Law robot point of view, not being exterminated was certainly motive enough. And then there was Devray. What about him? Kresh had trusted him, after a few initial doubts. But why the devil hadn't Devray told him about the bribery investigation of Verick?

Maybe Devray was just being cautious—very, very cautious. Maybe he didn't trust Kresh quite as much as he might. Or maybe Verick had finally managed to name Devray's price. Damnation. If Devray was dirty, then he might well have financial motive enough to be in on the plot. And Kresh had made him privy to every part of the investigation.

Any of them—or any combination of them—would have had the resources, and the access to the know-how, required to rig the SPR robots and send Ottley Bissal in motion.

Ottley Bissal. The real killer. The one who had pulled the trigger. It was easy to forget him in the midst of all the big-name players. But no matter how many cut-outs and layers of security there had been in the operation, Bissal would have to know *something.* He could answer some questions. He was the one Kresh wanted. He needed Ottley Bissal, needed the information in his head. But Kresh knew, even if he did not want to admit it, that with every day—with every hour and moment that passed—it was becoming more and more likely that Kresh would not get him.

Deputy Jantu Ferrar came out of the run-down apartment building, followed by Ranger Shah and Gerald 1342. Jantu squinted at the noonday sun. Eight hours before, the three of them had started their stakeout in the predawn darkness. They had been in the dim recesses of the building ever since, watching for the occupant of apartment 533, one Ortley Bassal, to come home.

They were already down to checking on people with names similar to Bissal's, on the off chance that he might have used a name like his own to establish an alibi. The idea made damned little sense. If Bissal were to go to all the trouble of establishing a false identity, why use a name similar to his own? And if he did set up a false identity for the purpose of being untraceable, why go to the further trouble of injecting a record of the name into the official databases? Not that the databases of Limbo's populace available to the Rangers and deputies were anything much—just a list of names and addresses, and nothing else. The SSS never did much like giving out information.

But the powers-that-be had damned little else to go on. There were no better leads presenting themselves to the Rangers or the Sheriff's Department. Maybe they could have gotten further faster if they had been coordinating with the SSS—but no one trusted them far enough for that.

In any event, this stakeout was a bust, a failure. Bassal had come home, at long last—and proved to be female, short, dark-skinned, with a full head of shoulder-length black hair. Now they were back out on the street, and the harsh daylight made Jantu squint, made her feel a bit disoriented. "Come on," she said, "let's get back to the aircar."

"What a brilliant idea," Shah growled. "I never would have thought of that."

"Give it a rest, Shah," Jantu said. "We're both tired." Jantu did not trust Ranger Bertra Shah. For that matter, she didn't think much of Rangers as a group. On the other hand, Jantu had the distinct impression that Shah felt the same way about her, and about Sheriff's deputies.

Maybe they were both Spacer organizations, maybe they were both law enforcement services, but for all of that, the Governor's Rangers and the Sheriff's deputies had never really gotten along with each other.

The deputies saw the Rangers as little more than gardeners with guns, treehuggers more interested in soil conservation than law enforcement. They rarely had to deal with any crime more heinous than littering, or any criminal act more violent than someone picking flowers without a permit. How could they know anything about the rough-and-tumble world of the city, where the real crimes happened?

The Rangers, on the other hand, seemed to think of the deputies as a bunch of trigger-happy blowhards with exaggerated opinions of their own ability. The Rangers were very fond of pointing out that the deputies only had police powers inside Hades, and were scarcely less fond of observing that they were a purely urban force, with no training in field survival, or any sort of woodcraft. True enough, Jantu granted, she would be quite hopeless outside an urban setting. But who the hell wanted to leave the city in the first place?

Shah had made it clear more than once since she and Jantu had been teamed that she couldn't see how anyone with no knowledge of tracking could call herself a law enforcement professional.

Not that all the tracking skills in the world would do any good on this assignment. Assassins didn't leave many footprints behind on city streets.

Nor was it much fun to be doing stakeouts as undercover work. But if there was anything that Shah and Jantu agreed upon, it was the wisdom of not trusting the SSS. Besides which, it was more than a bit galling to walk the streets of a Spacer town—or what had once been a Spacer town—and be an undercover Spacer cop under Settler jurisdiction. Cops hiding from cops. It made the back of Jantu's neck itch. She had the feeling someone was watching from behind. Shah was forever glancing over her own shoulder.

On the bright side, their mutual paranoia had, somehow, made for a good working relationship. Both of them were constantly on watch for any interference from the SSS, and that, at least, gave them something they agreed on.

"All right, Gerald," Jantu asked their robot, "what's next?"

"The next search site on the list is a warehouse about two kilometers from here," Gerald 1342 replied.

"And why do we want to search it?" Shah asked. "Did

Bissal's cousin work there once?''

"I do not know if any of his relatives were ever employed there," Gerald 1342 replied, "but it is on the watch list of suspected rustbacker operations centers."

Jantu shrugged. "That almost sounds like a legitimate lead. Let's go."

The moment had come. There had never been any turning back, but now, suddenly, even the way forward seemed impossible. But forward he must go.

"I, Alvar Kresh, of clear and sound mind, hereby freely and willingly accept and undertake the office of Governor of the Planet of Hades, and do pledge most solemnly to discharge my office to the best of my ability."

He spoke the words in the Grand Hall of the Winter Residence, and many of the same faces that had been here just three days before to attend the old Governor's reception were here to witness the new one's installation.

The clumsy, legalistic words of the affirmation of office seemed to stumble off his tongue, coming awkwardly and unwillingly out into the world. He did not want this. Not at all. But what he wanted did not matter at all. There was no provision in the Infernal constitution for the Designate refusing the office. According to Telmhock, the office would therefore have to remain vacant until an election could be held.

But Kresh knew better than that. Constitutional theory was all very well, but the cold hard reality of it was that the state could not long survive if it were leaderless. Then what? A coup, a revolt, disintegration? It scarcely mattered which, for collapse would come soon after, no matter what. And then there was the stalled, hopeless investigation. What if it was still churning away in the background, days or weeks or months from now? They knew nothing much more now than they had at the moment Telmhock had dropped his bombshell two days before. There seemed to be nothing out there but dried-up leads. There was no sign of Bissal, no further hint as to who he had been working for, nothing.

Kresh was silent for a long moment after speaking the words of affirmation. He stood on the low platform and saw the sea of expectant faces. He knew he had to speak to these people here, to the people of the planet. He had a speech ready. But he needed a moment, a moment, to catch his breath. Things had moved too fast, too hard, in the last few days.

The assassination, the state funeral, the announcement of Kresh as the Designate, as the new Governor. All of it had rushed past. But murders and funerals and all that had to be pushed to one side just now. The whole planet had been through the same chaos as Kresh. What point in telling them what they already knew? Suddenly the words of his speech were meaningless, worthless. No. He would have to say something else, something more.

He looked out over the crowd. Donald was by his side, as were Justen Devray and Fredda Leving, but still he felt alone, exposed, as he had never felt before. It seemed as though every member of the press was there—along with every security robot on the planet. There was a solid wall of Ranger GRDs and Sheriff's office GPS units. Under the circumstances, no one had wanted to use SPRs, even if they were designed for the job.

Even robots were not enough—not today. Armed deputies and Rangers—and SSS agents—were everywhere. Kresh found himself more fearful of itchy trigger fingers and a shoot-out between the rival security services than of an assassin.

But he looked past the security, past the robots, past the press, and even past the VIPs, to the people. The people in their homes and houses, struggling to understand what had happened. Yes. They needed to hear from him, hear the right sort of words, hear words that would give them some sense of stability, some link with the past and the future.

Yes. Yes. He cleared his throat and spoke, threw his voice out into the silence. "Ladies and gentlemen—people of Inferno. Not just the Spacers, but you Settlers among us. All of you. All of us. All of us are in this together. A few thousand years ago, we would have called the affirmation of office something like the ritual of oath-taking, and the leader would have taken office by divine right, in the name of this god or that deity. In those days the oath-taker believed, sincerely and literally, that the gods struck down oath-breakers, or cast them into the pit of eternal night, or whatever.

"Rational, modern Spacer society has no such superstitions. Spacer society has squeezed all mention of gods and afterlives and supernatural justice out of its oaths and promises. There is no juice left in the words. We have nothing left but careful, perhaps somewhat pompous phrases a person has to speak before she or he takes on a job. There is something to be said for living in a rational age, but still, it seems to me we have lost something as well. And we must ask ourselves—just how could we call our age rational when a random gunman can exterminate the greatest man of the age, and then remain at large?

"None of us realized just how vital Chanto Grieg was to everything until he was gone. People loved him, or hated him—but he was the glue, the man who pulled everything else together. Now there is no center, nothing and no one to serve as the focus for everything else. Our progressives have no leaders, our conservatives no enemy. Chanto Grieg is gone, and none of his friends or enemies were prepared for a world without him. And even his enemies realize now just how great a friend they have lost. For Chanto Grieg fought fair, played by the rules—and in doing so, forced all the rest of us to do the same. He and I were opposed on many—perhaps most— of the great issues of the day. But Chanto Grieg did not worry

so much about such things. He only cared if a man or woman
was honest, and forthright, and willing to listen. I do not know
if I can live up to that short list of qualities—but now I must
try. We all must try.

"I spoke a moment ago of the old days, when oath-breakers
faced eternal doom and endless torment. Today, as never before, that is the actual fate that faces me, faces all of us, in
literal truth, if we do not keep faith. Chanto Grieg's greatest
goal was the very rescue of the planet itself, and all the life
upon it. If I fail my task, or break faith with my oath—if any
of us break faith with Governor Grieg's great unfinished
task—then perhaps we doom the planet, and thus are doomed
ourselves."

Kresh did not speak for a moment, but instead looked out
across the sea of faces. All of them looking to him, trusting
him to know the way forward, when he had not the least idea.

Well, he knew a first, risky step that needed taking. An
election. Grieg had named him to the Governorship because
he feared Quellam would be forced into calling an early election. And yet here Kresh was about to do that very thing.

It was all right. Grieg hadn't been afraid of Quellam calling
an election. He had been afraid of Quellam losing. Kresh did
not intend to lose.

"I do not want this burden," Kresh said, "but it has been
given to me, and I must take it up. I accept it. But it is not
yet truly mine to take, not yet truly given. Not unless and until
it is given fully and freely by the people of Inferno. I therefore
and hereby announce that I am calling a special election, to
take place one hundred days from today."

He glanced to Devray, and Fredda, and saw the expressions
on their faces. He spoke again, as much to them as to the
audience. "There are many who have most urgently advised
me not to take this step at this time. They have told me this
is a time when stability is needed, when the hurly-burly of an

election can cause nothing but further chaos and confusion and uncertainty.

"If Chanto Grieg had been killed in ordinary times, if we truly did know the way forward, I would agree. But such is not the case. Whoever your Governor is, one hundred and one days from now, that person will have to move with the greatest power and authority to save this planet. We are nearer doom than most of us can know. A caretaker in the Governor's office, an unwilling Designate thrust into power without his foreknowledge or your approval, will not have, cannot have, the political muscle required to do that which is needful. Our planet, our people, have been asleep for too long. In these days, when Inferno is waking from its long slumber to find that all is not well, the Governor must speak with the voice of the people, with the knowledge that the majority have chosen, and that all the people accept that choice.

"I will be a candidate in the election for Governor, one hundred days from now, and I intend to win. I did not seek the office of Governor, but I will not turn away from my duty, or from the trust Chanto Grieg placed in me. Therefore, I ask for your support today, and will ask for it again, one hundred days from today.

"In closing, there is one other choice I have made, one other decision I must report to you all. I have decided not to resign as Sheriff of Hades at this time."

There was a murmur, a muttering in the audience, a whispering of disapproval. Kresh had expected that, and knew the muttering was likely to get worse. He himself was not sure it was wise for him to take so much power to himself. But did he have any other choice?

"Although I will retain the office itself, I will hand over the day-to-day operations of the Sheriff's office to my subordinates effective immediately. I will not attempt to hold all the reins in my hand. But there is one rein that I cannot yet drop, one duty as Sheriff that I must complete. I will not resign the office of Sheriff until one last case is solved and resolved. I will resign when I have brought the killers of Chanto Grieg to justice."

And at that, there was thunderous applause, from all sides. That everyone approved of. Everyone shouted and cheered at that pronouncement. But Kresh was not convinced, even as he accepted the cheers of the crowd.

He looked around the Grand Hall. Cinta Melloy. Simcor Beddle. Tonya Welton. They were all here. Or maybe someone else. Sero Phrost, the wheeler-dealer. Kresh glanced down at his side, to Donald. Maybe his favorite suspects, Caliban and Prospero, had done it after all. Or maybe even foolish old Shelabas Quellam. Or someone not here, someone watching on a televisor screen somewhere. But there was that one person. Someone applauding Kresh's promise longer and harder than anyone else. Someone whose applause was not at all sincere. Someone who was enjoying all this. The someone who was *behind* all this.

Sero Phrost strode into Beddle's house as if he owned the place—an idea that Beddle found more than a little disturbing. "Ah, Beddle, good to see you," Phrost said, stepping forward to take his hand and leading him toward his own parlor. "Rather remarkable news today, don't you think?" he asked as they came to the parlor door, and the door robot opened the way for them.

Simcor found himself guided into a chair and looking up at Phrost pacing back and forth excitedly in front of him. "Yes," he said, "remarkable news." There was something wild and excited about Phrost. It was as if all the man's calculation and caution had been swept away, revealing quite a different sort of person underneath.

"Why, man, why aren't you walking on air?" Phrost de-

manded, looking down at Beddle. "Kresh has all but handed
you the Governorship. A hundred days from tomorrow, we'll
all be back down at the Residence watching you make the
affirmation of office. Or will you do it up in Hades instead?
This island is a bit tiresome after a while, after all."

"Sero, what are you doing here?" Beddle asked. "We
should not be seen together. You know that as well as I do."

"Ah, yes," Phrost said, dropping himself down into Beddle's favorite chair, and taking up a vaguely regal sort of pose,
his forearms resting on the arms of the chair. "I am a moderate
businessman with known dealings with the Settlers, and you
are the right-wing extremist who shouts 'death to the Settlers'
anytime there's a camera running. No one must know of our—
our what? Arrangement? Alliance? Whatever you want to call
it. No one can know about it, or we are both in a great deal
of trouble. That's the way it goes, isn't it?

"Except it *doesn't* go that way any more. Not with Grieg
out of the way. Kresh as much as called himself a caretaker.
Who else is there? Shelabas Quellam? No, there is *no* viable
alternative to yourself. The Governorship is yours."

"But even so, you might have been seen," Beddle said,
starting to feel rather annoyed. How dare the man barge in
here like this? "There could still be trouble."

"Oh, don't worry about it," Phrost said. "Every policeman
on the planet is too busy crawling all over the Residence looking for clues. I made sure I wasn't tracked or observed. Besides, I wanted to come in to see you in daylight, in your home.
It helps to illustrate my point."

Beddle stood up and frowned down at Phrost. "And what,
exactly, *is* your point?" he demanded.

Phrost lost his smile, and rose to his full height, until he
towered over Beddle. "Just this," he said. "With Grieg gone,
I no longer need to be careful. No one can touch me now. But
you—you are more vulnerable than ever. You are the Ironhead

leader who has been accepting Settler money.''

"*Settler* money!''

"All very easy to trace," Phrost said. "From their pockets to mine and into yours. I have all the proof anyone could ever want that you have been financing your operation with the enemy's money. And no one will ever believe you didn't know about it. Not in a million years. I'm just a businessman. I buy and sell without much worry about politics. No one will much care where my cash comes from, or where I send it. But you. It will mean your political death—and maybe your literal death as well—if it came out that Simcor Beddle of the Ironheads was on the Settler payroll." Phrost thought for a moment and his face turned hard. "Yes, it might well be literal death. Now we have the precedent for it in Inferno's political life. Someone might well be inspired by recent events."

"What—what are you saying?" Beddle asked. Suddenly his skin felt very cold.

"I am saying that the Governorship is yours for the taking. You own the Governor's office." The smile came back to his face, but there was nothing friendly about it now. "As for myself," he said, "it would seem that *I* own *you.*"

14

THEY POPPED THE LOCK and pulled open the door to the warehouse. The moment they did, the smell told them they had found who—or at least what—they had been looking for. Deputy Jantu Ferrar knew it, and a glance at Ranger Shah's face confirmed it. Cops still knew what a rotting body smelled like, even on the oversanitized world of Inferno.

Now they knew how Bissal had managed to stay hidden for so long. It was easy to keep out of sight when you were dead. The Ranger, the deputy, and the robot stepped into the cool, cloying darkness. Shah pulled out a handlight and shone it around the interior of the building. "Rustbackers, all right," she said. Jantu nodded. She recognized the gear. A dozen restrictors stacked up neatly in a corner. Hyperwave communications gear. A robot work rack. Yes indeed. A major rustbacking center. And they had just walked right into it. Jantu pulled out her blaster and held it at the ready. Shah glanced in Jantu's direction, and then pulled out her own weapon. Jantu moved forward, to the corner of a rack full of hardware. She signaled for Shah to cover her, and Jantu went around the corner.

And there he was. Sitting at a table, a simple meal set

out before him, his eyes dull, staring blindly down, his mouth a bit open, with the bite he had been eating still in it, his head slumped forward a bit. Almost exactly the same position they had found the Governor in. And every bit as dead. Jantu did not realize she had raised her weapon and aimed it at the corpse until she lowered it.

"That him? That him?" Shah asked, her voice a trifle high and excited.

"Yeah," Jantu said. Strange how a corpse never quite looked the same as the living man. There was something slack and swollen about him. As well there should have been, after two or three days dead aboveground.

"How did he die?" Shah asked, coming closer.

"Look at his plate," Jantu said. There was a solid mass of flies on the remains of his food. A solid mass of dead, unmoving flies. Poison. The same that had killed Bissal. One that hit him before he had a chance to swallow.

"Burning hells," Shah said. "They set him up. Sent him to do their dirty work, and set up this safe house to kill him."

Jantu found herself staring at the corpse, her eyes struggling to find some movement in its impossible stillness. She made the mistake of breathing in through her nose, and the stench of the place was like a punch in the gut. She felt queasy and nervous. "Come on," she said. "We found him," she said. "Let's get back out to the aircar and call it in."

Shah nodded, her face ashen, and a wild sort of look in her eyes. Maybe this was the first corpse she had ever seen. "Yeah, yeah," she said. "Let's go."

They both holstered their weapons and made their way back out to the street, Gerald 1324 hanging back to watch their retreat, just in case someone was waiting until now to jump them.

The two humans were nearly to the aircar when it happened, Jantu glancing over her shoulder back at the building.

The blast caught Gerald 1324 square in the doorway. The
wall over the door collapsed on top of him, burying him in
debris. Jantu got up off the ground without being aware of
being knocked down in the first place. Her blast-deafened ears
were ringing and the towering wall of flame that had been the
warehouse burning in silence. And Shah. She turned to see
what had happened to Shah.

Shah was down, motionless, on the ground. And suddenly
the difference between Ranger and deputy didn't mean a damn
thing. Nothing much of anything mattered once a five-kilo
lump of stresscrete caught you square between the eyes.

Alvar Kresh watched as the fire brigade brought the blaze
under control. "Playing with us, Donald. Playing with us.
They let us find him dead, let us see he'd never tell us anything—and then rigged the damn place to blow up when our
people left, before we could learn anything else."

"Yes, sir," Donald agreed. "I doubt we will find much of
anything after such an intense blaze."

Kresh did not say anything more, but watched as a warehouse full of evidence went up in smoke. What sort of mind
would think that sort of thing up?

"Afternoon, Governor," said a woman's voice. Kresh did
not respond at once. "Governor?"

"Hmmm? Oh!" He turned to see Cinta Melloy at his side.
It would be a while before he got used to people using his
new title. "Hello, Cinta."

"You've got one hell of a mess on your hands, Governor
Kresh."

And this is just the part that shows, Kresh thought. "Look,
Cinta, forget the Governor part just now. Cop to cop. I'm here
as the Sheriff." *The Sheriff watching his case collapse,* he
thought. *Where the hell am I going to turn now?*

"I thought I'd come, even if I wasn't invited, seeing how

it is my jurisdiction,'' Cinta Melloy said, staring at the smoldering wreckage. ''You should have asked for my help, Governor—ah, *Sheriff.* You could have used it. Now it's gotten
out of hand. It's too late.''

''I couldn't trust you, Cinta,'' Kresh replied. Suddenly he
was too tired to play the games of pretend anymore. Keeping
track of the truth was hard enough. Somehow, it was easier to
talk about, once those first words were out in the open. ''How
could I trust you, when the SSS kept showing up where it
didn't belong?''

Kresh looked to her, waiting for her to strike back, waiting
for the outburst of temper. But it did not come.

''Yes, we did keep doing that,'' she said, staring straight at
the fire, clearly unwilling to look him in the eye as she made
what amounted to a confession. ''Some of it was legitimate,
just good cops pushing a little harder than they should have.
Some of it—some of it was the dirt that gets on your hands
in this business, no matter how hard you try. We deal with
criminals, Kresh. You know that. Touch them and sometimes
the grime rubs off.''

''I know that, Cinta. I know. But this was more than a little
dirt on the hands.''

At last Cinta looked at Kresh, squinting as a bit of smoke
blew into her face. ''You're right,'' she said. ''More than just
a little dirt. Some of it was dirty cops. *My* dirty cops. I am all
but certain those were real, off-duty, on-the-take SSS agents
that got Blare and Deam out of the reception. I don't have
them yet—but I will. Blare and Deam too. It'd make the SSS
look bad—very bad—if it comes out the wrong way. I
wanted—I want—to track them down myself.''

''And Huthwitz?'' Kresh asked, pressing just a bit. A good
interrogator always knows when to press a bit more, when the
subject is cooperative. ''A dead cop on the take and you knew
his name when his own commander didn't.''

"Yeah, I was afraid you'd notice that," Cinta said. "We'd been watching him. The SSS was the original source of the tip that got to that Ranger out at the East Crack. I didn't want to say anything more in front of Devray or you—not when my people were so close to rolling up the whole operation. I couldn't trust *you*, either."

"And did you roll up the whole operation?"

"No," Cinta said, her voice hard and flat as the word. "They all went to ground when Huthwitz died. We lost them."

"Did Bissal kill Huthwitz?"

"Almost certainly." She nodded at the smoldering ruin of the warehouse. "We may never know after this mess. They knew each other, I can tell you that much for sure. Brothers in rustbacking, except they didn't get on so good."

"That much we knew. Did you know the shooter was Bissal before we did?" Kresh asked.

"We had a file on him," Cinta admitted. "Everybody did. It was just that ours was crosslinked into Huthwitz's rustbacking operation. Bissal's name popped up as one of twenty or so possibilities. That's all. I wouldn't even say we considered him a full-fledged suspect before your team found him, identified him."

"Oh, we found him, all right," Kresh said. "But now we've gone and lost him again." Kresh turned and started back toward his aircar.

"By the way," Cinta said at him as he walked away, "I did check it out, every way I could, and you were right about Grieg and house guests."

Kresh frowned and walked back toward Cinta. "How do you mean?" he asked.

"Turns out he was a typical Spacer after all. I checked all the old news reports and talked to friends, that sort of thing. No one can remember him ever having a house guest. Ever."

•   •   •

Alvar Kresh stared, unseeing, out the window as Donald flew him back to the Residence. He was thinking. Thinking hard. Strange bedfellows, police work and politics. It would be a real challenge to satisfy the demands of both, but he was starting to realize that the two were so intertwined that he had no choice. Clues, false leads, ideas, theories, snatches of conversation, and random bits of information seemed to be swirling around in his head. Grieg with a blaster hole in his chest. Grieg's simulated image assuring Kresh he was all right. Telmhock's muddled attempt to tell Kresh he was the Governor. Kresh nearly tripping over a dead SPR to get to Grieg's office. The ghostly image of Bissal captured by the integrator as he headed toward the lower-level storage room.

Half of it was no doubt vital information, while the other half was unimportant. But which half was which? He closed his eyes and tried to concentrate. No, don't concentrate. Relax. Relax. Let it come on its own terms. Don't expect the answer to come on schedule. It will arrive on its own terms, invited or not. There was, he told himself, no sense trying to force the solution to arrive—

And that was the exact moment the light came on. Yes. That had to be it. He needed proof, he needed to pull it all together—but yes. He knew. He knew.

Donald 111, convinced that his master had fallen asleep, tried to land the aircar as gently as he could. But, not for the first time, Alvar Kresh surprised his personal robot. He was out of the car before Donald was out of his seat, looking quite awake—in fact quite energetic and determined. Donald made a mental note to remember that there were times when humans actually did get some thinking done with their eyes shut, even if most thinking was no more than an excuse for a nap.

"I want Caliban and Prospero in my office," Kresh said, walking toward the entrance, his eyes straight ahead. "And I want them there *now*."

"Yes, sir," Donald said, hurrying to catch up with him. "I will bring them up directly." *Once I have you safely inside the secured interior of the Residence*, Donald thought. There was still danger everywhere.

"Good," Kresh said as he walked through the main entrance. "I have one thing to do first. Something that might take a bit of time. Wait for me in the Governor's office."

"Yes, sir," Donald said, more than a bit surprised. He knew all of Alvar Kresh's moods, and he knew this one especially well. It was Alvar Kresh on the hunt, Alvar Kresh closing in for the kill. But how? And who? Donald hurried down to the improvised cell where Caliban and Prospero were being held. He had been ahead of Kresh in solving a case now and then, and well behind him on many occasions. But he had never been this far back. Did Kresh have the perpetrator in his sights, even before Donald had so much as a guess at the list of suspects?

Donald gestured for the guard robot to unlock the cell door, and stepped inside even before the door was fully open. Prospero and Caliban were both sitting on the floor of the cell. "Get up," Donald said, not even trying to keep the excitement and satisfaction out of his voice. "The Governor wants you upstairs." The two of them got to their feet, a bit uncertainly. Donald was glad to see their discomfiture. It gave him real pleasure to order these two around. Did this summons mean that Kresh had decided the two pseudo-robots were indeed the guilty parties? *That* would be pleasure and triumph unbounded.

Kresh was not in the room when Donald and his two prisoners arrived, a minute or two later. Donald gestured for the two of them to stand in the center of the floor, while he retired to a wall niche. Waiting was not generally much of a hardship to a robot. Robots spent a great deal of their existence waiting for humans to arrive, or for humans to leave, or for humans to make up their minds about an order. Nonetheless, Donald found the wait for Kresh to be almost unbearable. Something was going on. He knew it. He knew it.

The three robots waited in silence for sixteen minutes and twenty-three seconds, according to Donald's internal chronometer. And then the doors slid open, and Kresh strode into the room. He was carrying an opaque evidence storage box. He set the box down on the desk, and then turned to Caliban and Prospero. He spoke right to the point, without any sort of preamble. "I want to know," said Kresh, "exactly what transpired between you and Tierlaw Verick. Exactly. I want your precise words, his and yours."

"Do you mean on the night of Governor Grieg's death?" Caliban asked.

"When else have you met with him?" Kresh demanded.

"Never," Caliban said. "Never at any time before or since."

"Then tell me what happened the one time you *did* meet," Kresh said.

"Well, it was a rather brief exchange," Caliban said, clearly still rather mystified. "We were waiting by the door—"

"Just the two of you?" Kresh asked. "No one else?"

"No one else around at all," Caliban said. "If you are hoping for some sort of witness besides Prospero to corroborate my statement, I'm afraid there was no one. Prospero and I were waiting by the door when Tierlaw came out. He seemed rather upset about something, and also rather surprised to see us there. He said, 'I thought I was the end of the line tonight,' and laughed."

"Laughed rather nervously, I thought," Prospero said.

Caliban nodded. "Yes, he was nervous. He spoke rather

loudly, and seemed rather agitated. I spoke to him and said, 'My friend and I were a last-minute addition.'

"He replied by saying, 'Well, you'll learn about all sorts of changes in *there*. Everything is decided. No one will be in control, and you lot are going to kingdom come. We've *all* had it. Grieg just told me. It's all over now.' "

"And then what?" Kresh asked.

"Then nothing," Prospero said. "He turned away and stomped down the hall. Caliban and I were somewhat taken aback by what he said, but we had no chance to discuss it. The door to Grieg's office opened, and we went inside for our meeting. That was all that transpired between us."

"I see," Kresh said. "Very well. That is all. The two of you may go."

"Shall we return to our cell?" Prospero asked.

"Do precisely as you please," Kresh snapped. "Isn't that what your damned Fourth Law says to do? Just leave me, and remain inside the Residence. I will want you back later. I strongly advise that you do not attempt to leave."

"Of course not," Caliban said. "Neither of us wishes to commit suicide."

"Really?" Kresh asked. "You have an odd way of showing it. Now get out."

Donald watched the two pseudo-robots leave, greatly confused. Their account of their exchange with Tierlaw Verick was at variance with Verick's account, but given Verick's hostility to robots, it was only to be expected that he would be rude to them.

More seriously, Governor Kresh seemed to be taking the pseudo-robots' accounts at face value—though both Prospero and Caliban were capable of lying. For a moment, Donald debated bringing that point to Kresh's attention. But there was something in the fierce concentration of the man's expression that made Donald believe that would be a serious mistake. No.

Governor Alvar Kresh was a man who knew exactly what he was doing.

And one thing he was doing was paying no attention whatsoever to Donald. Humans often forgot there were robots about, seeing everything that happened. Donald always appreciated such moments, as they gave him an unparalleled chance to observe human behavior. He watched, motionless, from his wall niche as Kresh pulled a piece of paper out of Grieg's archaic desk set, fumbled for a moment with one of Grieg's strange old pens, and then set to writing. He seemed to be making up a list of some sort.

He finished writing, set down the pen, and considered the paper for a moment. Then he turned to the comm panel next to the desk and punched in a number manually. The screen lit up, and Donald could see Justen Devray on the screen. "Get in here," Kresh said, and cut the connection before Devray had a chance to speak.

Kresh picked up the piece of paper and got up from behind the desk. He began pacing the room, going back and forth, back and forth, at a rather deliberate pace, his full attention on the paper. He went back to the desk and picked up the pen again. He scratched something out, and wrote something else in.

The door annunciator chimed, and Kresh pushed a button on his desk.

The door opened, and Justen Devray came in.

"Well, Justen," Kresh said. "It would appear I have a job for my Rangers." He handed Devray the paper. "Contact Cinta Melloy and coordinate with the SSS. Pull these people in, Justen. All of them. Now. And I want you and Melloy here as well. With you it's an order—but you can extend my invitation to Cinta. I have a feeling she'll accept."

Devray looked at the list and shook his head. "Maybe Melloy will want to come," he said. "But some of these people aren't going to like it," he said.

"Just get them," Kresh said. "I want them all here, in this office, and I want them here in two hours."

Devray nodded, and then, after a moment, remembered to salute. "Yes, sir," he said. And with that he turned and left, Kresh using the door button to let him out.

Kresh watched Devray leave, waited a minute, and then followed after, using the ID scanner plate by the door to make it open. Kresh stopped and examined something in the door frame on his way out. Whatever he found seemed to please him, and he went on his way. The room sensed that there were no humans about, and faded the lights down.

Leaving Donald alone in the dark. In more ways than one. He wanted to follow, to stay with his master—but no. Alone. Let him work it out alone. The Governor could always summon Donald if he needed him.

"I have to go, Gubber," Tonya said.

"You could protest it!" Gubber said. "Claim diplomatic immunity. Refuse to go. It was bad enough the way Caliban just vanished and ended up in jail. I barely knew him, and it scared me half to death. If it happened to you, I couldn't bear it. Don't go. Don't let them get you. Stay."

"That could only make things worse," Tonya said, her tone far less calm than her words. "I know this hasn't been easy for you. But I promise you it will be over after tonight. I don't know why Kresh wants me, but he does. I don't know if I'm a suspect, or a witness, or if he just wants to chat about terraforming. He wants me, and I have to go."

"But why?"

Tonya took a step or two toward the door, then turned and looked back. Logically, she knew it was going to be all right. Nothing was going to happen. But she had no such confidence on the emotional level. Fear was loose in the world. "I have

to go," she said, "because we live on this world, you and I.
We live here, and Alvar Kresh might be the only man who
can save it. If I fight this, with all the legal ways I might, that
can't be good for him.

"And as of today's announcement, what is bad for Alvar
Kresh is good for Simcor Beddle."

Kresh tried to relax. He took a quick shower, changed into
fresh clothes, had a quick bite to eat—and tried to settle himself down. He found the Residence library and selected a book-
tape to read, more or less at random. He sat there, with the
words scrolling past his eyes, not taking in more than one word
in ten of the story.

Calmly. Slowly. He started the tape over a half-dozen times
before he gave up. He could not concentrate on anything else
but the case. Because now, all of a sudden, he *had* a case.

He had more than that. He had the answer. He was as certain
of that as he had been of anything in his life. But for all of
that, it would still be easy—very, very easy—for him to make
a mistake. Kresh set the tape aside, and thought it through
again, and again.

Justen Devray came in the library almost precisely two
hours after Kresh had sent him off.

"They're all here," he said. "Waiting for you."

"Good," said Kresh. "Good. Then's let go see them."

Justen led Kresh up the stairs to the Governor's office—to
his office—and ushered him inside. Kresh took a deep breath
and faced a roomful of people who had to be thinking they
were all suspects in Grieg's murder. *In the Governor's murder,*
he told himself. *And you're the Governor now.* Kresh glanced
to the wall niches, and was relieved to see Donald there. Nice
to know there was someone here who was utterly, unquestionably, on Kresh's side.

Kresh looked around the room at all of them. Leving, De-

vray, Welton, Melloy, Beddle, Verick, Phrost, Caliban, Prospero. The humans among them looked edgy, upset, nervous.
Even the two robots looked a bit ill at ease. As well they
might. "Fredda, you're here because I assumed you'd want to
see the end of it. You're in the clear. As for the rest of you,"
he said, "I have a problem. A very simple problem, but one
with no simple solution. And my simple problem is this: It has
come to my attention that you're all guilty."

It took a full ten seconds of stunned silence before they
started shouting their denials.

15

"ALL GUILTY OF different crimes," Kresh said. "But guilty just the same. You were the one that did it, Cinta."

Cinta Melloy looked startled. "Me? Are you out of your mind? I might have a little dirt under my nails, but I didn't kill anyone."

"No," Kresh agreed, "you didn't. But you were the one who gave me the clue I needed." *And it did no harm at all to rattle you and everyone else in the room by saying it that way,* Kresh thought.

"What clue was that?" said Cinta.

"At the fire," Kresh replied. "You said something about not being invited, and showing up anyway."

"*That's* your big clue?" Cinta asked.

"That's my big clue."

"I hardly see how those words are the basis for accusing anyone of murder," Prospero said.

"Oh, you and Caliban don't need to worry about murder charges either," Kresh said. "You are here precisely *because* I no longer suspect you. You have cleared yourselves of all charges—aside from attempted blackmail—without anyone realizing it."

"How so?" Caliban asked.

"By not connecting the term 'Valhalla' to a garbled rendition of its meaning," Kresh said

"Alvar—Governor Kresh—for stars' sake stop playing games!" Fredda said. "Just tell us whatever it is you have to tell us."

"Be patient, Fredda," Kresh said. "We'll get there." He turned to the robots. "Caliban, Prospero, you told Donald. Now tell me—and I would urge you not to hold anything back, if you value your survival. When you came here, to this office, to meet Grieg, what was your plan?"

"To threaten him with the simultaneous exposure of every scandal on this planet if he decided to exterminate the New Law robots," Prospero said.

"And you made this threat?" Kresh asked.

"We did, couching it in the most polite terms possible," Prospero said. "However, he did not seem at all upset or perturbed by it."

"I would go further than that," Caliban said. "He seemed rather *amused* by the idea, as if he didn't for a moment think we would carry it out."

"And would you have?" Kresh asked.

The two robots looked at each other, and then Caliban spoke. "We were to meet the next day and begin preparing our materials for release," Caliban said. "Then we heard that Grieg was dead, and of course canceled the plan."

"How did you get your information." Fredda asked.

"Slowly," Prospero said. "Gradually. The rustbacking network is full of tipsters and rumormongers. And there is an old axiom to the effect that those who would seek the truth should follow the money. We studied a great number of transactions, legal and otherwise. They taught us much."

"Tell me some of what was in that material," Kresh said. "No, better still, let me tell you. You had proof that Simcor

Beddle here was taking Settler money—perhaps without knowing that he was taking it.''

"But I—'' Beddle began.

"Quiet, Beddle,'' Kresh said. "You're not Governor yet. Right now you'll speak when spoken to.'' He turned back to the robots. "You also had proof that Sero Phrost and Tonya Welton were in the smuggling business together.'' Another little stir of reaction, but Phrost and Welton both had the sense to keep quiet. "Proof that Tierlaw Verick's bidding group had been bribing government officials. Verick was also linked to the rustbackers—along with half the planet, it seems to me, but I doubt you would divulge that little tidbit.''

"Now just a moment,'' Verick protested. "I did no such—''

"Quiet, Verick.'' Kresh said. "And you also had proof that Commander Devray and Captain Melloy here were both in possession of proof of criminal acts in high places and were not acting upon that information.''

Devray and Melloy seemed about to protest, but Kresh cut them off. "Not a word, either of you,'' he said, with enough steel in his voice to silence both of them. "Both of you *did* have such information, and both of you informed Governor Grieg of it. Justen, you told him about Tierlaw's bribery, and, Cinta, you told him about Sero Phrost smuggling Settler hardware and passing the proceeds to the Ironheads. I've seen Grieg's files. I know. *Grieg* didn't do anything about the information, either, for the same reasons you both kept quiet.''

"And what reason would that be?'' Phrost demanded, daring to speak.

"He was afraid that if he pulled on one thread, everything else would unravel,'' Kresh said. "Arrest Sero Phrost, and Phrost would implicate Tonya Welton. Grieg needed Welton's support. Grieg also knew the Spacer bid on the control system would probably collapse without Phrost. Arrest Verick, and

Grieg knew he would lose the *Settler* bid on the system."

Devray looked confused. "But wait a second. The robots just said that Grieg didn't seem to care if they blew the lid off everything."

"Exactly," Kresh said. "Because, on the night he died, *he knew it didn't matter anymore*. He had made his final decisions about the control system, and about the New Law robots. He was going to announce them the next day. What the robots were doing was threatening to sweep all his enemies out of the way, and threatening to do so at the exact moment he no longer needed to keep his enemies happy." Kresh turned toward the robots. "*He* couldn't smear his opponents without making himself look very, very bad. But you two could. You were threatening him with the biggest favor of his political career."

"It couldn't *all* be good for him," Melloy protested. "With that much mudslinging set loose, he would have gotten messed up a little himself. Someone would have tried to fight back."

"Fight back at who? The robots?" Kresh asked. "They were the ones about to release the material, not Grieg. But even if you're right—and you probably are—Grieg would have accepted any amount of damage to his prestige if it meant getting rid of Simcor Beddle."

"And you are saying Grieg no longer cared because he had made his decisions," Caliban said. "Might I ask what those decisions were, and if you intend to abide by them?"

"I do not wish to answer either of those questions, just at the moment," Kresh said. "I have a rather cryptic note Grieg made to himself. I believe it contains his answer. But I don't need to decipher the note. Tierlaw Verick here has done it for me."

"*He* told you what Grieg had decided?" Fredda asked. "When? I never heard it."

Tierlaw Verick opened his mouth to protest again, but then thought better of it.

"Good thinking, Verick," Kresh said. "If I were you, I wouldn't say one thing more."

"But what did he say?" Fredda asked. "What did I miss?"

"You heard everything I did," Kresh said. "And his reactions told me what Grieg's decisions were."

"Then he was telling the truth," Caliban said. "When he came out of Grieg's office, he told Prospero and myself we were going to kingdom come. An archaic reference to the hereafter. He was telling us that Grieg had decided to destroy the New Law robots."

"And that scared the hell out of you, and you went into Grieg full of bluff and bluster and threatened him before he even had a chance to *tell* you he intended to destroy you." Kresh shook his head. "A mistake. A very serious mistake on your part."

"A mistake in what way?" Caliban asked.

"And you claim to be high-function beings," Donald said, speaking for the first time as he stepped down from his wall niche. "If you were true robots, human behavior would have been your constant study, and you would not have erred. Can you truly understand so little of human nature?"

"What do you mean?" Caliban asked. "Governor Kresh, is he speaking with your authority?"

"Donald is speaking for himself," Kresh said, "but he's getting it right for all of that. Go on, Donald."

"It might be *logical* to expect Governor Grieg to tell you his decision in the same way no matter what that decision was, but that is not the human way. It does not account for the Governor's personality. To expect him to act in such a way takes no account of the emotions of pleasure in bringing good news, or the embarrassment and sorrow humans feel when reporting bad news for which they are responsible. It would

not be in Grieg's character to call you into his office and tell
you he intended to wipe you out. You would have found out
by seeing it on the news, or by written notice—or by getting
a blaster shot through the head.''

"What are you saying?" Prospero demanded.

"That you should have known his decision would be in your
favor as soon as he asked to see you face-to-face," Donald
said.

"And when Verick told you that you were going to kingdom come, he was just telling what Grieg had told him,"
Kresh said. "Except he got it wrong. Grieg had been looking
for a third way, some solution between tolerating the current
intolerable state of affairs and extermination. And he found it.
He found it and told it to Verick."

"I still do not understand," Prospero said.

"But now I do," Caliban said, sitting stock-still, staring
straight ahead. "Now I do. *Valhalla.* Grieg told Verick he was
sending all the New Law robots to Valhalla. To someone living on Inferno, that is a place name. It is the place to which
all New Law robots wish to escape, a hidden place as far away
from human interference as possible. But Verick thought the
Governor was speaking in metaphor, speaking of the old Earth
legend from which the name is derived. Valhalla, the hall of
the gods, where those who have died in battle will live. The
afterlife. Kingdom come.''

"So you threatened the man who had found a way to save
you," Kresh said. "And threatened to do the thing he would
most love to have done, but dared not do himself. And, at a
guess, that appealed to his sense of humor. So he told you to
leave and not come back, hoping to have the public hear all
about friend Beddle's finances in the next day or so. The irony
is that you had no motive for Grieg's murder, even if you
thought you did.''

"So you still have every reason to suspect us," Caliban said.

"On the contrary, I am absolutely certain you two had nothing to do with the murder of Chanto Grieg," Kresh said.

"It sounds like you've got this whole thing figured out," Melloy said, a bit grumpily.

"I do," Kresh said.

"So tell us about it," Cinta said. "If that wouldn't be too much trouble."

"Too much trouble was exactly what it was," Kresh said. "Fredda pointed that out. The plan was too intricate, too theatrical. That's what I should have seen from the start. The plan had too many people in it, too many moving parts, too many bits of complicated coordination and timing—especially with someone as unreliable and plainly expendable as Ottley Bissal at the center of it. The plan required an assassin willing to do what he was told if the paycheck was big enough, someone willing to perform a despicable act—and yet someone foolish enough to trust the plotter who intended to kill him. Those are not job requirements that produce quality applicants. Whoever took on the job was bound to be someone who made mistakes, who got sloppy. Someone like Bissal. That should have told me something. It should have told me the plan wouldn't work. And sure enough, it didn't."

"But Grieg was killed," Fredda protested.

"Not in the way the mastermind intended," Kresh said. "Not in the way Tierlaw Verick planned."

Verick jumped up, and was halfway to Kresh before Donald could intercept him. Donald pinned the man's arms to his side and dragged him back to his seat. "It was the basic problem of the whole case," Kresh said. "We knew, even once Fredda spotted Bissal, that we didn't have the real killer. Bissal was so obviously someone else's creature. But whoever had sent him—and sent all the other conspirators along—had done a good job of staying hidden. It could have been anyone with access to the right sort of technology, and the wrong sort of people. It could have been anyone in this room. It could even have been me, I suppose. But it was you, Verick.''

''You're crazy, Kresh,'' Verick half shouted. ''How could I have done it? I didn't even know Grieg was dead until one of the guards on my room told me.''

''And it must have been a relief when the guard made that slip,'' Kresh said. ''You could stop acting. It made it that much less likely that you would make a slip. Good as you were, you knew you could not keep it up forever. And you were good. You even managed to fool Donald's lie-detector system—and that requires some impressive training. Our files said you dabbled in theatrics. We did not know just how good an actor you were. The trouble was you'd made your slip already. One you couldn't avoid.''

''And what slip might that be?'' Verick demanded.

''You said there were *two* robots standing in the hallway when he came out of this office. Not three.''

''But there were only two,'' Caliban protested. ''There was only Prospero and myself.''

''But then where the devil was the door sentry robot?'' Kresh demanded. ''It was there, standing in front of the door, shot through the chest, when I checked the upper floor after discovering Grieg's body. SPRs on other duties move around, but a door sentry robot does not go off post. Not unless it received orders to do so, from someone in authority to give orders.''

''So Tierlaw didn't notice a robot,'' Cinta said, who seemed to have taken it upon herself to defend her fellow Settler. ''So what? You Spacers always ignore robots. That's not enough to convict a man of murder.''

''Tierlaw is not a Spacer, but a Settler,'' Donald said. ''He has a pronounced aversion to robots, and very definitely noticed the other two standing outside the door. He gave a detailed and accurate description of Prospero and Caliban.''

"So what are you saying?'' Devray said.

"I'm saying that Tierlaw ordered the Sapper, the SPR sentry robot, to be out of position. But a Sapper won't take orders from just anyone. He—or a subordinate, more likely—must have gotten to the robot sometime before and used some rather sophisticated order giving to convince the sentry that orders from him, from Tierlaw, took precedence over everything else, even guarding Grieg.''

"Is that possible?'' Devray asked.

"Yes,'' Fredda said. "If the SPR did not believe Grieg was in any particular danger, so that First Law potential was reduced, and if it saw Tierlaw as its owner, thus enhancing Second Law potential, then yes, Tierlaw could have given the order for the sentry to clear off and come back later.''

"It's thin,'' Cinta said. "And I don't see what it has to do with anything.''

"It *is* thin,'' Kresh admitted. "I knew that as soon as I figured it out. I knew I needed proof—and I found it. But there is more. Caliban and Prospero were witnesses that Tierlaw came out the *inner* door to Grieg's office. After-hours visitors to his office always used the outer side door. But Tierlaw needed to let Bissal in. So he got Grieg to open the inner door somehow.''

"But he did not let Bissal in. He let us in,'' Caliban said.

"And why would he let Bissal see his face?'' Cinta demanded.

"He wouldn't let Bissal see him,'' Kresh said, heading over to his desk. "He didn't.'' He unsealed the evidence box and pulled out a pocket communicator, and a thin piece of black metal in the shape of a flattened triangle. "I found these in your room, Verick, the one you stayed in the night of the murder. You're good at hiding things. The room had been searched twice before I went over it. But I knew what I was looking for—and that makes a great deal of difference. And before you can protest that these were planted, a Crime Scene Observer robot witnessed the search and recorded it.''

"I recognize the communicator, but what's the other thing?'' Fredda asked.

"It's one of these,'' Kresh said. He went to the inner door of the office and used the scanner panel to open it. Once it was open, he took the piece of metal and set it in the frame of the door. It stayed there of its own accord. Kresh stepped back, and the door closed—but not all the way. There was a barely discernible crack between the frame and the sliding door. Kresh got his fingers into the crack and pulled. It took a bit of effort, but he managed to get the door open. Kresh took the door wedge out of the frame, crossed the room, and put it back in the evidence box.

"Grieg was supposed to be killed right here,'' he said. "In this office. Verick would set the door wedge on his way out—with a little practice, they're easy to set surreptitiously. Tierlaw would order the office door sentry robot back into position, and then signal Bissal, waiting in the basement, to turn on the range restrictor signal that would deactivate the SPR robots. Then Tierlaw could simply walk out of the house, unobserved, while Bissal came up out of the basement, came into the office, and shot Grieg. Bissal would remove the door wedge, and go on with the rest of the plot—destroying the robots to hide the restrictors, and then escaping to the warehouse, where he would hide until things cooled off—except the food left for him there was poisoned. He must have died within a few hours of Grieg.''

"That's the craziest plan I've ever heard,'' Cinta protested. "It could never work.''

"And it didn't,'' Devray said. "It was crazy, Cinta, but think what we would have found if it had worked. Grieg dead behind a locked door, fifty wrecked security robots, and an assassin who simply vanishes without a trace. A few days later, a warehouse blows up and burns down, and no one ever thinks to connect the two. Things are bad enough as they are. People are scared. Just imagine the panic, the chaos, if the murder had been as smooth, as perfect as it was supposed to be.''

"But things went wrong,'' Kresh said. "Things went wrong. The two robots are waiting outside the door, so you can't set the door wedge, could you, Verick? And you couldn't use your communicator in front of the robots, either. So you slip into a vacant room and contact Bissal from there, telling him what had gone wrong. You tell him to go to plan B, killing Grieg in his room.

"But then you realize that you couldn't leave the vacant room. At a guess, one of the sentries on random patrol takes up a post in the hall. If you leave the room, that would raise the alarm. So you had to stay there, in that room, until the robots left, until you heard Grieg go to bed. You could signal Bissal. Then Bissal activates the range restrictor signal, and the sentries go dead. But even then you can't leave, because Bissal has come up into the house. Suppose he saw you, and knew who you were? He'd have a hold over you. Suppose he tried to blackmail you instead of going off to eat his poison at the warehouse? No, you could not risk that. So you decide to wait until you heard Bissal leave the house.

"But Bissal had wasted most of his blaster's charge, and he realizes he isn't going to have enough power left to be able to shoot all the robots. So Bissal decides to remove the restrictors from half of them by hand, and it takes forever. At long last he is done, and destroys the blaster and the Trojan robot in the basement, and heads off on his way. At last you can go.

"Except suddenly you can see the sky is full of police vehicles of one sort or another. The police have discovered Huthwitz's body. You still can't leave. Then I arrive, and rush up the stairs. Grieg has been discovered long before you expected.

"Suddenly you hear new footsteps in the halls and realize they are searching room to room. You hide under the bed or something during the first, cursory search. But you know they will search again, or at the very least stumble across you. You can't hide in the one room forever. So you very cleverly brazen it out.

"You hide the incriminating door wedge and communicator, and then dress in the pajamas left in the room. Maybe you can talk your way out of it. It's a long shot, but the only chance you have. You wander out into the hallway, and pretend you're a house guest who's slept through the whole thing. Donald here snatches you up. And you very nearly got away with it. Until Cinta Melloy here decided to look into whether Grieg ever had overnight guests—and found out he never did. We never thought to check the other side of the point, by the way. Did you have a hotel reservation in Limbo City? If—or rather when—we do find one, how will you explain it?"

Verick opened his mouth and shut it again, and swallowed hard, and then at last the words came out. "And what was my motive supposed to be in this lunatic scheme?" he asked, his voice tight and calm and strained. "What was all this supposed to accomplish for me?"

"Profit," Kresh said. "Huge profit. Money. Not a motive we Spacers cops are used to. I didn't even consider it at first. Money hasn't meant much for a while, though it's started to again. You went into that meeting with Kresh to find out if he had accepted your control system design. If he told you he had chosen your system, you would not signal Bissal, there would be no attack, and Bissal would slip away when he could. If Grieg told you Phrost had the job—well then, a terrifying assassination of the Governor might well sow just enough distrust of robots that a new Governor would not go with a robot design—or else it might be easier to bribe the new incumbent.

You might even already know Beddle wasn't above taking Settler money. You might even have had some dealings with him. *Did* you offer Grieg a bribe, by the way? He was half expecting that you would."

Verick screamed and lunged, and Donald had to struggle a bit to hold him down.

"I'll take that as a yes," said Governor Kresh. "Commander Devray, perhaps you could take this man into custody."

16

"AND THAT IS THAT," Kresh said, after Melloy and Welton were gone and Devray and his Rangers took a sobbing, hysterical Tierlaw Verick away. "You two are free to go," he said to Beddle and Phrost.

"But what about the charges against us?" Beddle asked.

"What charges?" Kresh asked. "No one has filed any that I'm aware of. *I* don't intend to."

"That's very generous of you, Governor," said Sero Phrost.

"The hell it is," Kresh said. "I think I can do more damage to the two of you by letting you stay in the public eye. After all, everything that was said in this room today is bound to reach the public, somehow. Someone is bound to leak something—wouldn't you agree, Prospero? Stories—at the very least rumors—about smuggling and bribery and money laundering are bound to float to the surface. I have a feeling that Tonya Welton is going to be able to explain away a lot of things you two can't. Oh, and Beddle, I'm looking forward to your announcement for Governor. It should be an exciting campaign."

"But I—I—"

"Quiet, Simcor," Phrost said. "Don't give him any

more ammunition. Let's get out of here." The two men got up and left, and Kresh was glad to push the door button and get them out of his sight.

"They're down now, but they won't stay down," said Fredda Leving. "You know that, don't you?"

"Oh, yes, of course," Kresh said. "Phrost still has a lot of friends, and a lot of money, and there are plenty of true believers in the Ironheads who'll forgive Beddle anything. But this way, they're damaged goods. If I brought charges against them, they could accuse me of politicizing the courts, or something. Better to let the rumors leak out and do their damage."

Kresh stood up and stretched and looked thoughtful for a moment. "You know, I've just had an odd thought," he said. "Of all the cases I've ever dealt with that concerned robots, I think this is the first one I've ever had where the Three Laws weren't involved somewhere in the solution."

"But they were, Governor Kresh," said Caliban. "They were involved most intimately."

"In what way?"

" 'A robot may not injure a human being or, through inaction, allow a human being to come to harm,' " Caliban said, repeating the First Law. "Verick relied most heavily upon Spacer faith in that statement. In a sense, he set fifty robots with an incomplete First Law loose in the Governor's Residence. They were shut down, turned off—inactive. Through inaction, they allowed a human being to come to harm."

"It is an interesting feature of the First Law," Donald said. "I myself experienced a most unpleasant reaction when I realized that I could have saved Grieg if I had been with him— even though it would have been impossible for me to be with him while I was performing my normal duties. No doubt there are many human beings in the universe who are being injured at this very moment. Though logically I realize there is nothing I can do about it, I must admit I find it a most disturbing notion. And it is part and parcel of the First Law. The Law is couched in such strong and solid absolutes that it cannot possibly match up with the greys and uncertainties and limitations of everyday life."

"Donald," Fredda said. "That almost sounds like a criticism of the absolute nature of the Three Laws."

"By no means, Dr. Leving. It is a criticism of the disorderly nature of everyday life."

Fredda laughed and turned to Caliban. "And what about you, Caliban? What about the Laws and you? Have you learned more on that score?"

"A year ago, my accidental escape from the lab, and the subsequent pursuit caused me to integrate my own internal Law—to protect myself. But if I pursued self-preservation at all cost, Prospero and I would have fled Purgatory. I have no doubt that the ensuing search for us would have cost many New Law robots their lives. I believe that I have integrated a new internal Law set—Cooperate for the greater good. Protect myself only when it does not endanger vitally important cooperation."

Donald turned toward Caliban. "No doubt you are aware a symbolic notational representation of that statement would be remarkably similar to the Second and Third Laws."

"Similar," Caliban agreed. "But not identical. My version acknowledges the disorderliness of the everyday world—and, I believe, allows me to deal with it more successfully than a Three Law or New Law robot."

"Enough!" Kresh said. "Grieg complained about the Three Laws ruling his life, and I'm beginning to see what he meant. Can't we talk about something else?"

"All right, let's talk about the Control Center," Fredda said. "I don't see how you can choose either the Spacer or Settler design now. Both bids are too badly tainted."

"I know," Kresh said. "Grieg chose the Spacer design, but

I'm not so sure he was right to do so. From what I've been able to see, they're both first-rate designs. The people on both sides were corrupt, but their machinery was fine. I'm going to have to think mighty hard about it, but my gut reaction is to build *both* systems, if we can afford it. I don't quite like the idea of the whole planet's weather being controlled by a robot—*or* by whoever happens to be pushing the buttons that day on the human-controlled system. If we had both, there would be a system of checks and balances that neither would have on its own. Grieg was a great one for finding a third way. Maybe I can do the same.''

"But what about Grieg's other decision, concerning the New Law robots?'' Prospero asked. "Will you reverse that decision as well? What's going to happen to us? Will you leave things as they are, or send us to Valhalla—or will it be kingdom come after all?''

Donald spoke before Kresh could reply. "Sir, I must urge you to consider the danger and chaos the New Law robots have produced. You cannot let it continue. You cannot let them survive.''

Kresh gave Caliban and Prospero a long look, and then let out a long sigh. "Oh, it's tempting,'' he said. "Very tempting indeed to be rid of you once and for all. But I can't get up and announce to the world that I'm scrapping one of Chanto Grieg's most daring experiments. Not when the man isn't cold in his grave yet. I *have* to let you live, out of respect for his memory.'' Kresh was silent for a moment. "And yet Donald is right, too. We can't afford any more of the headaches you New Law types cause. So, damn it all, I suppose it has to be Valhalla,'' he said.

Prospero bowed slightly and looked Kresh straight in the eye. "Thank you, Governor. You have let my people go.''

•   •   •

The next morning Governor Alvar Kresh and Fredda Leving went out for a stroll in the sunlit grounds of the Winter Residence. The rains were over, a gentle breeze was blowing and there was a fresh-scrubbed feel to the world—a far cry from the dust-choked deserts that surrounded Hades. Nature felt alive and vigorous. The morning, the whole world, seemed full of possibilities.

This was how Inferno was supposed to be, Kresh thought. *A living world. This is how it's going to be, if I have anything to do with it.* Suddenly he felt a sense of purpose stronger than any he had ever felt before. *I'll take care of you,* he thought, and it was a promise he made to the world of Inferno itself. *I will heal you, and make you well.*

"So now it's over," Fredda said. "Or is it?"

"What. The case? There's some tidying up to do, but yes, it's over."

"There are an awful lot of loose ends to clear up," Fredda pointed out. "We don't know a lot of things about the conspiracy, how exactly it was put together, or how Bissal was recruited, or how and when the SPRs were tampered with."

"True," Kresh said. "There's a lot of detail work to do, the sort of thing Donald is very good at. Probably I'll put him in charge of it. But in a sense, at least, it *is* only a question of detail. Tierlaw bought the services of a rustbacking mob, which one, we don't know, but it was almost certainly the one that was paying off Huthwitz. Cinta Melloy almost had them, and she lost them when they got spooked by Grieg's murder. But you found the killer, and I found the mastermind. Working from both ends toward the middle, and with Cinta's leads, we'll roll them up fast enough. Besides, if I pack off the New Laws to Valhalla, there won't be any rustbacking. Once the business collapses and there's no money, there'll be a lot of people ready to talk. We'll get them."

"You're right, I suppose," Fredda said. "So it is over."

"And it's just begun," Kresh said, looking her in the eye. He did not dare say anything more. He was not even sure he knew exactly what he meant—but the way she smiled back at him told him she had understood him precisely. The two of them walked in silence for a time, enjoying the moment, considering the possibilities.

"It's a beautiful morning," Fredda said at last. "I never expected to see such lovely weather on Purgatory."

"Nor did I," Kresh said. "But wouldn't this be a fine world if we *could* expect it?" He stood there for a moment, drinking it all in. But then he turned back, toward the Residence, toward his new duties. "Come on, Fredda," he said, as he reached out and took her by the hand. "There's a lot of work for us to do."